Praise for KAREN SCHALER

"Schaler's smart, appealing protagonists will
keep readers turning the pages, and the plotting is
pitch-perfect, leading to an inevitable but
charming happily-ever-after."
—*Publishers Weekly*

"How *A Christmas Prince* screenwriter Karen Schaler
became a holiday publishing darling."
—*Entertainment Weekly*

Praise for Karen's *Christmas Ever After*

"A wonderfully festive setting...The cast is charming
and the atmosphere's enchanting."
—*Publishers Weekly*

Praise for Karen's *Christmas Camp*

"VERDICT a charming movie-to-book crossover
that would be right at home on the Hallmark Channel
and a winner for fans looking for a touching holiday read."
—*Library Journal*

Praise for Karen's *Finding Christmas*

"For Schaler, creating these fantastical
holiday stories comes naturally."
—*Money*

A ROYAL CHRISTMAS FAIRY TALE

KAREN SCHALER

HAWKTALE
PUBLISHING

Cover design by Mary Ann Smith
Edited by Entrada Publishing
Interior design by Ramesh Kumar Pitchai
Chapter title and chapter opener © Vector Tradition SM/Shutterstock

Library of Congress Cataloging-in-Publication Data has been applied for.

ISBNs 978-1-7347661-4-1 (trade), 978-1-7347661-5-8 (hardcover), 978-1-7347661-6-5 (ebook)

PUBLISHER'S NOTE

The recipes in this book are meant to be followed exactly as written. The publisher and author are not responsible for any of your adverse reactions to the recipes found in this book, or for your individual allergies or health issues that may require medical assistance.

A ROYAL CHRISTMAS FAIRY TALE

*This book is dedicated to everyone
who is ready to create their own
fairy tale and happily ever after.
I hope this inspires and reminds you
that anything is possible
if you just believe…*

Chapter 1

The European-style Christmas market looked like a Christmas dream come true, right in the middle of Manhattan, and Kaylie Karlyle was on a mission to catch the crooks who were trying to mess with Santa.

It was twilight, or what Kaylie liked to call magic hour, when the day eased into the night, right before the first stars made their appearance, and the hundreds of white twinkle lights from the Christmas market were illuminating the dancing snowflakes that were just starting to fall.

It was also one of the best times of the day to shoot video and Kaylie, an investigative television reporter, was counting on her photographer, Rachel, to capture everything that was about to happen.

It was just a week until Christmas, and the sooner she could get her story on the news, the better.

Kaylie, with Rachel by her side, weaved her way through dozens of festive Christmas stalls selling everything from hand-made winter hats, mittens, and sweaters, to vintage Christmas ornaments, crafts, and sweet and savory holiday treats.

Each one of the stalls was decorated with matching fresh, fragrant evergreen garlands that made you feel like you were walking through an enchanted forest.

Adding to the magic and merrymaking, Christmas carolers dressed like they'd just stepped out of a Charles Dickens novel were joyfully singing, "We Wish You A Merry Christmas."

But Kaylie was too busy being laser-focused on getting her story to appreciate any of what was happening around her.

Kaylie picked up her pace. "Okay, Rachel, we're almost there. You know the plan, right?" But when Kaylie turned around to get Rachel's reaction, Rachel had disappeared. "Rachel?"

She was looking around for Rachel and not watching where she was going when she ran right into someone.

"I'm so sorry," Kaylie said as she whirled around and found herself looking right into the eyes of Santa Claus. He looked like a wonderful old-world Santa. He was wearing a long red velvet coat that was elaborately trimmed with gold embroidery. His long white beard appeared to be as real as the twinkle in his eyes.

"Ho! Ho! Whoa!" Santa said with a big belly laugh. "Looks like someone is in a hurry."

"I'm really sorry," Kaylie said. "I didn't see you. I was looking for my photographer."

Santa held up a Polaroid camera. "How about a picture with me instead?"

Before Kaylie could answer, Santa happily snapped a selfie of them and gave her the picture. "Merry Christmas," he said. He then pointed to his nose and then her. "You might want to slow down a little, enjoy the season. It's Christmas, the most wonderful time of the year." He gave her a little wink before he headed for a group of children who were waiting for him.

Kaylie laughed as she tossed the Polaroid picture into her tote bag and then spotted Rachel over at a stall of Christmas sweaters. As she hurried over, she noticed all the sweaters Rachel was looking at could have been strong contenders to win an ugly Christmas sweater contest. Rachel smiled when she saw her coming and she held up a sweater that had a giant grinning reindeer on it. There were brown fuzzy antlers sticking out on both sides.

"Look what I found," Rachel said, excited.

"I thought I lost you," Kaylie said.

Rachel flashed her a guilty grin. "Sorry, I couldn't resist. These sweaters were calling my name. Check this one out." Rachel quickly held up another sweater. This one had blinking red and green Christmas lights. Before Kaylie could comment, Rachel was already reaching for a third sweater. "And I love this one, too. Everything's stuck on with Velcro, so you can move everyone around and create your own Christmas scene." Rachel put a snowman and a gingerbread boy into Santa's sleigh. "I can't decide which one I like best."

Kaylie laughed. "Come on, we gotta go. You can shop after we get the story." When Kaylie took off walking again, Rachel hurried to catch up.

"Good, because I still haven't finished my Christmas shopping," Rachel said, giving the sweaters one last look over her shoulder.

"You're really thinking of buying one of those for a Christmas present?" Kaylie asked. "For who?"

Rachel grinned back at her. "For me."

Kaylie laughed. "Seriously?"

"Yes," Rachel said with conviction. "Don't you always buy yourself something for Christmas?"

"Uh, no," Kaylie said.

Rachel gave her a surprised look. "Well, you should. I always try and find something unique, and this place is full of some really cool things." She spun around, taking it all in. When she spotted a giant stuffed candy cane, she eagerly ran over and picked it up. "Like this. Don't you love it?"

Kaylie laughed. "No. I like to eat my candy, not decorate with it."

"Ah, so you like candy canes," Rachel said. "Good to know. I thought you boycotted all things Christmas."

Kaylie frowned. "You make me sound like a Grinch."

"You don't decorate. You don't have a tree. You never come to the TV station Christmas party. That sounds pretty Grinchy to me."

"First of all, I love the Grinch," Kaylie said. "Think about it. The poor big green guy, he was just bullied and misunderstood. But he came around in the end, that's what really matters, right? So, I don't have anything against Christmas. I've always just worked the holiday, so it's like any other day. I don't get together with my parents because they do their annual Caribbean trip; they hate the cold and love the beach so it's a win-win for them. They always invite me and my sister, of course, if we want to come, but…"

"But let me guess, you never do," Rachel finished for her.

"That's because work comes first for both of us," Kaylie said. "I always volunteer to take the reporter shifts for people who have kids, so they can be with their families for the holidays. My sister, Amelia, is stationed in Germany. She runs a family readiness program for the Army. She helps families who have loved ones who are deployed. Christmas is always a tough time for military families when they're apart, so it's one of her busiest times of the year. We all decided more than ten years ago that it's just easier to get together sometime in January or February when it fits all our schedules. Make sense?"

"I guess so," Rachel said. "I just think it's kind of sad that you're missing out on all the Christmas magic, like this." Rachel grinned as she picked up an endearing stuffed gingerbread boy and wiggled it back and forth in front of Kaylie. "He could be your Christmas date."

Kaylie laughed as she held up her hands to keep the gingerbread boy away. "Thanks, but I'll pass."

"You're so picky. Is it his big round eyes or his short little arms?" Rachel asked, giving the gingerbread boy a hug. "Because I think he's adorable. But seriously, when was the last time you went on any kind of date?" Rachel put the gingerbread boy down and they continued walking. "Oh, wait, I know what you're going to say. You've been too busy working. I'm starting to sense a theme here. You know what they say about all work and no play?"

"That it gets you promoted to your dream job," Kaylie said as she linked arms with Rachel. "Now let's go get this story. You know the drill?"

"Of course," Rachel said with a confident smile. "I start rolling as soon as you walk up to the booth selling the vintage Santas."

"The *fake* Santas," Kaylie corrected her.

Rachel shook her head, dumbfounded. "I still can't believe someone would make counterfeit Santas at Christmas. Who does that? That's gotta be bad Christmas Karma, right?"

"One hundred percent," Kaylie agreed. "Especially because they're selling them as one-of-a-kind, handmade, collectible art from Europe. And they're really crossing the line when they're saying all the proceeds are going to help a children's charity."

Rachel frowned. "That is just so wrong."

Kaylie nodded. "I know, and that's why we're about to make things right."

"And this is why I love doing stories with you," Rachel said. "You always go after the bad guys, even at Christmas."

"Especially at Christmas," Kaylie jumped in. "What kind of investigative reporter would I be if I didn't?"

"And that's why you're getting your new series, *Kaylie on Your Side*. When are they going to announce it?" Rachel asked.

Kaylie's eyes lit up. "Bob said tomorrow night at the Christmas party. I can't wait. This is everything I've been working for and dreaming about, and why I went into journalism. I've always wanted to have my own series to help people who can't help themselves. I've had the name, *Kaylie on Your Side*, ready to go forever and I already have the first month of story ideas planned out. There's even talk of the series possibly getting nationally syndicated. This is my chance to show what I can do and hopefully finally get a network job. The bigger the audience, the more people I can help."

"If anyone can do it, you can," Rachel said. "I've never seen anyone work so hard. You're the most dedicated person I know."

"Thank you," Kaylie said with a smile. "That means a lot, and this promotion couldn't come at a better time. My rent just went up again and my student loans are coming due and I'm running out of my savings and—"

Kaylie suddenly stopped talking and pointed at the stall she'd been looking for. "There it is!"

The stall was set up along the edge of the Christmas market to try and look like it was one of the approved vendors when it wasn't. She noticed how it had even tried to copy the signature garland and twinkle lights to match the rest of the stalls, but if you looked closely, you could see the garland was fake, just like the Santa figurines they were selling.

She'd gotten tipped off a week ago that someone was going to different Christmas markets and holiday events around New York City, selling what they claimed to be one-of-a-kind collectible Santas to raise money for a children's charity. The person had bought a Santa and had given it to Kaylie to check out. It turned out the tipster had been right. Everything about the Santa was fake and there was no charity.

Kaylie had done stories like this before, where people tried to sell counterfeit designer purses, wallets, and watches, but trying to sell a knock-off Christmas decoration was a first. If Kaylie had it her way, this would also be the last.

She gave Rachel a quick look to make sure her camera was rolling. When Rachel nodded and gave her the thumbs-up, Kaylie confidently approached the Santa stall.

"Excuse me," she said, getting the attention of the guy behind the stall. "I'm Kaylie Karlyle with Channel Six Action News." She picked up one of the grinning Santas. "I need to talk to you about your Santas…"

Kaylie and Rachel stood in front of a giant TV monitor in the newsroom and watched their Santa story wrap up on the evening news. When it was done, Rachel held up her hand for a high-five.

"Nice job, Kaylie."

"Right back at ya," Kaylie said. "That last shot you got of the look on that guy's face when he knew he was busted was priceless."

"That guy won't be selling any more fake Santas anytime soon," Rachel added. "He's definitely on the naughty list and will be getting coal in his stocking."

Kaylie laughed. "Because you don't want to mess with Santa."

"Or Kaylie Karlyle," Bob said as he joined them. "Great job, both of you."

Kaylie smiled back at him. "Thanks boss, and thanks for giving me the extra time to go after this story."

"You delivered like you promised," Bob said. "It turned out great."

For Kaylie, getting praise like this from Bob meant everything to her. He wasn't just her boss, the news director at the TV station, he was her mentor. He was the one person she always trusted and turned to for advice.

She knew she wouldn't be where she was today if Bob hadn't taken a chance on her five years ago when she'd first moved to New York City, and had been struggling to find a job.

She'd been working as a local TV reporter in Phoenix, but had always dreamed of working for one of the top networks as a national correspondent. She knew those jobs were fiercely competitive and to have any real shot at it, she needed to be where the networks were. So, she'd moved to Manhattan, determined to take any freelance job she could in the business and do whatever she could to prove herself until she could land a full-time gig.

She also knew the competition would be fierce for any job, so she'd come to the city with a plan.

As an investigative reporter, she knew what every news director wanted was an exclusive story that they could beat the competition with. So, while she was in Phoenix, she worked all her national sources until she'd found an exclusive story she could pitch in New York City to try and help convince someone to give her a shot as a freelancer.

But even with an amazing story, it had proven a lot more challenging than she had hoped. All the media outlets she'd reached out to wanted the story, but they also wanted one of their established reporters to do it because Kaylie wasn't known or trusted in the market. No one was willing to give her a shot.

With her savings running out fast, she was about to start waitressing when she'd met Bob in a coffee shop. He was in line in front of her to place an order and she'd noticed he was wearing a Channel Six Action News jacket.

She had overheard him talking to the barista, and when she learned he was a news director she'd been trying to meet but could never get past his gatekeeper assistants, she had literally followed him down the street to the TV station. The faster he walked, the faster she had pitched him her exclusive story and several other stories she'd come up with.

When he'd politely told her he didn't have any freelance openings, she hadn't given up. The next morning, she'd camped out at the same coffee shop where she'd met him.

She'd had a hunch that this could be his daily coffee fix. Her hunch had paid off. For the next week, every morning, she'd meet him at the coffee shop and walk back with him to the TV station, pitching him new stories she'd come up with the night before.

Impressed by her tenacity and her ideas, he'd finally given in and hired her on a trial basis to do just one story and see how it went. Kaylie had taken the opportunity and run with it, never looking back.

When Bob told the story now, he always joked that he only hired her so he could finally drink his coffee in peace again.

After the first story went well, he'd started her out working only two days a week, as an overnight freelance reporter on the weekends. It was a brutal schedule that she never complained about. Within a year, her dedication, determination, and drive earned her a full-time staff position.

She would always be grateful to Bob for giving her a chance when no one else would. He pushed her hard. He was never easy on her, but she knew all the challenges he threw her way meant he believed she could handle it, and she always did. She'd do whatever it took to make sure she never let him, or the station, or herself, down.

That's why this promotion she was about to get, having her own weekly branded series, *Kaylie on Your Side*, meant everything to her.

Bob had told her on her first day working at the station, that her job as an investigative reporter was to be a watchdog for society, to give a voice to people who couldn't stand up for themselves.

It was a responsibility she had taken to heart and lived by.

Her goal was to always make a difference by uncovering scams and secrets so she could shine a light on the truth. Some days she was taking down multi-million-dollar Fortune 500 companies involved in fraud, and other days, like today, she was helping people not buy a fake Santa for a children's charity that didn't exist. She felt every story was important and that people deserved to know the truth.

As she looked around the newsroom now, one word came to mind. Home. This is where she spent all her time, and there was no other place she'd rather be.

She turned back to Bob, feeling energized and excited. "You know, I have this great idea for a follow-up to this story I wanted to run by you. I just got a tip on another charity scam we need to go after right away and…"

"Kaylie, wait," Bob interrupted. "Let's go in my office and talk." He was already walking away.

Kaylie looked surprised. She couldn't remember the last time she was in Bob's office. He was always out in the newsroom with everyone, and rarely held office meetings.

"Is everything okay?" she asked.

Bob got to his office and opened the door for her and then closed it behind them.

Now Kaylie was getting nervous. Bob never shut the door unless it was something serious.

As she entered, her eyes were immediately drawn to the blinking red lights on Bob's five-foot Christmas tree in the corner. Every year his tree had a new theme. This year the theme was elves, and they were on the tree in all shapes and sizes.

"If all those elves make presents, you're not going to have to do any Christmas shopping this year," Kaylie said with a laugh, trying to ease the tension she was feeling. When Bob didn't laugh back, her heart started to race and her stomach twisted into a knot. "Bob, what's going on? Is this about my series?" She wrung her hands together. They suddenly felt cold and clammy.

Bob took a deep breath and looked her dead in the eye. "Yes, and it's not good news."

Kaylie's legs suddenly felt like jelly. She sat down in the nearest chair. "What is it? Just tell me. Do we have to move the start date back?"

"Kaylie, I'm sorry. There's not going to be a series."

For a moment, Kaylie couldn't breathe. She felt like someone had punched her in the stomach. "What?" she asked, her voice cracking. She cleared her throat and took a deep breath. "What do you mean?"

"The station has been sold," Bob said.

"I heard the rumors that it might be," Kaylie said.

Bob nodded. "We all knew it was coming, but we didn't know the new owners would be making so many cuts."

"What kind of cuts?" Kaylie asked with growing dread.

"We're losing the first hour of our weekend morning news and they're cutting the nightly six-thirty news…"

"What?!" Kaylie exclaimed, horrified. "People love the weekend morning news, and our investigative stories are in the six-thirty newscast. Are we going to have to move them to the five o'clock news now? What does the rest of the investigative team think about this?"

When Bob didn't answer her right away, she felt her blood run cold.

"Bob?"

"We also have to cut staff, a lot of it. The new owners decided they didn't need a whole investigative team. They only want one person…"

Kaylie shook her head. "No…"

"They want to keep Tim," Bob added. "Because he's been here twenty years and everyone knows him."

"And the rest of us on the I-team?" Kaylie asked, her voice shaking. "Me, Randy, and Judy?"

"I'm sorry," Bob said. "There was nothing I could do."

Kaylie reached out and held on to Bob's desk to steady herself as she felt the world she had so carefully built for herself come crashing down on her.

Chapter 2

Kaylie was at one of her favorite wine bars with Rachel, The Wine Vine. But she wasn't exactly following the mantra written on a sign that said *Only Wine No Whining Allowed*.

"I still can't believe it," Kaylie said, depressed. "A few hours ago, I was celebrating an upcoming promotion, and now I'm unemployed and have no idea what I'm going to do about my career or how I'm going to pay my bills." Kaylie frowned when she picked up her wine glass and it was empty.

Rachel quickly motioned for the bartender to pour them another round.

Usually, this was Kaylie's favorite place for happy hour. It was cute and cozy and right around the corner from the TV station. She didn't even mind how the bar always went all out to decorate for Christmas. There was upbeat Christmas music playing, a giant Christmas tree in the window that had ornaments made out of wine labels, and glittering white and silver snowflakes hanging from the ceiling. The vibe was festive and fun, but right now Kaylie wasn't feeling any of it.

She took a deep breath and tried to steady her raw nerves. "Rachel, I don't know what I'm going to do. I'm freaking out. I had a plan and now everything I planned is gone…"

"Okay, you just need to breathe," Rachel said. "We're going to figure this out."

Kaylie nodded and tried to put on a brave face, but she still felt like she was drowning.

Rachel reached out and gave her hand a reassuring squeeze. "You're sure there's no way there's any job for you at the station? Can't they keep you on as a general assignment reporter, or a writer, something, anything?"

Kaylie shook her head. "Bob says they're cutting everything. You're lucky you still have your job."

Rachel nodded and looked grateful. "Oh, I know. Thankfully, they always need photographers. I still can't believe how many people got laid off today."

"And a lot of them are here," Kaylie said, looking around the bar. When Kaylie saw a few people from the TV station that still had their jobs, they gave her a look of sympathy. But it only made her feel worse. She didn't want to be pitied. What she wanted and desperately needed was her job back.

Rachel tried again to wave the bartender over, but he was the only person behind the bar and he was hustling, pouring drinks as fast as he could for the growing crowd.

But when Kaylie held up her empty glass, the bartender hurried right over.

"Seriously?" Rachel muttered. "He must be a fan." But Rachel's frown turned into a bright smile when the bartender got closer. He was hot.

"Sorry to keep you waiting." He gave Kaylie a sexy smile and filled her wine glass to the very top. "It's on the house, and my name's Rick if there's anything else I can do for you…"

Rachel held up her empty glass, but Rick only had eyes for Kaylie.

Kaylie was clueless. She was going through emails on her phone.

Rachel cleared her throat. "Excuse me? May I also get a refill, please?"

"Of course, sorry," Rick said. He was still looking at Kaylie as he poured Rachel's wine. "I'm here if you need me for anything else."

"Uh, huh," Kaylie said. "Thanks." She never looked up from her phone.

As soon as he walked off, Rachel snatched Kaylie's phone from her.

"Hey!" Kaylie exclaimed, trying to get her phone back. "What are you doing?"

Rachel laughed. "What are you doing? The bartender, Rick, was totally hitting on you."

"What? No…" Kaylie shook her head.

"Uh, yes," Rachel countered. "Wow, you're even more far gone than I thought. I swear, the most eligible bachelor in the world could walk in here, and all you'd be checking out is his watch to see if it's counterfeit in case there was a story there."

Kaylie started looking around the bar at all the guys. "You know, that's not a bad idea. I bet you a lot of the watches here are fake. There's a new scam going on around Times Square and…"

"Stop." Rachel laughed. "Enough about work. You know what you need? A little work-life balance, because if you had a life, you would have noticed that the bartender was hot."

"I've been doing just fine," Kaylie said. "I've been concentrating on what's important. You have to go after your dreams if you want to make them come true. So, yes, I work a lot, but that's how I'm going to get where I need to be."

Rachel sat back. "Really? And how's that working for you right now?"

Kaylie, not amused, crossed her arms in front of her chest and stared back at Rachel.

Rachel leaned in. "Too soon? Sorry."

"Way too soon," Kaylie said. "Look, if you want to worry about me, worry about helping me find a job. That's what I really need right now."

Rachel was still eyeing the sexy bartender. "That's not all you need."

Kaylie picked up a menu, glanced at it, and quickly put it back down. She then grabbed one of the candy canes out of a glass mason jar on the bar. She peeled the wrapper off and took a big bite and then another. She was stress eating and didn't care.

"Seriously," she said. "I was planning to start having more balance in my life, or whatever you want to call it, after I got this promotion," Kaylie took another bite of her candy cane that was already half gone. "I just needed to focus on one thing at a time. That's the only way I can get things done. Work has to come first then everything else will follow. I learned that when I graduated college."

"What do you mean?" Rachel asked.

"I had this college boyfriend, Steve, we were great together."

"And?" Rachel asked.

"We graduated and both got jobs in different states," Kaylie said. "We tried to make the long-distance thing work, but it was hard with our schedules. Finally, we had to pick our careers or each other."

"And you picked work," Rachel said.

Kaylie nodded. "And it was the right choice."

"No regrets?"

"Never," Kaylie said. "I always think we're exactly where we're meant to be. He went on and got married and has two kids. He's happy."

"And you?" Rachel asked. "Are you happy?"

Kaylie sighed. "I was, until I got laid off a few hours ago."

"A job is a job," Rachel said. "It can't keep you warm at night, or go to dinner and movies with you, or…"

Kaylie held up her hand. "Stop. I get it. I hear you, but I think everyone is different and needs different things. What I need to make me happy is work, so right now I just feel…lost. I just have to regroup and figure out what to do."

Rachel moved Kaylie's wine glass closer to her. "No, what you need to do right now is try and relax. Give yourself a minute to catch up with what's happened. It's a lot, and I'm here if you need me."

Kaylie picked up her glass and held it out to Rachel. "To good friends. I don't know what I'd do without you."

Rachel clinked her glass to Kaylie's. "Good thing you'll never have to find out. Cheers."

Just as Kaylie was about to drink, an alert went off on her phone. When she glanced at her phone and saw it was Bob, she checked it quickly. Her eyes grew huge.

"No way." Her eyes lit up with hope.

"What?" Rachel asked, trying to read Kaylie's text.

"Bob says he might have a job for me!"

"That's amazing. Already?" Rachel said. "I knew he'd come through for you."

"Oh…" Kaylie's voice trailed off, and she frowned as she read the rest of the text.

"What?" Rachel asked.

Kaylie put down her phone. "The job's not at the TV station. It's for a friend of Bob's who owns an online magazine. It's just a quick freelance assignment, a puff piece feature to interview some family about their Christmas traditions."

"Oh…" Rachel tried to hold back a laugh but couldn't. "Your favorite kind of story. A feature story and a Christmas story. You hit the jackpot."

"Right?" Kaylie sighed. "I haven't done a feature since college, and even then I was never very good at them, and Christmas, really? A story about Christmas traditions, what was Bob thinking?"

"Uh, maybe that you need a job and it's a week before Christmas, so most people probably aren't hiring until the New Year—that's what he was thinking," Rachel said.

"You're right," Kaylie said. "What am I saying? I should be thankful for any job right now. I just don't want to take a job I can't do and let his friend down."

Rachel laughed. "You have taken down some of the top criminals in New York City I'm sure you can write a Christmas feature story. Have a little faith, my friend, and remember, if all else fails, 'tis the season."

"For what?" Kaylie asked, confused.

"For Christmas miracles, of course," Rachel said, like it should have been obvious. "You just have to believe."

Kaylie laughed. "Oh, wow, did you just get all that from some holiday fortune cookie?"

"No," Rachel said, completely serious. "Those are words I live by, so you're welcome."

Kaylie laughed louder. If there was one thing she could always count on, it was Rachel making her laugh. She picked up her phone and texted back Bob to tell her more.

His text back to her was almost instant.

"Bob says it will just take a few days to do the story, but I need to stay over Christmas."

Rachel frowned. "That's a bummer."

"No," Kaylie said, reading more of the text. "No, it's actually a good thing. They'll pay me double time because I would be working the holiday and…" Her eyebrows rose with interest. "The story's in Eastern Europe. I'd have to leave tomorrow."

"That's pretty last minute," Rachel said. "But Europe's cool. Think of the frequent flyer miles. You're always saying you want to travel more."

"All I'm thinking about is the overtime," Kaylie said.

Another text came in from Bob that asked: *Are you in?*

Kaylie looked at Rachel.

Rachel nodded, looking excited. "Go for it."

Kaylie took a deep breath and texted back: *I'm in.* She picked up her wine glass and waved at the bartender. "Hey, Rick, we're going to need another drink."

Less than twenty-four hours, and two plane rides later, Kaylie found herself jetlagged and blurry-eyed in Eastern Europe, stepping off a private jet that had just landed on a tiny airstrip somewhere in the middle of a snowy mountain range.

It was early in the morning, and a stretch of thick, dark clouds was blocking the sunrise.

Kaylie shivered as a blast of icy wind hit her full force and gratefully took the hand of the pilot who was waiting at the bottom of the stairs to help her.

"Thank you," she said as she wrapped her black scarf even tighter around her.

"You're welcome," he said. "And please be careful. It's a little icy out here, so watch your step."

Just as he said these words, her black leather riding boots slid on the slick tarmac. He grabbed her arm just in time to keep her from falling.

She laughed. "And thank you again. If I'd known I would be up in the mountains, I would have worn some different boots."

She'd been surprised that after her first commercial flight landed in London, she was picked up and transferred to a private jet airport just outside the city. She was even more surprised when she'd found out she would be taking a private jet for the rest of her journey and that she would be the only passenger. It only added to the mystery that had started right after she'd accepted the story assignment from Bob.

When she'd started asking him about the family she'd be interviewing and for more details about where she was going in Eastern Europe, Bob had barely given her anything. He'd said the family she was featuring had asked she only be told all the details once she arrived to protect everyone's privacy. Kaylie had heard about things like this before from other reporters who had interviewed celebrities, prominent CEOs, and politicians, so it had her imagination working overtime trying to guess who this family was.

When Kaylie had gotten on her second flight, the private jet, she'd tried to get some more information. She'd asked the pilot where they were going, how long it would take, and if he knew the family she'd be doing a story on.

But the pilot had merely given her a discreet smile and told her that they would be arriving at their destination *soon* and that she should just relax and enjoy the flight.

Since relaxing wasn't something she embraced, Kaylie had turned her attention to the friendly flight attendant to try once again to get some answers. Unfortunately, the chatty flight attendant had clammed up as soon as Kaylie started asking questions about who owned the jet and where they were going.

Never one to give up easily, she had continued to ask vague questions during the flight, but so far, she was still as much in the dark as she'd been when she left New York.

All the secrecy had Kaylie's investigative senses firing on all cylinders. In her experience, secrets usually meant someone was trying to hide something. Maybe, she thought, her fluff piece would turn out to be more interesting after all. A girl could dream.

She stood on the tarmac gazing up into the sky, blinking away the snowflakes that fell on her lashes and were covering her black wool coat.

The pilot followed her gaze. "It looks like we made it just in time," he said. "A storm front is on the radar and it looks like it's going to roll in here tonight. That could shut the airport down for days."

"Airport?" Kaylie looked around, confused. All she saw was one small hangar and a quaint brick building that was decorated with red and gold Christmas lights. "What kind of airport is this?"

"A private one," the pilot answered, making her even more curious.

When another blast of wind swirled around her, she rubbed her arms to stay warm.

The pilot motioned to the brick building. "You go ahead and get out of this cold. Your car should be waiting for you out front. I'll have someone bring your luggage."

Kaylie's teeth were starting to chatter. "Thank you so much." She moved as fast as she could, being careful not to slip, toward the building. She was about to go inside when she saw a black town car pull up.

"Thank goodness," she said, shivering. She was starting to go numb. When the car stopped, she eagerly ran up to it. She grabbed the back door just as another gust of wind blew her scarf into her face and blinded her. She practically fell into the car, landing right on the lap of a very surprised man.

"What the…" the man exclaimed, grabbing her hips.

"Oh my God!" Kaylie, horrified, locked eyes with the man. For a moment, she forgot she was sprawled across some stranger's lap, because he was one of the most handsome men she'd ever seen. His eyes were green with gold flecks. He had thick, black, wavy hair and a chiseled jaw that had just enough stubble to look sexy. She was staring at his full lips when someone grabbed her arm and pulled her out of the car.

"What are you doing?!" a large, stern man in a long black coat demanded.

"I'm so sorry," Kaylie said, still dazed. "I thought this was my car. I couldn't see because of the snow and the…"

The man quickly shut the door so the handsome stranger disappeared.

Kaylie tapped on the black-tinted window, trying to see the passenger again. "I'm really sorry…"

But it was too late. The man who had yanked her out of the car was already back in the driver's seat, and the car sped off.

Kaylie, still shaken, watched it go.

"Miss Karlyle?"

Kaylie spun around and found another formidable-looking man staring at her. He was holding her luggage.

"I'm your driver, Thomas, if you're ready to go."

"Did you just see that?" Kaylie asked, embarrassed. "I thought that was my car. They probably think I'm some kind of crazy person."

"Right this way, please," was all Thomas said as he walked toward the other side of the building where Kaylie saw another black town car waiting.

As Kaylie hurried to keep up with him, her boots kept slipping and sliding. As she fought not to fall, she was suddenly hit with a rush of nerves.

What have I gotten myself into? she wondered. She was in the middle of nowhere, freezing, and she had no idea where she was or where she was going. She was usually up for any adventure, but at this moment, she was cold, tired, hungry and had already humiliated herself once.

This was not the start she was hoping for.

When she caught up with Thomas, he was already holding the passenger door open for her. She cautiously peered inside but didn't move.

"Is everything okay?" Thomas asked.

Kaylie looked around inside the car. "Just making sure I don't run into any more surprises." Kaylie got into the car. "I hate surprises."

After Thomas shut her door, Kaylie could have sworn she heard him laugh.

Chapter 3

As they drove down the picturesque, snowy, winding, tree-lined, mountain road, Kaylie kept holding her phone up, trying to get a cell phone signal. She'd promised Bob she'd text him when she arrived, but she wasn't getting any signal at all.

She saw Thomas watching her in his rear-view mirror.

"I'm having a hard time getting a signal," she explained.

"That's because cell service is pretty spotty around here, especially after a storm," Thomas said as he slowed down to take a sharp curve around a mountain.

"Around here being?" Kaylie asked, still trying to figure out where she was. "Where are we exactly? What mountains are those?"

Thomas looked amused. "We'll be there soon."

Kaylie nodded. At this point, she wasn't surprised by him also dodging her questions.

She put down her phone and peered out the window. She tried to catch a glimpse of her surroundings, but she couldn't see anything past a thick forest of trees.

Kaylie felt like she was in a winter wonderland. All around her, everything was white and sparkling with fresh snow. Icicles in all shapes and sizes were hanging off of snow-covered tree branches, and every once in a while, a ray of sunshine would make it through the clouds, illuminating everything.

When they finally drove out of the forest, Kaylie's breath was taken away when she saw a magical lake in front of them that was glittering gold with the reflection of Christmas lights coming from a charming village. The village was made up of brick buildings and winding cobblestone streets. All along the lake there were lit-up Christmas trees decorated with bright red ornaments. Even the boat dock was decorated with Christmas wreaths and garland. But the real showstopper was the magnificent castle on the hillside, overlooking the lake, that was lit up with white twinkle lights, looking like something right out of a fairy tale.

"Wow," Kaylie whispered, blinking several times to make sure she wasn't dreaming. But when she opened her eyes, the village and castle were still there, looking more enchanting than ever.

Not caring that it was still snowing and freezing, she quickly put down her window and started taking pictures with her phone.

"That's Swan's Gate Castle. It was built in the 1600s. It's our crown jewel in Tolvania," Thomas said with pride.

"Tolvania?" Kaylie questioned.

"We're a very small sovereign state," Thomas said with a smile. "This is where I grew up. This is my home."

"It's beautiful," Kaylie said. "Like something out of a storybook. Can you visit the castle? Is it a museum? I'd love to get a look inside."

Thomas shook his head. "No, I'm afraid not. It's not a museum."

"That's too bad," Kaylie said. "Maybe while I'm here I can get some more pictures from the outside."

Thomas nodded. "Maybe."

Excited, Kaylie scrolled through the photos she just took. She was happy to see she'd gotten a few great shots that captured the dreamlike way the Christmas lights from the village reflected off the lake.

In her sixth-grade photography class, she'd been told she had an eye for finding the light and a gift for framing pictures. She had always loved trying to find the best way to capture what she was seeing and feeling.

She could still remember the day she'd come running home from school and had announced to her parents and sister that she wanted to be a photographer. She wanted to travel the world and tell stories with her photographs.

Her family had thought it was a great idea. Her parents had always encouraged her to go after her dreams, whatever those dreams might be, and from that day on, she had become the family photographer, taking pictures of anything and everything she could find.

Her love of photography had also been inspired by her time spent with her grandma, Patricia, who loved to travel. She smiled, remembering how they'd spend hours together going over old issues of *National Geographic* magazines at the library. She had been just eight years old when they'd started to keep a special journal together. They had called it their *Someday Trips* where they'd write down all the places they found in the magazines that they wanted to visit someday and take their own pictures of. They continued to add things to the journal all the way up to the week before her grandma had passed away. Kaylie had been a freshman in college.

The fact that they had never had a chance to take one of those *Someday Trips* together was one of Kaylie's biggest regrets.

They always thought they had time and would do the trips when she was on a summer break, or after graduating college. When her grandma had suddenly passed away, Kaylie was heartbroken. She had never looked at their journal again. She'd also changed her career course, deciding that being a foreign photojournalist wasn't very realistic because there were so few jobs. She had put away her cameras and her photography dreams. She switched her major to broadcast journalism and focused on being a TV reporter, where someone else like Rachel would capture the images and she would just write the stories.

"And we're here," Thomas announced as he slowed down the car, bringing Kaylie out of her reminiscing.

When Kaylie looked up from the castle pictures on her phone, she was stunned to find they had pulled up to the castle's massive front door.

"Oh, I'm sorry. I didn't mean I wanted to get pictures right now of the castle," Kaylie rushed to explain. "We can keep going."

Thomas got out and opened her door for her. "We have arrived."

"But I'm supposed to be meeting the family I'm interviewing," Kaylie said, not budging.

"Yes," Thomas said. "This is where I was told to drop you off."

Kaylie's eyes grew huge as she got out of the car. "This is where I'm meeting them? Well, that's cool. I guess it makes sense. They also want to show off your crown jewel."

Kaylie, in awe, started taking pictures of the impressive entryway with its massive twenty-foot double-sided wood-carved door. On each side of the door were two beautifully decorated Christmas trees that had white twinkling lights, red velvet ribbons, and red and gold glass ornaments. On the door itself was a huge wreath. It was covered with pretty pinecones, bright red holly berries, and was topped off with another lovely red velvet bow.

Kaylie admired the brass door knocker that had two swans' necks arching toward each other, creating a heart. "This must go with the name of the castle, Swan's Gate. Nice," she said to herself. She was just about to knock when the door suddenly opened.

Staring back at Kaylie was a cute ten-year-old girl who had a very curious but stern look on her face.

Kaylie, smiling, bent down so she was eye to eye with the little girl.

"Well, hello there," Kaylie said in a cheerful voice. "Who might you be?"

The little girl studied Kaylie and crossed her arms in front of her chest. "The princess," the little girl said, tilting her chin up proudly.

"I see," Kaylie said as she fought back a laugh. She was getting a kick out of how serious the girl was about playing her make-believe game.

"And you are?" the little girl asked in a voice that sounded much older than she was.

Kaylie grinned back at her. She was ready to play along. "Well, if you're the princess, then how about if I'm the queen?"

The little girl frowned. "No."

"Because I'm afraid that role is already taken," a woman's voice said behind the little girl.

This time Kaylie did laugh out loud. She was loving how everyone was getting in on the royal ruse.

As the door opened wider, Kaylie got her first glimpse of the woman standing behind the child. Kaylie guessed she was in her sixties. The woman looked flawless in her stylish winter-white pantsuit. She smiled back at Kaylie.

"You must be Miss Karlyle," the woman said with a polite smile.

"I am," Kaylie said, excited. "But you can just call me Kaylie. Are you"—Kaylie checked her phone where she had her notes written down—"Isabella? That's the only name I have for the family I'm supposed to meet. I hope I'm in the right place?"

"You are," the woman said, smiling back at her. "I'm Isabella."

Kaylie quickly held out her hand. "It's so nice to meet you."

Kaylie saw the little girl's eyes grow huge. When the woman didn't take her hand, Kaylie, embarrassed, quickly dropped it, realizing too late that handshakes must not be a custom here.

"It is our pleasure to meet you, too," the woman said and looked down at the little girl. But the little girl wasn't smiling. She was looking Kaylie up and down like she was dissecting her from head to toe.

Kaylie squirmed under the scrutiny. She hated to admit she was starting to feel a little intimated by the child. This was by far the most somber little girl she had ever seen. The girl's perfectly tailored navy-blue pants and matching jacket looked more like something you'd find on an adult going for a business interview.

The girl looked up at Isabella. "She's the queen."

"Oh, right, sure," Kaylie said, hoping to win the child over. She winked at the girl.

She could totally play this game. "Let's see," Kaylie said with a thoughtful smile. "If she's the queen and you're the princess, then maybe I can be a duchess or a countess, I'm not really sure the difference."

"No, you can't," the little girl said with authority.

"What's going on here?" a stern male voice behind Kaylie had her jumping before she turned around.

"You!" she exclaimed. She couldn't believe it. She was staring into the eyes of the same gorgeous guy she'd seen at the airport and had literally fallen into his lap. His green eyes flashed a warning that had Kaylie stepping back. He was even more handsome than she remembered, but right now all he was looking was annoyed.

"What are *you* doing here?" he demanded.

Isabella's perfectly-shaped eyebrows arched up. "You two have met?"

The little girl watched the adults, looking more intrigued by the second.

"No," Kaylie said.

"Yes," the man said.

They stared at each other before Kaylie turned to Isabella. "We didn't officially meet, but I accidentally tried to take his car at the airport."

The little girl did not look pleased, but Isabella was smiling.

"Really," Isabella said with a laugh. "That had to be interesting."

The man took a step toward Kaylie. "You still haven't answered my question. Who are you?"

Kaylie stood up straight and met his stare. "I'm Kaylie Karlyle from New York City, and you are?"

"The prince," the little girl answered for him. When the girl walked over to him, he relaxed for the first time and leaned down and gave the little girl a heartfelt hug and a kiss on the cheek.

Kaylie shook her head, impressed. "Wow, you all really take this royal role-playing to a whole new level. Okay, I'm game."

She did a silly mock bow to the prince. "Your highness, it's my greatest honor to meet you." She started laughing.

There was an awkward silence when no one else laughed.

The man walked past Kaylie into the castle and stood next to Isabella, giving her an incredulous look. "Mother, what is going on here? Who is she and why is she here?"

The little girl looked at Kaylie. "Father, don't be mad. She's American, from New York City, she doesn't know any better. Right, Grandmother?"

The queen, still smiling, nodded. "That's right, my darling, I'm afraid she doesn't."

Kaylie waved her hands. "Uh, hello. You know I am right here. I can hear you. I don't really know what's going on here, but I was just trying to play along…"

"Play along?" the man asked, confused. "Play along with what?"

Kaylie pointed at the little girl. "She said she was a princess." She pointed at Isabella. "And that you were the queen." Kaylie turned to the man. "And that you were the prince." Kaylie laughed. "Obviously, our little princess here is playing make-believe. I mean, we *are* in a castle, so I get it."

"Make-believe?" the man asked, confused. He turned to Isabella. "She's kidding, right?"

Isabella simply shrugged. The little girl did an identical shrug.

As he raked his fingers through his thick, wavy hair, he gave them both a disapproving look. "Seriously, you two are incorrigible."

Isabella stepped forward. "Miss Karlyle, I am sorry for the confusion. Let me formally introduce you to my family. This is my son, Prince Alexander, and my granddaughter, Princess Anna…"

"And my mother is the queen, Queen Isabella," Prince Alexander interrupted as he locked eyes with a stunned Kaylie.

The queen nodded. "And this is our home, Swan's Gate Castle, and we are officially known as the Royal Family of Tolvania."

Kaylie's mouth dropped open. "No! Shut the front door!"

"Shut the front door?" the queen asked looking confused.

Kaylie hurried to explain. "It's an American saying, like you're kidding, no way, for real…"

"We're real," Princess Anna chirped in. "Aren't we, Father?"

The prince locked eyes with Kaylie. "Very real."

Kaylie shivered, but not just from the cold.

A handsome caramel-colored dog, a Vizsla, ran up and sat down next to the princess. He gazed up at the princess with adoring sweet brown eyes.

"And this is Blixen, my dog, he's real, too," the princess said as she petted him.

Kaylie smiled and held out her hand to Blixen. He stepped forward, sniffed it, gave her a once over, seemed to approve, then happily licked her hand. Kaylie was charmed. "His name is Blixen. Blixen, like the reindeer?"

"Yes," Anna replied, as she gave Blixen a big hug.

"What a wonderful name," Kaylie said as she scratched behind his ears. He wagged his tail, looking like he was loving it.

The corner of Princess Anna's lips twitched. It was the closest thing to a smile that Kaylie had seen from her.

The queen opened the door wide. "Well, before we…*shut the front door,* please come in, Miss Karlyle. I will explain everything."

As Kaylie entered the castle, the prince turned to the queen. "Mother, I'm also looking forward to you explaining *everything.*"

Chapter 4

Once they were all inside the castle and the queen shut the door, she addressed her son.

"Alexander, I'm sure Anna's governess, Ms. Meyers, is looking for her. Why don't you take Anna back to her studies?"

"I want to stay," father and daughter said at the exact same time, with identical stubborn looks on their faces.

"Anna, I'm sure you don't want Ms. Meyers to be worried about you, do you?" the queen asked. "Or to get behind in your schoolwork right before Christmas break?"

Anna thought about it for a second. "No, I don't want that."

"That's my girl." The queen gave Anna a nod of approval.

Anna glanced over at Kaylie. "Will she be staying with us, Grandmother?"

The prince jumped in. "No."

The queen corrected him. "Yes, Anna, Miss Karlyle will be staying with us for a few days."

When the prince gave his mother a disbelieving look, Kaylie watched as the queen met his stare without blinking. The prince ended up looking away first.

The queen gave Anna a loving look. "Alexander, please take Anna back to Ms. Meyers."

The prince took Anna's hand. "And then I'll be back so we can talk." As the prince and princess walked away, the princess looked over her shoulder at Kaylie.

Kaylie waved at her.

The princess gave her a disapproving look.

Kaylie couldn't help but laugh as she watched them disappear around the corner.

"Wow, tough crowd."

The queen gave her an apologetic look. "I'm very sorry about all that. They're both very protective and serious by nature…"

Kaylie nodded. "I can see that. I think they're suspicious of me."

"They are that way with all strangers. Don't take it personally," the queen said. "Now you can see why I wanted you here. Please follow me."

But Kaylie didn't *see* or understand anything as she followed the queen down a long ornate corridor that was decorated with a half-dozen fragrant Christmas trees.

She was still trying to come to grips with the fact that she was inside a real castle with a real royal family. She knew no one was ever going to believe it. She didn't even believe it. Her mind was whirling with a million questions as she followed the queen into a beautiful drawing-room.

The setting was grand but still modern. All the walls were wallpapered in a rich red tone that was accented with gleaming gold trim. Despite all the inspiring landscape paintings and unique pieces of art, the real showstopper was the view from the floor-to-ceiling windows. From the windows, you could see a picturesque lake that was nestled up against a snow-covered mountain range.

Kaylie couldn't help herself. She took out her phone and walked up to the window and took a few pictures.

"Incredible," she whispered, taking it all in.

"This is one of my favorite views of our lake," the queen said as she joined her. "It's Lake Charles, named after my great-great-grandfather, and that mountain range is called Glacier Ridge."

Kaylie took another picture. "It really is magical."

"Like a fairy tale," the queen said, "especially at Christmas-time with all the snow."

"And when it comes to Christmas you certainly have some beautiful decorations from what I've seen so far," Kaylie said.

The queen looked pleased with the compliment. "Thank you. We have decorations that go back centuries. They all have a story."

Kaylie nodded. "I can imagine. I look forward to learning more."

"That is good to hear," the queen said. "I wanted to talk to you about what you'll be writing…"

They were interrupted when an attractive woman, Kaylie guessed her to be about the same age as she was, wearing a black chic dress with a pretty red silk scarf entered the room holding a silver serving tray. On the tray were two beautiful crystal mugs filled with hot chocolate. There was also a snowflake plate with some breakfast pastries. There were delectable-looking mini quiches, muffins, and croissants.

The queen gave the woman a grateful look. "Elsa, wonderful, thank you. You can set that down right on the coffee table."

"Is there anything else I can get you?" Elsa asked.

"This will be all for now. Thank you, Elsa," the queen answered.

As Elsa left the room, the queen motioned over by the impressive gray stone fireplace where Elsa had dropped off the tray. As Kaylie followed the queen over to a red velvet settee, she could imagine curling up next to the fire with a good book and thought she could happily live in this room forever. All the space and natural light was a huge contrast to the minuscule studio apartment she had in New York City. What she appreciated the most was, that while the room was undeniably luxurious, it was also still warm and inviting, making it the perfect cozy combination.

"Do you travel a lot?" the queen asked, taking a seat next to Kaylie in a regal red and gold wingback chair.

"Not as much as I'd like," Kaylie said. "My job usually keeps me pretty busy in New York City."

The queen nodded. "And you enjoy it?"

"The city or my job?" Kaylie asked, but then answered her own question. "I actually love both. The city is so full of life and always changing. You're never bored. There's always something to learn, something new to do and my job, now that I think about it, is the same. It's always changing, too, because I never know what story I'll be doing. Every day it's like I'm starting over with a new challenge. I guess you could say it keeps me on my toes."

The queen picked up a hot chocolate and handed it to Kaylie. "So, you like new experiences and trying new things?" the queen asked.

"I do," Kaylie said, before taking a sip of her drink. Her eyes lit up. She took another sip, savoring the taste. "This chocolate is amazing. It's so rich and bold and a little bit…spicy, I think, maybe?"

The queen looked impressed. "Yes, that's because it has some chili peppers in it. I'm glad you like it. It's from our chocolate shop in the village. Jean Pierre is an award-winning chocolatier carrying on his family's chocolate-making tradition by always blending unique ingredients together. He creates a new hot chocolate every year for Christmas. We can't wait to see what he comes up with next."

"I can see why," Kaylie said, still marveling at how delectable the hot chocolate was. "And these?" she asked, picking up and admiring a mini quiche before taking a bite.

"Those are all from Chef Jake," the queen said proudly. "We are very lucky to have him. He's always brilliant at putting together a menu for our Christmas tea, another tradition of ours."

"They're delicious," Kaylie said, popping the rest of it into her mouth. When she put down her plate, she noticed a family picture on the table. It was in a classic silver frame. It looked like it had been taken in the same room they were in, right next to the stunning ten-foot Christmas tree that was in the corner. As Kaylie admired the real tree, she noticed it looked like it was decorated almost the same as the tree in the picture, with red glass hearts and garland made out of a collection of small glass gold beads.

In the picture standing next to the tree, dressed in formal festive wear, was the queen in a dazzling silver ball gown. Next to the queen was Princess Anna in a pretty pink Cinderella-style dress, Prince Alexander in a white tux and tails, and a pretty woman in a red sparkling ball gown that Kaylie guessed to be the prince's wife. Blixen was also in the picture. He was wearing a red bow and sitting dutifully at the princess's feet. They all looked like one big happy family.

"That is one of my favorite pictures," the queen said, picking up the photograph that Kaylie had just been studying. "It was taken three years ago. It was the last Christmas we had with Sophia, Anna's mother, my daughter-in-law."

When Kaylie gave the queen a questioning look, the queen took a deep breath before continuing.

"We lost Sophia right after Christmas. She had a long battle with cancer. She lived each day to the fullest and had so much love for everyone. We all miss her very much, especially at Christmas, because this was her favorite time of year and she believed in creating magical memories and honoring traditions. She had me promise I would always make sure that Anna and my son continued to celebrate Christmas, the joy, the love, the laughter." The queen's voice trailed off. Her eyes looked sad. "But it has not been easy to keep that promise."

Kaylie could feel the queen's pain. "I'm so sorry. I can't imagine how hard this must have been on all of you."

"My son and Sophia had a great love," the queen continued. "He wasn't always like this, so serious and guarded, but after Sophia passed, he changed, and because of that, unfortunately, so did Anna. My granddaughter had to grow up very fast, and my son threw himself into his work. I think it helps him forget his pain and brings him comfort. I'm very proud of him. He's so passionate about helping our people, just like his father was. My husband passed away when Alexander was in college and Alexander immediately stepped up to help fill that void. But now I worry about my son and granddaughter. There is more to life than just work."

Kaylie listened, thinking about how Rachel had just said the same words to her back in New York.

"I want Anna and my son to have every happiness in life. They both deserve that," the queen said. "When my husband passed away, the last thing that was on my mind was replacing him with anyone else. He was the love of my life, so I understand Alexander not wanting to replace Sophia, but Anna is so young, it's hard to see her growing up without a mother."

"But she has you," Kaylie said. "She's very lucky."

The queen looked pleased. "Thank you for saying that. My granddaughter has my whole heart. Right now, she's ten going on forty. It's like she has the weight of the world on her shoulders and, in a way, she does. She will follow in her father's footsteps and will run our nation someday, as queen, that is her legacy, but that is hopefully years away. While she can, I want her to grow up and experience the joy of being a child. I want her to laugh and play, have fun, and to be a free spirit."

Kaylie's eyebrows arched.

"You're surprised?" the queen asked.

Kaylie answered honestly. "Yes. You always hear about royal families and all the pressure to be a certain way, all the formality, all the rules. I guess I don't think of any member of a royal family having a free spirit and getting to do whatever they want, when they want."

"Oh, don't misunderstand me, we have rules we must follow to keep up appearances because our people expect that and look forward to it as something they can count on," the queen said. "But we're a very small sovereign state here in Tolvania, and we're a modern royal family. My father, King George, was very progressive, even in his time. He always believed that as a royal family it was our duty, for the best of our people, to find the balance between tradition and progress. Yet, I worry that perhaps we've become too modern..."

"What do you mean?" Kaylie asked.

"I run our home with a very small staff," the queen said.

Kaylie looked surprised. "But this is a very big castle."

"It is, and I have help when I need it for housekeeping and things like that, but I don't have a staff of maids, butlers and doormen and ten people in the kitchen. I like to keep things simple, for a lot of reasons. For example, I can open my own door when someone knocks, if I'm the one closest to it."

"Unless your granddaughter gets there first," Kaylie said with a smile.

The queen chuckled. "Yes, although she knows she's not supposed to do that. I'm sure she saw you on the security camera. We have a lot of security cameras, but still, one can never be too careful, especially with a child."

Kaylie nodded. "I agree."

"I told her someone from New York City was coming and she has been very curious," the queen said and then glanced around the room. "While I believe in tradition, I also believe in updating when necessary, to keep up with the times, and that's what I just did recently when we completely renovated the castle, including all twenty bedrooms. All of the upgrades and changes were needed, to be sure to preserve the castle for future generations and for comfort. We created a gourmet kitchen with the leadership of Chef Jake. He also helped us update and expand our wine cellar so we could host special wine dinners, and we added a state-of-the-art sound system throughout the castle and updated the ballroom for our dances and concerts we host."

"It sounds wonderful," Kaylie said.

"It is, or should I say, it was," the queen said with a sigh. "Unfortunately, we haven't hosted any events since we lost Sophia. It didn't seem right the first year, and then the years just slipped by so fast, and now here we are. And it's not just the events here at the castle that we're missing."

The queen walked over to the Christmas tree and carefully took down one of the red heart glass ornaments and held it up to the light. "We also used to host special events during holidays for the village. There were so many Christmas events and traditions everyone loved, and they have been very missed, but now this year we are bringing them back for the first time since we lost Sophia. I think it's so important that Anna experiences these Christmas traditions that are part of her heritage and who she is, traditions that her mother loved so much," the queen said as she put the heart ornament back on the tree, making sure it was illuminated by the white twinkle lights. "And that's why you're here, Miss Karlyle."

"Please call me Kaylie," Kaylie said with a smile. "And yes, I understand this story is to be about your family's Christmas traditions."

"In part," the queen said with a smile.

There was something about the queen's smile that made Kaylie nervous. "In part? There's more?"

"Yes," the queen said, giving Kaylie her full attention. "My family needs you."

Kaylie's eyes grew huge. "Me? How?"

The queen looked into her eyes. "We need you to take our royal Christmas traditions and create a Christmas fairy tale for the princess that I can give her on Christmas at our special family Christmas dinner."

When Kaylie's jaw dropped to the floor, the queen didn't miss a beat.

"By using all our traditions and customs to create this fairy tale, we'll have a story we can continue to hand down for generations. A fairy tale that's full of heart and a happily ever after. It's just what my granddaughter needs, and I'd like you to write it."

Kaylie, in shock, stared back at the queen. "You're not serious…"

"I'm very serious," the queen said.

When Kaylie saw that she really was serious, she started to panic. She stood up and started pacing as she tried to process what the queen was saying. "You want me to use your traditions and write a fairy tale?"

"Yes," the queen said, excited. "A Christmas fairy tale."

Kaylie laughed a nervous laugh. "But I'm a journalist, not an author. I write stories for the news. I've never written a children's story in my life."

Kaylie knew she was talking faster and faster, but she couldn't help herself. She had to make the queen understand that a huge mistake had happened. She wasn't the writer they were looking for. They needed an author. She felt terrible about it, but she couldn't pretend to be someone she wasn't.

"Yes, I know all about your journalism career," the queen said. "Bob told me all about it."

"Bob? You know my boss, Bob?" Kaylie asked. She was getting more confused by the second.

"Yes, and he assured me you would be the perfect person for the job," the queen said with a confident smile.

Kaylie stopped pacing. "Then Bob's nuts, and trust me, I love Bob, but he is way off base this time. I don't know what he was thinking." She got out her phone. "We should call him right now and straighten this out." She checked her phone and frowned. "I can't get a signal."

"It's the snowstorm," the queen said. "It happens. Please sit back down. Let's discuss this."

Kaylie sat down and rubbed her throbbing temples. "Okay, let me start over. I'll just cut to the chase. I'm a news reporter, an investigative reporter, and honestly, even doing a feature story about your Christmas traditions was going to be a stretch for me, and that was *before* I found out you were a *royal* family…" Kaylie laughed. It was a high-pitched nervous laugh.

The queen patiently waited for Kaylie to continue.

Kaylie took a deep breath. "Bob never told me you were royal. I get it, you wanted your privacy. That totally makes sense. I don't blame you, but I don't have any experience covering royal families. It's not what I do, unless you're involved in some kind of scam." Kaylie abruptly stopped talking and stared at the queen. "You aren't, are you? Involved in a scam?"

"No, we are not," the queen said patiently. "But to your point about you not reporting on a royal family, a family is a family," the queen said with conviction. "Royal or not, we're people. We're mothers and fathers and grandmothers, we have blood and bones just like anyone else."

"Except your blood is *blue,*" Kaylie said quickly. "I mean, not literally, of course, but you have royal blood so that changes everything."

"Does it?" the queen asked. "How? We live and love and laugh the same."

Kaylie jumped up and held out her arms, looking around. "You live in a castle. That is not normal. None of this is normal…"

The queen, unfazed, continued to smile back at Kaylie.

Kaylie could see she needed to take a different approach. She took a deep breath and walked over to the queen and tried again. "Okay, let me put it another way. Royal or not, as a journalist I deal in facts, not fiction…"

"And the facts would be our real-life Christmas traditions," the queen said with a growing confidence that was making Kaylie even more nervous.

She rushed on. "But I wouldn't even know how to begin turning real-life facts, your Christmas traditions, into a fairy tale. That's just not in my skill set…"

The queen locked eyes with her. "But you're a storyteller, right?"

Kaylie opened her mouth, tried to find the words, couldn't, so snapped it back shut.

"You tell stories for a living," the queen continued. "You research and you use that research to tell a story, and that's all I'm asking you to do, to use our Christmas traditions to tell a story for my granddaughter."

"But you want a *Christmas fairy tale*," Kaylie said, making it sound like the queen was asking her to lasso the moon, because as far as Kaylie was concerned, she was.

"Yes," the queen said. "I want a fairy tale."

"And that's the problem," Kaylie said. "I didn't read fairy tales growing up. Nope. I was more of a realistic kid. I liked to read mysteries and stories about real places and real people. Fantasy and superheroes and all that stuff wasn't my thing. I've never even read *Harry Potter.*"

When the *Harry Potter* reference didn't bother the queen, Kaylie started to panic even more. She was frantically searching her brain, trying to find another way to help the queen understand. Her eyes lit up. She knew just what to say. Confident, she put her hands on her hips and locked eyes with the queen.

"At Halloween, I never wanted to be a queen or princess, or anything royal. I've never even worn a crown or tiara." Kaylie said. She was sure that should do the trick.

"We can fix that," the queen said, amused. "You can borrow one of my tiaras if you like."

"No," Kaylie said, exasperated. "That's the point. I would not like that. Nothing about being royal is something I would like." Kaylie snapped her mouth, embarrassed to have blurted out what she was thinking out loud. "I'm really sorry," she said and meant it. "I don't mean to insult you, and your family, but I don't know how else to say it. You have the wrong girl. This isn't something I can do. It's not a good fit for me. I can't do it."

Kaylie collapsed on the settee, exhausted, and stress-ate two more quiches.

The queen, undeterred, smiled back at her. "Bob thought you could, and I have faith in you, too."

"But I don't have faith in me," Kaylie said. "Not for this. I don't want to mess this up. This is obviously very important to your family. So, trust me, you need a real author who does this kind of thing, and I need to go back to New York City."

The queen got up and walked to the window and motioned for Kaylie to join her. When Kaylie stood next to the queen, she followed the queen's gaze outside but all she saw was a blur of white whirling snow.

"No one is going anywhere today," the queen said. "Not with this storm."

"Oh, no…" Kaylie's heart sank. She stepped closer to the window and touched the freezing glass, feeling trapped. She was trapped inside a castle, only this wasn't a fairy tale, Kaylie thought, it was a nightmare.

Chapter 5

"Mother, we need to talk…"

Kaylie heard the prince's voice as he entered the room and quickly turned from the window and saw he looked like he was on a mission.

The queen gave him a patient smile. "Of course. Come in and join us."

"Alone," the prince said, giving Kaylie a pointed look.

"I would love to go, but I have no idea where to go," Kaylie said, locking eyes with him. "Because apparently I'm stuck here."

"What are you talking about?" the prince said.

"She's talking about the storm," the queen answered for her. "I was just about to explain to Kaylie that there's only one road to our airport and how we close it when a storm comes, so no one will be flying until it's safe."

"She can't stay here," the prince said with conviction.

Kaylie watched as the queen tilted her head with a smile that looked like more of a warning. "Kaylie will be staying here as our guest, as planned," the queen said.

Kaylie saw the prince's jaw clench. She could feel his displeasure from across the room. She felt a chill down her spine, even though the room was toasty warm from the fire.

"As planned?" the prince shot back. "I didn't know anything about this *plan*."

"Neither did I," Kaylie said. "Join the club."

"So, it's settled, and you will stay here with us," the queen said, smiling at Kaylie.

Kaylie was still trying to process everything. "I really don't want to impose…"

"Too late," the prince said under his breath, but Kaylie caught it, as did the queen.

"Alexander." The queen gave him a disapproving look. "Where are your manners?"

The prince crossed his arms in front of his chest. "You might want to ask Miss Karlyle about her manners. She's the one who tried to give me a lap dance at the airport."

The queen's eyebrows arched as Kaylie's face blazed red hot from embarrassment.

"What? No!" Kaylie sputtered. "That's not what happened." Frantic, she turned to the queen. "I mean, I did fall into his lap, that's true; I couldn't see. It was windy, but I did *not* give him a lap dance."

The queen's eyes widened with even more amusement.

Kaylie rushed on, desperate to explain. "I thought his car was mine and it was snowing and I jumped in…"

"And landed on my lap," the prince finished for her.

Kaylie glared back at him. "I didn't see you." She turned to the queen. "I really didn't see him. I couldn't see anything and I promise you, I've never done a lap dance in my life…" She spun back around and faced the prince. "And even if I had, it wouldn't have been for someone like *you.*"

"What? Someone royal?" the prince asked with a laugh.

"No, someone rude!" Kaylie fired back at him.

The queen chuckled. Kaylie could see she was enjoying the heated banter.

"Alexander, how do you even know what a lap dance is?" the queen asked. Her eyes were twinkling with laughter. "Are you talking from experience?"

"Mother!" the prince exclaimed, looking appalled.

The queen laughed. "You started it."

The horrified look on the prince's face was so priceless, Kaylie couldn't help but laugh, too.

The prince, frustrated, walked over to the fireplace and added another log to the fire.

"Alexander, Kaylie is a journalist…"

The prince, stunned, dropped the log he was holding. "A journalist? You've invited a journalist into our home after you know what they've done to this family…"

The queen interrupted him. "She's not paparazzi, she's a feature reporter I've hired to help research some of our family's Christmas traditions."

"Actually, I don't usually do features; I'm an invest…" But Kaylie didn't have time to finish before the prince jumped in again.

"Why does she need to research our Christmas traditions." he asked, giving Kaylie a look of distrust.

"Because they're important for us all to remember and we haven't been doing that these last few years. We haven't been celebrating Christmas at all and I don't want Anna to forget how special it is, and you know Sophia wouldn't have wanted that either. All you've been doing is working right through the holidays like you want to forget it all, but we can't and shouldn't forget."

Kaylie saw a flash of pain cross the prince's face before he quickly looked into the fire.

"There's nothing wrong with working," the prince said. "It's our duty. That's who we are. That's what our people expect."

The queen walked over and looked into his eyes. "But our first commitment should always be to this family, to each other. We can't help others if we can't help ourselves." She took the prince's hand. "Put 'family first,' is what your father would always say, remember?"

Kaylie watched the prince's eyes soften for a moment.

"I remember," the prince said quietly. He kissed his mother's hand before letting it go. "But times have changed and we have even more commitments now. I'm just trying to live up to Father's legacy, like he wanted, and someday Anna will carry on that tradition."

The queen lovingly put her palm against the prince's cheek. "Son, I know you've done an amazing job and you're teaching Anna all about duty and honor…"

The prince nodded.

"But…" When the queen continued, the prince's smile faltered. "There's more to life than just work, and this Christmas I want Anna to see that. I want her to learn that what's most important at Christmas is being with family and the people you love and opening your heart to the Christmas spirit." The queen looked deep into the prince's eyes. "And Anna isn't the only one I want to enjoy this Christmas. She learns by your example, so you need to show her how special Christmas can be."

"But my schedule is filled back-to-back until the first of the year, you know that," the prince said.

The queen nodded. "Yes, I do, and that's why I've made some adjustments."

Kaylie's eyes widened as she watched the prince's mouth drop open.

"Adjustments?" the prince asked, looking annoyed. "What do you mean by *adjustments*?"

The queen crossed her arms in front of her own chest, mimicking him, and took a step toward the prince as she locked eyes with him. "May I remind you that I still run this family? If adjustments need to be made, I will make them."

The prince immediately dropped his arms and his attitude. "Of course. I understand."

"Do you?" the queen asked. "Because sometimes I feel like you've taken on all the responsibility of this family and you use that as an excuse to stay so busy that you're hardly a part of this family anymore."

Kaylie winced, seeing the prince take the direct hit.

"I don't ask you to do a lot for me," the queen continued. "But this Christmas, I need you to support me on this."

The prince looked confused. "On what?"

"On celebrating Christmas again," the queen answered.

Kaylie shifted from one foot to another. She felt very uncomfortable being in the room when such a private conversation was happening.

"And I've decided," the queen continued. "Things are going to be very different for us this Christmas." The queen turned and smiled at Kaylie. "And Miss Karlyle—Kaylie—is going to help us."

Now Kaylie felt even more awkward. She wished the ground would swallow her up so she didn't have to deal with the disapproving look on the prince's face. She looked around but felt trapped, and then decided maybe she could appeal to the prince and get through to the queen that way. She felt like the prince clearly didn't want her there any more than she wanted to be there.

"As I told your mom…" she started.

"The queen," the prince quickly corrected her.

"Yes, sorry, of course, as I told the queen, I'm a reporter. I don't write books or children's stories."

"Children's stories?" the prince asked, looking confused. "What does that have to do with anything?" He looked from his mother back to Kaylie.

Now it was Kaylie's turn to stare at the queen. "You didn't tell him? I thought you said your *family* wanted me to do this?"

The queen brushed off Kaylie's concern with another charming smile and Kaylie couldn't believe it when the queen motioned for her to tell him. She took a deep breath and ripped the proverbial Band-Aid off.

"Your mother wants me to write a fairy tale for your daughter for Christmas."

"What?" the prince said, almost choking. He looked stunned and furious all at the same time.

The queen didn't blink. "Kaylie will be using our Christmas traditions to create a customized fairy tale for Anna, so our traditions can be preserved for generations to come. Isn't it a wonderful idea?"

The prince looked at the queen like she was insane. "I don't understand what's happening here."

"That makes two of us," Kaylie said and turned back to the queen. "And you do realize Christmas is only a few days away. No one can write a children's book that fast."

The queen waved off her concern. "I'm not asking for a full book, just a fairy tale using our family's Christmas traditions. I'd like to give it to my granddaughter on Christmas to start a new family tradition. Then, after Christmas, we'll hire an illustrator to create some beautiful pictures for your story and have it made into a little book."

"I am so confused," the prince said, raking his fingers through his thick, wavy hair.

"This might help," the queen said as she walked over to an exquisite antique writing desk and picked up a fancy scroll with a red satin ribbon tied around it. She handed it to the prince.

"What's this?" he asked, looking even more baffled.

"Open it up and see," the queen urged. Her eyes danced with anticipation.

As the prince unrolled the scroll, it went on and on until he finally couldn't hold it anymore. He dropped one end and it tumbled all the way to the floor.

"Whoa," Kaylie said, seeing all the writing on the scroll. She leaned in to get a closer look at what was written.

"Tolvania Christmas Traditions." the prince read out loud. "What is this?"

The queen laughed. "You just read what it is."

Kaylie looked impressed. "Are these all really your Christmas traditions?"

"Only my favorites," the queen said. "We have hundreds, but these are the ones I'd like you two to concentrate on."

"*Us* two?" Kaylie asked, startled.

The prince gave Kaylie an apprehensive look. "What does she mean *us*?"

Kaylie held up both hands in self-defense. "Hey, don't look at me. She's your mom. I don't know what she's up to."

The queen laughed. "Kaylie, you said you don't think you're qualified to do this…"

"That's right," Kaylie said, relieved that the queen was finally getting it.

"And Alexander," the queen continued. "You don't think you have the time to bring back a bunch of Christmas traditions."

The prince also looked relieved. "That's right, I really don't."

"Well, you're both wrong," the queen said. "And since I'm the queen and this is my castle, we're going to do things my way."

Kaylie's smile disappeared when she realized the queen wasn't kidding. The queen continued. "The fact of the matter is there's a snowstorm outside, so for the time being, Kaylie, you must stay with us and during this time I see no reason why you, Alexander, can't show her some of our Christmas traditions. This way, Kaylie, you can make an informed decision on whether you can write this fairy tale or not."

"But I've already said," Kaylie started but was interrupted by the prince.

"Mother," the prince said. "I told you I don't have time to, to…play holiday tour guide." The prince glanced at Kaylie. "No offense."

"Some taken," Kaylie said.

The prince held up the scroll and its long list of Christmas activities. "I can give you a dozen reasons why I can't do this."

The tense moment was interrupted when Princess Anna entered the room. "Father, is anything wrong?" she asked. "I'm done with my studies and I would like to take Blixen for a walk." Blixen was right next to the princess. When he heard the word *walk*, his ears perked up and his tail started wagging.

The queen happily motioned toward the princess. "Alexander, you have all your reasons why you think you can't do this, well, there's your one reason why you must. Your daughter. Do I need to give you more?"

Kaylie felt uncomfortable watching mother and son battle it out so, instead, she turned her attention to the princess.

"What topics are you studying right now?" she asked the princess.

"English literature and history," the princess answered in a matter-of-fact voice. "I've also been learning about global warming."

"Wow," Kaylie said, surprised and impressed. "That's a lot, and you're how old?"

"Ten and two months and four days," the princess answered. "Tomorrow I'll be studying archaeology and Renaissance art."

Kaylie laughed. "Okay, now you're just messing with me."

The princess didn't laugh back. Confused, she looked at her father for help.

"Wait, seriously?" Kaylie asked.

The queen nodded. "You see what I mean. Time to add a little fun into the curriculum."

"Fun?" The princess frowned. "What do you mean?"

The queen walked over to her granddaughter and took Blixen's leash from her. "How about you and me and Blixen go for a walk in the gardens out back, where Miles always shovels a path for us. It's snowing pretty hard out there. We'll have to bundle up. How does that sound?"

"I would like that," the princess answered politely. "Blixen loves the snow."

Blixen barked his approval.

The queen laughed. "Then it's unanimous. While we do our walk, Alexander, you can give Kaylie the tour."

"Tour?" Kaylie asked, fearing whatever the queen was going to say next.

"Yes, around the castle, so you'll know your way around. It's quite large but don't worry, Alexander will show you everything. Won't you, Alexander?"

Alexander opened his mouth to say something but then saw Anna watching him. He promptly shut his mouth. "Of course." When he tried to smile, Kaylie could tell it was forced and was only for the princess's sake.

"Anything in particular you'd like me to show Miss Karlyle?" the prince asked the queen.

She motioned toward the scroll he was still holding. "Anything that's on the list that's one of our Christmas traditions. You might want to take it with you so you don't miss anything."

The prince held up the huge scroll. "You've got to be kidding me. There are dozens of things on this list."

The queen laughed. "I am kidding."

The prince looked relieved.

"I sent you an email with the list so you'll have it on your phone. You don't have to carry the scroll around," the queen said with a bright smile. "I just thought the scroll was a fun idea."

"So much fun," the prince grumbled.

Kaylie hid a laugh, seeing that the princess was watching them closely.

"You two enjoy your tour. I look forward to hearing all about it," the queen said as she guided the princess and Blixen out of the room.

As soon as the queen and the princess were gone, Kaylie turned to the prince. "Does your mother, the queen, always get her way?" she asked, exasperated.

"What do you think?" the prince answered as he quickly rolled up the scroll and handed it to Kaylie.

"I think I'm in trouble," Kaylie said, shaking her head. "Big trouble, but wait, why are you giving me this?"

The prince was already heading for the door. "Because I have work to do."

"But I thought we were supposed to do this *together*?" Kaylie called after him. "What about my tour?!"

"I'll have Elsa do it," the prince said as he sailed out the door and laughed.

The next laugh Kaylie heard was the queen's as she walked into the room with the sheepish-looking prince.

"Apparently this one didn't quite understand today's game plan," the queen said, giving the prince a look.

The prince looked away. "I thought you were going for a walk with Anna."

"I am," the queen said. "She's changing into the proper clothes."

"So, you were just waiting for me?" the prince asked in disbelief.

The queen laughed. "I know you well, my son. Now please, don't embarrass either of us anymore. You're being quite rude to our guest. Apologize, Alexander."

The prince rolled his eyes. "Mother, I'm not twelve."

"Then stop acting like it." The queen gave the prince a little nudge.

"I'm sorry, Miss Karlyle," the prince said. "Sorry, that you got tangled up in this family drama."

"Don't you mean Christmas celebration?" the queen offered.

"I give up," the prince said with a sigh.

The queen patted his cheek. "Good choice."

This time Kaylie did laugh and that had the prince turning his attention to her. "It is really a shame that you came all this way, from New York City, under false pretenses for a job that you're clearly not qualified for."

The prince's blunt words startled her. Even though she'd been saying the exact same thing to the queen, that she wasn't qualified to write a Christmas fairy tale, having the prince say it was a whole different story. He didn't know her. He didn't know anything about her.

She held up the scroll that the prince had tossed at her.

When the prince gave her a look that said *don't do it*, she looked even more determined as she let the scroll unravel, dropping to the ground. She quickly scanned the top Christmas traditions on the list. One immediately jumped out to her.

"This tradition, about upside-down Christmas trees, what's this one all about?" she asked.

The prince shrugged. "I have no idea. Never heard of it."

They both looked at the queen who was smiling, remembering.

"Ah, the upside-down Christmas trees," she said, her eyes lighting up with joy. "That is one of my favorite traditions that we haven't done in years."

The queen gave Kaylie a hopeful look. "Would you like to hear more about it?"

At that moment, Kaylie knew if she said yes, she'd be going down the Christmas Rabbit Hole with the queen.

But when she saw the prince behind the queen vehemently mouthing the words *no, no, no* and shaking his head, she made up her mind.

She looked back at the queen. "I would love to hear more." Kaylie's smile grew when she saw the prince throw up his hands in frustration and look at her like she was nuts.

Chapter 6

"Wonderful." The queen beamed back at Kaylie. "You're going to love this tradition. It's something you actually have to see to really understand and appreciate, and it will be perfect for the fairy tale..."

"Wait, I didn't agree to write the fairy tale," Kaylie interrupted. She walked over to the window and peered out at the snow that was still falling. "But while I'm snowed in here, I can still learn about your Christmas traditions, because that's the story I'm supposed to do for the magazine and that's a story I can still do. I'm sure people will be very interested to see what kind of Christmas traditions a royal family has and get a rare glimpse inside a castle like this at what royal life is really like."

The prince, looking upset, stepped forward. "You're not going to be writing about my family's Christmas traditions or anything about my family at all. We don't talk to the press. Ever!"

"Alexander is right," the queen said. "We value and protect our privacy. I'm sure you can understand that, Kaylie. I invited you here to write the fairy tale that will exclusively stay with our family. No one else will see it."

Kaylie, flabbergasted, stared at the queen. "But that's not what I agreed to."

Before the queen could respond, the prince jumped back in. "Mother, there's no sense sharing any of our Christmas traditions with this journalist if she can't do what you wanted. You heard her, she's not an author. I say she leaves as soon as possible and we all put this unfortunate misunderstanding behind us."

Kaylie, her head throbbing, sat down on the settee. The jetlag was definitely catching up to her because she couldn't think straight. All she knew was that she wanted to call Bob immediately and find out what in the world was going on.

"I disagree," the queen told the prince as she carefully pulled out a large red leather photo album from the bookcase and sat down next to Kaylie. Embossed in gold across the top of the album, Kaylie saw the words *Christmas Memories*. As the queen flipped through the pages, Kaylie saw all the photographs were vintage black and white.

The queen's face lit up with joy when she found the page she was looking for. She pointed to an old black and white photo of a grand ballroom that was decorated for the holidays.

When Kaylie leaned in for a closer look at the picture, she did a double take when she saw a bunch of beautifully decorated upside-down Christmas trees hanging from the ceiling. "Why are those trees upside-down?"

"Aren't they marvelous?" the queen asked, eagerly. "They were cut down right from our forest here in Tolvania. Twelve trees to represent the twelve days of Christmas."

Kaylie's eyes grew huge. "They're real?"

"They are," the queen said proudly.

Prince Alexander looked over the queen's shoulder to check out the picture. He looked perplexed. "Why did someone hang Christmas trees upside-down in our ballroom?"

"It's a family tradition dating back centuries. This is part of your history, and Anna's, too," the queen answered as she flipped to another page showing even more photos that included some close-ups of the fabulous upside-down trees and all their pretty ornaments.

Kaylie instantly noticed the glass heart ornaments.

"Are those the same heart ornaments that you have on the tree in here?" she asked.

"They are," the queen said. "Those ornaments are another tradition for our family and Tolvania. They're hand-blown from our glass blower in the village and they represent the heart of Christmas. A new collection is released every year for Christmas and people buy them and give them to the people they love the most. They bring good luck in love and life, well beyond Christmas."

"The hearts I knew about," the prince said. "But I still can't believe our family would invent such a crazy tradition of turning Christmas trees upside-down."

"Oh, we didn't invent the upside-down Christmas tree idea," the queen said. "That tradition was started back in the seventh century."

"The seventh century. Seriously?" Kaylie asked, fascinated.

The queen nodded, smiling. "The upside-down Christmas tree idea all started with a Benedictine monk, St. Boniface, in Germany around the seventh century. But then the idea to hang Christmas trees upside-down became really popular in Poland around the twelfth century in a tradition called podlazniczka, where they'd also wrap up little treats of candies, fruits, and nuts in pretty shiny paper to hang on the trees."

"Wow, that's so cool," Kaylie said. Her journalistic mind always appreciated learning something new, but she quickly noticed the prince didn't seem as impressed.

"Then how did we end up with this tradition?" the prince asked. "And why haven't I ever seen one of these infamous upside-down trees?"

The queen handed him the photo album and pointed to a date at the top of the page. "These pictures were taken on December 19th, 1964, right before our Christmas ball. I was just a young girl, around Anna's age, but I still remember it so well because this was the first year I was allowed to go with my father to cut down a tree to use. I was so excited…"

The queen was interrupted when the princess entered the room and overheard the conversation.

"You cut down a Christmas tree, Grandmother?" the princess asked with wide eyes.

"I did," the queen said with a radiant smile. "And it was a big, beautiful Christmas tree, and my father and I had so much fun." The queen gave the prince a pointed look but he was still checking out the photos in the album and totally missed her not-so-subtle hint.

Kaylie knew what the queen was hoping, so she thought she'd help her out. "Would you like to cut down a Christmas tree with your father?" Kaylie asked the princess.

The princess's eyes lit up.

The prince almost dropped the photo album.

"I would. I would like that very much," the princess said quickly, looking hopefully at her father.

The queen gave Kaylie a grateful smile. "And I think that's a wonderful idea."

The prince shook his head, frowning. "No, it's not. We don't have time to go traipsing around the forest, cutting down trees.

We have a Christmas tree right here, and others around the castle. We're just fine. We have enough."

"You can never have enough Christmas trees," the queen said.

The princess looked down at her shoes. "That's okay, Father. I'm very busy, too, with all my studies."

Kaylie's heart went out to her.

When the queen gave the prince a disappointed look, Kaylie could see the prince knew he was trapped.

He sighed before walking over to his daughter. He kneeled down to her level and took her tiny hands in his. "Anna, is this something you'd really like to do? To go into the snowy, cold, wet woods and find a tree?"

"It's okay," the princess said. "I know we're very busy."

"But if we had the time?" the prince asked.

The princess looked up quickly. The hope was back in her eyes. "If we had the time, I think it would be a good thing to do since Grandmother says it's a tradition and you're always saying it's our duty to do things. I think this is one of those things."

Kaylie hid her laugh. She admired the princess's fast thinking and smart argument.

"I definitely think it's one of those things," the queen said, giving her granddaughter a proud look. "Splendid. Then it's settled. You will all three go find a Christmas tree that will make the perfect upside-down Christmas tree decoration for our ballroom."

"All three of us?" Kaylie blurted out, shocked.

"Yes." The queen nodded. "This will give you a wonderful chance to take part in one of our traditions for that story you're working on." The queen winked at Kaylie, making sure that the princess didn't see.

Kaylie opened her mouth to protest but then saw the princess watching her closely so she said nothing. She realized just like the prince she'd been outplayed once again by the queen.

"You can go tomorrow morning," the queen said. "It is supposed to stop snowing by then."

Kaylie jumped to attention. "But I'm hoping tomorrow the roads will be clear so I can get to the airport."

The queen wrinkled her perfect nose. "That probably won't be happening by the morning. We have a very small road crew, so things don't move very fast around here. So, while we wait, you can all get the tree."

The princess grinned back at her grandmother. "Yes, we can."

Kaylie was left speechless. Clearly, she was no match for the queen and young princess.

"Wonderful." The queen beamed. "Now, Anna, we should be taking Blixen for his walk."

Blixen barked and wagged his tail and then spun around in circles and barked again.

"We're ready," the princess said.

Kaylie couldn't help but be charmed by Blixen. She missed having a dog but knew, with her long work hours, it wouldn't be fair. A fur-ever friend was just one of the things she had to sacrifice to get ahead in her career, and that list of sacrifices seemed to be getting longer every day.

The prince zipped up the princess's coat and wrapped her scarf around her snugly before kissing her on the cheek. "It's cold out. Don't stay out too long."

"I won't, Father," the princess said. "And I'll keep an eye on Grandmother, too."

The prince chuckled. "Good idea. She needs someone to keep an eye on her." The prince gave his mother a knowing look.

Kaylie nodded, thinking the prince was right. This queen was a force to be reckoned with.

When the prince headed for the door, the queen's eyebrows arched. "Alexander, where are you going?" she asked. "You still need to give Kaylie the tour."

The prince didn't slow down for a second. "Yes, I know, and I will, but first I have to quickly reschedule some calls."

Kaylie stepped forward. "You know, this jetlag is really starting to catch up to me. Since I'm staying the night, would it be okay if we did the tour in the morning, before we get the tree? This way I can make some calls, too, and get some rest, and be all ready to start fresh tomorrow."

"Of course," the queen said. "You've had a long journey. I can have Elsa take you to your room and have a meal brought up later, if you like, so you can relax and settle in."

"That would be perfect," Kaylie said, relieved.

"Brilliant," the queen said. "Let's all meet for breakfast at eight o'clock, and Kaylie, if there's anything else you need, please just let us know."

Kaylie smiled back at the queen. "I will, and thank you for everything."

As if on cue, Elsa entered the room. "I would be happy to show you to your room now."

Kaylie gave Elsa a grateful smile. "That would be great." As she started to follow Elsa, she stopped when she got to the princess and leaned down to pet Blixen. She whispered in his ear. "You two have fun in that snow."

Blixen barked and wagged his tail.

"And be careful out there," the prince added.

Kaylie couldn't help but notice how much the prince's face had softened when he looked at his daughter. The genuine smile he gave the princess completely transformed his face, making him even more handsome.

Kaylie's heart beat faster. She tried to mentally shake herself and get a grip, reminding herself that the last thing she needed was to have a silly crush on the prickly prince. He had made it crystal clear that he didn't want anything to do with her and he wanted her gone as soon as possible.

Then there was also the fact that he was a prince and she was no Cinderella.

Her head knew all of this, of course, but her heart, she was finding, had a mind of its own, and that's what was making her nervous.

Chapter 7

As Kaylie followed Elsa up a grand staircase, she was captivated by all the family photos on the wall where everyone looked relaxed and happy. She paused in front of a photo of the prince. He was behind the wheel of an impressive sailboat. His hair was wind-tossed and he was smiling like he didn't have a care in the world.

"The prince loves to sail," Elsa offered. "I'm told when he was young, his father used to take him out on our lake in a small boat and teach him what to do. The prince used to sail all over the world, but unfortunately not anymore."

"Too busy working?" Kaylie guessed.

"And other things," Elsa said.

"I always loved photography and thought I'd travel the world taking pictures, but work got in the way of my wanderlust," Kaylie said with a wistful smile. "Maybe someday." A picture of the princess and a puppy caught her eye. "Is this Blixen?"

Elsa nodded. "The one and only. She got him for Christmas and they're best friends. Here are some more of the dynamic duo together." Elsa pointed out more adorable pictures of the princess and Blixen.

"I love that these photos are all candid and casual, not posed and perfect," Kaylie said as they continued up the stairs.

"I agree," Elsa said. "This wall used to have all these huge formal family oil paintings dating back well over two hundred years, but when the queen did her last renovation, she decided to move those more formal paintings into the Great Hall, leading to the ballroom. She said this way, guests coming for events at the castle could see and appreciate the family's legacy, and the family, meaning the paintings, could see who was coming to the castle."

Kaylie laughed. "I love that. The queen is so…surprising. You always hear about queens being very stern and stoic and so serious as the matriarch of the family."

Elsa nodded. "Well, there is no doubt our queen is the matriarch, and a fine leader at that, but she has always led with her heart. She genuinely cares about everyone in Tolvania, just like she cares about her own family. She's special that way, and we all adore and appreciate her."

"Would that be the queen's husband?" Kaylie asked, pointing at a lovely picture of the queen riding a horse with a handsome man. They were both smiling at each other and looking very much in love.

"Yes, that's Prince Randolph," Elsa said. "He also led with love. We all miss him very much, especially the queen. They had a great love story."

"I can't imagine what it would be like to love someone like that," Kaylie said with a wistful sigh.

"Do you have a special someone?" Elsa asked, and then looked embarrassed. "I'm sorry. I shouldn't be asking such a personal question."

Kaylie laughed. "Don't worry. When it comes to my love life, I'm an open book. A book, I'm afraid, that hasn't even been written yet. When it comes to having one great love, those pages are all blank. I guess you could say my love story is a work in progress."

"Well, as long as you're making progress, that's what matters," Elsa said with a thoughtful smile.

Kaylie bit her lower lip. "Well, okay, I may have overstated the *progress* part, but I know that love and meeting the right person will happen when it's meant to happen. Once I've gotten my career set up and I have enough time to really focus on a relationship, that's when I'll find love."

Elsa laughed as she continued up the stairs.

Kaylie followed her, taking two stairs at a time. "What's so funny?"

"Just the idea that you think you can schedule love for when it's convenient for you," Elsa said, but in a kind voice. "I don't think it works that way. Love usually hits you when you least expect it, whether you're ready or not."

"But what if you're not ready?" Kaylie asked, worried.

"Then I think you have to listen to your heart, even if your head hasn't caught up yet," Elsa answered. "Because your heart always knows. You just need to trust it."

"But what if your heart is wrong?" Kaylie asked. "I mean, come on, you have to admit the heart can be a little flaky. The heart told me I loved Timmy Tyson in first grade because he gave me a Valentine. But then I found out he also gave the exact same Valentine to Carey, Mindy, and Megan. I was crushed. My heart totally failed me on that one."

Elsa let out a small laugh. "The same Valentine? Really?"

"Yes," Kaylie said. "So not cool."

"Not at all," Elsa agreed. "But your heart didn't fail you. The fact that you were heartbroken meant your heart worked. Your heart was just young and still in training, but every heartache teaches us something so that when the right person does come along, our heart will be ready."

Kaylie thought about it for a second. "So, you're saying you have to crash and burn a few times before you find real love?"

Elsa shook her head. "It just depends on what your journey is. Everyone is different. My parents met in eighth grade and they are still happily married."

"Your dad apparently didn't give three other girls the same Valentine," Kaylie grumbled.

Elsa laughed. "No, he did not."

"And what about you?" Kaylie asked. "Have you trusted your heart and found the one? It sounds like you're talking from experience."

Elsa nodded. "I guess you could say that I, too, am a work in progress, but I'm keeping my heart open, so I'm ready when it's my turn to find love."

Kaylie thought about Elsa's words. "I don't think I know how to keep my heart open."

"Well, then just make sure it's not completely closed, so love can still sneak in then the rest will work itself out," Elsa said.

"Are you sure you're not a writer?" Kaylie asked. "You should be writing romance novels or self-help books, or both. I know I'd buy them."

Elsa laughed. "I've been the queen's assistant since I was eighteen, and there's no job I'd rather have because it's different every day. She keeps me on my toes. I never know what to expect next."

"I bet," Kaylie said, looking back at the picture of the queen. "She's really something."

Elsa nodded. "And she's my family."

When Kaylie looked surprised, Elsa continued.

"It's true," Elsa said. "I may not be royal, but she treats me with respect and kindness, and I can honestly say she's not just my employer—she's my friend, and more. My mother passed away when I was eighteen. That's when the queen hired me. At first, I thought it was just great timing, because I had to sell my mother's house and I had no place else to go, but now looking back, I know she was trying to help me. I was very lost in so many ways and she helped give me purpose and find my way."

"That's a wonderful story, and says so much about her," Kaylie said as she followed Elsa down the hall. She found herself liking the queen even more. Then she thought about Bob, her boss until she was laid off. She realized in some ways he had also been there for her when she needed it the most. He had helped her find her way and he was also always keeping her on her toes professionally, like this surprise freelance assignment that she couldn't wait to talk to him about.

When they finally arrived at the end of the hall, Elsa proudly opened the door to a room and motioned for Kaylie to step inside. "Welcome to the Ruby Room," Elsa said. "This is one of my favorites."

Kaylie's eyes grew huge as she entered the most enchanting bedroom she'd ever seen. It somehow managed to look regal, chic, and comfortable all at the same time. It was a beautiful blend of old and new, with rich ruby-red walls and thick velvet curtains that added a touch of drama. But what Kaylie couldn't take her eyes off of was the fabulous hand-carved four-poster bed that looked like something the queen's great-great-grandmother might have slept in. Draped across the bed was a luxurious-looking fluffy white bathrobe. On the upper right-hand side of the robe, by the collar, there were two swans forming a heart embroidered in gold. It was the same work of art with the two swans that Kaylie had seen on the castle's front door knocker and she guessed it must be the family's crest.

Her eyes were drawn up when she saw that all across the ceiling there was a canopy of twinkling white Christmas lights. There was also a Christmas tree in the corner that was decorated with red ornaments that looked like sparkling ruby gemstones in all shapes and sizes. Kaylie thought that was pretty clever, since her room was the Ruby Room. In the corner was a pretty gray stone fireplace that already had a fire roaring. Facing the fire was a cozy sitting area. Kaylie suddenly had the urge to wrap herself up in the bathrobe and sit by the fire in one of the giant snow-white wingback chairs that had red velvet heart pillows. She turned and smiled at Elsa. "This room is heaven. I could live here forever."

"Careful what you wish for," Elsa said. "Swan's Gate Castle has a way of getting under your skin and into your blood."

"Ouch," Kaylie said and laughed. "That sounds painful."

"Only when you have to leave," Elsa said with a smile. "If there's anything else I can get you, just use the phone and dial zero. We're still old school around here and use landlines because we do have a lot of problems with our cell towers when we get stormy weather." Elsa motioned toward an antique telephone sitting on a nightstand next to the bed. "I know it looks like a decoration, but it actually works."

Kaylie held up her phone and checked for a signal. She was excited when she got a few bars. "I think I'm finally getting something." A second later, the signal was gone. Kaylie frowned. "And now it's gone. How is the Wi-Fi? I do a lot of video calls on my phone."

"Also comes and goes, but if you need to make a call back to the U.S., or anywhere, feel free to use our phones."

"If I get the Wi-Fi working, is there a password I need to use?" Kaylie asked.

"The password changes all the time," Elsa told her. "Right now, it's Christmas Spirit. The queen picks it. Just use a capital C and capital S."

"Christmas Spirit, I shouldn't forget that," Kaylie said as she was already trying the password on her phone.

"No, you shouldn't," Elsa replied with a smile as she headed for the door. "I will let you get settled in."

"Thank you so much," Kaylie said. As soon as Elsa was gone, she started taking pictures of her room. "Rachel, Miss Christmas, is going to love seeing all this," she said to herself.

A pretty white wooden music box on the dresser grabbed her attention. It had a red heart painted on the top along with little pieces of painted holly with red berries. When she opened the box, the song "Silent Night" started playing. In a rush, Kaylie quickly shut the box and took a picture of it before moving to her nightstand to get a picture of a beautiful crystal angel that was holding a red heart.

"There is definitely a Christmas heart theme going on here," Kaylie said as she took a picture of the angel. "Who are you going to give your heart to, little angel? I hope whoever they are, they're worth it."

After she was done taking pictures, she checked her cell signal again and saw she had a couple of bars. It gave her hope that she'd be able to call Bob with a video call because she wanted to see his expression when she asked him what on earth he was thinking, sending her to a castle to write a fairy tale.

Her first two attempts to make the call failed, but the third call connected. When Bob's face popped up, she dived right in.

"Bob, why am I at a castle, and why didn't you tell me my story was about a royal family? Oh wait, I can't actually report on the family, but I'm supposed to use their traditions to write a fairy tale?! This is next-level crazy. What have you done?!"

Bob chuckled. "Well, hello to you, too, Kaylie. Aren't you just feeling the Christmas spirit?"

Kaylie's eyes narrowed. "No, Bob, I'm actually not, because I've been too busy trying to figure out what I'm doing here."

Bob laughed loudly.

"You think this is funny?" Kaylie shot back at him.

"No, I think *you're* funny," Bob said. "Who else would be complaining about getting to spend Christmas in a magnificent castle with a career-changing opportunity?"

Kaylie stared into the phone. "Career-changing opportunity? What are you talking about? I don't want to be a children's author, I'm a reporter."

"You're a storyteller," Bob said. "And this is a great story."

"Okay, now you sound like the queen and how do you know the queen anyway? And what about the magazine story? Was that all just a lie? I am so confused." Kaylie plopped down on her bed.

"What question do you want me to answer first?" Bob asked patiently.

"How about the big one?" Kaylie replied. "How did you ever think writing a fairy tale was something I could do?"

"You've spent your career telling other people's stories, negative, difficult stories, stories that can suck the life and hope right out of you. When I heard about this freelance job, I thought it could be just what you needed to refuel and reboot your creative juices and try something different," Bob said.

"Why would I want to try something different when I'm good at what I do now?" Kaylie asked, baffled.

"Because that's how we grow," Bob answered. "And right now, you don't have your old job."

"But I'm going to find a job again," Kaylie said with conviction.

"Of course you are," Bob agreed. "But in the meantime, you told me you needed to work and that you'd take any assignment, so I found this one for you. You're welcome."

Kaylie laughed because she didn't know what else to do. "So, you're saying you think I should be a children's author now?"

"I'm saying you can be anything you want," Bob replied. "Don't put limits on yourself. Be open-minded. Any time you're writing, you're using your creative talents. You don't want to be pigeonholed into only one lane going forward. You have to branch out, be adventurous and see where this path will take you. That's what storytellers do. You gather experiences to help tell your stories. You never know if what you see, who you meet, or what you do, could someday help you down the road with another story, whether you're reporting investigative news or writing a feature. The key is to just keep writing anything and everything every single day. Writing is like a muscle, use it or lose it."

Kaylie rolled her eyes. "Okay, now you sound like a bad fortune cookie."

"You know what you need?" Bob asked her.

"I'm sure you're going to tell me," Kaylie answered.

"You need to try and have some fun. It's Christmas," Bob said. "Be a little merry. Go get jolly. Stop being a Grinch." Bob's signal faded in and out.

Kaylie jumped up and started pacing, holding her phone up high. "Bob? Bob? Are you there? I'm losing you…" A second later the signal was dead.

Kaylie stared at the blank screen for several seconds. Fun and Christmas weren't two things that went together in her world. What *did* go together was Christmas and work. She grabbed her computer out of her bag, sat back down on her bed, and started writing down bullet points under the headline *Royal Christmas Traditions*. She put down what she'd learned about so far…

Upside-Down Christmas Trees
Heart of Christmas Heart Ornaments
Christmas Ball
Christmas Hot Chocolate

"Wow, that's already a lot of Christmas," she said to herself before starting another column where she wrote the headline *Christmas Fairy-Tale Ideas*. She stared at the column for a full thirty seconds. She had nothing. Frustrated, she shut her computer and grabbed the fluffy white bathrobe and headed into her bathroom.

When she got there, she found a giant marble bathtub calling her name. On the counter, there was a selection of bath salts and bubble bath oils in beautiful crystal containers. As she picked up each one, she laughed when she saw they were all in a Christmas theme. "Peppermint Christmas Bliss, Frankincense and Myrrh, Winter Wonderland, Candy Cane Kisses…" Kaylie shook her head in amazement. "Wow, this royal family really goes all out to make sure everything is Christmassy."

Still, she couldn't resist picking up the red and white bubble bath named Candy Cane Kisses.

"Okay, I'll play."

She turned on the water and poured half of the container into the steaming hot water. She frowned when she didn't see any bubbles right away so she poured the whole thing in and set the empty container on the edge of the tub.

"Maybe this will help bring me some fairy tale inspiration."

When she went back out to the bedroom, she quickly changed into the robe and laid back on her bed for a moment, staring up at the canopy of Christmas lights twinkling above her. "What have I gotten myself into?" she asked, sighing. As her eyes fluttered shut, she told herself she'd just rest her eyes for a minute.

Moments later, she was fast asleep as the bathtub continued to fill with water…

Chapter 8

The sound of shattering glass in the bathroom woke Kaylie up. It took her a second to remember where she was, and when she did, she panicked and bolted upright.

"Oh, my God! The bathtub!"

She jumped out of bed and ran into the bathroom and then went sliding across the floor when she hit a bunch of soapy bubbles. Just as she feared, the bathtub was overflowing, and the beautiful crystal bottle that had held the bubble bath was shattered on the floor.

Kaylie ran for the bathtub, jumping over the glass, and turned off the water. She almost disappeared into the tub of bubbles as she fished around trying to open the drain so the water could start going down. By the time she was done, she was soaked from head to toe and had bubbles all over her.

Horrified, she saw the floor that was also covered with water and bubbles. She tried to use all the towels to push the sudsy water into the shower, but only succeeded in creating a bigger mess.

"I need a mop and a bucket, something, anything," she panted, looking around. When she couldn't find anything, she checked the time on her phone. It was past eleven o'clock and she didn't want to bother Elsa or admit to anyone she'd been such a fool.

"I'll just find something myself," she muttered as she hurried out her bedroom door, leaving a trail of dripping water behind her.

Ten minutes later, she was still wandering the halls, searching for the kitchen, or some kind of storage room that might have buckets and mops, when Blixen appeared.

He looked about as surprised to see her as she was to see him.

Kaylie knelt down. "It's okay, Blixen, I'm just looking for the kitchen."

When Blixen raced off, Kaylie followed him, hoping he wouldn't start barking and wake everyone up. She was surprised and relieved when Blixen led her right to the kitchen. "You are a good boy," she said, petting him. "Thank you, Blixen."

Blixen wagged his tail, looking like he was loving the attention.

Kaylie looked around the kitchen in awe. It had all the latest state-of-the-art appliances and looked like something from a cooking show. It was also beautifully decorated for Christmas with garlands and wreaths that were lit up with white lights. There was even a Christmas tree in the corner that was decorated with cute Christmas-themed cookie cutters tied with red ribbons.

"Wow, the queen was right. This really is a gourmet kitchen. I'd almost be inspired to cook in here." She glanced at Blixen. "Okay, maybe not, but it's still really cool."

Kaylie's heart stopped when she heard footsteps. She didn't want to be caught prowling around, looking like a drenched rat. Then she saw the pantry door ajar and quickly slipped inside just in time. Peeking through a crack in the door, she covered her gasp with her hand when she saw the prince enter the kitchen. He was the last person she wanted to run into.

She noticed he was also wearing a robe, but one that was a rich crimson color that had the same gold embroidered swan crest on the front. He was wearing chocolate brown leather slippers.

"Blixen, what are you doing in here?" the prince asked and looked around. "Are you with anyone?"

When Blixen barked and ran over to the pantry, Kaylie jumped back and accidentally tripped over something on the floor and fell into the shelf. "Ouch," she cried out in pain just as a bag of flour fell off the shelf, dumping its contents all over her.

When the prince flung open the door, Kaylie looked as embarrassed as the prince looked shocked.

"What on earth is going on in here?" the prince demanded.

"Looking for a mop and bucket," Kaylie said with as much dignity as she could muster. As she tried to brush the flour off her, it just mixed with the water from her soggy, sudsy bathrobe, making a gooey, pasty mess.

The prince gave her a suspicious look, "For what?"

Kaylie wiped some flour out of her eyes. "There's been a little incident. But I can clean it up, no problem. I just need a mop..."

"How *little*?" the prince asked, as his eyes narrowed.

An hour later, Kaylie and the prince stood in Kaylie's bathroom, both holding mops and both of them dripping wet. The bathroom looked much better but Kaylie knew she was a hot mess. She gave the prince a grateful look. "I really appreciate all the help."

"You should have just called someone to come clean this up," the prince said, wringing out the sleeve of his bathrobe.

"I didn't want to wake anyone up. This was my mess to clean up, and besides, you didn't call anyone either," Kaylie said, giving him a pointed look.

"My castle. My job," the prince said with a straight face.

"I'm sure you have many jobs, but I doubt janitor is one of them," Kaylie said.

"My job is to do anything that needs to be done," the prince said as he took her mop and picked up the buckets and headed for the door.

He was just about to leave when Kaylie called out to him, "Do you think we could keep this whole thing to ourselves?"

"Meaning?" he asked.

"Meaning, not tell the queen, your mother," Kaylie answered. "I don't want her thinking I almost flooded her castle."

"But you did," the prince said.

"Only my bathroom," Kaylie quickly replied.

The prince shook his head. "Who knows if this leaked downstairs."

Kaylie's eyes grew huge. "Are you serious?! Did it go through the floor? What's underneath me?"

"My mother's bedroom," the prince said as he crossed his arms.

"No…" But when Kaylie saw the prince crack a small smile, she glared at him. "You're just kidding. You, Mr. Serious, pick *now* to make a joke. That wasn't funny."

The prince chuckled. "It was kind of funny. You should have seen your face." He turned to leave. "I'll see you in the morning. Try not to do any more damage between now and then."

"I can't make any promises," Kaylie called out after him. She heard him laugh as he left the room.

Chapter 9

When Kaylie woke up the next morning hugging a red heart pillow, it took her a few seconds to remember where she was. She was in a castle, in Tolvania, with a real-life queen, princess, and prince, where the prince was far too handsome for his own good. And the real kicker, she was expected to write a fairy tale based on the royal family's Christmas traditions. She was also supposed to go this morning and help chop down an upside-down Christmas tree.

She laughed to herself. *If this doesn't sound like a make-believe story, I don't know what does*, she thought. She'd even gotten the Cinderella part down when she'd been mopping the floors last night after the whole bubble bath fiasco. Only she had been mopping floors with a real-life prince who could give Prince Charming a run for his money when it came to good looks. For the actual *charming* part, Kaylie thought Prince Alexander could use some work.

She did have to admit that while he was far from warm and inviting, he had handled the whole bathroom situation very well. She'd been surprised that once he'd gotten over the shock, he hadn't yelled at her or blamed her for anything. Instead, he'd focused on solutions and had worked right alongside her to clean up the mess. She liked that while he was a prince, he'd also shown he was more than ready to roll up his sleeves and get his hands dirty, literally, if something needed to be done.

When she checked the time on her phone, she bolted up in bed. It was five minutes after eight o'clock. She was supposed to meet everyone at eight for breakfast. She could've sworn she'd set her alarm for seven to give herself enough time to get ready, but had apparently forgotten in the chaos of the previous night.

She quickly threw on some black pants, a black sweater, and some black riding boots and washed her face and brushed her teeth in record time. She raced out of her room and when she got to the bottom of the stairs, she found Blixen waiting.

"Are you making sure I get to the dining room?" she asked Blixen with a laugh. "Okay, lead the way."

When Blixen took off and she had to run to keep up with him. "Wait for me!"

She was breathless by the time she followed Blixen into the dining room and was relieved to find only the prince and princess at the table. At least she wouldn't have to explain her tardiness to the queen.

"I'm so sorry I'm late," she said, catching her breath.

"You slept in," the princess said.

"My alarm never went off," Kaylie answered as she quickly took a seat next to the princess. "I thought I set it but I must have done something wrong. It was a crazy night."

"Yes, it was," the prince said. His expression gave nothing away.

The princess reached for a silver domed cover that was on a platter in front of Kaylie and took it off with gusto.

"Christmas gingerbread pancakes," the princess said, excited. "They're Chef Jake's specialty and my favorite, and he made them so you could try them, too."

Kaylie's eyes grew huge as she stared at the giant stack of star-shaped pancakes and blissfully inhaled a delectable warm, spicy, ginger, and cinnamon scent.

"I'm honored," Kaylie said and meant it. She wasn't usually a breakfast person, but this morning she was going to make an exception. Her mouth was already watering. She picked up a fork and brought a pancake over to her plate.

The princess beamed her approval as she held up a red crystal dish. "And don't forget to try them with the cream cheese frosting."

Kaylie laughed. "Wait, is this breakfast or dessert?"

"Both!" the princess grinned back at her and moved the frosting closer to Kaylie.

"When in Rome," Kaylie said as she put a big dollop of frosting onto her pancake.

"Or Tolvania," the prince said, watching her. "We only do this for special occasions at the holidays. Usually, our breakfasts are much healthier. We can get you something else if you like."

"Oh, no," Kaylie said. "If I'm going to go for it, I'm going all in. Are these another Christmas tradition?"

"Yes." The princess nodded. "My grandmother loves them, too."

Kaylie eyed her pancake. "So, they're fit for a queen. Well, then I'm sure they are delicious." As she took her first bite, she quickly found out why everyone loved them so much. They were incredible, a little spicy, a little sweet, the perfect combination, she thought. When she saw the princess closely watching her, she gave her an enthusiastic two thumbs up.

"I told you she'd like them." The princess turned to her father with a victorious smile.

The prince laughed. "It does appear you've found another fan of Chef Jake's famous Christmas gingerbread pancakes."

"Absolutely," Kaylie agreed, grinning. "I need to carb load for our little Christmas tree adventure this morning."

"And have energy for your tour," the princess said. "We have a big castle."

Kaylie laughed. "I can see that. I might have to stay all Christmas to see everything here." When the prince frowned, she rushed to continue. "Don't worry. That was a joke."

The prince didn't crack a smile. "I'm afraid I have some news that isn't a joke. My mother just got an update and it's going to take at least another day to clear the roads and make sure the runway is okay and safe to fly. You won't be able to leave later today," the prince said. "I'm sorry."

I bet you are, Kaylie thought, knowing the prince wanted her gone as much as she wanted to leave.

"So, the new plan is that my mother would like me to give you a tour of the castle this morning and show you as many of our Christmas traditions as possible that are on her list," the prince said.

"She doesn't still think I'm writing the fa…" Kaylie caught herself just in time when she saw the princess staring at her. "The feature story on Tolvania?"

The prince shrugged. "You'd have to talk to her about that."

To stop herself from saying something she'd regret, she quickly stabbed another bite of pancake and stuffed it into her mouth.

"After your tour, we can go get our upside-down Christmas tree and then decorate it," the princess said merrily.

"What?" The prince frowned. "Decorating the tree isn't in the schedule."

The princess laughed. "Father, everyone knows you have to decorate the tree. You'd better put it in the schedule right now."

Kaylie laughed.

When the prince gave her a look, she just shrugged. "What can I say? She's right."

"She is absolutely right," the queen agreed as she entered the room. She turned her attention to Kaylie. "I hope you slept well?"

Kaylie stole a glance at the prince. She was relieved when he didn't say anything. "I slept very well. The ruby room is a real gem, pun intended. Thank you so much."

The princess looked at Kaylie's empty plate. "You should have another pancake. Having two is our tradition."

"Seriously?" Kaylie asked, looking at the queen.

The queen nodded.

Kaylie happily put another pancake on her plate. "Then who would I be to fight tradition?"

The queen chuckled. "Just remember you said that."

Fifteen minutes and another pancake later, Kaylie was walking with the prince down a long hallway on the same floor as her bedroom. She kept checking to see if her phone could get a signal, but she was having no luck.

"You can put away your phone," the prince said. "You're not going to need it."

"I need it to take some pictures."

The prince stopped walking abruptly and the angry look on his face had Kaylie taking a step back.

"We need to set some ground rules right now before we go any further," the prince said through gritted teeth. "You will not be taking any photographs of me or anyone in my family ever, is that understood?"

"But I wasn't going to take any of the family, only..."

"Do you understand?" the prince interrupted.

Kaylie was so surprised by his harsh tone she just nodded and quickly put away her phone.

As the prince kept walking, she could see he was still extremely tense and guarded.

"You know we don't have to do this tour if you don't want," Kaylie called after him.

The prince kept staring straight ahead. "Tell that to my mother."

Kaylie's mouth snapped shut. She hated feeling like a burden, but she also hated having to deal with the queen.

As they walked side by side, she could literally feel the tension radiating off the prince. She knew she had to do something to try and lighten the mood or it was going to be a miserable morning. She stepped in front of him and held out her hand. "Truce?"

The prince looked surprised. "Are we battling?"

Kaylie gave him a look. "It kind of feels like it." When she saw him stare at her outstretched hand but make no move to take it, she rushed on. "Am I allowed to shake your hand, or am I supposed to curtsy or bow? Exactly what do you do here in Tolvania?" When she asked the question, she was serious. She had absolutely zero experience interviewing anyone royal and the last thing she wanted to do was make a fool of herself. She felt like she had already started to go down that road and was trying to reroute and redeem herself.

When the prince finally took her hand in his, she was just as startled by his gesture as she was by the spark she felt when he touched her. Her eyes flew to his. Her heart raced.

"We are allowed to shake hands," he said, locking eyes with her. "It's our way to determine if the person we're meeting is a friend or foe."

Since his expression gave nothing away Kaylie couldn't tell if he was kidding or not. She shook his hand with a firm grip.

"Okay, then, what vibe are you getting from me? Friend or foe?" Kaylie asked.

When he wouldn't let go of her hand and looked into her eyes, Kaylie felt a jolt of electricity. She stared back at him, breathless.

"That is to be determined," he said as he dropped her hand and continued down the hall.

For a moment, Kaylie just stared after him and tried to reassure herself that her heart was only racing because she was totally out of her element, in a foreign country, in a castle with a royal family, hired to do an assignment she wasn't qualified to do. That had to be it, she told herself.

"So how are you going to determine if I'm a friend or foe?" Kaylie asked. She just couldn't let it go. "I ate the pancakes—doesn't that make me friend-worthy?"

"Hardly," the prince scoffed. "Anyone worth their weight usually eats at least three pancakes."

"But Anna said two was tradition," Kaylie exclaimed. When she saw the twinkle in his eyes, she playfully slapped his arm. "Stop joking around."

The prince, stunned, stared at the arm Kaylie just slapped.

"Did you just *hit* me?" he asked, dead serious.

Kaylie cringed. "I did. Sorry. I was just kidding around and got a little carried away."

"You don't hit a prince," he said with authority. "And there's a punishment for hitting a member of the royal family. It looks like our first stop will be the dungeon."

Kaylie laughed loudly. "Good one."

But when the prince didn't blink, Kaylie could feel a sense of dread wash over her. She rubbed her hand that had hit the prince, imagining what it would feel like in shackles. She shuddered as her always-overactive imagination conjured up all kinds of horrors that could be waiting for her in the dungeon.

"I really am sorry," Kaylie said, telling herself to stop being so ridiculous. She kept waiting for the prince to crack a smile to show he was just pulling her leg, but his expression stayed stern.

He walked to the end of the hallway and stopped at a bookcase.

She gasped when he took a book off the shelf and the entire bookcase moved to the side, revealing a dark staircase going down that disappeared into the darkness.

"Wait, there's really a dungeon? You weren't kidding?" Kaylie asked with growing dread.

"After you," the prince said as he motioned toward the stairs.

Chapter 10

Kaylie took a step back. "You know, I don't really need to see the dungeon. I'm not a dungeon kind of girl. I don't like dark spaces," she rushed on, talking faster and faster. "I'm a little claustrophobic. I need a lot of natural light. I think I might even have that seasonal disorder. You know, the one where you get depressed when it's dark and gloomy during the winter?" Kaylie knew she was babbling but she couldn't help herself. "So, I'm good staying up here," she finished with a smile, crossing her arms in front of her chest. "So, what else do you have to show me? I know we need to keep on schedule. We have a lot to do and I didn't see dungeon on your mother's list. So, let's go."

When Kaylie continued to walk down the hall, the prince called out after her.

"First things first," he said, pointing at the staircase again.

She gave him a long look. "I'd really rather not."

"But you will. After you," the prince said. His expression was impossible to read.

Kaylie took a deep breath and walked slowly over to the bookcase and peered into the darkness. She got out her phone and turned on the flashlight app to light the way. But this only made her more nervous when she saw the stairs leading into what looked like a dark hole.

"Prince Alexander, what are you doing?" Kaylie whirled around when she heard Elsa's voice.

"Just giving Kaylie her tour," the prince answered.

Kaylie turned to Elsa for help. "He's insisting I go into your dungeon because I hit him."

"What?" Elsa asked, concerned.

"I was only kidding around," Kaylie tried to explain. "It's what we do in America. We slap each other on the arm or pat them on the butt…"

The prince's eyebrows arched.

"But I didn't touch his butt. I swear!" Kaylie realized she was only making things worse. She took a deep breath and tried to get a grip. "When I hit his arm, it was just a playful thing, a light tap, really. I didn't mean any disrespect."

"So, you're taking her to the *dungeon*?" Elsa asked the prince.

"Yes," the prince said proudly.

Elsa slapped the prince's arm. "You stop giving Kaylie a hard time."

"Ouch!" The prince rubbed his arm.

Kaylie's jaw dropped. She pointed at Elsa. "You just slapped him, too!"

"I did and I'll slap him again if he keeps this up," Elsa said. "It turns out we have the same tradition here in Tolvania if someone is being a pain."

The prince gave Elsa a look. "Looks like I need to take you *both* to the dungeon."

"I'd like to see you try it," Elsa threw back at him.

Kaylie was fascinated watching them banter. "You two sound just like brother and sister."

Elsa laughed. "Can you imagine?"

"Oh, no, never," the prince said, making a face like it would be the most horrible thing in the world.

Then the prince and Elsa both started laughing.

Kaylie was fascinated to see how the prince's whole face changed. He looked younger, happier, like a completely different person.

The prince surprised Kaylie even more when he put his arm around Elsa. "Actually, Elsa is like a sister to me."

"And he's the big brother I never wanted," Elsa continued as she put hers around the prince. She looked at Kaylie. "Okay, I agree, you need to show Kaylie the dungeon."

"What?" Kaylie sputtered. "I thought you were on my side."

Elsa was already walking away from them. "Have fun."

"Elsa, wait. I'd rather go with you," Kaylie called out after her, but Elsa had already disappeared around the corner.

"Come on," the prince said. "Like you said, we have a lot to see."

When he stepped into the stairwell and flipped a switch, the stairs were flooded with light that came from a stunning chandelier.

Kaylie breathed a sigh of relief to see the staircase was actually quite beautiful and had stopped looking like something out of a horror movie. She breezed by the prince, slapping him on the arm again, as she headed down the stairs. "I bet you got a kick out of scaring me," she said.

He nodded as he followed her. "I did."

When they got to the bottom of the stairs, Kaylie found herself standing in the entryway of a magnificent dining room. Kaylie took it all in. It was festive and fantastic, decorated for Christmas with fragrant evergreen garlands and wreaths.

Overhead there was a canopy of white twinkle lights strung across the beamed ceiling. There was also a giant Christmas tree in the corner that was decorated with shiny gold bows to match the gold Christmas lights. There was also a unique garland that was made up of wine corks that were strung together and had little red bows separating each cork.

Running the length of the dining room was a shelf that displayed empty wine bottles that were filled up with tiny white lights that glistened and glowed. In the center of the room was a giant, gorgeous, live edge wooden dining table that was set for two dozen people in an enchanting Christmas theme. There was a table runner made up of evergreens, pinecones, and boughs of holly with bright red berries. There were gold candelabras with white candles waiting to be lit, crystal wine glasses waiting to be filled, and regal tall back red velvet chairs waiting to be sat in. As Kaylie moved closer to the table, she couldn't resist picking up one of the white china plates that had the two golden swans embossed on it. They were the same swans that Kaylie had seen on the door knocker and on her bathrobe, where the necks were gracefully arched facing each other to form a heart.

The prince joined her.

"That's our family crest," he said with pride. "You'll see it all around our Tolvania village."

"It's really cool," Kaylie said. "And clever. I like how you have two swans making the heart."

"You know, swans actually have quite the royal history, and not just for our family," the prince said.

"They do? How so?" Kaylie asked.

"There are stories of swans dating back more than 10,000 years ago," the prince explained. "They have always been very prestigious, and owning swans was a sign of nobility, just like having a hawk or hounds for hunting. The swans were celebrated for their elegance and beauty, representing the idea of tranquility and grace."

Kaylie looked skeptical. "Tranquility? Really? Because all I know about swans is from the ones in Central Park in New York, and they're not tranquil at all. They're mean. If you get too close, they come after you and hiss at you."

The prince nodded. "They do have a reputation for being very protective of their young, but that is a good trait, is it not?"

Kaylie gave it a thought and nodded her head. "Yes, I guess so, but that still makes them a little scary."

"They're also delicious to eat," the prince added.

"What?!" Kaylie asked, grabbing her stomach, looking disgusted. "You eat your pets? Oh, that's just wrong…"

The prince laughed. "First, I didn't say anything about the swans being *pets* and I personally don't eat them, but back in the day, in some royal circles, swans were very popular to have for a feast, especially at Christmas. In England there's even the story that Henry III had forty swans at his Christmas celebration at Winchester in 1247. It was popular to have a swan feast up until the eighteenth century."

"That's both fascinating and disgusting," Kaylie said. "I mean, I can understand eating a Christmas goose, but a swan, no thanks."

"That's too bad, because that's what we're having for a dinner," the prince said.

For a second, Kaylie believed the prince until she saw the twinkle in his eye. She pointed at him. "There you go again, trying to make a joke."

When they shared a smile, Kaylie felt that spark again that sent shivers all the way to her toes. Confused and embarrassed, she quickly looked away and mentally checked herself. Just because the prince was handsome, and even more so when he smiled, she couldn't allow herself to fall under his spell, especially because she knew she'd be the last person he would ever try matching up with a glass slipper.

She turned her attention back to the plate she was still holding. "Does this crest mean anything in particular for your family?"

"It does," the prince said, gently tracing the outline of the swan crest with his fingers. "And it's also connected to Christmas."

Kaylie waited for him to explain more but instead he walked over to a small, black, shiny panel on the wall that lit up when he touched it. Christmas music filled the room.

Kaylie looked around in surprise. An orchestra was playing "Silent Night..."

Silent night, holy night
All is calm and all is bright...

The prince turned the music down a little. "This is one of my mother's latest additions with the remodel. It's a high-tech in-wall stereo system."

"Wow, it's impressive," Kaylie said, looking around for some huge speakers, but she didn't see any.

The prince nodded. "She loves music, especially Christmas music, and she wanted to make sure it could be heard everywhere. You even have it in your bedroom, and a word of warning—the only thing that's playing right now is Christmas songs."

Kaylie laughed. "Well, I won't be listening to any Christmas music, that's for sure."

"Not a fan of Christmas music?" the prince asked.

"Or Christmas," Kaylie said quickly. It came out before she could stop herself. "I mean, I'm no Scrooge, contrary to what some people might say, but Christmas just isn't my thing. I've always worked during the holidays, so it's like any other day for me. I try and avoid all the holiday hoopla and can't wait for it to be over. It's such a distraction. My favorite day is December 26th."

"Interesting," the prince said, studying her.

Kaylie squirmed under his scrutiny. "What?"

"I thought all you Americans went crazy for Christmas," the prince said. "The amount of money you spend every year on decorations, and food, and presents is in the billions. It's legendary. And if you don't like Christmas, why in the world would you accept a job to write a Christmas fairy tale for my daughter?"

When Kaylie stared back at the prince, she knew she needed to pick her words wisely, because the last thing she wanted was for the already-suspicious prince to think she was there for the wrong reasons. She knew that could be disastrous.

Chapter 11

She took a deep breath before starting. "Honestly, I'm here because I needed a job. I needed the money. Trust me, I had no idea when I first took this freelance assignment that it had anything to do with writing a fairy tale, or coming to a castle, or dealing with a royal family. That would be the last thing I'd ever want to do."

When she saw the prince's surprised look, she realized how rude her words must have sounded. She hurried to fix her blunder. "Sorry, no offense, but you know what I mean."

The prince stared back at her. "No, not really."

Kaylie took a deep breath before trying again. "I don't usually cover feature stories."

"About Christmas?" the prince asked.

"About anything, especially Christmas," Kaylie answered. "I don't do any kind of puff piece stories."

The prince looked confused. "Puff piece stories?"

"You know, those feel-good, lighthearted stories, simple stories that you usually see at the end of the news," Kaylie said. "We sometimes call them our kicker stories when we try and leave everyone with something positive."

"And you don't do these kinds of positive stories?" the prince asked as he started examining the crystal wine glasses on the dining table and holding them up to the light.

"I do positive stories that help people, but not those kind of positive stories about things that aren't important, like Christmas decorations and traditions and stuff like that. I cover the news at the top of the newscast. The top stories. The ones that matter most. In my reports, I cover things that are happening to people that need to be fixed. I right the wrongs. I do the serious stuff."

"So, you don't believe Christmas stories are important stories?" the prince asked in a tone Kaylie thought was starting to sound a bit judgy again.

She frowned. "You're making me sound like the Grinch. I just think stories that help people are more important than doing stories about the latest Christmas decorating trends. The series I was going to do was called *Kaylie on Your Side*. I help people who need it the most. I think that should make people feel really good, right? That's why I'm an investigative reporter."

The prince's head jerked up from the wine glass he'd been studying. "An investigative reporter…"

Kaylie was surprised by his sharp tone and the way he said *investigative reporter*, like it was something wretched.

Kaylie held up her hands in self-defense. "I already know where you're going with this. Don't worry, I don't sneak around trying to dig up dirt on celebrities or royal families. I'm not paparazzi. I'm one of the good guys."

The prince's eyes narrowed.

She hurried to continue. "I'm what my boss likes to call a watchdog for society. I help people who can't help themselves, people who are getting scammed or ripped off. I go after the bad guys. I try and make things right."

"I see," the prince said.

But the way he said it had Kaylie thinking he didn't really see at all and, for some reason, that really bothered her. This wasn't the first time, and she knew it wouldn't be the last, that she had to defend what she did for a living. People usually fell into two camps; they either totally got it and were thankful for the kind of reporting she did, or they just thought of her like the paparazzi, someone who only cared about selling the story and grabbing headlines.

She couldn't even count the number of times Bob had told her it didn't matter what other people thought, she knew the truth. But still, it sometimes hurt depending on who was judging her. Right now, she knew the prince was definitely forming an opinion and by the look on his face, it wasn't a good one. She walked over to him until they were toe to toe. "I'm really good at my job and I help protect a lot of people."

"And my job is to protect my family and Tolvania from reporters," the prince said, staring her down.

For a moment, Kaylie thought she saw something flicker in the prince's eyes that went beyond judgment and disdain. It almost looked like…pain. And then in a second, it was gone.

"It must be exhausting," the prince finally said.

"What?" Kaylie asked, more confused than ever.

"Always trying to fix things for people," the prince answered. "Because if you're Kaylie come to the rescue, or whatever you call it, then you're taking on everyone else's problems and being the morality police."

Kaylie gave him a shocked look. "Who said anything about being the police?"

"I believe you just did," the prince said.

She crossed her arms in front of her chest. She was exhausted trying to play mental hopscotch and word games with the prince.

"Then you didn't hear me right," she fired back at him.

The prince didn't miss a beat. "Didn't you just say a second ago that you were society's 'watchdog'? That sounds like policing to me."

Kaylie hated that her own words had trapped her and that he was taking something positive she'd said and twisting it into something negative. He was making it sound like the only person she was helping was herself. She tried to think of a better way to help him understand. Her eyes lit up.

"You say you're protecting your family and Tolvania, right?" Kaylie asked him.

"Yes, always," the prince said.

"So, that means you're Tolvania's watchdog," Kaylie quickly added.

The prince thought about it. "In a sense, yes."

"So, in a way, we're the same," Kaylie said.

"We are not the same," the prince said with conviction. "I would never be anything like a reporter."

Kaylie's jaw dropped open. "Wow, don't hold back."

"It's not personal," the prince said.

Kaylie looked at him like he was nuts. "It's personal to me because I am a reporter and proud of it."

"And that's the problem," the prince said. "My life, my family's life, is private. We don't talk to reporters, ever. My mother invited you here to write a fictional story, not dig up dirt and create lies about our lives."

Kaylie's eyes grew huge. "What in the world are you talking about? I'm not here to do any of that. I don't lie in my reports. I hate liars. It's why I do what I do, to expose liars. I'm not here to do a news story about you or anyone else. I don't even have that job anymore. I told you, I came here thinking I was doing a feature story for an online magazine about a family's Christmas traditions."

"But yet, you just told me you don't do feature stories," the prince jumped in. "You're not making any sense. Which one is it? Why are you really here?"

Kaylie's head was spinning. She pulled out a dining room chair and sat down to try and calm her jangled nerves. She rubbed a throbbing temple and took a deep breath. As she played back the conversation she'd just had with the prince, she realized he had every right to be confused. She had told him two different stories. She had made such a big deal about never doing feature stories and being an investigative reporter, no wonder he was suspicious about her intentions. She motioned to the chair next to her. "Can you sit for a moment, please?"

The prince sat down but he didn't look happy about it. "I'm listening," he said.

She took another deep breath before she dived in. "First of all, I owe you an apology."

The prince's eyebrows raised.

Kaylie nodded. "You're right. I've been talking in circles."

"Yes," the prince agreed.

"The short version is, I was an investigative reporter and I just lost my job, right before a big career promotion. My job is everything to me and I truly do it to help people. It's how my parents raised me and my sister, to always give back. They are both retired teachers who always volunteered for so many different causes. So, my sister and I grew up volunteering, too. We worked at senior centers, hospitals, after-school children's programs, literacy programs. We volunteered at our local library because that's where my parents always took us to get books when we were growing up. Libraries are still my happy place. We come from pretty modest means, but when I was at the library, by reading different books, I could go anywhere and have anything. The stories I read were my escape and I knew I wanted to write my own stories someday." Kaylie paused. She knew she was rambling and she definitely wasn't telling the short version, but when she nervously looked up at the prince, she was relieved to see he was listening intently to everything she was saying.

She gave the prince a guilty look. "Sorry, this wasn't supposed to be my entire family history."

"It's fine, please go on," the prince said.

She nervously unfolded and folded a gold cloth napkin on the table. "I'm sure you have your reasons for not trusting the press, but I'm not here to hurt you or your family. I'm here because I lost my job and I didn't have any other job offers." Kaylie, upset, dropped her head into both hands.

It was so silent between them, you could hear a pin drop. The prince finally cleared this throat and stood up.

"Can you do this job?" he asked. "Write a fairy tale for my daughter?"

Her head jerked up. When she looked at the prince, his expression was impossible to read. "I don't know," she answered him honestly. "I've never done anything like this before."

The prince studied her. "You strike me as the kind of woman that can do anything she sets her mind to."

Kaylie was surprised by his compliment. "Are you saying you think I can write this fairy tale?"

"I'm saying it doesn't matter what I think," the prince answered her. "It matters what *you* think. My mother brought you here for a reason. I have no control over that…"

"But you want me gone?" Kaylie asked bluntly, already knowing the answer.

"What I want right now is to finish this tour because that is what my mother asked me to do," the prince said. "Would you like to continue?"

As Kaylie stared up at the prince, she didn't know what she wanted or what she was going to do about going or staying, but she did know she was tired of feeling sorry for herself and fighting the hand fate had dealt her, starting with her losing her job. She knew complaining about it wasn't going to get her job back or make her feel any better. She also knew she had to stop being upset about the fact that she was stuck at a storybook castle, in Europe, with a handsome prince, because there were definitely worse fates to have. She always lived by the motto, it wasn't what happened to you but how you handled it that mattered, and lately she knew she hadn't been handling it very well. She also knew she needed a holiday attitude adjustment if she was going to try and do any writing about Christmas. It wasn't going to be easy, but she wasn't a quitter. She knew she had to try.

She stood up from the table and took a deep breath. "Okay, let's continue with the tour." But when a new Christmas song started to play, "The Christmas Waltz" with Frank Sinatra, she froze as she listened to the lyrics…

It's that time of year
When the world falls in love
Every song you hear seems to say
Merry Christmas
May your New Year dreams come true…

Kaylie caught her breath as a memory from a long time ago came rushing back to her.

Chapter 12

The memory "The Christmas Waltz" song had unlocked was from more than twenty years ago, on Christmas Eve, when she was just a little girl dancing with her dad to this same song. Her big sister Amelia and her mom were watching as she had eagerly stood barefoot on the top of her dad's shoes and held on tight as he twirled them around the room. She had been laughing and happy as she looked up at the string of snowflakes dangling across the ceiling that she'd made with her sister.

"Is everything okay?" the prince asked, watching her.

When Kaylie realized her eyes were filled with sentimental tears, embarrassed, she quickly brushed them away. "I'm fine. Allergies. They always act up when I fly."

Kaylie could tell by the look on the prince's face that he wasn't buying her lame excuse, but she was thankful when he didn't push.

"You like this song," he said.

She nodded. "I haven't heard it in years. It's my dad's favorite. We used to dance to it together. I'd forgotten about that."

"That's the thing about Christmas songs—they have a way of bringing back memories," the prince said, looking like he was speaking from experience. "My mother always says Christmas songs are something we grow up with at the holidays. They're always around us and become part of our traditions, and that's why she loves Christmas music so much. She says it's another way to remember, like looking at old pictures, Christmas music can bring back so many memories."

Kaylie nodded and wondered if that was why she never liked listening to Christmas music anymore, because it reminded her of past Christmases when her family used to all get together. She was still sorting through her feelings when the prince walked over to a massive black wrought iron two-sided door that also had the swan crest on it.

"Are you ready?" he asked.

She gave him a suspicious look. "That depends on if that's a dungeon or not."

"You're just going to have to trust me," the prince said with a hint of a smile.

Kaylie walked toward him. "Yeah, like you, I don't really trust people."

"Then perhaps we have more in common than I thought," the prince said. "Do you like wine?"

Kaylie's face lit up. "Does a bird have feathers?"

When the prince looked confused, she rushed to continue. "You know, birds, feathers, were talking about swans earlier. I was trying to go with the theme. Anyway, yes, I love wine."

"Then you can thank my mother," the prince said. "Our wine cellar is on her list of things she wants you to see."

Kaylie walked past him into the cellar. "I knew I liked your mother." She made a decision that no matter what happened, going forward she was going to make the best of it.

This is an adventure, she told herself. *I can do adventure. I love adventure. I live for adventure. Bring on the adventure.*

She was still smiling from the power of positive thinking when the prince joined her inside a huge wine cellar that took her breath away. The cellar went on for days and Kaylie guessed there had to be more than a thousand bottles of wine.

"Wow, this is impressive," she said, taking it all in. She felt like she'd stepped back in time to hundreds of years ago. The cellar had a curved ceiling made up of exposed rock that matched the stone walls. The floor was a worn red brick and vintage oak wine barrels were being used as tables to display different wines and wine glasses. There were floor-to-ceiling wine racks, and every slot was filled with bottles of wine.

"And I think it's bigger than the little wine shop I always go to by my apartment, and it's definitely a lot bigger than my apartment."

The prince gave her a curious look. "Really?"

"Oh, yeah," Kaylie assured him. "I live in a tiny studio, a lot of us do in the city, but it's fine because you're never really in your apartment except to sleep. At least, that's how I am. I eat out all the time. Why would I cook when New York has some of the best restaurants in the world? Plus, I have a wine bar downstairs, so that's like my living room. It's great."

The prince shook his head and frowned. "A living room with a bunch of strangers."

"But that's the best part," Kaylie continued. "This way I'm always meeting new people. I never know who I might have a glass of wine with. It's exciting and keeps things interesting. There's never a dull moment when you live in Manhattan. I meet someone new every single day."

"Well, I don't think I can offer you anything that exciting," the prince said. "But I can show you around our wine cellar."

"Sounds great." Kaylie smiled back at him. "I've never met a wine cellar I didn't like."

"So, you've toured many?" the prince asked.

Kaylie laughed. "No. This is my first, but I'm sure if I did, I would like them all." She followed the prince as he led her down one aisle that opened up to an area where there was another beautiful hand-carved wooden dining table. This one had seating for twelve but there were no place settings. In the middle of the table was a gleaming three-foot gold candelabra that was surrounded by fresh evergreens, holly, and red berries. It matched all the Christmas wreaths that were at the end of each wine aisle.

She ran her hand lightly across the table as she walked around it. "This is really something."

"That table is two hundred years old," the prince said proudly. "My mother has remodeled most of the castle, but down here we all agreed it was best to keep things the way they've been for centuries. History never goes out of style."

"It sure doesn't," Kaylie agreed.

"Okay," the prince said, turning to leave. "Are you ready?"

Kaylie didn't move. She put her hands on her hips. "Uh, not so fast. Aren't we missing something here? From what I've heard, any tour of a wine cellar usually involves some wine tasting. Am I right? Since this is my first tour, I want to make sure I do things right."

The prince arched an eyebrow. "In the name of research?"

"Of course," Kaylie said as she walked over and picked up a wine glass and tapped her fingernail against the crystal. "So? Are you going to help a girl out?"

"It's early," the prince said.

"It's five o'clock somewhere," Kaylie countered.

"What kind of wine do you like?"

"A big, bold, spicy red," Kaylie answered quickly. "It can be a Bordeaux or a California Cab or a Spanish Rioja or a peppery Zinfandel. I'm open to any wine that's complex and interesting and tells a story."

"Says the storyteller," the prince said as he walked along a row of wines. "Have you ever written about wines?"

"No," Kaylie said. "That would fall into the feature fluff category and, so far, I haven't run across a scandal that involves a winery, but never say never, right?"

The prince frowned and headed for the door.

"Wait, we're leaving?" Kaylie asked. "What about the wine tasting?"

"We still have a tour to do and we need to keep on schedule," the prince answered.

Kaylie reluctantly put down her glass and followed the prince back into the dining room. "About this schedule. I saw that epic list of your mother's. It would take two lifetimes to do all of that."

The prince nodded. "We do have generations of Christmas traditions here at the castle and in our village of Tolvania, so we'll do the best we can. We're lucky we only got my mother's favorite things she wants to be considered for the fairy tale."

"How many Christmas traditions do you have?" Kaylie asked.

"Hundreds."

Kaylie shook her head in amazement. "You sure love your Christmas. So what else do I need to see down here, minus the dungeon?"

"My mother wants you to see the Christmas Room," the prince said with a sigh.

Kaylie laughed. "You have a room called the Christmas Room?"

"We do," the prince said. "Follow me."

As she followed the prince down another long winding corridor, she knew she'd never be able to find her way back to the staircase on her own. "This place is huge," she said.

"We have dozens of passageways that connect to all different areas of the castle," the prince said, picking up his pace.

Kaylie hurried to catch up to him. "Like secret passageways?" she asked, fascinated.

"Well, I don't know if you'd call them a *secret* since everyone knows about them." The prince stopped in front of a massive fifteen-foot antique, hand-carved wooden door that had the swan crest in the middle of it.

Kaylie touched the carving. "Nice." She then noticed an old vintage key sticking out of the lock on the door.

"Go ahead," the prince said, following her gaze. "You can open it."

Kaylie eagerly turned the key and the door creaked as it opened. When she stepped inside, she gasped. "Whoa!"

Chapter 13

"Are you kidding me?" Kaylie asked, captivated. She couldn't believe what she was seeing. She walked into the room and slowly spun around, taking it all in. Her brain searched for the right words to describe it all.

A Christmas Disneyland.
A Christmas Time Capsule.
A Christmas Dream.

Then she knew. "This is like a Christmas fairy tale," she said in a voice filled with wonder. "It's magical."

The prince nodded and smiled. "That's what my daughter says, too, but really, this is just an old storage room filled with Christmas decorations from years gone by, many, many years gone by."

Mesmerized, Kaylie looked at all the vintage Christmas decorations. Even the stacked-up storage boxes of decorations were a festive red and gold. Kaylie didn't think it looked like a storage room at all. As she walked around, she felt like she was walking around an upscale department store that was filled with Christmas treasures everywhere you looked.

She stopped in front of a life-sized army of wooden nut-crackers that were all wearing elaborate costumes. She saluted the nutcracker closest to her. "At your service," she said merrily.

"Careful," the prince said as he joined her. "You'll get recruited into the Christmas Brigade."

"Is there really such a thing?" Kaylie asked, intrigued.

The prince shrugged. "I have no idea, but don't mention it to my mother—she'll start one."

Kaylie laughed as she walked over and admired a collection of snow globes in all shapes and sizes. "Wow, these snow globes are pretty amazing."

The prince picked up a snow globe that was on a golden pedestal. He shook it and held it up so Kaylie could watch the mesmerizing mixture of snow and gold glitter softly fall.

She leaned in closer to study the scene inside the snow globe and was charmed. "This is the castle, right?"

"It is," the prince said, handing her the snow globe so she could get a better look. "It's actually a gift my mother commissioned from a local artist, Carl, to do, and gave to me when I was away at college so I would always remember home."

"The likeness is amazing," Kaylie said. "All the detail work is incredible." She carefully handed it back to the prince. "But I imagine no matter where you go, you could never forget all this, the castle, your home."

The prince nodded. "You're right. Even though I don't do much traveling anymore."

Kaylie gave him a surprised look. "Really? Why? You're so close to so many incredible places here in Europe. I would think you'd be traveling all the time."

Kaylie caught a faraway look in the prince's eyes before he left her side and walked over to a bookcase filled with Christmas music boxes. She waited for him to comment but when he didn't say anything, she decided it was best to drop it.

With a child's excitement, she walked toward a giant gingerbread house and stepped inside and peeked out the window at the prince. "This is so cool," she said. "I feel a little like Hansel and Gretel…"

The prince glanced over at her. "Or maybe the wit…"

"Hey," Kaylie stopped him before he could say the word *witch*. "Do not even think about calling me that."

The prince cracked a hint of a smile. "I was just going along with your line of thinking."

"Well, I never think of myself as a witch," Kaylie said. "I've been called a lot of things but not that, thank you very much."

The prince raised his eyebrows. "Are you sure about that? I mean, if you go after criminals, I'm sure they have some pretty choice names for you."

Kaylie nodded. "Maybe, but never a witch to my face, and I'd never be the kind of witch to stuff some kids into an oven."

"I sure hope not." The prince laughed. "Remind me to keep Anna far, far away from you. I've already seen the damage you can do in a bathroom."

"Touché," Kaylie said with a laugh.

As Kaylie continued to check out the gingerbread house, she started to crave gingerbread cookies. "Where are the cookies to go with this house?

The prince looked confused. "What do you mean?"

Kaylie stepped out of the house. "Gingerbread cookies, gingerbread house, don't they go together at Christmas?"

The prince looked surprised. "For someone who doesn't do Christmas, you certainly seem to know a lot about Christmas traditions."

"Sure, I know about them, but that doesn't mean I do them anymore," Kaylie said.

"Did you ever?" the prince asked. "Do Christmas traditions?"

Kaylie headed toward a giant bright red Santa sleigh. "Sure, I've done Christmas. I just don't do it anymore. Been there. Done that," Kaylie said.

Ignoring the prince's questioning look, she jumped up into the sleigh, sat down, and grabbed the worn leather straps from the driver's seat. "Giddy up," she said merrily, bouncing the straps up and down.

"Giddy up?" the prince asked. "Seriously? Because I don't believe that's what Santa says to motivate his reindeer."

Kaylie laughed. "Oh, and you know this because you and Santa are besties? Please, tell me all about this special friendship. I'm fascinated."

"I'm afraid that's privileged information between me and Santa Claus," the prince said with a mock seriousness that had Kaylie laughing again.

"That sounds just like something my dad said to me once when he told me he was one of Santa's helpers when I caught him dressed up in a Santa suit," Kaylie said. "I was around eight and I had so many questions."

"I bet," the prince said. "That could have been a disaster."

"Except my dad is always quick to come up with a story. His imagination is pretty incredible," Kaylie said. "He told me something about how it was a secret between him and Santa and I, of course, believed him."

"That must be where you get it from, your storytelling ability," the prince said.

Kaylie thought about it and liked the idea. "Maybe it is."

"So, if he dressed up like Santa Claus, it sounds like your family really got into the Christmas spirit."

Kaylie looked wistful. "We used to." Her voice trailed off when, for a moment, she went where she never allowed herself to go, back to memories of her Christmas past when they still celebrated Christmas as a family.

"Is everything Okay?" the prince asked.

Kaylie was jarred back to the present. "Yes, great. Sorry. What were you saying?"

"I was asking if you'd ever taken a sleigh ride in Central Park, in New York?" the prince asked.

Kaylie shook her head. "No. We don't have actual sleighs but we do have carriage rides, but I've never taken one of those either." Her eyes went to a big shiny speedometer in front of her that was labeled *Christmas Spiritometer* and showed increasing levels of Christmas spirit. She turned back to the prince. "Where did this sleigh come from? And don't say the North Pole."

The prince shrugged. "I'm not sure. It's been around as long as I can remember."

As Kaylie went to step out of the sleigh, the prince held out his hand to help her. When she put her hand in his, she felt a spark and her pulse quickened. For a moment their eyes locked before they both quickly looked away. Kaylie willed herself to breathe as her heart raced.

That's when she saw a glass shelf filled with angels and walked over for a closer look. It gave her a chance to catch her breath and get a grip. The last thing she needed was to fall for a guy who had blatantly told her he didn't like what she did for a living and wished she wasn't there. The fact that he was a prince just made any infatuation or crush she might have even more ridiculous. She admired the angels that were in all shapes and sizes. "These are beautiful," she said. There were glass angels, porcelain angels, carved wooden angels, bronze angels, gold angels, silver angels, every kind of angel you could imagine.

"They're our Christmas angels," the prince said proudly, joining her.

She was instantly drawn to one of the smallest angels. It was only about three inches tall and it was made of glass with a gold halo and gold wings. Captivated, she carefully picked it up and cradled it in her hand. "This one's exquisite."

She was surprised when the prince took the angel from her and carefully put it back on the shelf. "They're all collector's items. Many are priceless. They are very special to us."

Kaylie clasped her hands together and quickly took a step back from the bookcase. "I'm sorry, I shouldn't have touched anything."

"It's all right," the prince said. "You didn't know. These angels go back many generations. Each one represents a different Christmas celebration and a different year. This is another of my mother's favorite family traditions and a tradition we share with everyone in Tolvania. Every year a different artist from the village is selected, by the people of the village, to create that year's angel that is displayed here at the castle on Christmas Eve for the ball."

"That must be a great honor for the artist," Kaylie said.

"And for us," the prince replied. "We keep the angels here, for safety, but we always say they're Tolvania's angels. They are displayed for special occasions. Some of the angels are in museums all over the world. They're recognized as one of the oldest royal Christmas traditions."

"That's a wonderful tradition," Kaylie said as her eyes were drawn back to the little glass angel she had been holding. She then looked around the room. "And you have enough Christmas decorations to decorate the village five times over."

"Probably more like one hundred times over," the prince corrected her. "These are just some of my mother's favorites. I'm sure she'd love it if you included them in the fairy tale, if you decide you can do it."

"You make it sound so easy," Kaylie said with a sigh. She walked over and stood in the middle of the nutcracker army. "Maybe these guys can help me write it."

"They already have a job," the prince said. "The nutcrackers will all be busy guarding over our Christmas Eve ball."

"Where do the sleigh and gingerbread house go?" Kaylie said.

"In the town square," the prince replied. "People love taking pictures with them, and Chef Jake even dresses up like a giant gingerbread boy and hands out his special cookies. He's quite the hit."

Kaylie laughed. "No way. Next, you're going to tell me Santa shows up with his reindeer and takes off in his sleigh."

The prince rolled his eyes. "No."

"Thank goodness, finally some sanity," Kaylie said.

"The reindeer are already with the sleigh, waiting for Santa to bring the bag of toys. Everyone knows that," the prince said with a smug smile.

"Stop it," Kaylie said, grabbing a wreath and flinging it at him like it was a Frisbee. "Who knew Prince Alexander was a comedian."

"Alex," the prince said, catching the wreath before it hit him.

"Really?" Kaylie asked, flattered to be on a first-name basis with the prince. "Okay, Alex."

"Prince Alex," the prince said. "You can call me Prince Alex."

Kaylie sighed. "Got it." *I should have known better*, she thought.

The prince headed for the door. "We need to go."

"To stay on schedule," Kaylie said.

"No, because it's five o'clock somewhere," the prince said.

"Wait...seriously?" Kaylie asked, excited, as she hurried to catch up with the prince as he headed for the door.

Chapter 14

When the prince led her back into the wine cellar dining room, Kaylie was already rubbing her hands together in anticipation, until the prince stopped at the Christmas tree.

"This is what I wanted to show you," the prince said.

Kaylie frowned. "Really? The tree?"

The prince nodded. "It's on my mother's list of traditions to show you."

"Uh, I've seen Christmas trees before," Kaylie said, glancing longingly at the wine.

"But have you seen *these* kinds of ornaments?" the prince asked as he walked over to the tree and took one of the wine cork ornaments off the tree and handed it to her.

When she examined it, she saw it was written on with red ink. "Dec 7th, 1997, K and S."

"For years, during the holidays, everyone who joins us for a wine event here signs the cork from the wine they try and they become ornaments for all our Christmas trees in the wine cellar," the prince said.

Kaylie handed him back the cork and studied another one that was hanging from the tree. "This one says Dec 17th, 1980, Bob and Fran."

"We have hundreds of corks, and for some of our friends that come year after year, it also becomes a holiday scavenger hunt. They go around looking for their cork ornaments on our trees and anyone who finds theirs gets to take home a bottle of wine."

Kaylie was suddenly more interested. "Okay, I could get behind that."

"Then I think you should have your own wine cork," the prince said and then held the wine cellar door open for her. "After you."

Kaylie happily slipped by the prince. "Does every castle have a wine cellar?" she asked.

"Only the good ones," the prince said as he let the door shut behind them.

As Kaylie sipped her glass of wine, she thought about how enjoyable the last half-hour had been. After the prince had helped her pick a bottle of wine, a big, rich, and bold Bordeaux, he'd surprised her with a wine tasting that included a delicious cheese board with Brie, Gruyère, Gorgonzola, and her favorite Manchego cheese from Spain.

Instead of sampling the wine in the wine cellar, the prince had taken her to a more casual room that was set up like a living room. There were lots of whimsical, cozy chairs and couches surrounding a grand stone fireplace. She'd picked the chair closest to the fire that had red and white stripes and reminded her of a giant candy cane.

"The Bordeaux is to your liking?" the prince asked as he watched her take another sip.

Kaylie nodded. "Very much. It's exactly as you said it would be, big and bold, but still rich and chocolaty, with a hint of plum and black cherry. It's spicy but not too much."

"I'm glad you approve," the prince said with a smile. "It comes from Saint-Émilion, one of my favorite appellations in the Bordeaux wine region of France. It's a Grand cru, from a winery there that's owned by a friend of the family."

"Great friends to have, because this is wonderful," Kaylie said with a sigh of contentment. "And I loved the cheeses you picked to pair with it. Are you a chef *and* a prince?"

When the prince laughed, his eyes crinkled at the corners. "Oh, no, I'm no chef, but I do appreciate good food and wine and so does my mother, and that's why we're lucky to have Chef Jake with us."

"Chef Jake of the infamous Christmas gingerbread pancakes?"

"The one and only," the prince answered. "He's actually American, like you."

Kaylie's eyes widened. "Really?"

"Yes," the prince said. "Why do you act so surprised?"

Kaylie shrugged. "I don't know. I guessed because of the way you reacted to me being here."

"I don't have anything against Americans."

"Ah, only American journalists, got it," Kaylie said but kept her tone light. She didn't want to go down that road again. She decided to quickly change the topic. "So, did Chef Jake show you how to put this delicious cheese board together?"

The prince nodded. "He did…"

"He's lying," a man said, laughing, as he walked into the room. "He didn't do any of it. I did. We try and keep the prince out of the kitchen."

Surprised, Kaylie turned around to see an attractive man walk into the room. She guessed he was around her age. He was wearing a crisp, all-white chef's uniform, minus the hat.

When she gave the prince a questioning look, the prince just shrugged, trying to look innocent. He failed. She turned back to the newcomer. "Let me guess, you're Chef Jake?"

"At your service." Chef Jake grinned back at her. "And you have to watch the prince. He's always trying to take credit for my work."

"What? That's not true," the prince jumped in. He tried to look indignant but then ended up cracking a smile. "Okay, maybe it's a little true. Kaylie, please meet Chef Jake Sullivan, our master chef."

"Pleased to meet you," Chef Jake said, holding out his hand to Kaylie.

She happily took it. "Very nice to meet you, too." She then gave the prince the side-eye. "I should have known something was up when he appeared with this magnificent cheese board."

"He's famous for trying to take credit for my work," Chef Jake said. "Like the time I had to make an elaborate dinner for him and his date and he made me hide in his bedroom when she came over early so she wouldn't know he didn't make it."

"The dinner was a hit," the prince said.

"And I was stuck in your bedroom for hours. You still owe me for that," Chef Jake said.

Kaylie watched the exchange fascinated. "So, you two are…"

"Old college friends," Chef Jake finished for her.

"And best friends," the prince continued. "Then and now."

"And I'd love to stay here and reminisce, but the queen wanted to go over some menus with me for her Christmas tea coming up," Chef Jake said. "It was very nice to meet you, Kaylie, and you be careful with this one. Don't say you weren't warned."

Kaylie laughed as Chef Jake left the room.

"Don't listen to him," the prince said. "Jake thinks he's the only one who should be in his kitchen, but I'm actually pretty talented in the kitchen myself."

Kaylie looked surprised and laughed. "Really? Because he said I shouldn't trust you. I'm not sure who to believe. I'm usually really good at reading people, it's what I do for my job all the time, but you, Prince Alexander, I can't figure you out."

The prince's smile disappeared. "Do you *read* all the people you interview?"

Kaylie saw something in his eyes change. Gone was the guy who had just been joking with his buddy. Now his eyes held a steely glint that gave her a chill, and not in a good way. She answered him quickly. "Of course. I have to be able to read someone if I'm going to interview them. This is the only way I can figure out what they're really thinking and where they're coming from so I can get what I need from them."

The prince frowned. "Get what you *need* from them?"

"You know, for my story," Kaylie tried to explain as she saw the prince's frown deepen. "It's my job to communicate with people so they'll talk to me. That way they open up and tell me things they might not have told me otherwise."

"So, you're trying to get people to tell you their secrets?" the prince asked with growing concern.

Kaylie laughed to try and lighten the mood that had just taken a drastic turn. "Why are you always finding a way to put a negative spin on what I do?"

"I'm just trying to state it like it is," the prince said. "It sounds like you'll do anything for a story."

"You say that like it's a bad thing," Kaylie said, fighting to stay calm. She felt like she was coming under attack. "I'm just doing my job."

The prince's eyes narrowed. "So, you *are* one of them," he said as he stood up.

"One of who?" Kaylie asked. She was confused by the prince's accusatory tone.

The prince locked eyes with her. "That's what you've been doing with me this whole time, isn't it? You've been trying to read me and gain my trust so you can learn my secrets. You act all friendly, asking a million questions, buttering me up, and then when my guard is down, you're going to go in for the kill. I'm done with this." The prince headed for the door.

Kaylie jumped up. "You think that's what I'm doing with you?" she called after him. "Really? That's insane. You're judging me but you don't know who I am or what I really do."

The prince stopped and turned. "Really, because I think you've just explained yourself very well about what you do as an investigative reporter and how you'll do anything to get your story. Trust me. I heard you loud and clear." He turned back around and left the room.

Kaylie, baffled, stared after him. She turned to one of the nutcrackers and threw up her hands. "What did I do?" She took a deep breath to calm herself and then realized if the prince left without her, she'd never figure out how to get back upstairs. "Wait for me," she yelled as she ran out the door. When Kaylie caught up with the prince, his jaw clenched and he stared straight ahead.

She couldn't figure it out. She thought she was finally getting along with the prince and was even enjoying herself, and the next minute he was looking at her like she'd stolen Santa's bag of toys. She was so confused. He knew she was a reporter, and he'd made it clear he didn't like reporters, but she thought they'd come to an understanding that she was only there to write a fairy tale. It really bothered her how hurt she felt, and she was mad at herself for caring so much.

The whole way up the stairs, Kaylie tried to think of what she wanted to say to the prince, but by the time they got to the top, she still hadn't come up with anything.

When he shut the door behind them, he didn't even look at her. He checked his watch and frowned and started walking down the hall. "We're running late. We need to speed up this tour," he said, frostier than ever.

Kaylie didn't move.

The prince turned around and stopped when he saw Kaylie wasn't following him.

"Are you coming?" he asked.

Kaylie stood her ground. "No."

"No?" the prince asked, looking annoyed.

Kaylie locked eyes with him. "No, because you're upset. I don't know why, but obviously you don't want to continue this tour."

"I never wanted to do this tour in the first place," the prince said, crossing his arms.

Kaylie blinked twice. "Wow, okay, way to be blunt. Well, neither did I. So, I see no reason to continue, since you're acting so tortured. Maybe you have one of those here too, a torture chamber, but I'm not interested in being made to feel like I'm a huge imposition."

"My mother wants us to do the tour," the prince said, impatiently checking his watch.

"I'll deal with your mother," Kaylie said and, with her head held high, she stormed past the surprised prince.

"Your room is the other direction," the prince called out after her.

Kaylie clenched her hands into fists and just kept walking. She wasn't sure where she was going but she wasn't about to go hide out in her room. And that's when she heard it.

Christmas music from the stereo system had started playing. It filled the hallway with the joyful sound of Christmas carolers exuberantly singing…

We wish you a Merry Christmas
We wish you a Merry Christmas
We wish you a Merry Christmas and a happy New Year…

"Bah, humbug," Kaylie grumbled as she picked up her pace.

Chapter 15

The prince shook his head as he watched her go. "Unbelievable," he said to himself. Part of him wanted to stop her
because he didn't like the idea of her roaming around the castle
on her own, but his ego wouldn't let him chase after her.

She was one of the most infuriating women he'd ever met.
And she was good, he thought, really good, because she'd
almost had him believing she was actually there for all the right
reasons, and that she wasn't just another reporter out to exploit
his family. He knew he needed to keep an eye on Kaylie, but
there was no way he was going to do it. However, he knew the
perfect person for the job. He needed to go find Elsa, who he
called the 'Fabulous Fixer' because no matter what the mess,
Elsa could always figure it out.

He walked further down the bookcase and pushed a new
section that opened to another secret hallway that led him
down a long corridor.

"So, what? You just let Kaylie take off on her own?" Chef Jake
asked with a laugh as he took a cookie tray filled with freshly-
baked gingerbread boys out of the oven.

The prince picked up a cookie from a cooling rack and
snapped its head off. "I did."

"Where did she go?" Chef Jake asked.

The prince shrugged. "I have no idea. I sent Elsa to go try and find her. It's not like she could get that far. You wouldn't believe how impossible she is. All she cares about is her career and work. She'll do anything to get ahead."

"Uh, the workaholic part sounds a little familiar," Chef Jake said, giving the prince a pointed look. "Was she really *that* bad because she seemed pretty nice to me?"

"Trust me, under that pretty smile is a tenacious reporter who will stop at nothing to get her story," the prince said.

"Ah, ha!" Chef Jake pointed at him. "So, you think she's pretty, that's the real problem here…"

"What are you talking about?" the prince asked, losing his patience. "Look, it doesn't matter what she looks like. She's a barracuda just waiting to bite."

"Not all reporters are like that," Chef Jake said.

"No, she literally told me she's exactly like that," the prince countered. "She said she'd stop at nothing to get a story and her whole plan was to get people to trust her and open up so she could learn their secrets."

Chef Jake put another cookie sheet into the oven. "Really, she said all that?"

The prince nodded as he picked up another cookie. "She did. She's one of them, Jake. I know she is."

"But what if she's not?" Chef Jake asked. "Maybe you've got this figured out all wrong."

The prince shook his head. "I don't think so. I need you to be on my side on this."

"I'm always on your side," Chef Jake quickly responded. "I wouldn't have come here as your head chef if I wasn't on your side."

"We both know you came because Sophia sweet-talked you into it," the prince said with a smile. "You spoiled her in college, always making her favorite meals and desserts. I don't think she would have married me if you hadn't come along as part of the package."

Chef Jake laughed. "Probably not."

The prince looked around and sighed. "I miss her, Jake, especially this time of year. She loved Christmas so much and many of my favorite traditions include her. That's why I couldn't stay here after we lost her. It was too hard. You know that first Christmas I took Anna to the British Virgin Islands because we both needed an escape. I thought it would give us a chance to relax at the beach and try to heal. When the next Christmas rolled around, I just went back to the Caribbean again. It was easier."

"I know it's hard," Chef Jake said. "This being your first Christmas back at the castle since Sophia passed away."

"There are just so many memories here," the prince said.

"But memories can be a good thing," Chef Jake said. "I think that's why your mother did all this, wanting a special gift for the princess. We all miss Sophia but I really think she would have loved this fairy tale idea. You know how much she loved trying to make Christmas special for your daughter."

"I know," the prince said. "But we didn't get our happily ever after, did we? I don't know if I want Anna believing in fairy tales. I don't want her to get disappointed and hurt any more than she already has been. She lost her mother, Jake, she lost everything."

"No, she didn't," Chef Jake quickly said. "Anna still has *you*. I know these last few years have been incredibly hard for both of you..."

"For all of us," the prince said quietly.

"Yes, for all of us, but don't you think it's time for Anna to start enjoying Christmas again and learning more about why her mother loved it so much?"

"Anna doesn't really care that much about Christmas," the prince said, putting down the cookie he was eating. "It's not a big deal for her."

Chef Jake gave him a pointed look. "You really think that? She's just following your lead because she knows you haven't liked celebrating Christmas. She's very smart and intuitive but she's still a child, Alex. She should be enjoying Christmas. I've seen how her face lights up when she's talking to your mother about Christmas and helping her decorate and plan the events."

"I haven't seen that," the prince said, frowning.

"Maybe because you haven't wanted to," Chef Jake said.

The prince raked his fingers through his hair and started pacing around the kitchen. "I've really messed this up for Anna, haven't I? I've been so busy working lately, I missed seeing any of this."

"You haven't messed anything up," Chef Jake said with an encouraging smile. "I'm just saying I think it's time for you, and for Anna, to start making your own Christmas memories. If there's any time of year for hope and healing, this is it."

"Are you a chef or a therapist?" the prince asked, only half-joking.

Chef Jake came and patted him on the shoulder. "I'm anything you need me to be. That's what friends are for."

The prince knew Chef Jake was right. He had never intentionally meant to cut Christmas out of Anna's life but that's exactly what had happened when they spent their last couple of holidays in the Caribbean at their family's vacation home.

He remembered how his mother had wanted them to stay in Tolvania but when she had seen how hard it was for him, she'd agreed he should go. She'd supported him doing whatever it took to help them get through the impossibly difficult time.

The prince smiled a little, remembering how much Anna had thrived and healed during their time in the Caribbean. They'd spent all their days together, just the two of them, boating and swimming in the beautiful turquoise sea and exploring all the sugar-white sand beaches. Anna was his entire world, and all he wanted was for her to be safe and happy.

But if he was being completely truthful with himself, he knew those island Christmas getaways were just as much for him as they were for Anna. He was the one who had a hard time dealing with all the Christmas memories. He counted on how, when they went to the Caribbean, they didn't do any Christmas activities but treated it like a wonderful beach vacation. There was no talk of Christmas, past, present, or future.

There had been times when he had wondered if Anna was missing out on celebrating Christmas but he'd convinced himself that he was doing the right thing. He planned that someday when the memories weren't so painful, he would share some of her mother's favorite Christmas traditions with her.

That time had come faster than he had hoped when a hurricane took out a large portion of the compound earlier that year. Since the repairs were still happening that meant this Christmas they'd have to stay home at the castle.

He had asked his mother to keep things low-key, but apparently, her definition of low-key was very different as she had gone ahead and planned a lot of Christmas events that she'd expected him to be a part of. The fact that she'd also invited a journalist to stay with them was still something he couldn't understand. He knew she was only doing what she thought was best for him and her granddaughter, but bringing a stranger into their home, a reporter no less, had thrown him completely off guard. And now he had to deal with the fact that his daughter apparently loved Christmas as much as her mother and grandmother.

He knew, no matter how complicated his relationship with Christmas was, he owed it to his daughter to make sure she had the kind of Christmas she truly wanted, and if that meant doing all the holiday traditions to make her happy, that's what he was determined to do.

"I need to fix this with Anna, don't I?" The prince asked the question already knowing the answer.

Chef Jake put some gingerbread cookies on a cute Santa plate and handed it to the prince. "This might help. They're her favorite."

"Thanks," the prince said as he took the plate, but still looked worried.

"Look," Chef Jake said. "Your mother is a smart lady. I'm sure she checked Kaylie out. She'd never bring paparazzi here. She hates them as much as you do for what they've done to your family, and she would never do anything to hurt Anna. I know you want to protect Anna but you don't want to protect her so much that she doesn't have a chance to live her life. She's just ten years old. I think your mother is just trying to bring some Christmas magic into her life."

The prince nodded. He knew Jake was right. He knew Anna had inherited her mother's vivid imagination and love of a good story. So, no matter how he felt about fairy tales and believing in happily ever after, he knew his mother had gone to a lot of trouble to bring a writer here, even if, in his opinion, she had picked the wrong writer for the job.

"So, maybe you want to ease up on her," Chef Jake said.

"My mother or the reporter?" the prince asked.

"Both," Chef Jake answered.

The prince nodded as he looked down at his plate of gingerbread cookies.

"Don't even think about it," Chef Jake said. "Those are for Anna."

"And she's going to love them," the prince said as he headed for the door. "Thank you."

"Anytime," Chef Jake said with a smile. "You got this. You're a great dad."

"And you're a great friend," the prince said as he left the kitchen.

Chapter 16

After Kaylie had stormed away from the prince, she was pretty proud of herself for only taking two wrong turns before finding her way back to the drawing room. When she'd found it empty, she'd decided to take a seat by the fire and start coming up with her plan B.

She knew she had been immature to stomp off in a huff, but something about the prince just kept getting under her skin. She hated to admit how much it hurt that he thought she was sneaking around, undercover, doing some kind of negative story about his family. She was upset with herself for believing that even for a second he was starting to warm up to her. He was still as icy as the weather outside and, just like the weather, there was nothing she could do about it.

"So, now what do I do?" she muttered to herself as she stared into the fireplace and watched the flickering flames. Restless, she got up and walked over to the window. The snow had stopped and for the first time, she got a clear view of the lake without all the whirling snow getting in her way. Mesmerized, she leaned closer to the glass to take it all in. "Wow," Kaylie said softly. It was so picturesque it looked like something on a postcard.

All along the lake, there were snow-covered trees decorated with white twinkle lights and bright red round ornaments.

As she looked closer, she saw Blixen run out to the end of a wooden dock on the lake. The dock was also festively decorated with white lights and Christmas wreaths that had big red bows.

Kaylie laughed when Blixen started barking and saw the princess join him, followed by the queen. They all looked like one big happy family. She was still watching them when the queen saw her looking out the window and waved. Kaylie waved back. "Your Royal Highness, we need to have a little chat," she said out loud and was surprised when someone answered her back.

"A chat about what?" Elsa asked as she entered the room.

Kaylie spun around and was partly relieved and partly disappointed that it was Elsa and not the prince.

"Is Alexander giving you a hard time?" Elsa asked with a knowing look.

Kaylie laughed. "That would be an understatement. He has made it very clear he doesn't want me here."

Elsa joined her by the window. "Don't take it personally."

Kaylie raised an eyebrow and looked confused. "Well, it feels pretty personal."

"And I assure you he doesn't hate *you*," Elsa continued. "What he doesn't like are reporters and the media, and he has good reasons." When Elsa walked over by the fire and sat down on the settee, Kaylie joined her, taking the chair across from her.

"I'm listening," Kaylie said.

"When the prince's father died, the media wasn't very kind," Elsa said with a sigh. "They tore the prince to pieces, questioning the kind of king he would be, saying he wasn't fit to be king."

Kaylie winced. "They actually said that?"

Elsa nodded. "And a lot worse, unfortunately. They called him a playboy prince who cared more about his social life than his royal duties and his family. They didn't let up, and everything they reported were lies or twisted half-truths. They were relentless. It was horrible. The queen had just lost her husband, the love of her life, and now the media was attacking her only child. The prince wasn't worried about himself as much as he was worried about how all the negative press was upsetting his mother, making an impossible time even more heartbreaking."

"So, what did he do?" Kaylie asked.

"He left to try and protect her," Elsa said. Her voice was filled with sadness. "He was at a university in England, but when the media wouldn't stop hounding him, he took a year off and disappeared."

"Disappeared?" Kaylie asked. "What do you mean?"

"Exactly that," Elsa said. "He got on a plane and after trying to go several places in Europe and still not being able to completely shake off the paparazzi, he finally found his escape."

"Where?" Kaylie asked.

"Africa," Elsa answered. "He made sure the paparazzi thought he was in South America and then he quietly traveled to a small village in Southeastern Africa, in Malawi, and volunteered at a local orphanage where no one knew who he was."

Kaylie listened, fascinated. "He just randomly went to Malawi?"

"Oh no," Elsa said. "The prince never does anything randomly. His father had gone to Malawi to volunteer when he was the prince's age. It's one of the poorest African countries, and it had a great impact on Prince Randolph, so he always told his son that one day they would travel to Malawi together and volunteer and help the Malawi people."

"But they never had a chance to do that," Kaylie said quietly, thinking about the trips she never got to take with her grandma.

Elsa shook her head with regret in her eyes. "No, they didn't. So, Prince Alexander went as a way to honor his father's memory."

"How long was he gone?" Kaylie asked.

"More than a year," Elsa replied.

"But wasn't that hard on the queen, having him so far away for so long?" Kaylie asked.

Elsa nodded. "It was, but she wanted what was best for him. She could see how all the negative press was destroying him and she wanted him to have a break, away from all of this, away from the pressure that someday he would be king."

"She's very wise," Kaylie said.

"And very loving," Elsa added. "She would do anything for her family. I remember the queen told me this would be her son's one chance to escape this life he was born into and live his own life the way he wanted. The prince loved being in Malawi so much. He always talked about the kindness of the Malawi people and of course, that's where he met Sophia, his wife."

"He met her in Africa?" Kaylie asked, surprised.

Elsa nodded. "He did. Sophia was volunteering as a teacher at the same orphanage where he was helping to build a new school. It was meant to be. Sophia was taking a gap year from Harvard and after the year was up, when Sophia went back to Massachusetts to finish college, the prince went, too, and finished his studies at Harvard."

Kaylie's eyes grew huge. "The prince lived in America?"

"He did," Elsa said. "And he flew under the radar for a long time. Everyone simply knew him as the guy who volunteered in Malawi with Sophia. He would always tell me these amazing stories about his time at Harvard. He had such a great time exploring Cambridge and Boston.

"And that's where he met Chef Jake," Kaylie said, putting two and two together.

"That's right," Elsa said. "And they've been best friends ever since. But after he and Sophia graduated, he knew it was time to come home. When he brought Sophia back to Tolvania, everyone fell in love with her just like he did. She was this positive force, full of laughter, and light. She always made people feel good. People loved being around her. I know I did."

"She sounds amazing," Kaylie said.

"She was. She brought out the best in everyone, especially the prince. She even somehow managed to win over the paparazzi."

Kaylie looked skeptical. "How?"

"By being so nice," Elsa said. "They really did have a perfect love story, so there was no dirt to dig up anymore on the prince's dating habits. So, the paparazzi got bored and moved on to torture someone else and finally left our family alone. But then Sophia passed away and they came back with a vengeance."

"Oh, no," Kaylie said covering her mouth with her hand. She felt sick. "What happened?"

Elsa looked upset as she stood up and walked closer to the fire. For a moment she only stared into the flames, not saying anything.

Watching her, Kaylie could feel her pain. "It's okay. We don't have to talk about this."

Elsa turned to face Kaylie. "I'd like to share what happened with you so you have a better understanding of the prince."

Kaylie nodded and waited for Elsa to continue.

Elsa took a deep breath before continuing. "After Sophia passed away, the paparazzi came after Prince Alexander again, hard. A lot of the reporters were still angry that the prince had disappeared and ditched them so they started reporting all these stories about how he had been unfaithful to Sophia and had a mistress and didn't care about his daughter, Princess Anna…"

Kaylie jumped up. "But none of it was true!" Even though she barely knew the prince, she felt like he'd never do something like this.

"No, of course none of it was true," Elsa agreed. "The prince would never have done something like that to Sophia or Anna. Sophia was the love of his life. Everyone knew that, including the paparazzi, but a great love story doesn't sell newspapers and magazines, a scandal does. They made the whole thing up and the story made headlines and went viral. Different reporters would put their nasty, hateful twist on the story, until it just kept getting bigger and uglier and even more hurtful."

Kaylie joined Elsa by the fire. "I'm so sorry. I can't even imagine the pain this caused for all of you."

Elsa nodded. "It was unforgivable, especially because now he had Anna. The reporters even got a picture of her crying and made up stories about how depressed she was. It was a nightmare."

Kaylie felt sick to her stomach. "What did the prince do?"

"He worked with the queen and a new special law was passed banning paparazzi from Tolvania."

"Did it work?" Kaylie asked.

"Only as long as he stayed here in Tolvania, where he was protected," Elsa said. "He always loved to travel but he had to stop. He knew anytime he left Tolvania, the paparazzi reporters were standing by, wanting to sink their teeth into him."

"So, he's trapped," Kaylie said, feeling a rush of sympathy for the prince and princess.

"In a sense, yes," Elsa said. "But please keep this between us. He doesn't share this with anyone, but I thought you should know so you could understand a little better what you're up against. It doesn't excuse him from being rude to you, but hopefully this will offer a little insight. You're media. You're everything he has run from his entire life."

"It all makes sense now," Kaylie said, shaking her head, as Elsa's story sank in.

"Even now the prince is still constantly looking over his shoulder, waiting for another reporter to stab him in the back with some scandalous untrue story," Elsa continued.

"And then I showed up on his doorstep," Kaylie added. "I'm surprised he didn't chase me off with a sword and dagger."

Elsa laughed a little. "If he had one, he might have."

"But what I don't understand is, why am I here then?" Kaylie asked. "I am a reporter. Everything this family hates. What was the queen thinking? Why would she..."

But Kaylie's sentence was cut off when the queen entered along with the princess and Blixen.

"I will be happy to tell you exactly what I was thinking a little later," the queen said as she motioned to the princess who was playing with Blixen. "Kaylie, you're finished with your tour already? I find that hard to believe. Where is my son?"

Kaylie looked to Elsa for help but luckily the princess walked over.

"Did you see the Christmas Room?" the princess asked.

Kaylie quickly nodded. "I did. It was amazing."

An older woman wearing black pants and a pretty blue sweater entered the room. She had the kind of warm smile and demeanor that made you feel at ease immediately.

"Ms. Meyers, please come and meet our guest, Miss Kaylie Karlyle," the queen invited.

"She's from New York City," the princess chimed in.

Ms. Meyers joined them. "That's a wonderful city. It's a pleasure to meet you, Miss Karlyle."

"Kaylie, please," Kaylie said with a smile. "It's nice to meet you, too."

"Ms. Meyers has been part of our family since Anna was born," the queen said. "We don't know what we would do without her."

"I feel the same," Ms. Meyers said. "And now I believe it's time for your art lessons, princess. Did you find some inspiration on your walk with your grandmother?"

"I did," the princess answered, excited. "The Christmas trees down by the lake. I want to paint those."

Ms. Meyers held out her hand to the princess. "That sounds like an excellent idea. Shall we get started?"

"Yes," the princess said, eagerly taking Ms. Meyers's hand.

"It was a pleasure to meet you, Kaylie," Ms. Meyers said.

"You as well," Kaylie responded.

"I'll stop by and see what you're creating a little later," the queen said to the princess.

"Thank you, Grandmother," the princess said as she walked away with Ms. Meyers, with Blixen following close on her heels. They were going out the door when Anna turned around and looked at Kaylie.

Surprised, Kaylie waved. She was even more surprised when Anna shyly waved back. Kaylie was still smiling when they disappeared out the door and then she saw the queen watching her.

"My granddaughter has taken a liking to you," the queen said.

Kaylie, surprised, turned back to the queen. "Really? You think so?"

The queen had a satisfied look on her face as she nodded. "Yes, I do. She doesn't usually warm up to people very fast. She's very cautious."

"Like her father," Kaylie said. The words were out of her mouth before she could stop herself.

The queen nodded thoughtfully. "Yes, like her father." The queen gave her and Elsa a shrewd look. "Is there something I need to know about today's tour that obviously isn't finished?"

Kaylie had no clue what to say, so she said nothing. She tried not to flinch when the queen studied her closely.

"So, where is my son?" the queen asked.

Elsa came to the rescue. "He went to get the next part of the tour ready for Kaylie, so I've been keeping her company telling her about some of the Christmas events we have coming up."

The queen's eyebrow arched. "I see. So, Kaylie, what event are you most looking forward to?"

Oh crap, Kaylie thought as she looked over at Elsa, and then threw out the first thing that came to her mind. "The gingerbread house event, that one sounds really cool."

"The gingerbread *event*?" the queen asked, giving Kaylie a questioning look. "What event, exactly, is that?"

The prince entered the room with a smile. "I told Kaylie about how we make gingerbread cookies and hand them out in the village and how people take pictures with the gingerbread house," the prince said.

"Yes, that event," Kaylie jumped in, giving the prince a grateful look.

"That's not one of our events," the queen said. "It's something we do, but not an event."

"It's my fault," Kaylie jumped in. "You have so many things you're doing, I'm getting it all mixed up." Kaylie jumped when her cell phone all of a sudden started beeping with alerts. She quickly grabbed it out of her pocket. Her eyes lit up. "It's working!" she exclaimed. "My cell phone is finally getting a good signal."

"They must have fixed the cell tower," the queen said.

Kaylie's eyes grew huge as she scrolled through more than a dozen text messages. There were several from Rachel and her former boss, Bob. One of the texts from Rachel said *911*. That was their code for 'call me ASAP, it's something important.' She held up her phone. "I really should return some of these messages. It's my boss, or I should say, my former boss, and friend. I don't want them to worry about me. I'm supposed to check in."

The queen nodded. "Of course. Please go call your friends and then you can meet my son and granddaughter back here at three to go get the upside-down Christmas tree."

Kaylie and the prince exchanged an awkward glance.

"I really don't need to go," Kaylie jumped in. "This sounds more like a father-daughter thing to me."

The queen frowned. "But you told Anna you were going. You don't want to disappoint her. It's all she has been talking about this morning, going with *both* of you to get her first upside-down Christmas tree."

"There you have it," the prince said. "That's settled." He locked eyes with her as if daring her not to agree.

"If you're sure," Kaylie said, her voice cracking.

"I'm sure," the prince said.

Kaylie felt a shiver go down her spine. She knew she was the last person the prince wanted to spend time with, but she forced herself to keep smiling. She was stuck. If she didn't go now, she'd be the bad guy, and she didn't want to disappoint the princess or the queen. She could deal with the prickly prince for a few hours. She'd certainly dealt with other difficult people in her career.

She gave the prince her sweetest smile. "Okay, great, then I'd love to come." *Two can play at this game,* she thought, and felt some small satisfaction when she saw his jaw clench.

"Then we will see you soon," the prince said.

"It's a plan," she said as she started to walk out of the room. When she felt the prince's eyes drilling into her back, she had to force herself not to run. When she got to the door, she glanced over her shoulder and saw she'd been right.

The prince was watching her like a guard dog getting ready to pounce.

Chapter 17

Kaylie headed back to her room as fast as she could while also checking texts on her phone. Her cell signal had started going in and out again and she wanted to call Rachel as soon as she could. Rachel rarely used their *911* text code, but when she did, Kaylie knew something important was going on.

When she got to her room she burst through the door, only to find a surprised princess and Ms. Meyers staring back at her. "Whoa," Kaylie exclaimed, equally surprised to see them. She looked around and quickly realized she wasn't in her room at all. The room she was in was filled with art supplies.

"I am so sorry," Kaylie said. "I thought this was my room."

"That's no problem," Ms. Meyers said kindly. "Your room is at the end of the other hall, down that way," she said and pointed. "Don't worry, it happens all the time."

"No, it doesn't," the princess corrected Ms. Meyers.

Kaylie couldn't help but laugh. She loved the princess's honesty. "I'm sure it doesn't. I'm just terrible with directions and I was looking at my phone and…" She stopped talking when she saw some wonderful paintings on the wall of the castle, the lake, and Blixen. She walked over to get a closer look. "These are great," she said, drawn in by the vibrant colors.

"The princess is very talented," Ms. Meyers said.

Kaylie's jaw dropped when she stared at the princess. "You did all these? No way!"

"I did," the princess said with a hint of a smile.

"Seriously?" Kaylie asked, glancing back at the paintings. "Because these are really good." She would have never guessed a ten-year-old had done them. She pointed at the Blixen painting.

"So, Blixen, this is you?" Kaylie asked. "You look very handsome."

Blixen barked and wagged his tail.

Kaylie walked over to where the princess and Ms. Meyers were sitting at a table together. "What are you guys working on now?" When she got closer, she was impressed when she saw the princess was painting a row of Christmas trees with bright red round ornaments.

"The trees down by the lake," the princess answered.

Kaylie pointed to a large star at the top of one of the trees. "I like your star."

"Thank you," the princess said and rewarded her with a smile. "I wanted the star to be big enough so people in heaven could see it, like my mother and grandfather."

Kaylie's heart went out to her. "I love that, and I'm sure they can see it. It's perfect."

The princess smiled back at her and then went back to painting.

Ms. Meyers walked over to where two easels were set up and motioned for Kaylie to join her.

As Kaylie walked over, she noticed right away that there was a regular-sized easel and a miniature easel set up next to it. On the regular-sized easel, Kaylie was charmed when she saw a beautiful painting of a snow-covered village. "Is this Tolvania?" Kaylie asked.

Ms. Meyers nodded proudly. "It is, and this was painted by Anna's mother, Princess Sophia."

"It's fantastic," Kaylie said. "So, this is where the princess inherited her talent. It makes me want to go to the village immediately."

"I think that was the plan, to draw people in," Ms. Meyers said. "And you will see when you go that Tolvania is even more magical in person. I think it's wonderful that you're here and what you are doing for Princess Anna and the family. It's going to mean so much to everyone. I know Sophia would have loved the idea of the princess having a special fairy tale. Sophia was so creative. The princess definitely takes after her. Where most children start off coloring, Anna skipped that and went straight to painting when she was two. Her mother said she had the gift and the two of them would spend hours painting together. It was really something special to see."

"I bet it was," Kaylie said and then pointed at a painting of Blixen that was on the smaller easel. He was standing at the end of the dock wearing a big red Christmas bow, looking adorable. "And this one?"

"The princess painted that. He's her favorite thing to paint," Ms. Meyers said.

Kaylie nodded, looking over at the princess and how Blixen was sleeping at her feet. "Those two make quite the pair."

Ms. Meyers nodded. "They are inseparable."

Kaylie watched the princess concentrate on her painting. "She's so focused on what she's doing. It's really something to see."

"Painting is her favorite thing to do," Ms. Meyers said. "Right after her mother passed away, she didn't want to paint anymore. It was heartbreaking to see, but then the prince got the idea to put a different picture her mother had done every day on the easel. He told the princess her mother was always with her and encouraged her to try and use the painting as inspiration to see what she could paint as a way of still painting together. It only took a few days before we found her in here painting on her little easel next to her mother's."

"So, it worked," Kaylie said, in awe.

"It did, and thankfully she has been painting ever since. But now it's hard for me to get her to do any other arts and crafts." Ms. Meyers chuckled. "Now she only wants to paint." Ms. Meyers glanced over at the princess. "Would you mind keeping a quick eye on her while I run and get a sweater for both of us? This room is a little chilly today."

"Of course," Kaylie said.

"I'll be right back," Ms. Meyers said as she hurried out the door.

Kaylie wandered back over to the princess who was still painting like she was in her own private world.

The princess gave her a curious look. "Do you paint?"

Kaylie pointed at herself. "Me? Oh, no. I can't even draw a stick figure, and you do not want to see me around any paint," Kaylie said with conviction. "That could be a disaster."

The princess got some paints and paint brushes off the counter and picked up two pieces of paper and sat back down.

"Sit," the princess commanded.

Kaylie instantly sat. She felt like an obedient pet when she saw Blixen wag his tail.

The princess slid a piece of paper over to Kaylie and handed her a paint brush.

Kaylie refused to take it. "Oh, no. I told you. I don't paint. I'd much rather just watch you. You're the real artist."

The princess waved the paint brush at her. "Don't be afraid. I'm going to show you how."

Kaylie sat up straight. "Who said anything about feeling afraid?"

The princess gave her a knowing smile. "You did."

Kaylie gave the princess a look. "How old are you again?"

"Ten," the princess said proudly. "Almost eleven."

"Going on forty," Kaylie said under her breath.

The princess heard her and giggled. She then waved the paint brush at Kaylie again.

Kaylie gave up and finally took the brush. Clearly, the princess had inherited her grandmother's tenacious personality, and she knew the sooner she got this embarrassment over with, the better. She'd always admired anyone who could draw or paint and tell a story that way. As far as her artistic talents were concerned, she knew she was lacking. She was more than happy to keep her storytelling to the words she wrote and spoke.

"I'll try on one condition," Kaylie said, seeing some scissors and picking them up. "That you do one of my family traditions with me. It's the only crafty thing I could ever do. It's really easy." She picked up a piece of white paper and started folding it and then quickly cut out a fantastic snowflake and held it up. "Voilà!" She was pretty impressed with herself. She hadn't made a snowflake since she was about the princess's age. She handed a piece of paper to the princess and the scissors. "Here, your turn."

"I haven't made a snowflake before," the princess said. Within seconds, copying what Kaylie had done, the princess cut out a perfect snowflake and held it up, proudly.

"Show-off," Kaylie said with a laugh.

The princess giggled. "That was easy."

"But we're not done yet," Kaylie said, picking up a red felt pen. "In my family, our tradition was to make snowflakes for our tree and write on each one a word that reminds us of what matters most at Christmas." Kaylie wrote the word *joy* on her snowflake and handed the princess the pen.

The princess quickly wrote the word *family* on her snowflake. "Can we make more and put them on our tree?"

"I don't see why not," Kaylie said, grabbing some more paper and handing the princess a sheet. They both started cutting out new snowflakes.

In no time they had a little pile of snowflakes that were ready to hang on the tree. Kaylie enjoyed every minute of it, until the princess picked up a paintbrush and handed it to Kaylie.

"A deal is a deal," the princess said. "Now it's my turn to teach you how to paint."

Kaylie frowned. "I thought you were going to forget about that."

The princess merrily shook her head as she dipped her paint brush into the green paint. "We will start with something really easy. You just do what I do, okay?"

"Easy for you to say." Kaylie eyed the paint. "You're a little Van Gogh. You know, the famous artist…"

"I have both my ears," the princess quickly replied.

When Kaylie looked surprised, the princess grinned back at her. "Ms. Meyers just told me about him yesterday in our art lesson, and about Monet and Renoir and…"

Kaylie waved her paint brush at the princess. "Yeah, yeah, okay. I get it. You're a genius, but are you a teacher? We shall see, because I'm not going to be an easy student."

"I can teach you. My mother taught me," the princess said with a confident smile. "And I taught Blixen to fetch. I'm a good teacher. Just don't be afraid. You can't be afraid when you do art. Just have fun; that's what matters most."

Kaylie took a deep breath. "Okay, but don't say I didn't warn you." She dunked her paintbrush into the green paint and twirled it around.

"Be careful, you don't want too much paint," the princess warned.

Kaylie frowned. "So, I'm messing up already?"

"No, you can't mess up with art, that's what Ms. Meyers always says. Everything we create is beautiful because we created it," the princess said, sounding all-knowing.

Kaylie was impressed. She wondered, if she'd had an inspiring art teacher who had encouraged her, instead of telling her all the things she was doing wrong, maybe she would have liked art more.

"You just have to believe it and then you can do it," the princess said.

As the green paint dripped off Kaylie's paint brush onto her blank piece of paper, she couldn't help but laugh. Now, not only was she getting a painting lesson from a ten-year-old princess, she was apparently getting a life lesson as well.

When Kaylie's phone lit up with a text from Rachel, the princess's smile faded.

"Do you have to go and work?" the princess asked in a matter-of-fact tone that sounded like she already knew Kaylie's answer.

Kaylie's heart went out to the princess as she imagined this happened to her all the time with her busy father.

"Hold on," Kaylie said, quickly checking her phone. It was another text from Rachel—another *911*. She quickly texted Rachel back. *I'm okay. I made it here. Are you okay? Can I call you later?*

As Kaylie waited for Rachel to text back, she saw the princess watching her. She admired how the princess wasn't pouting or looking disappointed.

She sighed with relief when Rachel's text came in.

I was just worried! Yes, call me later.

When Kaylie put away her phone, the princess looked surprised.

"You don't have to work?" the princess asked, confused.

Kaylie picked up her paint brush. "Oh, I'm planning to work, with *you*, because you said you were going to teach me to paint, and trust me, that's going to be work."

When the princess grinned, it lit up her entire sweet little face.

Kaylie smiled back at her. "Okay, teacher, show me what you got."

Chapter 18

The prince was carrying a plate of gingerbread cookies as he walked down the hall toward the princess's art room. He knew it was time to have a real heart-to-heart with his daughter.

When he heard laughing, he stopped outside the door and was surprised to find Kaylie and the princess inside the room, painting together, joking around, and having a great time.

"What in the world?" he said to himself, taking it all in.

He couldn't help but smile when he saw how happy his daughter looked. She was giggling, trying to show Kaylie how to paint something that Kaylie was clearly having trouble with. He stepped closer so he could listen in without interrupting them.

"There's no way I can paint an angel on the top of my tree," Kaylie said to the princess. "You're nuts."

The princess giggled. "I'm not nuts. You're just afraid you'll mess up."

"Uh, yeah, because I will," Kaylie said. "My tree is looking pretty fantastic and I don't want to push my luck by trying to add a tree topper that's an angel because that's *way* too hard for this beginner."

"No, it's not. It's easy. You can do it," the princess said with conviction. "Just watch me. First, you draw a circle for the head and then a triangle for the body and you have an angel. See, easy!"

"For you!" Kaylie laughed as she watched the princess effortlessly draw a simple and perfect little angel.

"Nope, I'm good. My tree looks just fine as it is."

"But it doesn't have a tree topper," the princess insisted. "Every Christmas tree needs a tree topper. Everyone knows that."

"That's not the way we do it in America. We don't have tree toppers in America, so I don't need to add one since I'm American."

The prince laughed as he entered the room. "Is that so?"

Kaylie almost fell off her chair from surprise. "Where did you come from? Another secret passageway?"

"Of course," the prince said. Seeing how nervous Kaylie looked, he reminded himself that he'd promised to try and give her a chance and be more open-minded. "Now what was this you were telling my daughter about tree toppers?"

The princess looked at her father. "She said they don't have them in America."

"Really?" the prince said, eyeing Kaylie. He watched her face flush red with embarrassment.

"Well, I may have exaggerated that a little bit," Kaylie said, avoiding the prince's stare.

The prince arched an eyebrow. "A little bit?"

Kaylie rolled her eyes. "Okay, maybe a lot."

The princess's eyes lit up. "So, you do have tree toppers where you live?"

Kaylie nodded. "Yes, we do."

"So, you were just afraid?" the princess asked.

The prince was amused by how Kaylie looked even more embarrassed after being called out by a ten-year-old.

"I'm not *afraid*," Kaylie answered. "I just don't want to wreck my masterpiece we've worked so hard on."

"You're afraid," the princess said with an all-knowing voice.

The prince watched Kaylie's mouth snap shut. He smiled back at her. He couldn't wait to see how she tried to wiggle her way out of this one. If there was one thing he knew about his daughter, while she was a dreamer, like her mother, she had also inherited his very logical way of thinking, and didn't let people off the hook very easily.

"Father, tell Kaylie what you always tell me," the princess pleaded.

The prince walked over to Kaylie. "We have a saying in our family that whenever you're afraid of doing something…"

"You just have to believe," the princess jumped in.

"And don't look back, just dive in," the prince finished for her.

"But what if I dive in and I drown?" Kaylie asked them both.

"Then my father will save you," the princess answered as if it were obvious. "Won't you, Father?"

"Of course," the prince answered. As he looked into Kaylie's eyes, he thought he saw a flash of something, maybe fear, or annoyance, or attraction? He wasn't sure. She had talked about how hard he was to read, but he also thought she was impossible to try and figure out. But one thing he did know, he hadn't seen his daughter this excited and happy in a long time. She was acting like a regular ten-year-old. It had him thinking about what his mother, Jake, and Elsa had all been saying about letting Anna enjoy her childhood by embracing some of life's simple pleasures without always having the pressure of knowing that someday she would be queen.

When he saw Kaylie eye the Santa plate he was holding, he held the gingerbread cookies closer to her, practically under her nose.

"Would you like one of Chef Jake's cookies?" he offered.

"They're gingerbread, my favorite," the princess said.

Kaylie gave the prince a suspicious look. "You didn't poison these, did you?"

The princess giggled. "No, he didn't poison them. He loves them, too." She took one off the plate and handed it to Kaylie. "Try it, you can trust me."

The prince couldn't help but laugh. Kaylie certainly did have a wild imagination and right now he knew she had a right to be suspicious after their argument.

Kaylie took the cookie. "I trust you, princess."

The prince didn't miss the look Kaylie gave him that definitely said she didn't trust him. He watched as she took a bite of the cookie, then nodded her approval.

"You're right, princess, these are delicious," Kaylie said.

"Told ya," the princess said with a big smile as she took her own cookie and took a big bite. "Thank you, Father."

"You're very welcome," the prince said.

The princess's face lit up and she turned to Kaylie. "You should do a gingerbread boy, like the cookie, as your tree topper."

Kaylie almost spit out the cookie she was chewing. "Wait. What?"

The prince almost felt sorry for her. "You should have done the angel, much easier."

Kaylie gave him a look. "Big help you are."

The prince sat down next to the princess. "Hey, I brought the treats. You should be thanking me."

The princess giggled, looking from her father to Kaylie then back to her father again.

"The only way I'm going to be thanking you is if you paint my tree topper, so I don't have to," Kaylie said, sliding her tree painting over to the surprised prince.

The princess's eyes grew huge. "Oh, you don't want to do that."

"Why?" Kaylie asked. "Because he's *afraid*?"

"No," the prince said. "Because I'm really good at painting…"

"Uh oh!" the princess said, covering her eyes.

"Finger painting!" the prince said, laughing as he started to reach for Kaylie's painting.

"No!" Kaylie exclaimed, grabbing his hands just in time. For a moment their eyes locked and the prince felt a spark like he hadn't felt in a very long time. He instantly pulled his hands away and tried to compose himself.

"I warned you," the princess said to Kaylie.

Kaylie stood up. "You sure did, and on that note, I'm going to leave you two to your cookie break and see if I can call my friend back."

When Blixen barked, eyeing the cookies, the prince shook his head. "Sorry, Blixen, no cookie break for you. Cookies aren't good for dogs."

"Unless they're dog cookies," Kaylie corrected him. "Then it's totally okay."

"Dog cookies?" the princess asked. "What are those?"

"They're yummy cookies made just for dogs with healthy ingredients. My friend, Gena, has a pet store in New York City that sells them."

"Can we go to New York City, Father, and get Blixen some dog cookies?" the princess asked, excited. She turned to Kaylie. "Would you show us around if we came?"

The prince was surprised by his daughter's request. It was the first time she'd asked to go anywhere outside of Tolvania since she was five and had wanted to go to California, to Disneyland, to see the castle and to meet the princess she was convinced must live there.

"I'm sure Kaylie is very busy. She has a very important job," the prince said.

"But earlier, when she got a text, she didn't work. She stayed here and painted with me," the princess said with a smile that lit up her face.

"Really?" the prince asked, surprised. He couldn't imagine Kaylie, who seemed so ambitious and career-focused, would put her work on hold for anyone, much less his ten-year-old daughter. When he gave Kaylie a questioning look, she smiled back at him. He searched her smile for signs that she was joking but he couldn't find anything. She looked sincere, confusing him even more.

"I did have a work call," Kaylie said. "But I was right in the middle of a painting lesson with your daughter and that was more important."

"See, Father?" the princess said happily.

"I do see," the prince said. Even though he realized he really didn't understand Kaylie at all. When Kaylie looked at him with a twinkle in her eye, he would have sworn he saw a challenge.

"Princess, if you come to New York, I would be happy to show you around my favorite city."

"Blixen, too?" the princess asked, excited.

"Blixen, too," Kaylie said with a laugh as she leaned down and pet Blixen. "But now I better go call my friend in New York like I promised. I'll see you guys at three to go get the tree."

As Kaylie headed for the door, the princess jumped up and stopped her and handed her the painting she'd done. "Don't forget your painting. You did a very good job and later I can show you the Christmas tree in the village close up and you'll see how much yours really looks like it. And I still need to give you another lesson so we can add a tree topper."

Kaylie pretended to look scared. "Oh, no, I was hoping you'd forgotten about that."

The princess laughed. "No, I'll never forget."

Kaylie leaned down so she was eye to eye with the smiling princess. "Thank you again for teaching me to paint. You're an excellent teacher. I had so much fun."

"Me, too," the princess said. She leaned in to whisper in Kaylie's ear. "And I won't tell anyone you were afraid."

The prince overheard her and marveled at how much his daughter had taken to Kaylie. He was grateful Kaylie was being so kind to her.

"Thank you," Kaylie said to the princess. "This will be our little secret." She held out her pinky finger to the princess. "Pinky swear?" Kaylie asked.

When the princess looked confused, Kaylie gently took her hand and linked pinkies with her. "This means we have a pact, a promise, a secret together."

The princess nodded, excited. "Yes, I pinky swear."

As the prince watched his daughter grin back at Kaylie, he started to worry that she was growing too fond of her. They didn't have a lot of visitors outside of their close circle of family and friends, and he didn't want his daughter forming an attachment to someone who was about to leave. He still couldn't get over how much she seemed to have bonded with Kaylie already in such a short amount of time, when she usually was so guarded with everyone else.

When he also saw Blixen give Kaylie an adoring look, he started to wonder if maybe, instead of a reporter, she was a witch who had cast a spell over his entire family. Or maybe she was a combination of both. A witch reporter, the most dangerous kind. He laughed at his own imagination. Clearly, all this fairy tale talk was messing with his brain.

"I'll see you guys later," Kaylie called out as she left the room.

The prince and princess watched her go.

"I like her, Father," the princess said with conviction.

The prince nodded. "I like her, too," he said, and was a little worried by just how much.

Chapter 19

When Kaylie got to her room this time, to be sure, she slowly opened the door and peeked her head inside. "Yup, my room," she said with a laugh as she entered. She was excited to see she was finally getting some decent cell service so she quickly tried to call Rachel.

Rachel's cheerful face popped up on the second ring.

"There you are," Rachel said. "I was beginning to think you'd been kidnapped!"

Kaylie laughed. "In a way I have been. You won't believe where I am." Kaylie held out her phone to give Rachel a look at her room.

"Nice digs," Rachel said, impressed. "I like your hotel."

"Oh, I'm not in a hotel," Kaylie said. "I'm in a *castle*."

Rachel burst out laughing. "Yeah, right. Good one."

"I'm serious," Kaylie said, plopping down on her bed. "I'm in a real-life castle. It's incredible."

"And next you're going to tell me you're hanging out with a handsome prince," Rachel said, still laughing.

When Kaylie just grinned and nodded, Rachel's eyes grew huge.

"Wait. What? No!" Rachel exclaimed. "You can't be serious. You're not really there with a *prince*!"

"No, I'm not here with a prince…" Kaylie started. "I'm here with an entire royal family! There's a prince, a princess, and a queen. There's even a royal dog, even though he's named after a reindeer, but they're all the real deal. They're the royal family of Tolvania."

"You've got to be kidding me," Rachel said, looking stunned.

"Nope, and it gets better," Kaylie said. "You know how Bob said this freelance gig was to interview a European family about its unique Christmas traditions?"

"Yeah…"

"Well, that's not exactly the assignment," Kaylie said as she got up and started pacing around the room.

"What do you mean?" Rachel asked. "I'm so confused."

"Join the club," Kaylie replied. "When I got here, I found out the queen hired me to come because she wants me to use their Christmas traditions, and there are zillions of them, to create a Christmas fairy tale for the princess."

Rachel's jaw dropped open. "No way!"

"Yes, way."

"What did you tell them?" Rachel asked, dumbfounded.

"That they were nuts," Kaylie said with a laugh. "I explained I don't write this kind of stuff, but there's a huge snowstorm, and I've been trapped here. I was just getting a painting lesson from the princess and we're going to get an upside-down Christmas tree. It's all so surreal…"

"The princess is the prince's wife?" Rachel asked.

"No," Kaylie replied. "The prince's daughter, Anna, who is a very mature and adorable ten-year-old."

Rachel looked like her mind was blown. "I'm having a hard time keeping up with all this…"

"Me, too!" Kaylie said. "The prince's wife passed away a few years ago. It's a really sad story and the paparazzi reporters have been stalking the family. It's horrible. I'll tell you all about it when I get home, hopefully tomorrow, as soon as it's safe to fly."

"Wait. You're coming home early?" Rachel asked. "I thought you were staying through Christmas."

"Did you not hear what I said?" Kaylie asked. "That was the original assignment when I thought I was doing a feature story, not writing a fairy tale, and the prince doesn't want me here…"

"But didn't you say the queen set this up?" Rachel asked.

"Yeah, without the prince knowing."

"Are they kicking you out?" Rachel asked.

Kaylie laughed. "No, but…"

"Then why on earth would you come back here? You don't have anything going on for Christmas. This is a paying job and you need the money. You're in a castle in Europe. Hello, this is like a dream come true…"

"But I'm not qualified for this job," Kaylie said. "I shouldn't be here…"

"You're a writer. You can write anything," Rachel countered.

Kaylie stopped pacing and stared into the phone. "Wow, now you sound just like the queen."

"Then I think I would like this queen," Rachel said. "What's she like? Is she one of the queens that are trying to marry her son to some suitable duchess or something like that to bring two powerful families together?"

Kaylie laughed. "Are you binge-watching the Royal Romance Channel again?"

"It's not a channel. It's a reality TV series," Rachel said, like it was much more impressive.

"Forgive me, of course." Kaylie rolled her eyes. "What was I thinking? I don't know if the queen is trying to marry her son off, but she doesn't seem like that. She's very modern and hip, and forward-thinking. She's formidable, don't get me wrong, but she's not stuffy or pretentious. She's very down-to-earth. If anyone has an attitude, it would be her son, the prince."

"What kind of attitude?" Rachel asked.

"You know, kind of hoity-toity, serious, all work, no play, that kind of attitude," Kaylie said. "It seems like the queen is trying to loosen him up and have him live a little."

"Now I know I would like this queen," Rachel said. "Maybe she can help you do the same, to loosen up and have some fun."

Kaylie rolled her eyes. "Very funny."

"Who's kidding?" Rachel said. "You need to stay there and see where this takes you."

"With a prince who doesn't trust me? I don't think so," Kaylie said.

"So, you can win him over. You win everyone over. That's your job," Rachel said. "A prince should be a piece of cake."

Kaylie laughed. "Not this prince. There's nothing sweet about him. He's all duty, no sugar. It's clear he loves his daughter very much, even if it looks like he works too much, like a lot of dads. He's fiercely loyal to his family and friends, and he seems to truly care about the people of Tolvania."

Rachel's eyebrows arched. "Sounds like you're one smitten kitten."

Kaylie laughed. "What in the world are you talking about? I'm not *smitten* about anything. I was just telling you like it is."

"And this prince, he's handsome, right?" Rachel asked.

When Kaylie didn't answer right away, Rachel pounced. "He is! I knew it! You've fallen for a prince! It's been forever since you've liked anyone, but when you fall, you certainly do it right. If you married him, would you be a princess, or since his daughter is a princess, how does all that work?"

"Stop!" Kaylie said louder than she meant to. "You're being ridiculous. You really should come here and write this because you're apparently very good at making things up."

Rachel grinned back at her. "Nope, this is your job, your journey, and your fate..."

"Oh, no," Kaylie groaned, rubbing her temple. "Please don't start telling me this is what it says in my horoscope or my tarot cards or..."

"Nope," Rachel stopped her. "This is what I'm saying as your best friend, and you should listen to me. You deserve to find love. I bet your sister agrees with me. What does she say?"

"Amelia? I haven't talked to her lately," Kaylie said. "She's always busy with work."

"And so are you," Rachel said. "But you're in Europe, you're probably just a quick plane or train ride away. Aren't you going to try and see her before you head back to New York once you're done with your job?"

"Honestly, this all happened so fast I hadn't thought about it," Kaylie said. "I just got here and nothing is like I planned and I really don't think I'm staying..."

Rachel's face became huge on the screen as she leaned in. "You have to stay. What are you going to do back here, eat boxed mac and cheese for Christmas dinner when you could have a royal Christmas feast?"

"Yeah, well, I'm not really into eating swans," Kaylie muttered.

"What?" Rachel asked, confused.

"Nothing, long story," Kaylie answered.

"I really think this is fate," Rachel said. "You don't want to ignore your destiny."

Kaylie laughed as she walked over to the window. "Rachel, you know I love you, but I think you're a little Christmas crazy right now. Maybe you've had too much eggnog, or you've overdone it on joy and merrymaking..."

"It's called Christmas spirit, Miss Scrooge," Rachel said with a laugh. "I have it and you need it, desperately. You can do this, Kaylie. This is the time of year when anything is possible..."

Kaylie gave up. "Okay, I'm shutting this down before you start going on and on about how you just *have to believe.*"

"Well, you do," Rachel said. "You might want to try. Seriously, it's not like you to run away from an adventure like this. The Kaylie Karlyle I know is never afraid of anything, so what are you afraid of now? Check this Tolvania place out and I bet there's so much material here to write a fairy tale it would be easy for you. Just get out of your own way and give it a try. It could open up a whole new world for you. You don't have to just be 'Kaylie, the investigative reporter' you know?"

"What if I like being 'Kaylie, the investigative reporter'?" Kaylie fired back. "That's the only person I've ever been."

"So, maybe it's time to broaden your horizons."

Kaylie laughed. "You sound just like Bob."

"Then maybe you should listen," Rachel said. "I'm just saying as your friend and your co-worker, you need to have some adventure in your life. I think you should stay and see what kind of Christmas traditions this Tolvania place has and see if you can sell it as a freelancer. Everyone's always looking for some great Christmas content. You can get the story up right away online."

"You really think I could sell that story?" Kaylie asked. Her wheels were already turning.

"I do. I'll put out some feelers to see if any of the editors I know are looking for a last-minute Christmas feature. Get lots of pictures and video and let me see what I can do."

Kaylie's face lit up. "That would be amazing. Thank you. I could really use the money. But it might be too late. I already told everyone I wanted to leave first thing tomorrow as soon as the storm cleared up."

"But you can always tell them you've changed your mind and that you'd love to stay at least a few days," Rachel said.

Kaylie nodded as she looked out the window at the Christmas trees along the lake and watched how their white twinkle lights sparkled. "Maybe, we'll see. I'm sure the queen would be thrilled. This was all her master plan, but then I'd still have to write this fairy tale with just a few days before Christmas…"

"Fairy tales can be short, around a thousand or two thousand words, whatever works," Rachel said. "It's not like you're writing a full-length novel. The illustrations are a big part of it and you're not doing them."

"Right…"

"So, think about it," Rachel said. "Don't just instantly run back here. I know you can do this. I'll check in tomorrow. Good luck!"

"Thanks," Kaylie said. "I'll need it." After Kaylie hung up, she walked over and picked up the little crystal angel that was holding the red heart. "Can I really do this?"

Chapter 20

It was just three o'clock when Kaylie rushed down the stairs and found the prince and princess waiting for her by the door.

"Who is ready to get an upside-down Christmas tree?" Kaylie asked, smiling at the princess.

"I am! I am!" the princess replied, raising her hand, unable to hold back her enthusiasm.

The prince eyed her black leather riding boots. "You're not going to get very far in those," he said.

Kaylie frowned, knowing he was right. "I thought about that, but these are the only boots I brought. I didn't know I was going to be hiking in the woods."

When the queen entered the room holding a pretty pair of snow boots that were white with white faux fur trim, Kaylie knew she shouldn't be surprised. The queen always seemed to think of everything.

"These should work a lot better," the queen said. "You're around a size nine, right?"

Kaylie was impressed. "Eight and a half, but how did you know?"

The queen smiled as she handed her the boots. "Just another skill I have."

"Look, they match my boots," the princess said proudly as she modeled her mini version of the boots the queen had just given Kaylie.

"They sure do," Kaylie agreed and turned back to the queen. "Thank you so much for letting me borrow these."

"You're welcome," the queen said, smiling warmly back at her. "But you're going to need more than just the boots."

Elsa walked in holding an arm full of additional winter wear that included a pretty white ski jacket.

"I think you should be able to find everything you need in here," the queen continued. "You'll need a good hat, gloves, a warm sweater and coat. It can get chilly out there in the woods."

"Thank you again so much," Kaylie said as she took the clothes from Elsa and found a place to sit and started taking off her boots.

"Well, we couldn't send you out there unprepared," the queen replied. "Please let me know if there's anything else you might need. I look forward to hearing all about your quest for the perfect upside-down Christmas tree when you return."

The prince adjusted the princess's pretty pink knit hat that had a white fluffy ball at the end. "Are you ready?"

The princess grinned up at him and nodded. "But Kaylie needs a hat, too."

Kaylie looked through her things and held up a big white furry hat that matched the white fur trim on the jacket Elsa had given her.

"I have one right here." When Kaylie put on the hat, it slid over her eyes.

The princess giggled as Kaylie fought to fix it.

"So, we're ready," the prince said.

"We're ready!" Kaylie and the princess said at the same time, then laughed together.

When Blixen trotted into the room, he was wearing a bright red Christmas sweater with the family's swan crest in white.

"Cool sweater, Blixen," Kaylie said. "I want one of those."

The princess laughed. "I don't think that would fit you."

"Bummer," Kaylie said as she eyed Blixen. "But maybe I should try it on to make sure. Oh, Blixen, let me see that pretty sweater of yours…"

Blixen took off out the front door.

Kaylie quickly followed him and so did Anna. The princess was laughing, sounding like an excited ten-year-old ready for an adventure.

It was one of those perfect clear, crisp, and cool winter days as Kaylie, the prince, the princess, and Blixen trekked through the forest.

Kaylie was in awe as she took in the scenery. It was like a magical winter wonderland.

All the trees were glistening in the sunlight with a blanket of fresh snow. It was so peaceful that Kaylie felt a sense of calm that she hadn't felt in a very long time. She tried to remember the last time she had taken a break away from the hustle and bustle of New York City to just walk around and enjoy the surroundings instead of being in a rush to get somewhere.

When she'd first moved to the city, she'd walked in Central Park almost every day. But the busier she got, the less time she had for the park, and now she realized how much she'd missed it. As she inhaled the fragrant scent of evergreens, she felt invigorated.

The prince stopped walking. "Everyone okay? We don't have much farther to go."

"I'm great," Kaylie said, taking advantage of them stopping to snap a few quick pictures of the breathtaking scenery. "What about you, princess?"

"Me and Blixen are great, too," the princess said with a big smile.

Blixen wagged his tail and barked as he ran a circle around them.

The prince took the princess's hand and continued walking until they reached an area that had a group of towering fir trees. "Okay, I think this looks like a great spot to find our tree."

"I'll go find it!" the princess exclaimed as she ran into the trees. Blixen was right on her heels.

Kaylie smiled, remembering how much she'd loved picking out her family's tree when she was little.

The prince took off his backpack and pulled out a portable, folding bow saw and then turned to face her.

Kaylie jokingly took a step back. "You and a sharp weapon. Should I be nervous?"

The prince chuckled. "You're safe."

Kaylie laughed. "Thank goodness."

"But seriously, Kaylie, I want to thank you for coming with us today," the prince said. "Anna has really been looking forward to this so it means a lot to her and me. I know earlier today, when we were doing our wine tasting, I said some things, and I may have judged you harshly…"

Kaylie was surprised. She hadn't seen this coming. For once she didn't know what to say. As she waited for the prince to continue, he looked like he was trying to choose his words carefully.

"I worry about my family, their safety, and privacy, and I don't like surprises," the prince said. "When you showed up as a reporter, and because my family has been terrorized by reporters in the past, I jumped to all kinds of conclusions about you. It wasn't fair, you didn't deserve that. I know it's not fair to judge all reporters by the ones I've known, but the scars run deep. It's not an excuse, just an explanation. I hope you will accept my apology?"

Kaylie was impressed. It took a real man to admit he was wrong and his words meant a lot to her, especially after knowing all he'd gone through with the press.

"I will accept your apology," Kaylie said as she looked into his eyes. "I'm truly sorry about what's happened to you and your family with the press. I can't imagine how painful that was and still is. You have every reason to be cautious and protect your family. I respect you for that and apologize, too, for over-reacting. I feel like I'm always trying to defend what I do, but that's no excuse for me to be rude to you."

When they shared a smile, Kaylie felt like they had a breakthrough.

The prince took off his glove and held out his hand. "Truce?"

Kaylie was surprised that this time it was the prince who was offering the truce. She nodded slowly. "I would like that." When she took off her glove and put her hand in his, the warmth she felt from his touch made her whole body tingle. Her eyes flew to his and Kaylie felt like they were the only two people in the world until Blixen ran up and barked, interrupting the moment.

"I found one!" the princess called out from inside a group of trees.

The prince laughed as he started walking. "We'd better go see what my daughter has found. Do you think there's any chance she's found a nice small tree?"

Kaylie burst out laughing. "No chance at all."

A few moments later, when they found the princess, Kaylie had been right. The princess was proudly standing next to a tree that was at least twelve feet high.

The prince's eyes grew huge. "That's the one you want?"

The princess nodded vigorously. "Isn't it perfect?"

When the prince looked at Kaylie, she was smiling, too.

"It is pretty perfect," Kaylie said.

The prince shrugged and laughed. "Okay, then." He held up his bow saw. "Who wants to make the first cut?"

The princess's hand shot up into the air. "Me! Me!"

Kaylie laughed and looked at the prince. "Looks like you two are about to start a new Christmas tradition."

A few hours later, when Kaylie was back at the castle in her room, changing into some dry clothes, she still couldn't believe they'd been able to drag the giant tree out of the forest. She'd been impressed that the prince had packed a tarp in his backpack to put the tree on so it could slide in the snow. When she'd asked him where he'd gotten the great idea, he'd confessed that the queen had given him the tip because that's what she used to do with her father.

After they had all taken turns cutting down the tree, Kaylie had surprised herself by saying they needed to do snow angels. Growing up it was something she always did with her sister and her parents at Christmas, but she hadn't thought about it in years.

The princess had loved the idea and even though Kaylie knew the prince wasn't so sure, he'd played along and they all lined up, arm's length apart, and had fallen back into the snow at the same time. There was a lot of laughter as they all moved their arms and legs making the snow angels as Blixen ran around them barking. When they'd carefully gotten up, Kaylie had been amazed at how perfect the angels looked. She and the prince were on the outside and the princess was in the middle, and all their angel wings were touching. But the moment Kaylie remembered the most was when the princess had stood back and looked at the three angels and taken her hand and said they were a snow angel family.

As they were heading back to the castle, dragging the giant tree behind them, the prince had suddenly stopped walking, saying he needed a break. But when that break was really the prince making a snowball and throwing it at Kaylie, an all-out snowball fight erupted with the princess on Kaylie's side.

The prince never had a chance when Kaylie and the princess both tackled him and started stuffing snow down his jacket, and even Blixen jumped on him and started licking his face. When the prince finally surrendered, Kaylie had claimed they'd won because they'd had *girl power* and she and the princess had high-fived. For the rest of the trip, the princess had used her two new favorite words, *girl power*, anyplace she could find a fit, and even when it didn't fit.

Kaylie couldn't remember an afternoon when she'd had this much fun. As she looked out her window and watched the Christmas trees along the lake cast their glittering reflection on the water, she was hit with an overwhelming urge to share this beauty with someone.

She got her phone and tried to call her sister Amelia. She knew it was a long shot trying to catch her. They always scheduled their calls because they both were so busy with work. She couldn't believe it when Amelia answered immediately.

"Kaylie? Is that really you?" Amelia asked with a shocked smile.

"Amelia! It's me!" Kaylie said as she felt a rush of love and her eyes welled up with tears.

"What's wrong? Is everything okay?" Amelia asked, concerned.

Kaylie laughed and quickly brushed her tears away. "Sorry, everything's fine. I'm fine, so are Mom and Dad. I just miss you…"

Now it was Amelia's turn to get emotional. "I miss you, too."

"I made a snow angel today," Kaylie blurted out. "Just like the ones we all used to make."

Amelie looked surprised. "In New York?"

Kaylie shook her head. "No, I'm not in New York." She flipped the camera so she could show Amelia the magical view of the lake she'd just been admiring. "You're never going to believe where I am…"

An hour later Kaylie was having dinner with the queen, prince, and princess, and telling them all about talking to her sister.

"My sister's doing great," Kaylie said, feeling grateful. "She really loves Germany and her job in the Army leading a soldier and family readiness group, where she helps support people who have family members in the service. She's always so busy, but we're going to see if there's a way I can see her before I go back to New York, since I'm already in Europe."

"I think that sounds like a wonderful idea," the queen said.

"So, you'll see her after Christmas," the princess said with a smile.

"Kaylie was planning to go home tomorrow," the prince said.

"What?" the princess asked, looking crushed. "Why? You were supposed to stay here for Christmas with us. Isn't that what you said, Grandmother?"

The queen nodded. "Yes, that was the plan, and what I would still like and hope will happen."

"But then we had the mix-up about me writing a…" Kaylie stopped when she saw the princess staring at her. "About the job I was supposed to do here." She felt awful for disappointing the princess and the queen.

"Would you like to stay with us for Christmas?" the prince asked.

His question caught Kaylie completely off guard. When her eyes flew to his, she thought he looked sincere. "Yes," she said, before she had a chance to think about it. "Yes, I'd like to stay." As soon as the words were out of her mouth, she wondered what she'd just done.

"So, you will stay?" the princess asked, looking like she was holding her breath.

Kaylie looked at the queen and the prince. They both nodded. She took a deep breath. "Yes, I would love to stay."

The princess clapped, excited. "This is going to be the best Christmas ever, so much better than being in the Caribbean..." She quickly covered her mouth with her hand, looking guilty. "I'm sorry, Father."

The prince looked at the princess with love. "There is nothing to be sorry about. Of course, you love it here for Christmas. This is your home. Your Christmas traditions are here, and this is where we will be celebrating Christmas from now on. How would you like that?"

The princess's face lit up with joy. "I would like that *very* much."

The queen's smile was radiant. "Well then, now that that's settled, we have a lot still to do, starting with decorating that upside-down Christmas tree you all got today. Who is with me?"

The princess's hand shot up and Kaylie laughed when she saw the prince put his hand up too, so she did the same, and the queen raised her hand as well.

"It looks like we have a unanimous decision," the queen said, picking up her wine for a toast. "To Christmas."

Kaylie and the prince picked up their wine and the princess picked up her crystal water glass and they all said at the same time, "To Christmas."

Later that night, as Kaylie sat on her bed with her computer on her lap she thought about the last few hours.

Never in her life could she have imagined being in a ballroom, in a European castle, or any castle for that matter, decorating an upside-down Christmas tree with a prince, princess, and queen, but that's exactly what she had been doing.

She'd been amazed at the ingenuity and engineering it took in order to decorate a Christmas tree that was going to hang upside-down from the ceiling.

The tree was placed in the center of the ballroom, temporarily replacing a crystal chandelier. It had been hung with a wire and pulley system so it could be lowered enough for them to all decorate it and then get hoisted back up to the ceiling when they were all done. For the tree lights to work they had been plugged into where the chandelier had been. It was genius, and the most stunning and unique Christmas decoration Kaylie had ever seen. She knew she could write a whole story about upside-down Christmas trees and knew she had to include it in the princess's fairy tale.

She'd even been brainstorming how she could put an upside-down Christmas tree up in her own tiny New York apartment, using LED lights that ran on a battery, so she didn't have to mess with the electrical. She still had some logistics she needed to work out, but she was determined to try and have one for next Christmas. It would be the first Christmas tree she'd put up in years.

She let out a happy sigh thinking again about her call with her sister. She hadn't realized how much she'd missed her until her face had shown up on her screen and she'd heard her voice. When they'd hung up, they both promised to try and do better about calling more often.

Now that she'd agreed to stay through Christmas, she knew the clock was ticking and she needed to get started working immediately to create the princess's fairy tale. She was thankful for her journalism experience, where she had to write new stories every day. It had turned her into a fast writer, but reporting on things that were actually happening and creating imaginary things in your head were two very different things.

Kaylie took a deep breath and told herself she just needed to concentrate on trying to embrace all things Christmas, and if that meant following a snowman down the Christmas Rabbit Hole, then she was ready to dive in and go for it.

Staring at her computer, she'd been surprised and relieved that once she'd started working on the fairy tale, inspired by her magical day, her fingers had flown over the keyboard. Within no time she had four pages of ideas of things she wanted to include in the fairy tale, and there were more things she wanted to write down before she went to sleep. "This just might work," she said happily to the little crystal snow angel that was lit up in the moonlight.

Chapter 21

Kaylie woke up in the morning to find her computer next to her on her bed and realized she must have fallen asleep while still working on ideas for the princess's fairy tale.

She was excited thinking about how much progress she'd made. Still, she knew there were a lot more traditions on the queen's list for her to do. She had a busy day scheduled that started after breakfast, when she was set up to go with the prince to Tolvania so he could show her around the village. Also, on the agenda was a Christmas tea tasting with the queen and princess, and a special tree lighting ceremony that night that the queen had promised to tell her more about. Smiling, she grabbed her computer and went back to work on the fairy tale.

Kaylie arrived downstairs at a quarter to ten, fifteen minutes before her scheduled time to meet the prince, and was surprised to find him already waiting for her.

"You're early," he said.

She laughed. "And so are you. I'm excited to see Tolvania."

"And I'm looking forward to showing you," the prince said and held the door open for her.

When Kaylie got outside, she saw the same car and driver that had brought her to the castle.

"Good morning, Thomas," she called out to him happily.

"Good morning." Thomas smiled back at her. "So, it looks like you got your Christmas wish after all."

Kaylie stared back at him, confused. "My Christmas wish?"

"When I brought you here," Thomas continued. "You said you wished you could see inside the castle and take pictures."

"What?" the prince asked, sounding alarmed.

Kaylie rushed to explain. "I meant like a tourist taking pictures because it was so beautiful. I asked if there were any tours, didn't I, Thomas?"

"Yes, you did," Thomas said as he opened the back door for her.

The prince looked relieved. "Thomas, can you take us to the village square? I'd like to show Kaylie the gingerbread house and sleigh now that they're set up."

"Of course," Thomas said.

"Will the reindeer be there?" Kaylie asked in a teasing voice.

"Of course not," the prince answered. "They're still in the North Pole getting ready for Christmas Eve."

Kaylie and Thomas both laughed.

As they drove away, Kaylie saw the queen looking out the window, watching them. Kaylie waved and the queen waved back.

When they arrived at the village square, Kaylie saw people gathered around the gingerbread house, taking pictures. It looked even more magical in its new setting. It was decorated with red and white twinkle lights and set up on a pretty red platform surrounded by snow-covered Christmas trees. She couldn't wait to get her own pictures and jumped out of the car as soon as it stopped.

When Thomas opened the door and the prince got out of the car, people started to instantly gather around him. Kaylie expected to see the prince tense up but was surprised when he did just the opposite. With a genuine smile he interacted with everyone, talking with them and shaking their hands, asking them about their families. Kaylie also noticed that no one took a picture of the prince or even had their phones out. As she joined Thomas, who was standing on the fringe of the crowd watching the prince, she was still in awe.

"They adore him," Kaylie said.

Thomas nodded. "They sure do. We all do. He's a wonderful prince. He does so much for the village. He truly cares about everyone here."

"And no one takes pictures." Kaylie said, amazed. "I knew there were rules for the paparazzi…"

"And those rules apply to everyone who lives in Tolvania, and anyone who visits," Thomas explained. "No one is allowed to take pictures of the royal family, the prince, the queen, and especially the princess. This is the only way to ensure that photos aren't accidentally or intentionally leaked to the press. Nowadays, with social media, one picture can go around the world in seconds."

"That's true," Kaylie said. "Working in media, I always thought that it was a good thing to have a story go viral so it could reach as many people as possible, but I can see why, if you wanted privacy, that wouldn't be so great."

"Exactly, so these rules are for the family's privacy and their safety. This solution has worked very well for us," Thomas said. "And if there are ever any problems, I am here to deal with them."

"As the prince's driver?" Kaylie asked, confused.

"As his head of security and one of the royal family's body-guards," Thomas replied.

Kaylie's eyes grew huge. "Really. A bodyguard? That's your job?"

"Yes," Thomas said. "My father was a bodyguard for Prince Alexander's father, and his father before him also served the royal family, so it's a great honor to be following in my family's footsteps. There are several security guards, of course, to protect the family, but I've been with them the longest," Thomas said with pride.

As Kaylie watched Thomas keep a watchful eye on the prince, she could see how dedicated he was to his job.

When the prince turned and motioned for her to join him, she could feel the buzz of curiosity from the crowd. Self-conscious, she stepped forward and joined the prince with a nervous smile.

"Everyone, this is a friend of the family, Kaylie Karlyle from America. She wanted to see our village and how we celebrate Christmas."

Kaylie was greeted with so many warm and generous smiles, she instantly felt her nerves disappear. "Hi everyone," she waved with her fingers together and a little flip of her wrist and then, embarrassed, quickly put her hand down, wondering if they thought she was trying to imitate the queen's wave. Then she wondered if this queen even really waved like that in the first place. She mentally shook herself because she was starting to feel like Rachel, making royal assumptions based on what she'd seen in the movies.

As she followed the prince though the crowd, she was touched by everyone's kindness and good wishes.

"Merry Christmas," a young mom holding her infant daughter called out.

"Welcome to Tolvania," a second woman said.

An elderly man gave her a kind look. "Enjoy your visit."

"Thank you." She smiled and waved at everyone. "Thank you all very much. Merry Christmas."

As they cleared the crowd and walked toward the village square, her eyes were drawn to an awe-inspiring church. It had a steeple that was decorated with pretty Christmas wreaths and garland. The largest wreath, with a big red bow, was right above the church door. There was a golden light coming from inside the church that lit up the windows and reflected onto the lake.

Right next to the church was a beautiful towering Christmas tree that Kaylie guessed had to be at least thirty feet high. It was decorated with the same red glass ornaments she had seen on the Christmas trees lined up along the lake, but this tree also had gorgeous gold glass ornaments and cute ornaments that looked like little gold Christmas presents wrapped with a red bow.

"You approve?" the prince asked her.

Kaylie realized she was smiling ear to ear. "I do. It's fantastic."

The prince nodded. "Wait until you see it lit up tonight."

"I'm looking forward to it," she said, and held up her phone tentatively. "I'd love to get some pictures of all the decorations to show my family and my friend Rachel, she's a photographer and loves Christmas. I know she'd be thrilled to see all this. Is it okay?"

The prince hesitated a moment before answering. "Yes, that would be fine."

Kaylie gave him a bright smile. "Thank you!" She happily ran up closer to the tree and started taking pictures. She began with some close-ups of the different ornaments and then kneeled down on the ground to get an extra low angle, making the tree look even more massive than it already was. She used the same angle to get some shots of the church so she could get as much into the frame as possible. With each picture she took, she could feel the prince's eyes on her. Not wanting to push her luck she wrapped up her photo session and walked back to him.

"Thanks again. That was great," she said with a smile. "I think I got some cool shots."

"You like taking pictures," the prince said.

"I do," Kaylie said without hesitation. "Especially when I'm someplace like this where everything is so incredible. My grandma and I used to talk about traveling the world, and how we would take pictures of our favorite places. We even had a journal we called our *Someday Trips Journal* that we'd keep a list of all the places we wanted to go that we'd found in magazines and by watching travel shows. My grandma started it when she was about the princess's age, and then passed it down to me for us to do together."

"And where did you go?" the prince asked.

Kaylie's smile faded. "Unfortunately, my grandma passed away before we could do any trips together."

"But you still have your *Someday Trips Journal,*" the prince said. "You can still do those trips."

Kaylie sighed. "If I ever have the time. My job keeps me pretty busy, or at least it did, and hopefully will again soon. I'm not even sure where that journal is anymore…"

"Well, like my mother always says, you make time for the things that matter most," the prince said.

Kaylie nodded but wondered if she would ever find the time for one of those *Someday Trips* and the thought that she might not, suddenly made her feel sad.

"Shall we continue?" the prince asked, bringing her back to the present.

Kaylie shook herself mentally. "Yes, of course."

As they began walking down Tolvania's quaint cobble-stoned streets, Kaylie was captivated by the village's charm. She was surprised but pleased by what a wonderful tour guide the prince turned out to be. He was very passionate and knowledgeable about the history of the village, and was an animated storyteller.

In the heart of the village, Kaylie had been happy to find Tolvania had its own small, enchanting, outdoor Christmas market where different artists were selling their Christmas crafts and collectibles out of festive stalls. It reminded her of a miniature version of the Christmas markets she'd just been at with Rachel in New York. She tried to take it all in as she followed the prince who was zigzagging around the stalls.

But she stopped suddenly when she saw a stall with painted ceramic Santas. It had a sign that said the Santas were hand-made and that all the money from the sales would be going to Tolvania's college scholarship fund. Her eyes narrowed. They looked similar to the Santas she'd just reported on being fake in Manhattan.

"Unbelievable," she said. "It even happens here."

"What even happens here?" the prince asked, confused.

"This," she said, pointing at the sweet Santas. "They're all fake."

The prince laughed. "What are you talking about?"

"I'll show you." Kaylie picked up a Santa figurine and turned it over, looking for the tell-tale signs that it was mass-produced, not handcrafted as advertised. When she saw the Santa figurine was signed by the artist, she laughed. "Oh, they're good," she said, looking at the prince. "They're using the old bait-and-switch routine."

The prince looked even more perplexed. "Bait-and-switch?"

"You know," Kaylie said. "These scam artists put a couple of *real* Santas out front for people to check out but when you go to actually buy one, they give you one of the fakes that's in a box or something. They tell you they want to make sure you get a good one, one that no one else has handled. Ha! It's the oldest trick in the book. They do the same thing for jewelry, purses, sunglasses, you name it. Then you're stuck with a piece of junk and no money actually goes to any charity and these crooks cash in on their scam, lining their greedy pockets."

The prince looked alarmed. "What are you talking about?"

"I'll show you," Kaylie said as she rushed behind the booth and started searching through boxes. "I know the fakes are here somewhere."

When the booth owner, a teenage boy of about seventeen, returned, he looked just as surprised as the prince to see Kaylie rummaging through his things. She was tossing bubble wrap out of a box.

"Did I do something wrong?" the teen asked the prince.

The prince put his arm around him. "No, you didn't do anything wrong, Lucas. Miss Karlyle here is the one who is doing something wrong. Kaylie, Kaylie, stop it!"

Kaylie finally looked up and saw the prince with the teen.

"What?" she asked, exasperated because she couldn't find the fake Santas.

The prince motioned toward the concerned teen. "This is Lucas. He is one of our most talented artists in Tolvania. He has been given a scholarship to attend one of the top art schools in Europe. These are his Santas. He's carrying on his family's Christmas tradition, of more than a hundred years, of making these Santas."

Kaylie's eyes widened. "What? You mean these Santas are *real*? This isn't a scam? What about the charity?"

"The charity is the same scholarship Lucas was given, and it's his family's way to pay it forward and help another student," the prince said.

Kaylie gulped as her face flamed red with embarrassment. She turned to Lucas. "I am so, so sorry. I'm a reporter and I just did a story about fake Santas and…" Kaylie stopped talking when she saw that Lucas's face had gone ghost white.

Lucas turned to the prince. "I swear I don't know who she is. I don't know any reporters…"

The prince gave him a reassuring pat on the back. "That's okay, Lucas. I know. She's actually staying with us."

Lucas looked visibly relieved.

"And I'm an idiot," Kaylie rushed to continue to apologize. "I'm really sorry. Your Santas are amazing. You're amazing. I'm sure your family is…"

"Amazing," the prince finished for her. "Yes, we got it."

"It's okay," Lucas said. But Kaylie could see he still looked uncomfortable and nervous.

She turned to the prince. "How can I make this better?"

Chapter 22

A few minutes later, they were walking away from Lucas's stall and Kaylie was carrying a bag full of the Santas that she'd bought, after also giving Lucas all the cash she had with her to donate to the Tolvania's college scholarship fund.

She felt so foolish for jumping to conclusions and insulting Lucas like that and upsetting the prince. She stole a glance at him as they walked together in silence down the street.

"I really am sorry," she offered.

The prince nodded. "I know. It was a mistake. A very big mistake. Let's just move on and not mention this to my mother."

Kaylie looked relieved. "I would appreciate that. Where to next?"

"Do you like chocolate?" the prince asked.

"Even more than wine," Kaylie responded quickly. "So, yes, I love chocolate."

"Excellent," the prince said and picked up his pace. As they quickly made their way down several more winding streets, Kaylie found herself unable to resist window shopping. She wasn't usually a big shopper, but for some reason, every cute boutique shop in Tolvania was calling her name. When she saw a shop called Imagine This, she couldn't help but stop.

The Imagine This store window was filled with beautiful Christmas snow globes that Kaylie couldn't take her eyes off of. Each one had a different Christmas theme with the village of Tolvania featured in many of them. There was even a snow globe that showed people skating on an ice rink surrounded by trees with twinkling white lights.

"I want to go there," she whispered, gazing at the skating rink.

"Do you skate?" the prince asked, startling her as he joined her.

"I used to," she answered. "My whole family did on Christmas day."

"A tradition," the prince said.

Kaylie nodded. "Yes, I guess you could say it was one of our traditions." She leaned closer to the window to get a better look. "These look like the ones I saw in the Christmas Room."

The prince nodded. "Yes, many of them came from here. Carl and his family have been making these special snow globes for generations. He and his family are known for creating scenes from around Tolvania, so it's a keepsake people like to have."

Kaylie gazed longingly at them. "I can see why."

"Would you like to go in?" the prince asked.

Kaylie's face lit up. "Really? Do we have time to stop?"

"We will make the time," the prince said. "Why don't you go inside while I run across the street to the jewelry store to check on a Christmas gift? How about we meet back up in ten minutes? Is that enough time?"

"More than enough. Thank you," Kaylie said, excited. She was already heading into the shop. As she entered, the jingle bells hanging from the doors made a cheerful sound and had a man in his sixties looking up from the snow globe he was crafting. His smile was warm and welcoming.

"Merry Christmas. May I help you?" he asked.

As she looked around the tiny shop, she felt like she was being given a big, warm Christmas hug. There was a fragrant pine scent from all the real Christmas trees, wreaths, and garlands that decorated the shop, along with all the red and gold sparkling Christmas lights.

"Yes, hello," she said, doing a slow spin, taking it all in. "I love your shop."

The man joined her. "Thank you. I'm glad you like it. I'm Carl, I'm the owner."

"I'm Kaylie. It's very nice to meet you. The prince was just telling me that you and your family have been making these snow globes for years."

Carl raised an eyebrow. "The prince?"

Kaylie nodded as she walked toward a table of snow globes that all had different scenes of the castle inside. "Yes, I'm staying with the family. I'm a…" she caught herself just in time before she said the dreaded seven-letter word, *reporter*. "I'm a family friend."

Carl nodded but still looked curious. "From America?"

"Yes, New York City," Kaylie said with pride. She picked up one of the snow globes and shook it gently, watching the snowflakes dance as they fell.

"So, you're here for all our Christmas activities, like our special tree lighting ceremony tonight."

"Yes," Kaylie said. "And I saw one of your snow globes at the castle. The one the queen had made for the prince when he went away to college."

Carl's smile grew. "I made that one myself."

Kaylie walked over to the table where Carl had been working. "So, you create all these different scenes from around the village and then make them into snow globes?"

"That's right," Carl said with pride. "I specialize in creating custom snow globes."

"What are those?" Kaylie asked.

"People will have a special Christmas memory in mind that they want to remember and I'll make that for them," Carl said. "Let me show you."

Kaylie watched him pick up a snow globe that was on his work table.

"This is one I just finished." He handed it to Kaylie so she could get a better look. "If you look closely inside, you'll see a family of four, two parents pulling two little girls on a sled."

"Yes, I see it. That's so cute," Kaylie said.

"That's the Owens family," Carl said. "And one of their Christmas traditions is going sledding with their girls every Christmas morning, so they asked me to create that scene. See the matching pink hats the girls are wearing? Their Aunt Susan knitted them those hats."

"Wow," Kaylie said, impressed. "That's amazing. It's like you're capturing a moment in time forever. Like a picture, but so much better." She carefully handed him back the snow globe. "I'm sure they're going to love it."

"I hope so," Carl said modestly. "I'm creating two, one for each daughter, so they can always have the memory with them wherever they go as they grow up."

"Do you start by using a photograph?" Kaylie asked, fascinated.

"Sometimes," Carl answered. "And sometimes people just tell me their memory and any details they would like added and I sketch up my idea and show them, and once it's approved, we go from there."

"What a wonderful gift," Kaylie said. "The gift of a memory."

"Thank you," Carl said. "My great grandmother is the one who actually thought of it when she wanted to find a snow globe of our church in Tolvania. It's where she got married but no one had one, so my grandfather, who was an artist, decided to figure out how to make one for her and the rest, as they say, is Tolvania snow globe history. Now my two sons and daughter are helping with the business, and my granddaughter is just starting to get involved. She's already so talented. I'm sure she will outdo me in just a few years." He chuckled.

"She's lucky to have you as a teacher," Kaylie said as she picked up another snow globe. This one showed the Christmas trees down by the lake. Every detail, including the red Christmas tree ornaments, were included. "I love this one. This is the view of the lake from the castle."

"It is," Carl said with a smile. "If you like it, please accept it as my gift."

"Oh, no, I couldn't," Kaylie said, reaching for her wallet.

"Please, as an artist, we like knowing our work is going to someone who will appreciate it," Carl said. "It would be our honor to have one of our snow globes in New York City with you."

Kaylie held the snow globe to her heart. "Then it would be my honor and great pleasure to take this home with me." She looked around the shop. "And I think some more of your snow globes also need to come to America. I would love it if you could help me pick one out for my parents and sister, and a friend who loves all things Christmas."

"I would be happy to help you find some Christmas presents," Carl said.

"They actually won't be Christmas presents," Kaylie said. "We don't really exchange gifts anymore, but I will just give it to them when I see them next. Whenever that might be. We get together when we can. We're all so busy." Her voice trailed off when realizing how much she missed her parents and sister.

"Is everything okay?" Carl asked, watching her.

"Yes," Kaylie said quickly, but as she thought about it, her real answer should have been no, because it has been months since she'd seen her family.

"So, what kind of things do your parents like?" Carl asked. "Let's start with them."

Kaylie thought about it for a moment. "Ice skating. They love ice skating. It's how they met."

"Come with me," Carl said as he led her to a shelf of beautiful snow globes that all had different ice-skating scenes inside.

Kaylie's attention was immediately drawn to a snow globe that showed two ice skaters, wearing matching red jackets, hats, and mittens. They were skating hand in hand around a Christmas tree.

"No way," Kaylie said. She couldn't believe it.

"What is it?" Carl asked, looking concerned.

Kaylie carefully picked up a snow globe. "This one, of the couple, they're wearing red jackets. My parents have red jackets and my mom always makes my dad wear a matching red hat just like she does, whether it's Christmas or not. It's a standing joke in our family. So, this one is perfect. I can't believe it."

Carl's eyes twinkled as he nodded. "I always say the perfect snow globe will find you, you just have to know how to look with an open heart."

Kaylie, delighted, shook the snow globe and watched the snowflakes land on the skater's red jackets, turning them white. "They will love this." She looked hopeful as she turned to Carl. "My sister is in the Army. She's stationed in Germany and she always says what she misses most about the family Christmases we used to have is how we'd all make snowmen together. You don't, by chance, have a snow globe with snowmen?"

Carl grinned back at her. "Well, as a matter of fact, I do. It's just right over here."

Kaylie felt like she'd just won the jackpot for finding the most perfect presents ever and she wanted to capture this moment.

"Would you mind if I take a few pictures?" Kaylie asked.

"Be my guest," Carl replied. "There are so many wonderful Christmas things to take pictures of around Tolvania."

Kaylie grinned as she snapped some shots. "I'm starting to see that. Are you sure this isn't really a Christmas village? Because I've never seen anyplace with this much Christmas everywhere."

Carl chuckled. "Wait until you see the Christmas tree lighting tonight. It's like nothing you have ever seen before."

Kaylie's eyes lit up. "I can't wait."

A few minutes later, she was happily humming the Christmas song "Jingle Bells" as she walked out of the shop after having bought snow globes for her parents, Rachel, and her sister.

When she looked at her cell phone, she panicked, realizing the quick ten minutes she'd promised the prince had turned into a half-hour. "He is going to kill me," she said as she looked around for him and saw him across the street inside a jewelry store.

The shop was called Be Jeweled, and the window display was a giant Santa with a sign that said *Add Some Sparkle to Your Christmas.* She was relieved to see the prince was still shopping until she saw that he was talking to a striking woman about her age, wearing a chic fur coat. They were laughing and looking quite cozy together. Kaylie frowned when the woman gave the prince a hug and she saw how happy the prince looked.

Kaylie walked up closer to the jewelry store window. Her jaw dropped open when she saw the prince hold up a bracelet that sparkled with diamonds and then put it on the woman's wrist.

"What…" As she leaned in to get a closer look, she accidentally smashed her nose against the window. "Ouch," she yelped, rubbing her sore nose just as the prince looked her way. She jumped back from the window, hoping he hadn't seen her spying on him.

Moments later, he stepped out of the front door. "Kaylie? Is everything okay?"

Kaylie, embarrassed, quickly held up her shopping bags. "Everything's great. I've been…shopping."

The prince nodded. "I can see that. Are you ready to go?"

"Sure," Kaylie said. "If you're done in there? I don't want to take you away from anything or…anyone important." She glanced at the window and saw the woman the prince had been talking to was watching them.

The prince followed her gaze. "That's Madeline. Remember the winemaker I told you about? Apparently, she's just won another award. She's amazing."

"Uh huh," Kaylie said and thought this Madeline was both talented and beautiful, and wondered what exactly she was to the prince and why the prince had been putting a diamond bracelet on her wrist.

"Did you find what you were looking for in there?" Kaylie asked. She knew it wasn't any of her business, but she couldn't help herself from asking.

The prince smiled back at her. "I did, a Christmas present."

When the prince didn't elaborate, she didn't push, even though her curiosity was killing her. When he started walking, Kaylie joined him.

Kaylie fought to keep smiling and bit her tongue so she didn't ask him who the Christmas gift was for and if it was for the gorgeous woman he'd just been talking and laughing with. As she wondered if that was his girlfriend, she realized that she really knew very little about the prince's personal life, and figured that's exactly the way he wanted to keep it.

She had so many questions but knew she'd never ask them. The fact that she was a reporter meant the prince would always be on high alert with her. She knew she couldn't chance asking him any personal questions that weren't relevant to her fairy tale assignment and get his guard up again.

"We're here," the prince said, stopping in front of a quaint chocolate shop called Très Bon Chocolates, where the outside was decorated with a row of small Christmas trees that were all lit up with white twinkle lights.

As soon as the prince opened the shop door for her, Kaylie could smell the rich, mouthwatering scent of chocolate. As she stepped inside, she was charmed by all the festive holiday decorations and the fabulous Christmas-themed chocolates in the display case.

Along one wall, there was a row of giant three-foot candy canes, and strung across the ceiling were red and white Christmas lights. In the corner by the window, there was a Christmas tree that had a baking theme so there were tiny wooden spoons and measuring cups, mixing bowls, and chocolate molds of stars, angels, and wreaths. Kaylie especially appreciated the Christmas tree topper that was an exquisitely carved white chocolate angel. She had never seen anything like that before, but then she'd never been in a chocolate shop with a prince either.

Another thing she had never done before was meet a chocolatier who looked like the definition of tall, dark, and handsome, with his thick, wavy long hair and sapphire blue eyes that held the promise of mischief as he took her hand and kissed it. "Bonjour, ma belle. I'm Jean Pierre. Welcome to my shop, Très Bon Chocolates."

Kaylie didn't know what was more delicious: the chocolatier standing in front of her or the chocolates she saw behind him, but she knew she couldn't wait to find out.

Chapter 23

During the tour of his chocolate shop, the flirty Frenchman, Jean Pierre, had continued to compliment and charm Kaylie. She knew he was probably this way with all the women who came in, but she didn't mind it one bit. It was flattering and fun and great for her ego. She wished there was a handsome chocolatier in her New York neighborhood who had amazing chocolates and made her feel special and beautiful, because she'd visit all the time.

When they went in the back to see how the chocolates were made, she was surprised and impressed by how modern the operation was, considering how quaint the shop had looked when they'd first walked in. The area that had impressed her the most was where there were several artists meticulously decorating each chocolate truffle in a Christmas theme. They were painting on little holly branches, Christmas wreaths, gold and silver stars, and even tiny Christmas trees, and she also loved how each chocolate had a special Christmas name.

When Jean Pierre had first insisted that she try some, she'd felt guilty because they were all too pretty to eat, but in the end, her love of chocolate had won out and her favorites had been the Christmas Eve, a dark chocolate truffle with sea salt stars; the Ho! Ho! Holly truffles that had tiny holly leaves painted on them and were a creamy milk chocolate that melted in your mouth; the Christmas Snowballs, a pure, rich white chocolate truffle that had a refreshing hint of peppermint; and the Christmas Dream truffles that were infused with eggnog.

Jean Pierre had also made sure she tried his famous Berry Christmas treats, that were dark chocolate-covered cranberries with a hint of cinnamon, telling her they were a tasty Tolvania Christmas tradition that everyone had at the holidays.

As they made their way to the front of the shop, Kaylie glanced again at the chocolate angel tree topper. "Is that real chocolate?" she asked.

"Yes, it is," Jean Pierre said with pride. "It was my entry for Tolvania's annual Christmas angel contest, even though it doesn't really qualify because it would never stand the test of time, but it was a joy to make, and people love coming in to see it."

"I can see why," Kaylie said. "It's really beautiful. You did an excellent job."

"Thank you. It is beauty like yours that inspires me," Jean Pierre said as he took her hand and kissed it.

Kaylie blushed and was surprised to see the prince frown when he stared at her hand Jean Pierre was holding.

"We need to be going. We have a very busy day ahead of us," the prince said.

"It has been truly fascinating," Kaylie said. "I've learned so much."

Jean Pierre gazed into Kaylie's eyes. "I would be happy to give you another tour some evening after the shop closes when we have more time," Jean Pierre said with a smile that was both sexy and sincere.

The prince put his hand on the small of her back and started guiding her toward the door. "I'm afraid Miss Karlyle's schedule is very busy, but we appreciate all your time today, Jean Pierre. Thank you."

"You are very welcome, and it is always an honor," Jean Pierre told the prince. "Please tell the queen I will have all the chocolates ready for her Christmas tea, and that we're just finishing up her special Christmas Crown chocolates for the Christmas Crown event."

Kaylie's eyes lit up with interest. "The Christmas Crown chocolates? What are those?" She looked around. "Did I miss seeing those? And what's the Christmas Crown event?"

Jean Pierre gave the prince a surprised look. "You didn't tell her about the Christmas Crown event, our most beloved Christmas tradition in Tolvania?"

"She just arrived," the prince said. "There are many things to show and tell her. On that note, we really need to be going." The prince turned his attention back to Kaylie. "We don't want you to be late for the Christmas tea tasting."

As they started to leave, Jean Pierre went to the counter and picked up a small red canister and handed it to the prince. On the outside of the canister in gold letters, it said, "Tolvania Christmas Hot Chocolate."

"I almost forgot. For you. Your favorite."

"That is very kind, Jean Pierre. You always remember and we've just run out. Thank you so much. The princess will appreciate this, too," the prince said.

"I'm so glad," Jean Pierre said. "Merry Christmas."

"Merry Christmas," the prince and Kaylie said at the same time.

As soon as they were out of the shop, Kaylie started asking questions. "So, what is this Christmas Crown event? Do you guys have a crown with all your royal crown jewels in it, or what?" Kaylie asked.

The prince gave her a quizzical look. "How do you know we have crown jewels?"

"I don't. I was kidding. Wait… Do you have crown jewels?" Kaylie asked, getting excited.

The prince nodded. "Yes, we do. What kind of royal family would we be if we didn't?"

Kaylie couldn't figure out by his tone if he was kidding or not, but she knew one thing. If there were really crown jewels and a Christmas Crown, she wanted to see them. "Okay, so what's the Christmas Crown story? This definitely sounds like a Christmas tradition I need to know about."

Thomas pulled up in the town car before the prince could answer her.

"Did you have a good time?" Thomas asked, getting out of the car and opening the back door for her.

Kaylie slipped into the car. "I had a great time, and now the prince is about to tell me all about this Christmas Crown event."

"Ah," Thomas said. "It is the highlight of our Christmas celebration and…"

"And my mother is planning to tell her all about it," the prince said, before Thomas could say any more. "She tells the story the best."

"Of course," Thomas said with a smile. "It is quite a story."

The conversation was officially ended when the prince got in the car and turned up the volume on the radio that was playing the Christmas song "Hark! The Herald Angels Sing."

Kaylie sat back into her seat and couldn't wait to get to the bottom of this Christmas Crown mystery. It sounded like perfect material for the princess's fairy tale.

When they got back to the castle, the prince excused himself to catch up on some work while she did the tea tasting. She was about to walk inside the castle when a call from Rachel came in. She picked up immediately and laughed when she saw Rachel was wearing the ugly Christmas sweater from the market that had blinking red and green Christmas lights.

"I can't believe you went back and bought that sweater," Kaylie said.

"Don't you love it?" Rachel asked, modeling it.

"I have no words," Kaylie answered with a laugh.

"I'll take that as a compliment," Rachel said, grinning back at her. "So, what's happening in your magic kingdom today?"

Kaylie laughed. "A tour of the royal kingdom, of course, and now I'm getting ready for a Christmas tea tasting with the queen and princess."

"Of course you are." Rachel laughed. "I'm so jealous."

When Thomas saw she was on the phone, he had kindly come over and taken her shopping bags for her and went inside the castle, giving her some privacy.

"Tolvania really is so magical," Kaylie said with a blissful sigh. "It's so charming. It's like a storybook come to life."

"Did you see any sexy knights on horses?" Rachel asked, excited.

Kaylie laughed. "Uh, no. We're not in medieval times, but I did meet a fun, flirty Frenchman, a chocolatier. You would have loved him."

"Now I'm even more jealous," Rachel said. "I could talk about this all day, but I'm calling because I have some huge job news for you..."

Kaylie stopped walking. Her face lit up with hope. "Job news. For me?"

Rachel nodded. "Yes! You know my friend Gerry, the senior producer who works on the national news show *Tonight*?"

"Yeah, I've heard you talk about him before," Kaylie said.

Rachel rushed on. "Well, he's looking for some last-minute online Christmas features and I told him about your little royal adventure and he was obsessed! He's apparently been trying to get pictures and a story about that royal family forever."

Kaylie looked over her shoulder to make sure no one was listening and walked away from the castle's front door and lowered her voice. "That's because there's a ban on reporting about the family, and no pictures are allowed."

"What?" Rachel asked, confused.

"It's a long story. Bottom line, I can't do a story about the royal family. Period."

"What about this cool royal village you just visited? Is it off limits, too?" Rachel asked.

"No, it's just a village," Kaylie answered.

"So, I'll check with Gerry to see if he's interested in that story. It's not as sexy as the royal family, but it's royal family adjacent. It's worth a try. Do you have any pictures, video?"

"I did take some pictures in the village. Everywhere you look is a Christmas postcard. So, you're talking about a feature on Tolvania and the Christmas traditions?" Kaylie asked.

"Yeah," Rachel said. "If you think there's enough to do a story on..."

Kaylie laughed. "Are you kidding? This place is Christmas on steroids. I've never seen so many Christmas decorations or heard about more unique Christmas traditions. This place is more Christmassy than Santa Claus's North Pole, and I'm going back tonight for a tree lighting in the village that's supposed to be super unique."

"Okay, then, that sounds good. I'll see if Gerry bites," Rachel said. "Cross your fingers because this could be huge for you."

Kaylie had started pacing back and forth to keep warm. She looked confused. "Doing a Christmas feature on a Christmas town. How?"

"I saved the best part for last," Rachel said, smiling. "Are you ready for this? Gerry says they're also looking for a new investigative TV reporter to start in the New Year. They're adding another half-hour to their weekend news so they're adding some staff."

"What?!" Kaylie gasped and froze. "Are you kidding me? That's my dream job, to go national. What do I need to do? I need that job!"

Rachel laughed. "Hold on. There's apparently a ton of competition for it. Gerry says he needs someone who will bring him exclusive stories and I told him that's what you specialize in. I'm trying to get him to look at your resume tape."

"That would be amazing," Kaylie said. "Thank you. But you still want me to do this Christmas feature? I don't want Gerry thinking I'm some fluff reporter if he's going to consider me for this investigative job."

"Trust me," Rachel said, "Gerry's all about relationships and helping each other out and right now he needs some online Christmas content. You offer to help him with the feature, he looks at your tape, it's a win-win. But first, we have to sell him on this feature. So, send me lots of pictures and video, anything you have."

"I'm going back to the village tonight and I'll get video of the tree lighting and anything else I can find," Kaylie said, excited. "This is amazing. I can't thank you enough. You're saving my life."

Rachel laughed. "You don't have a life, remember? I'm saving your career. Just call me your agent. I'll be expecting my ten percent."

"If you help me get this job, I'll give you anything you want," Kaylie promised. The cell signal started to fade. "I'm losing you…"

"Go have fun tonight and get lots of good stuff…"

"Thank you, bye…"

Kaylie hung up and was over-the-moon happy. She had a shot at getting her dream job as a national reporter. Elated, she did a little victory dance and was still dancing around in the snow with her arms in the air when she heard the queen's voice.

"Kaylie, what are you doing out here? We've been waiting for you to do the tasting."

Kaylie froze. "Oh crap," she said under her breath. She'd totally forgotten about the time. She rushed toward the castle. "I'm sorry. I'm coming!"

Chapter 24

The queen held the door open as Kaylie zipped inside.

"I really am sorry," Kaylie said, looking guilty. "That was a co-worker from New York and she had some important news to tell me."

"Good news, I assume, by the way you were dancing around," the queen said as she started to walk toward the drawing room.

"Great news," Kaylie said, still beaming. "I have a lead on a new possible job as an investigative reporter for a national news show. It's a huge longshot, but I might have a chance."

"Then I wish you good luck," the queen replied. "If this is what you really want."

Kaylie, still on cloud nine, nodded vigorously. "Oh, it is. It's what I want more than anything. My job is the most important thing in my life."

As they entered the drawing room, Kaylie saw the princess sitting at a coffee table by the fireplace where a spectacular silver tea service was set up. There were exquisite crimson china plates and teacups that all had the gold swan crest. In the center of the table, there was a collection of three-tiered silver stands that were filled with festive treats, from scones, and chocolate éclairs, to gingerbread biscuits, and frosted Christmas cookies. There was also an assortment of mini-quiches and crust-free little sandwiches cut into the shapes of stars. Kaylie also immediately noticed a selection of Christmas chocolates from Jean Pierre's shop. Her smile grew even more when she saw sparkling crystal champagne flutes.

"Hello, Kaylie, welcome to our Christmas tea tasting," the princess said, smiling. She was the perfect little hostess.

"Well, hello, princess. Thank you so much for having me," Kaylie said.

Chef Jake and Elsa entered carrying even more trays of treats. Chef Jake had a warm smile for Kaylie. "We've heard you've been very busy visiting our village and cutting down a Christmas tree and even making snow angels…"

"And that there was even a snowball fight with the prince," Elsa said with a laugh.

"That we won," the princess said gleefully. "Because of *girl power*, right, Kaylie?"

Kaylie laughed as she took a seat next to the princess and they high-fived. "That's right."

"Of course," Elsa said. "That makes perfect sense. *Girl power* always wins."

The queen nodded. "Always."

Chef Jake chuckled. "Is that so? Well, remind me not to take any of you on."

Elsa gave him a knowing smile. "I thought you learned that a long time ago."

When Kaylie saw a spark between Chef Jake and Elsa, her smile grew, thinking about what a cute couple they'd make.

"Is there anything more I can get you?" Chef Jake asked the queen.

The queen gave him a grateful smile. "This looks wonderful. You've clearly outdone yourself again. Thank you both so much."

"My pleasure," Chef Jake said as he and Elsa headed toward the door. "Enjoy."

"Thank you," Kaylie said as she eyed all the treats. Her mouth was watering.

"Please, help yourself," the queen said, catching Kaylie's gaze. "We would love your thoughts on our tasting menu for our Christmas tea."

"Is there any special order I should try things in?" Kaylie asked, wiggling her fingers in anticipation.

"No, we're not that formal here," the queen said. "You just try whatever is calling out to you and tell me what you think."

Kaylie couldn't take her eyes off the gingerbread biscuits. "Well, honestly, these biscuits are calling out to me saying I need to try them because they're yummy."

The princess giggled. "They are talking to me, too, Grandmother."

"Then, by all means, let's all start with the gingerbread biscuits," the queen said. "It's an old family recipe. Very simple, only a few ingredients, with cinnamon and sugar sprinkled on top. They're a local favorite. I hope you like them."

Kaylie happily picked what looked like a puffy gingerbread cookie and took a bite and her eyes lit up with surprise. They were soft and chewy with just the perfect hint of ginger. "These are delicious."

"They're one of my favorites, too," the princess said. "Everyone loves them."

"So, tell me more about this Christmas tea, because I've never seen such amazing treats in my life," Kaylie said. "I've never really been a tea person, but I think I might convert if this is all part of it."

The queen smiled back at her. "We put on the Christmas tea every year to recognize and give thanks to our schoolteachers, medical staff, military, and first responders in Tolvania for all they do. It's a Christmas tradition my father started, and while I realize it's only a small gesture of our immense gratitude, I'm told that people very much look forward to it."

Kaylie was once again impressed by how many of the royal family's Christmas traditions included the entire village of Tolvania and focused on giving back and bringing people together.

"And we get to get all dressed up," the princess chimed in. "I have a new Christmas dress just for the tea, and Blixen also gets dressed up."

Blixen, who was sitting right next to the princess, wagged his tail.

Kaylie laughed a little. "Does Blixen have a Christmas tea sweater that he wears?"

The princess giggled. "No, of course not. He only wears his Christmas sweaters outside. But he does have a special red Christmas ribbon he wears when he dresses up, and even some bowties for formal occasions," the princess continued. "He loves dressing up, don't you, Blixen?"

When Blixen barked, Kaylie laughed.

"So, what did you think about our little village, Kaylie?" the queen asked.

"It was amazing," Kaylie answered, still in awe. "Everyone was so warm and genuine. They all love the prince and both of you so much. Everyone said to make sure to wish you a Merry Christmas from them."

"That's very kind," the queen said. "We have a wonderful, caring community. We are very blessed and you will get to see even more tonight for our tree lighting ceremony."

"I can't wait," Kaylie said. "You mentioned earlier it's very unique? I saw a giant tree in the center of the village that was all decorated. I'm guessing that's the one that's going to be lit up for the tree lighting?"

"That's the *first* tree," the princess said with a twinkle in her eyes. "There's more."

"More?" Kaylie asked, confused.

"Yes," the queen replied. "We start with lighting our main tree that you saw, but that's only the beginning of our ceremony. We then also light up the trees along the lake, one by one."

"With Christmas carols," the princess jumped in.

"Wait, what? How do you light up a tree with Christmas carols?" Kaylie asked, intrigued.

"It's a tradition that's almost two hundred-years-old," the queen answered. "We love our Christmas carols in Tolvania. They are part of our history and our heritage. We have Christmas carolers in the village during the holidays that stroll around, singing and bringing joy, but for the tree lighting night, they do more."

"It's my favorite part," the princess said, enthusiastically.

The queen gave her granddaughter a loving look. "As the tradition goes, after the carolers sing at the main Christmas tree lighting in the square, everyone in the village then follows the carolers down to the lake to our Christmas trees there."

"Like the one you painted that I helped you with," the princess said with a proud smile.

"Exactly," the queen agreed. "The carolers then start at the first Christmas tree along the lake and sing an abbreviated version of a Christmas carol and that tree is lit up. They then move on to the next tree and sing a new Christmas carol and *that* tree is lit up."

Kaylie looked impressed. "That's incredible. I've never heard of anything like this before."

"And it gets better," the princess said. "Because *we* get to sing with them."

"That's right, Anna," the queen said, smiling at the princess. "Everyone in the village gathers with candles and follows the carolers down to the lake and we all sing along as each Christmas tree is lit up with a new carol. We believe this is a way to bring light and love, and unite everyone together as we all fill our village with the sound of Christmas music. We always sing the classic carols because those Christmas songs are the ones that have their own unique history and story and we like to honor that."

"That's really beautiful," Kaylie said. Her mind was already spinning with ideas for how she could include all this in the Tolvania Christmas feature she was going to try and write for Gerry. She also knew this would be the perfect thing to get video of. Maybe, she thought, she could even interview some of the carolers, because it seemed like everyone in Tolvania had a special story to tell.

"You can sing with us," the princess said, bringing her back to the moment.

Kaylie laughed. "I'm afraid I don't know many carols and my voice is about as good as my painting."

"It's easy," the princess said with confidence. "You just sing what the carolers sing. I'll help you."

"And who picks the songs?" Kaylie asked.

"We do, as a family, together," the queen said.

"I always pick "We Wish You A Merry Christmas,"" the princess said proudly.

"What about Rudolph?" Kaylie asked. "That's one I know."

The princess giggled. "Of course, we pick Rudolph, that's Blixen's brother."

"Wait, what?" Kaylie asked with a laugh. "His brother?"

The princess looked at Kaylie like it was obvious. "Santa's reindeer, they're all brothers. They're all family."

Kaylie glanced at the queen who was smiling and nodding. "Of course," Kaylie said, joining in on the fun. "What was I thinking? You are right, and they are a great family."

"The best," the princess said. "Because they have so much Christmas spirit."

Kaylie laughed. "Christmas spirit, huh? So, that's pretty important?"

The princess laughed. "Of course, it's the *most* important, right, Grandmother?"

"Christmas spirit is the heart and soul of Christmas because it celebrates family, faith, friends, community, hope, and love," the queen said. "You can tell a lot about someone by the way they celebrate and honor Christmas."

The queen picked up a crystal champagne flute and handed it to Kaylie and then picked up her own. "And there's one more tradition you need to know about when it comes to our Christmas tea."

"What is that?" Kaylie asked.

"It's one I started," the queen said. "Where we always have a champagne toast."

The princess didn't miss a beat picking up her sparkling glass of water and holding it up.

"To Christmas spirit, and always keeping the true meaning and magic of Christmas in our hearts," the queen said.

"To Christmas spirit," the princess eagerly agreed.

When they both looked at Kaylie, she quickly joined in. "To Christmas spirit," she said, and even though it had been years since she'd even thought about Christmas spirit for herself, she found there was a place in her heart now that ached for it, and so much more...

"How do you like our Christmas tea tradition?" the princess asked, bringing her out of her daydream.

Kaylie held up her champagne glass. "I love it. I didn't know you could have champagne at a tea."

"That just makes it more special, don't you agree?" the queen asked.

"Absolutely." Kaylie said. "And that reminds me of another tradition I heard about this morning in the village, your Christmas Crown event. What is that?"

The princess's smile grew. "That is my favorite event!"

Kaylie laughed. "Wait, I thought you said the tree lighting was your *favorite* event?"

"That one is, too," the princess answered, happily. "I have a lot of favorites, but the Christmas Crown is so pretty and magical, I think it's my most favorite."

Kaylie's eyes widened. "So, there's a *real* Christmas Crown?"

"Oh, yes." The queen nodded. "The Christmas Crown is very real and very important to my family and to everyone in

Tolvania. My great-great-great-grandfather, Henry, had it made for his wife, Mary, so he could propose to her on Christmas Eve. Now, every Christmas Eve, we display the crown here at the castle and invite everyone from the village to come and see it."

"Because it's full of Christmas magic," the princess added, excited.

Kaylie laughed until she saw the queen and princess weren't laughing. Her eyes widened. She looked at the queen. "Magic? What do you mean by *magic*?"

The queen smiled back at her. "The kind of magic that makes Christmas wishes comes true."

The princess nodded eagerly. "That kind of magic. The very best kind."

"Wait, what?" But Kaylie's question was cut off when the prince entered the room, looking like he was on a mission.

Chapter 25

"I'm sorry to interrupt," the prince started right in.

"You're not interrupting, Alexander, we're just finishing up here," the queen said.

"I wanted to give you an update that everything is in place for the tree lighting tonight," the prince said.

"That's wonderful news," the queen said. "Let's all meet in here before we go tonight. I'd like to get some pictures of you and Anna all dressed up."

"I'm sorry, we'll have to do that after the event because I need to get to the village early in case anything is needed last minute. I'll meet you all there," the prince said as he quickly turned to leave.

Kaylie felt sorry for the princess when she saw how disappointed she looked, but was impressed that she never complained or said a word.

A few moments after the prince left, Ms. Meyers entered.

"It looks like you've all had a wonderful tea," Ms. Meyers said.

"It was delicious," the princess said, making them all smile. "And now you've come to get me to go upstairs." She turned to Kaylie. "I'm finishing a painting before we go to our tree lighting. I will see you later."

Kaylie once again was amazed at how mature the princess was. "By all means, go create your next masterpiece. Thank you for inviting me to tea."

"You only drank the champagne," the princess said. "Next time, you should try the tea, too."

The queen laughed and quickly covered her mouth with her hand.

After Ms. Meyers and the princess left, the queen picked up the champagne bottle that was in the ice bucket and poured herself and Kaylie more champagne.

"It would be a shame to let this go to waste," the queen said, lifting her glass. "Unless you'd rather have tea?"

Kaylie laughed. "No, champagne is perfect. Thank you. This really has been a wonderful day."

The queen stood up, holding her glass. "And it's not over yet. Please, bring your champagne and come with me. I have something for you."

Kaylie stood up. "For me? What is it?"

"A Christmas surprise," the queen said with a twinkle in her eyes.

A few minutes later, when Kaylie entered the queen's personal sitting room, she was once again impressed with the queen's design skills and how she gave the traditional royal décor, a modern twist so it felt fresh and inviting, not stuffy or pretentious.

For her sitting room, the queen had chosen soft shades of pink and gray to decorate with that made the room feel like a calming, peaceful retreat. Above the fireplace, on the mantel, there were wonderful candid family pictures of the prince and princess. She smiled seeing how happy and relaxed everyone looked.

"This is a lovely room," Kaylie said.

"Thank you," the queen said with a smile. "This room originally was very dark, decorated in the same deep red and gold tones you see throughout the castle. While those colors are a lovely part of our history, I felt like for this room it would be nice to brighten things up a little, and have softer colors. These color choices are inspired by a spa I visited in Switzerland that was so tranquil you could just feel your stress melt away. I wanted a place like that here so when things get too hectic or demanding, I could hide away in here and recharge and reboot."

"That makes perfect sense," Kaylie said. "You've done a marvelous job. You have quite the eye for design. I need to bring you back to New York so you can redesign my apartment, because I could definitely use a place to escape and reenergize."

"And how have you decorated it?" the queen asked.

Kaylie looked guilty. "You know, come to think of it, I haven't decorated it at all. I know that sounds terrible, but I'm working so much, I just think of it as a place to crash and get some sleep before I have to go back to work."

"Then where do you relax?" the queen asked.

Kaylie laughed. "Relax? What's that? That's not really a New York City thing."

The queen arched an eyebrow. "That doesn't sound healthy."

"Now you sound like my friend Rachel who is always telling me I need more work-life balance, but honestly I love my work so much, I don't mind," Kaylie said.

"Until you lost your job," the queen said.

Kaylie sighed. "Yes, and that has caused stress, that's for sure, but hopefully this new job lead will pan out and I'll be back on track soon."

"But is work enough?" the queen asked, watching her closely. "Don't you want a family, or someone special, a home, a place to start your own traditions?"

Kaylie shrugged. "I guess that hasn't been on my priority list. I mean, sure, everyone wants to have someone in their life that's special, but I've always said I'll get a life once I make it in my career, because right now that's where I have to put all my focus. I wouldn't have any energy left to work on a relationship, and I know they're a lot of work."

The queen gave her a thoughtful look. "Yes, they are, but they're also what life is all about. The people you love, your friends, and family—they are what really matter the most. Jobs come and go. You should work to live, not live to work. Maybe you shouldn't be in such a rush to get this next job if you haven't had a break in a while," the queen said. "You could take this time over the holidays to breathe a little and enjoy your life beyond your work. Christmas has a way of reminding people of what really matters the most, like family. Work will always be there, you can always find a new job, but your family might not always be there. You should appreciate them while you can."

When Kaylie saw the queen glance over at a family picture on the fireplace mantel that had her husband and the prince's wife in it, she knew the queen must be thinking about all she'd lost in her own family.

Kaylie thought about her grandma and how she'd give anything in the world to have one more day with her and do one of the *Someday Trips* that were in their journal. Maybe the queen was right, she thought. Maybe she needed to find a way to spend more time with her family while she still could.

The queen interrupted her thoughts by walking over to a cozy-looking window seat in the corner and picking up a beautifully-wrapped Christmas present. The present was in a big box that was about two feet wide and one foot tall. It was wrapped in shimmering gold foil paper with a giant red satin bow. She handed the present to Kaylie.

"What's this?" Kaylie asked, surprised.

"Just something I thought you might like to have while you're here," the queen answered with a smile. "You can call it an early Christmas present."

"You shouldn't have…." Kaylie started and then stopped when the queen held up her hand.

"You always accept a Christmas present graciously," the queen said. "There doesn't have to be a reason for them. It's Christmas time, and that is reason enough. It's the season for giving, and I only give gifts that I've put a lot of thought into, so please, open it."

Kaylie knew better than to argue with the queen so she sat down in the window seat and slowly started to untie the red ribbon. She was savoring the moment. This was also one of the loveliest wrapped presents she'd ever seen and it had been a while since she'd opened a real Christmas present. Her family stopped exchanging gifts when they stopped getting together and when they did finally all meet up sometimes, there were little things, like the snow globes she got them to exchange, but they were never called Christmas presents. With her friends, like Rachel, they always just went for drinks or dinner and called it a day.

When Kaylie finally opened the box and took out the white tissue paper, she gasped when she saw what was inside. In awe, she reverently pulled out a luxurious white fur coat and was speechless.

"Since we'll be outside for the tree lighting ceremony tonight, I thought this would be much more appropriate and nicer than my ski jacket you've been wearing," the queen said.

"Oh, but I couldn't," Kaylie said, shaking her head in amazement.

"Don't worry," the queen said. "It's not real fur. So, it's politically correct, and I think still very stylish and the most important thing is it will keep you warm. The princess and I will also be wearing our faux furs. The princess has a whole collection, she adores them."

Kaylie couldn't resist cuddling the fur coat and rubbing her cheek against its softness. "I can see why. This is so beautiful. I don't know what to say…"

"Just say thank you and enjoy it," the queen said, looking pleased. "I got you white because I noticed you already wear a lot of black."

Kaylie looked confused. "How would you…"

"We did a background check on you after Bob gave me your name, and in all your social media pictures you were wearing black, so I thought this would be a nice change," the queen explained.

Kaylie's eyes widened. "You did a background check on me?"

"Of course," the queen said. "You don't think I'd let just any journalist into our home to be with my family, trust them with our Christmas traditions and ask them to create this fairy tale for my granddaughter?"

"No, of course not," Kaylie said. She felt honored that she had passed the queen's scrutiny.

"Please, try the coat on, let's see if it fits," the queen said. "If not, we can take it back when we go into the village tonight and exchange it for another size."

As Kaylie slipped into the coat, her smile grew. "It's perfect. It feels so soft and luxurious. Now I'm the one who feels like a princess." She snuggled the coat with a blissful sigh. "Truly, thank you. This is such a thoughtful gift. It will also really come in handy back in New York City. I will treasure it always."

"I am so glad you like it," the queen said, looking pleased. She then walked over to a nearby table and picked up a smaller Christmas present that was wrapped identically to the first one. "Then you will hopefully enjoy this, too."

"Okay, seriously?" Kaylie said with a laugh as she took the present. "You have to stop."

"No, I don't," the queen said with attitude. "I'm the queen. I get to do whatever I want. At least that's what I tell my son all the time, even if he doesn't listen."

They shared a smile as Kaylie opened the next present. Kaylie couldn't believe it when, inside the box, she found a matching white faux fur hat to go with her fabulous faux fur coat and some festive red leather gloves that she noticed right away had the family's swan crest embossed in gold near each wrist.

"We have our Swan's Gate crest put on special pieces of clothing, so I thought you might like to have it on your gloves. All the family's gloves are like this."

Kaylie shook her head, marveling at her gifts. "I don't know what to say. This is so generous and thoughtful of you."

"Well, I want to thank you for being here and staying with us," the queen said. "I know for our privacy you weren't told the whole story about this job and I can see how that has caused you concern. I'm truly thankful that you've chosen to stay with us and help me make this a very special Christmas for my granddaughter. I've always trusted Bob, but now meeting you in person, I know he was right that you are the perfect person to create this fairy tale, and I want you to know how grateful I am. This means everything to me and my family."

"Thank you for having faith in me," Kaylie said, feeling a little overwhelmed by the confidence the queen had in her. The last thing she wanted to do was let the family down. Even though she had just met the royal family, she already felt a growing sense of responsibility to create a fairy tale that would help preserve the family's Christmas traditions for future generations.

"I have plenty of faith in you," the queen said, as if reading her thoughts. "You just need to have faith in yourself."

"Your faith in me is the best present of all," Kaylie said, and meant every word.

The queen nodded, pleased. "I'm sure you'd like to relax before we go tonight. I can take you back to your room."

"I don't know about relaxing," Kaylie said with a laugh. "But I could do some work on our story. I think I know my way to my room. I just leave here and turn right, right?"

"Left," the queen said with a smile. "Then just go to the end of the hall, take a right and an immediate left and go all the way to the end of that hall and your room is on the right."

"Fantastic," Kaylie said. "And thank you again for everything."

A few minutes later, Kaylie surprised herself by not getting lost. As she entered her room, she was surprised to see another call from Rachel coming in on her phone. When she answered, Rachel jumped right in.

"I have big news!" Rachel shouted, unable to contain her excitement. "You got the assignment!"

Chapter 26

"Wait, are you serious?" Kaylie asked, wide-eyed. "Gerry went for it? He wants a story on Tolvania's Christmas traditions…"

"Yes," Rachel said, excited. "I told him all about what you're doing and says he'll pay top dollar for it, but you need to have at least ten pictures they can choose from and a couple of good videos for social media promotion. And you need to work fast and send this in by Christmas Eve, noon our time, so in the evening your time. They're planning to run it Christmas morning."

Kaylie literally jumped for joy. "I can do that! This is amazing. You're amazing, Rachel. Best friend ever!"

"I think I'd rather be your agent so I can get that ten percent," Rachel said with a laugh.

"Whatever you want, it's yours," Kaylie said. "Especially if this gets me the news job."

"That's the plan," Rachel said. "Just impress Gerry and help him out with this last-minute Christmas story they need and you're on your way."

"I'll rock their Christmas stockings off," Kaylie promised. "I'm heading down to the tree lighting soon. Check this out." She held up her new fur coat and hat for Rachel to see.

"Wow!" Rachel said, looking impressed and envious. "Where did you get that?"

"The queen gave it to me. As a gift. Can you believe it?" Kaylie asked.

"I knew I loved this queen," Rachel said.

"She really is something," Kaylie agreed.

"So, for this story, Gerry said to make sure you include all the most unique royal Christmas traditions you can find that will be good clickbait," Rachel said.

"I know the drill," Kaylie said. "I have the tree lighting, Christmas chocolates, an upside-down Christmas tree tradition, there's a Christmas tea, a Christmas ball, and even a Christmas Crown event with a real crown. How is that for unique?"

Rachel's eyes lit up. "Hold the holidays, what is this *Christmas Crown*? Is this a real thing? A real crown?"

"Yes," Kaylie said. "And there's an amazing story behind it. So, I'm going to have a ton of great material."

"For the feature and the fairy tale," Rachel said. "I knew you could do this."

Kaylie shook her head in amazement. "I have to admit, working on the fairy tale has been easier than I thought, and getting to use my imagination and not having to only deal in facts has been fun, even though a lot of what I want to do will be based on the real traditions."

"I love it all," Rachel said.

"Just don't tell anyone I'm writing a fairy tale and feature stories. I don't want to wreck my killer reporter reputation," Kaylie said with a laugh.

"Mum's the word," Rachel said. "Be sure to have someone take a picture of you at the ball. I have to see what you're wearing."

Kaylie frowned. "Oh, I won't be wearing anything…"

Rachel's eyes lifted. "Well, look at you Miss X-rated going naked."

Kaylie laughed loudly. "I meant I won't be wearing anything because first of all I have nothing to wear, and second I'm here to work, not dance a waltz."

"But you *have* to go to the ball," Rachel insisted. "Reporter involvement, you're the one always saying some of the best stories are told first-person."

"Well, I couldn't, even if I were invited," Kaylie said. "My simple little black dress I always travel with won't cut it for a royal ball."

"So, be like Cinderella and figure it out. Where are those mice when we need them to make you something to wear?" Rachel asked.

"In your dreams, that's where," Kaylie said with a laugh.

"I have faith you'll figure it out," Rachel said. "I gotta go. Get lots of pictures and video. Can't wait to see everything. Talk soon."

When Rachel hung up, Kaylie caught her reflection in the mirror and smiled. Her eyes were sparkling with anticipation. She looked happy and excited. "This is your shot for a national reporter job. Bring on the Christmas cheer!"

An hour later, she was sitting on her bed, working on her feature story, when she heard a bark outside her door. When she opened it and found only Blixen, she was surprised.

"Well, have you been sent up here to get me?" Kaylie asked as she leaned down to pet his silky head.

He gazed up at her, panting.

She put on her fur coat and modeled it for him. "What do you think?"

Blixen barked and instantly eyed her fur hat on the bed. "Don't even think about it," Kaylie said to him.

Blixen tilted his head like he was listening to her and then took off down the hall.

"Hey, wait for me," she called out after him and grabbed her hat, gloves, and phone before running after him.

She was taking the stairs two at a time when she heard the princess call up to her.

"Don't run," the princess said. "We're not allowed to run down the stairs."

Kaylie tripped and had to grab onto the railing so she didn't fall. "Good rule," she called out and then held on to the railing the rest of the way down. When she got to the bottom, she saw the princess and the queen were also wearing beautiful white faux fur coats. The princess's coat was white with a black fur collar and cuffs, and the queen looked exquisite and very regal in her full-length white fur coat that also had an elegant hood.

"You two look fabulous," Kaylie said.

The princess grinned back at her. "You, too. We're all matching in our furs. We're twins."

"Triplets," the queen gently corrected her. "Triplets that will be late if we don't get going." Blixen barked when the queen opened the front door.

"Not this time, Blixen," the queen said, smiling. "I'm sorry."

When Blixen's head dropped sadly, the princess leaned down and gave him a hug. "I love you, Blixen. I'll tell you all about it when I get home."

As Elsa walked toward them, the princess gave her a hopeful smile. "You'll keep Blixen company, won't you, Elsa?"

"Absolutely," Elsa said. "Chef Jake and I might even have a special treat for him."

Blixen's ears perked up as he ran to Elsa.

The queen opened the door. "After you, Kaylie." When Kaylie saw the queen and the princess exchange a look, she wondered what they were up to this time. She didn't have to wait long to find out.

As she walked out of the castle, she gasped. In front of her was a magnificent horse-drawn carriage that was right out of a fairy tale. It was so grand it made Cinderella's carriage look tiny in comparison. This opulent carriage was a brilliant red, with gorgeous gilded gold accents that gleamed in the moonlight. A footman, that Kaylie quickly saw was Thomas, was wearing a regal red royal uniform. He was standing by the carriage door that was decorated with the family's swan crest.

Kaylie blinked several times. "Is this for real?"

The queen and princess joined her. "It is," the queen said with pride. "Very real. It belonged to my great-grandfather. We only use it for special occasions."

"And *this* is a special occasion," the princess said merrily.

"This is incredible," Kaylie said. "If you keep this up, I'm going to start believing in fairy tales myself."

"That's the plan," the queen said with a twinkle in her eyes.

With the help of Thomas, the princess got into the carriage first, followed by the queen. When it was Kaylie's turn, she was still trying to process that she was about to ride in a real royal horse-drawn carriage. As she took Thomas's hand, she couldn't believe this was her life.

"This is unbelievable," she whispered to him.

"Aren't you glad you didn't go home like you wanted to?" Thomas asked with a smile.

Kaylie nodded. "Very glad. This is all so crazy…"

"Or fate," Thomas said with a wink.

She was just settling into her seat across from the queen and princess when she saw the princess's face light up.

"Father!" the princess called out, surprised.

Kaylie turned and her heart started racing when she saw the prince exit the castle and head toward the carriage. He was smiling and looked dashing wearing a royal uniform that was red and gold that included a row of shiny medals across his chest.

"Surprise," he said as he climbed into the carriage and took the only available seat next to Kaylie.

"I thought you had to work and were meeting us," the princess said, confused but excited.

The prince gave his daughter a loving look. "I decided work can wait, but spending time with my daughter couldn't."

The princess leaned over and gave him a heartfelt hug. "I'm so glad you're here. Thank you for picking me. I love you."

"I love you, too," the prince said as he hugged her back.

Kaylie could see his eyes had misted up and this made her start to tear up as well as she thought about how powerful the love of a child was. When she looked at the queen, she saw the queen was getting emotional, too.

The prince took the princess's small hand in his. "I heard this is one of your *favorite* Christmas traditions. I didn't want to miss that."

"I didn't want you to miss that either," the princess said. Her eyes were filled with love.

Kaylie could see how much having the prince being there meant to the princess and it got her thinking about how often it was just the simple things that children needed the most, time spent with their parents, no matter what they were doing. She thought about how children didn't need fancy Christmas presents as much as they needed their parents to be *present*—that was the best gift of all.

When the carriage took off with a jolt, Kaylie, caught off guard, accidentally put her hand down on the prince's leg to steady herself.

When he jumped, startled, she pulled her hand away quickly. "I'm so sorry." But a second later, she fell into him again when their carriage hit a bump in the road. "Sorry again," she said, embarrassed.

The princess giggled.

"There's not a lot of give in these seats," the queen said. "I'm afraid you're in for a bumpy ride."

"But you get used to it," the princess added cheerfully as she held her grandmother's hand. "You can hold Father's hand if you like."

Kaylie's eyes flew to the prince's. "No, I'm fine. I'm good." Kaylie held up her hands to prove it, only another jolt of the carriage tossed her into the prince again. This time, one of her shoulders landed up against his chest. He was so close she could feel his breath on her cheek. Her pulse quickened and her face flushed red as she looked up at him and their eyes locked. The next jolt she felt wasn't from the carriage, but from a spark of attraction that ricocheted through her body.

"I'm sorry," Kaylie said to the prince in a breathless voice she didn't recognize. She cleared her throat. "It won't happen again."

"Where have I heard that before?" the prince asked, amused. "This is starting to remind me of our first meeting."

"Okay, I'm good now," Kaylie said with determination as she scooted as far away from the prince as she could and braced herself, with one hand holding the seat between herself and the prince as her other hand held on to the side of the carriage.

When she caught the queen's curious and all-knowing gaze, Kaylie promised herself that she would not fall into the prince again and, more importantly, she would not fall *for* the prince.

She reminded herself that she had a job to do, two jobs actually. She had to write the fairy tale and the feature story. She didn't have time for any distractions, and that included the prince, no matter how handsome he was. She shivered just thinking about him.

"You're cold," the prince said. He leaned down and pulled out a vintage trunk from underneath their seat. He opened it and took out two beautiful red and gold blankets and handed one to his mother and one to Kaylie. "This should help."

Kaylie watched the queen use the blanket for both the princess and herself and wasn't sure what to do with her blanket. The thought of cuddling up next to the prince and sharing it with him made her suddenly so warm she didn't feel like she needed a blanket at all anymore.

She awkwardly covered herself with half the blanket then left the other half of the blanket on the seat between them. "There's a lot of the blanket left if you'd like some," Kaylie said, pointing to it. "It's all yours." She scooted closer to the window.

The prince smiled, watching her. "I'm fine, but thank you."

When Kaylie nodded, she didn't know if she was more relieved or disappointed.

When they got to the village, Kaylie was awestruck to find the tree lighting ceremony was even more magical than she could have imagined. The pageantry and the beauty were one thing, but it was the genuine, authentic people of Tolvania who really made it special. She'd found herself completely caught up in the moment and enjoying every second of it. The princess had even convinced her to sing Christmas carols with everyone. Before she knew what was happening, she was happily singing "Jingle Bells" with the queen and princess, and even the prince joined in.

As they all four stood side-by-side, singing and gazing at the beautiful Christmas trees lined up along the lake, for a moment Kaylie felt something she hadn't felt in a long time. She felt what it was like to be part of a family. It made her happy and sad all at the same time. Happy because it felt wonderful to feel that connection again, and sad because she knew this wasn't real, that this wasn't her real family.

As they followed the Christmas carolers to the next tree that was going to be lit, Kaylie knew what she needed to do. She turned to the queen. "If you can excuse me for a minute. I need to make a quick call."

"Right now?" the prince asked, looking disappointed. "We're almost done."

"I won't be long," Kaylie promised.

"Do what you need to do," the queen said.

Kaylie gave her a grateful look and then hurried off. She headed for the church, hoping to find a quiet place to make her call. She suddenly stopped halfway there, realizing that she'd been having so much fun she'd completely forgotten to get video of the Christmas carolers like she'd promised Rachel she'd do for Gerry's story. She quickly got out her phone and zoomed in on the singing carolers and started recording.

She rushed to get all she could before the carolers stopped singing and also wanted to get some people from the village. As she panned from the carolers into the crowd, she saw the backs of the prince, princess, and queen come into frame. She smiled when she saw how sweet they looked as a family, arm in arm, singing together. When the carolers finished the song and the tree lit up, Kaylie captured it all and knew Rachel and Gerry would love it.

As the carolers moved to the next tree and started a new song, Kaylie hurried toward the church but found it was still too noisy to make her call. When she saw the church door was open, she slipped inside.

Chapter 27

L ooking around inside the church, she marveled at how it was even more impressive on the inside than the outside with its stunning stained-glass windows, the well-loved antique wooden pews, and a beautiful altar that was surrounded by bright red poinsettias.

After making sure she was alone so she didn't disturb anyone, she quietly sat down in a pew near the back and made her call. She nervously tapped her foot against the floor, waiting for an answer while the phone kept ringing and ringing. She was almost ready to hang up when her mom's face finally came on the screen.

"Mom," Kaylie said with a sigh of relief. "There you are."

Kaylie's mom, Kathryn, looked surprised and worried. "Honey, is everything okay? Are you all right?"

Kaylie nodded as she fought back a rush of emotion. Being with the prince and his family and seeing all they did and shared at Christmas together had her missing her own family so much. She knew she was probably being extra sentimental, surrounded by all the Tolvania Christmas cheer, but she hadn't felt like she could wait another moment to call her parents.

"I'm fine, Mom," she answered, even as her eyes started to fill up with tears. "I just wanted to call and say hi…" When her voice cracked, her mom looked even more worried.

"John, get in here," Kaylie's mom shouted. "Kaylie's on the phone. Something's wrong."

"Mom, I'm fine," Kaylie insisted. She hated upsetting her mom. "I just wanted to hear your voice and see you both."

"But you never call us unless you schedule a call because you're always so busy with work," Kaylie's mom said, still sounding concerned.

Kaylie's dad, John, got into frame. He appeared equally uneasy. "Is everything okay? Where are you?"

Kaylie stood up so she could show them.

"Are you in a…church?" Kaylie's mom asked, surprised. "Is this in your neighborhood?"

Kaylie turned the camera back to herself. "I am in a church, but I'm not in New York. I'm in Europe."

"Europe?" her dad jumped in. "You didn't tell us you were going to Europe. Is this for work?"

"Of course it's for work," Kaylie's mom answered before Kaylie could. "Kaylie always works the holidays, right, honey?"

Kaylie nodded. "Right, Mom. I'm actually doing a feature story about Christmas traditions…"

"A feature story?" Kaylie's dad asked with wide eyes. He seemed even more confused.

"About Christmas traditions?" her mom asked. "You don't even like Christmas."

Now it was Kaylie's turn to look baffled. "What do you mean, I don't like Christmas? I like Christmas."

"Since when?" Kaylie's dad asked. "Because you never want to celebrate it."

"That's because we're always all too busy," Kaylie quickly replied. "Amelia's stationed overseas and you guys always loved to go to the Caribbean."

She saw her parents give each other a look.

"What?" Kaylie asked them.

"We only go to the Caribbean because after Amelia left, you didn't want to celebrate Christmas anymore and we had no place else to go," Kaylie's dad said.

"But you love the beach," Kaylie jumped in. She was shocked when she watched her mom shake her head.

"Not really. We love Christmas in New England, at home in Vermont, but when you girls didn't want to come home anymore, we decided to try the Caribbean, hoping you'd come visit us there."

"Wait, what?" Kaylie asked, confused. "We thought you two loved being in the Caribbean because you didn't care about celebrating Christmas, that's what you always said."

"We said that so you girls didn't feel bad about working and not being able to make it home," Kaylie's dad answered. "We didn't want to put pressure on you or make you feel like you *had* to come home. You both seemed to like coming to the Caribbean in January so that's what we kept doing. But if you want the truth, we've really missed doing Christmas as a family with you girls."

"We miss you both so much," Kaylie's mom said, trying not to cry.

Kaylie's eyes filled up with tears. "I've missed you, too. I can't believe this. All these years, it has just been one big misunderstanding. Amelia and I thought you didn't want to celebrate Christmas and just go to the beach, and you thought we didn't want to celebrate because we were working all the time."

"But we understood you girls were working. We're so proud of you," Kaylie's dad said. "We think it's wonderful how you've always volunteered to work Christmas so your co-workers with children can be with them, and for Amelia being so far away in Germany and Christmas being a busy time for her to support military families."

Kaylie shook her head, trying to take it all in. "But I just talked to Amelia and she misses Christmas together at home in Vermont. She just told me she could put in to get Christmas off and come home sometimes around the holidays but didn't think any of us cared about celebrating so she never did it. That's why she always volunteers to work. This is crazy. We all were thinking the other one didn't want to celebrate Christmas, and never talked about it, but deep down we all wanted to."

"But you *did* have to work," Kaylie's mom reminded her. "At the TV station."

Kaylie nodded. "I did at first because I was the new reporter and had to pay my dues, but later, I could have taken the time off. I just figured I'd work and make the extra money and also help my co-workers because I didn't think my family cared about Christmas."

"We always cared," Kaylie's mom said. "I just honestly thought you didn't like Christmas. You were our little Grinch."

Kaylie laughed. "I think I just acted like that because I didn't have any other choice. We weren't getting together anymore, so it was easier to be all *Bah-Humbug*."

Kaylie's mom's eyes filled with hope. "Are you saying what I think you're saying? That you girls want to start celebrating Christmas again? Because that would be the best Christmas present ever."

Kaylie had to wipe another tear away. "Yes, Mom, that's what I'm saying. We want to celebrate Christmas as a family. Even if it's a different day, because Amelia can't get home right on Christmas, or I have to work, we can still celebrate Christmas and do all our traditions. Even if it is in January, as long as we embrace and honor Christmas, that's what matters most. It doesn't have to be anything fancy, as long as we're all together."

Kaylie's dad, excited, held up his cell phone. "I'm booking a flight right now back to Vermont."

"I didn't mean this year. Christmas Eve is tomorrow and I am working here and Amelia's working in Germany, so we can just wait until next year when we have more time to plan."

"Are you kidding?" Kaylie's dad said with a huge smile. "We're not going to let another Christmas pass without celebrating. We'll go home and get everything set up. We can get a tree and put up some lights and then when you girls can come home, whenever that might be, January, whatever, we'll celebrate Christmas then and start creating some new traditions together."

Kaylie felt her heart fill with joy. "That sounds perfect. I love you guys so much."

"We love you more," Kaylie's mom said.

"I'll come to Vermont as soon as I can. I might have some new job news to tell you about. Cross your fingers for me. I'll tell you more later." Kaylie got up and walked out of the church.

Kaylie's dad looked sentimental. "We're so glad you called, honey. Merry Christmas."

"Merry Christmas, Mom and Dad," Kaylie said, feeling so much love. "Merry Christmas."

Kaylie was still smiling as she walked back to the lake. When she passed people heading back to the village, she realized the tree lighting was over. She returned to where she'd left the royal family but only found the prince waiting for her.

"Where's your mother and the princess?" Kaylie asked, looking around for them.

"We were done and we couldn't find you and it was getting cold, so I had my mother take Anna back home while I continued the search for you."

"I'm sorry," Kaylie said. "I didn't mean to disappear like that. I went into the church looking for a quiet place to make a call."

"You made a call in the church?" the prince said. The disapproval in his voice was clear.

Kaylie frowned. "Yes, but no one was in there, so I wasn't interrupting anything or bothering anyone. I made sure of that." Kaylie stopped talking when she saw she was only making things worse. "I'm sorry. That probably wasn't very respectful. I won't do that again."

"Good," the prince said.

"But I called my parents," Kaylie blurted out, excited.

The prince looked surprised. "Are they okay?"

"They are and I am, too, now," Kaylie said. "We don't usually celebrate Christmas together but now we all want the same thing."

"And what's that?" the prince asked.

"What you have," Kaylie answered honestly. "To celebrate Christmas as a family, honoring old Christmas traditions, and creating new ones."

"But you are here with us this Christmas," the prince said, confused.

"I know, we're going to start next year," Kaylie said. "Even though my dad said something about them going to get a tree and putting it up for us when my sister and I come in January. That's crazy, right?"

The prince shook his head. "No, I think that's a father listening to his daughter about how she'd like to celebrate Christmas again and he's going to make that happen, no matter what. That's what fathers do for daughters."

This brought tears to Kaylie's eyes.

"I'm sorry," the prince said. "Did I say something wrong?"

"No." Kaylie smiled through her tears. "What you said was just right." She took a deep breath. "I don't know why I keep getting so emotional. I think singing all those Christmas carols with you and your family brought back so many memories of Christmas with my family and I realized how much I miss them. Your mother said something earlier about how we're not guaranteed time with the people we love the most, so I didn't want to waste another moment not telling them how much they mean to me and how much I love them. But I'm really sorry I disappeared like that. It wasn't planned, I promise."

"I understand," the prince said. "Time is precious."

When Kaylie looked up at him, she saw he really did seem to understand and for that she was grateful. She started walking toward the lake where all the Christmas trees were now lit, creating a dance of lights across the water.

"You know, being here, with you and your family, also reminded me of how much I've missed Christmas. I think I tried to pretend like it didn't matter but the truth was, it mattered so much and not celebrating hurt, so I just pretended I didn't care, if that makes sense?"

The prince nodded. "It does. I did the same thing after losing Sophia. It seemed wrong being happy at Christmas when she wasn't here with us. I felt…guilty, like I was betraying her in some way. But now I've realized the best way to honor her memory is to honor our Christmas memories together and be with my family and make sure my daughter always has a Christmas that's filled with love."

"You deserve that, too," Kaylie said without thinking, and then looked away, embarrassed.

"I think we all deserve love," the prince said.

When Kaylie looked up into his eyes, she saw compassion and understanding and then her pulse quickened when she also thought she might have seen something else…

The prince took her hand. "I'm really glad you're staying for Christmas."

"I am, too," Kaylie said in a voice she didn't recognize. It sounded breathless and full of longing.

As the prince stepped closer to her, her heart raced.

"You found her."

The prince abruptly dropped her hand and took a step back just as Jean Pierre, the chocolatier, walked up.

Kaylie, still dazed, looked at Jean Pierre, confused. "Were you looking for me?"

"Yes," Jean Pierre said, with his sexy smile. "I came to talk to you but then found out you were missing, so I have been part of the search party."

Kaylie laughed, surprised. "You had a search party looking for me?"

"Jean Pierre is exaggerating," the prince said.

Jean Pierre took Kaylie's hand, the same hand the prince had taken, and kissed it. "I am so glad we found you. We don't want to lose something so beautiful and special."

Kaylie held back a laugh at Jean Pierre's flowery words and was surprised to see that the prince seemed annoyed by them.

"But now that I've found you, I wanted to invite you to the shop tomorrow and show you the Christmas Crown chocolates."

Kaylie's eyes lit up. "That would be amazing…"

"Unfortunately, Kaylie's schedule is booked, but we appreciate the offer. If anything changes, we will be sure to let you know," the prince said.

Jean Pierre finally took the hint. "That would be wonderful. I hope to see you, Kaylie."

When he turned to walk away, Kaylie gave the prince a look. "That was a little rude, don't you think?"

The prince didn't look concerned at all. "No, it was the truth. We are very busy tomorrow. It's Christmas Eve and I know my mother wouldn't want you to miss anything."

Kaylie suddenly felt guilty. "I hope I didn't miss too much of the tree lighting ceremony."

"Only the grand finale and how we throw the last Christmas tree in the lake while singing the song "Oh, Christmas Tree," the prince said with a disappointed look.

Kaylie's jaw dropped. "What?"

When the prince started laughing, Kaylie's eyes narrowed. "Funny," she said and went to slap his arm but this time he caught her hand.

"Careful," he said. "You don't want to have to spend Christmas in the dungeon."

For an answer, Kaylie leaned down and grabbed some snow and threw it at him, making him release her hand.

"Ugh!" he exclaimed while Kaylie made a snowball and hit him in the chest.

"*Girl power*," she sang out as she held her hands up in victory and did a silly little dance. But when she saw the prince quickly make a giant snowball, she stopped dancing and started backing up. "You wouldn't…"

The prince grinned back at her. "Wouldn't I? You don't have my daughter as your partner in crime, so I'd say this is the perfect time for a re-match. Wouldn't you?"

For an answer, she took off running.

When she ran into a charming gazebo that was sparkling with white twinkle lights, she realized she was trapped and quickly held up both hands.

"Time out," she panted.

The prince laughed as he approached her slowly. He held up his snowball. "Time out? You can't call a time out. This isn't American football."

She started backing up. "Yes, I can. This gazebo is… off limits."

"Says who?" the prince asked.

"Says anyone who knows about gazebos," Kaylie flung back at him and then laughed at her own ridiculousness. But it worked. She was relieved to see the prince put down the snowball before he walked up to her and didn't stop until they were toe to toe.

Kaylie's heart raced.

"We do have some Christmas traditions that involve this gazebo," the prince said, never taking his eyes off her face.

"And what would those be?" Kaylie asked in a breathless voice.

When the prince pointed up and Kaylie saw the mistletoe, her heart stopped. Speechless, she looked into the prince's eyes. She knew he was about to kiss her, but she didn't move. She realized more than anything how much she wanted to kiss him. When he leaned in, Kaylie shut her eyes, but they flew open again when she heard Thomas come around the corner.

"Prince Alexander?"

They both quickly took a step back just as Thomas appeared.

"There you are. I thought I lost you for a moment. The car is parked around the corner when you're ready."

"I'm ready," Kaylie said as she rushed to join Thomas. Her head was a mess. Her heart was disappointed that they hadn't kissed, but her brain was telling her to wise up, and that she shouldn't fall for someone she could never have. She was mad at herself because she knew if they had kissed, nothing good would have come from it. They were from two entirely different worlds and after Christmas, just like Cinderella, she knew her time in this fairy tale would be up.

As they drove back to the castle in the town car, Kaylie's mind was in overdrive. She didn't want that almost-kiss to make things awkward with the prince. When they got out of the car and walked together to the door, she suddenly stepped in front of him.

"What was that all about, at the gazebo…" she blurted out before she could chicken out. She refused to let herself obsess about what that kiss could have meant and had decided she was just going to ask him.

When the prince gave her a blank stare, she felt embarrassed but determined. "The kiss. You almost kissed me," she said, louder than she'd wanted. She turned to make sure Thomas hadn't heard them.

Thomas was still standing by the car, waiting for them to safely get inside. To his credit, if he heard, he kept a straight face and had discretely looked away.

Kaylie stood her ground but lowered her voice and tried again. "What was that all about?"

The prince shrugged like it was no big deal. "I told you that was a Christmas tradition. That's all."

Kaylie's eyes grew wide as she tried to hide the hurt. "That's it?"

"A tradition is a tradition, and now, if you'll excuse me, I have a call I need to make and a lot of work I need to get done before all our events tomorrow. I'll see you in the morning."

As the prince walked away, Kaylie just stared after him. She wasn't going to say another word. The last thing she wanted was the prince to see how disappointed she was to find out their almost-kiss hadn't meant anything to him.

Chapter 28

Flustered, the prince paced around the kitchen and bit the head off a gingerbread cookie. "I don't know what happened."

"What happened is you almost kissed Kaylie." Chef Jake slapped him on the back. "Good for you!"

The prince, stressed, raked his fingers through his hair. "No, not good for me. And there's nothing to be happy about. That would have been a disaster."

"Why?" Chef Jake asked, confused. "You like her. Admit it. I haven't seen you like this with anyone since Sophia, and you know she wanted you to be happy. She would have liked Kaylie."

"None of that matters," the prince said, looking tortured. "I'm the Prince of Tolvania. I have a daughter who is a princess. My life is here. My responsibility is to my family."

"And Anna thinks Kaylie is great and your mother invited her here and they seem to get along, too, so I don't see what the problem is."

The prince snapped his cookie in two. "The problem is Kaylie lives in New York City. That's where her life is. She's a journalist. She is everything I've fought my whole life against. We have a ban against journalists here in Tolvania. She shouldn't even be here."

"But she's not here as a journalist, she's here as a writer, writing the fairy tale for Anna," Chef Jake said as he put some mini-quiches for the Christmas tea on a cookie sheet. "And writers can write from anywhere. I'm just saying, before you shut the door and create all these scenarios and get in your head about how this would never work, I think you should at least talk to her."

The prince shook his head. "No. There's no point. She probably doesn't even feel the same. We were both probably just caught up in the moment. I'm not going to embarrass this family."

Chef Jake gave him a knowing look. "Embarrass the family, or you?"

"It's the same thing," the prince said.

"You know, you're allowed to have a life," Chef Jake insisted. "And that includes falling in love again."

The prince laughed. "I'm *not* falling in love."

"Aren't you?" Chef Jake said, not backing down. "Because I think that's why you're stressing out so much. If you didn't care about Kaylie, none of this would be a big deal. I think you're just getting in your own way and making this a lot harder than it has to be."

The prince gave Chef Jake an incredulous look. "I'm a prince and a single father that's hard enough already."

"I'm just saying, talk to Kaylie, tell her how you feel. If she's not interested and your lives are too different to bridge the gap, fine, but at least you tried and will have no regrets. The Alex I know doesn't just give up so easily. You owe it to yourself to try. What do you have to lose?"

The prince stared back at him. "Everything. I have everything to lose."

Chef Jake sighed and shook his head.

"And what about you? When are you going to start taking your own advice and finally ask Elsa out?" the prince asked. "Talk about someone getting in their own way. You've had a thing for her since you got here."

"We're just friends," Chef Jake answered quickly.

"And that's the way it's going to stay, unless you do something," the prince said. "But you know she's like a sister to me. Don't mess it up."

"I don't know what you're talking about," Chef Jake said. "There's nothing to mess up."

"I'm just telling you, don't wait too long," the prince warned. "She's a catch and someone else is going to swoop in…"

"Who?!" Chef Jake demanded.

"I knew it!" the prince said with a laugh. "You've really got it bad, don't you?"

For an answer, Chef Jake threw a potholder at him.

Kaylie, upset, was pacing back and forth in her room, wearing her new fluffy white bathrobe the prince had gotten her to replace her drenched one from the bathtub incident. She was on her phone talking to Rachel.

"I still can't believe I almost kissed him!" Kaylie shook her head in disbelief.

Rachel had a grin a mile wide. "I think this is fantastic! You and the prince. I get to be in the wedding, right? Will you get to wear a crown? Will *I* get to wear a crown?!" Rachel's voice was bubbling over with excitement.

"Stop," Kaylie said, getting frustrated. "Haven't you been listening to me? That almost-kiss was just part of some silly Christmas mistletoe tradition—nothing more than that."

"But it meant something more to *you*," Rachel said. "You've fallen for this guy. I've never seen you like this with any other guy before. You *really* like him."

Kaylie groaned as she fell back onto her bed. "I do, I really do and I'm so mad at myself because this is a disaster waiting to happen. This is a horror story, not a fairy tale."

Rachel laughed. "Stop being so dramatic. Just tell the prince how you feel."

Kaylie sat back up. "Never! I'd get kicked out of here so fast it would make my head spin. He's already suspicious of me because I'm a reporter. He can never know how I feel. I just need to get a grip, give myself a reality check and get over this silly crush."

Rachel shook her head. "I don't think it's silly and I don't think it's *just* a crush. If you don't want to tell him the truth, at least be honest with yourself."

"I am being honest with myself," Kaylie insisted. "Nothing can come of this, regardless of how I feel. He's a prince. I'm a reporter, a profession he hates, end of story. There's no 'happily ever after' that's going to happen here for me. I just need to concentrate on doing my job, writing this fairy tale, and the Tolvania Christmas feature story, and getting that investigative reporter job and getting my life back on track. That's all I want."

"Are you sure about that?" Rachel asked.

Kaylie stared into her phone. "I'm sure," she said with conviction, even though her heart was telling her a different story. "And I gotta go. For Christmas Eve tomorrow, my schedule is packed with the tea, the Christmas Crown event, the ball, and everything in between, and I still have to write the Tolvania feature and the fairy tale. I have enough to worry about and just need to put the prince out of my mind…"

"Good luck with that," Rachel said with a laugh. "The putting the prince out of your mind part. For the feature story, don't forget Gerry needs it by tomorrow night your time. I already gave him the basic outline you sent me, so he's good with everything, and this gives you time to find out more about the Christmas Crown. As soon as you can, send me the pictures and videos so I can help pick the best stuff to send Gerry for promotions."

Kaylie breathed a sigh of relief. "Thank you, Rachel. I don't know what I'd do without you. I can send you all the pictures and video I have right now and then I'll call you in the morning. Let me know when the pictures come through. The internet can be iffy."

"Sound great," Rachel said. "I'm standing by."

As soon as Kaylie hung up, she started scrolling through all the amazing Christmas pictures she'd taken in the village and quickly sent the best ones to Rachel. When she got to the videos of the carolers and the tree lighting, she was relieved to hear the audio was great. You could hear the carolers clearly and could feel the joy from all the villagers who were singing along.

In her last video, she smiled when she saw the prince come into frame. He was standing with his back to the camera, between his mother and daughter, and had his arms around each of them and they had their arms around him. They looked just like all the other families singing who were having a wonderful time.

Even though she knew she could never use the video of the royal family in her story, she liked having it as her own personal memory of the night that had been so special. Leaving this video out, she highlighted all the other videos and sent them to Rachel.

She waited for Rachel to respond and a few seconds later, she got a thumbs-up emoji and then happily went to work writing her feature story. She had so many Christmas traditions she wanted to include about Tolvania. She was also excited to learn even more with all that was coming up tomorrow on Christmas Eve.

She refused to let her complicated feelings for the prince get in her way of doing a great job on the Christmas feature and the princess's fairy tale. She always prided herself on being a professional and never letting anything that was going on in her personal life interfere with the quality of her work. Granted, she hadn't had much of a personal life up to this point to get in the way of her career, but still, she was confident she could compartmentalize her feelings and channel all her energy into her assignments.

She knew the time was running out fast, but she'd never missed a deadline yet, and she wasn't planning to start now. She had just started typing when she heard a bark outside her door. She waited, thinking Blixen must have been going by, but when she heard the bark again, she got up to see what was going on.

As she opened the door, he trotted in, wagging his tail.

"Blixen, what are you doing here?" Kaylie asked as he stared up at her with his soulful big brown eyes. "Coming to check on me?" She laughed.

For an answer, Blixen headed back to the door.

"Okay, bye, nice seeing you," Kaylie said as she waved at Blixen. She waited for him to go so she could shut the door, but he didn't move. Instead, he sat down and barked again.

"Shhhh," Kaylie whispered. "You're going to wake everyone up."

Blixen stood up and turned around in a circle and stared back at her.

"I don't know what you want," Kaylie said.

Blixen ran into the room, grabbed her fuzzy white slipper that went with her bathrobe, and then raced out the door.

"Wait! Not my slipper." Kaylie ran after him and found him standing at the end of the hall with the slipper in his mouth.

Kaylie pulled her robe closer around her. She walked slowly toward him, talking in a soothing, coaxing voice. "Blixen, you're a good boy, aren't you?"

Blixen wagged his tail.

Kaylie was getting closer. "And you're going to give me that slipper back, right?"

Blixen wagged his tail even more.

"Fantastic," Kaylie said with a smile. "So, you can drop the slipper right there. Just drop it. That's right, drop the slipper…"

Blixen tilted his head like he was listening. He dropped the slipper.

Kaylie breathed a sigh of relief. "You're a good boy." But just as she leaned down to get the slipper, Blixen grabbed it again and took off down the stairs.

"No… Come back here!" Kaylie called after him in a whisper. When she got to the top of the stairs, she looked down and saw the slipper abandoned at the bottom. Blixen was nowhere in sight. She grumbled as she went to retrieve it. "Crazy dog." But just as she got to the last step, Blixen ran up, stole the slipper again, and took off around the corner.

"Seriously, Blixen?" Kaylie called out after him. "I'm going to tell Santa about this. He's not going to be pleased."

The next thing she knew, she was chasing Blixen into the kitchen. "Okay, now I have you trapped!" she said as she burst into the room. "You can't get away from me now…" She stopped dead in her tracks when she saw the prince in a crimson bathrobe pouring some hot chocolate into a giant Santa mug.

He was just as surprised to see her.

Embarrassed, she pointed at Blixen, who had dropped her slipper and was sitting in the middle of the kitchen staring at them both. "He stole my slipper, or your slipper, the slippers from my room."

"Ah, yes." The prince nodded, not acting a bit surprised. "He likes to do that. He always goes on the hunt for someone to play with after Anna goes to bed. Apparently, tonight he found you and your unfortunate slipper."

Kaylie put her hands on her hips and stared at Blixen. "Well, you're definitely on Santa's naughty list now."

Blixen just wagged his tail and laid down and start chewing on the slipper.

The prince held up his Santa mug. "I don't think you're getting that slipper back, but I can offer you some hot chocolate."

Kaylie inhaled, savoring the rich chocolate scent in the air. "Is this Jean Pierre's famous Christmas chocolate that I had with your mother when I first arrived?"

The prince picked up the gold canister Jean Pierre gave him when they'd visited his shop. "Actually, this is another flavor, mine and Anna's favorite."

"Let me guess," Kaylie said. "Gingerbread is involved."

The prince looked impressed. "Very good guess, yes, gingerbread is involved and so is cinnamon and vanilla and all sorts of other delicious ingredients that somehow make it rich but not too sweet."

"I'd love to try it," Kaylie said. "I can take it back upstairs and not bother you. I have a lot of work to do."

"You're not bothering me," the prince said, surprising Kaylie as he poured her hot chocolate into another adorable Santa mug and handed it to her. For a moment their eyes met and they shared a smile.

"Thank you," Kaylie said and took a sip of her chocolate. Her eyes grew huge.

"It's great, right?" the prince said.

"Delicious," Kaylie agreed. "You're turning me into a gingerbread fan."

For a moment they sipped their hot chocolate in silence, then they both started talking at once.

"About earlier," the prince said.

"About the mistletoe," Kaylie said at the same time.

"Please, you go ahead," the prince said.

But suddenly, Kaylie didn't know what to say. She'd promised herself to let it go and not think about the kiss that almost happened and just concentrate on work, but Rachel's voice was also in her head, encouraging her to tell the prince how she really felt. But right now, what she felt was confused. Nervous, she walked over to a plate of gingerbread biscuits and, without thinking, picked one up and took a bite.

"Oh, now you've done it," the prince said.

Kaylie turned around, surprised. "Done what?"

"Those are for the Christmas tea tomorrow, and we never have enough. They're very popular."

"So, I hear," Kaylie said. "I'm sorry."

The prince walked over and grabbed a red apron with the family's gold swan crest on it and tossed it to her. "Now we have to make more."

Kaylie almost dropped the apron. "Wait, what? It's late and I have a lot of work to do…"

"Then we better get moving. They're really easy," the prince said as he put on a matching apron. "And this is part of your work. This is on my mother's list of things for us to do. One of her favorite Christmas traditions is making Christmas gingerbread biscuits and I'm sure she'd like you to use this in the fairy tale."

Since the prince said this was work and on the queen's list, Kaylie didn't know how to say no. She looked at the apron she was holding. "I thought you said Chef Jake didn't like people in his kitchen?"

The prince gave her a look. "I'm the prince. This is my kitchen, not Jake's. He'll be fine. This is what my mother wants, so…"

Kaylie put on the apron. "So, we better get to work. You said this won't take long, right?"

"It won't take long at all," the prince said. "Easiest recipe in the world."

"Okay, but I'm warning you, I'm no Betty Crocker in the kitchen," Kaylie said.

"Don't worry. I know what I'm doing," the prince said with a confident smile.

But an hour later, when the prince caught his potholder on fire and the fire alarm went off, Chef Jake came running into the kitchen.

"What is going on in here?!" Chef Jake demanded.

The prince was putting out the blaze with a fire extinguisher, creating a huge mess.

Chapter 29

The prince tried to look dignified as he held the fire extinguisher. "I have everything under control. I was showing Kaylie how to make my mother's favorite Christmas gingerbread biscuits."

"You call trying to burn my kitchen down under control?" Chef Jake laughed.

Kaylie rushed to try and help the prince. "It's on our Christmas list of things the queen wanted us to do."

Chef Jake laughed even louder as he took the fire extinguisher from the prince. "No, trust me, the queen did *not* want the prince doing anything in the kitchen. Kaylie, you and I were going to make biscuits if we had the time. The prince had nothing to do with it. Everyone knows he's a nightmare in the kitchen."

Kaylie's eyes grew wide as she turned to the prince. "Really?"

"He doesn't know what he's talking about," the prince said as he crossed his arms in front of his chest.

Chef Jake's eyebrows arched. "Oh, really? What about that time in college when you tried to burn down our dorm?"

"What?!" Kaylie exclaimed.

"Oh, yeah, it's true," Chef Jake said. "He was trying to make an omelet, cooking bacon, when the grease caught on fire. He tried to put the fire out with water."

Kaylie cringed. "Even I know putting water on a grease fire will only make it worse."

"It ended up being fine," the prince insisted.

Chef Jake laughed. "Only after your mother made a very generous donation to the dorm and promised that you'd never set foot in the kitchen again."

The prince shrugged. "Like I said, it all turned out fine."

Kaylie turned and faced the prince. "Wow. I didn't know I was taking my life into my own hands being in this kitchen with you."

"Well, now you know," Chef Jake said. "If you see the prince in the kitchen, run!"

When Kaylie laughed, the prince just rolled his eyes.

"Okay, you two, very funny," the prince said. "Now let's clean up this mess before my mother sees it."

Chef Jake stepped over a pile of foam from the fire extinguisher. "You two go, I'll take care of this."

"No," the prince said. "That's not right. I made the mess. I should clean it up."

"And I can help," Kaylie said.

Chef Jake looked at Kaylie. "Honestly, the best way you can help is to get this guy out of here before he destroys anything else in my kitchen." Chef Jake noticed the batch of gingerbread biscuits they'd made before they'd caught the kitchen on fire. "Are these any good?"

Kaylie nodded. "They tasted really good to me."

Chef Jake picked one up, studied it, then took a bite. He chewed it slowly.

"Well?" the prince asked impatiently. "They're great, right?"

Chef Jake nodded. "Not too bad." He turned to Kaylie. "You must have made these, not the prince."

Kaylie laughed. "I only helped."

Chef Jake gave the prince a surprised look. "So, it looks like there's at least one thing you can make. I'll remember that when I need help again."

"Yeah, no," the prince said. "This was a one-time thing. Besides, remember, I'm a nightmare in the kitchen. I can't be trusted." He grabbed Kaylie's hand. "Let's get out of here while we still can."

Kaylie laughed as the prince pulled her out of the kitchen. "Sorry, Chef Jake." She heard Chef Jake chuckle as they left.

When they got into the hallway, the prince gave Kaylie a guilty look. "Sorry about all that."

Kaylie laughed. "Are you kidding me? That was the most fun I've had in a kitchen ever. I need to get this recipe. It really is easy. I think I could even do it. I want to make it for my family."

The prince laughed. "If I can make it, anyone can, and I haven't made them in years."

"Have you made them with the princess?" Kaylie asked.

"No," the prince said. "And I don't know if Jake will ever let me back in his kitchen."

"Yeah, good luck with that," Kaylie said. "But seriously, it could be a new Christmas tradition for you guys."

The prince thought about it. "She might like that."

"I think she'd love it," Kaylie replied. "You can see how much she loves spending any time with you. She was so excited to see you tonight. It's clear you mean everything to her. She's going to grow up so fast. This time you have with her now is so important."

The prince gave her a thoughtful look. "You sound like you're talking from experience."

Kaylie thought about it for a second. "I guess I am. My dad is a great dad, but he was always working to provide for our family."

"An honorable thing to do," the prince said.

"Yes, but really all my sister Amelia and I wanted was time with him, and we didn't get a lot of it growing up. We didn't need expensive vacations, or clothes, or presents, or any of that stuff, we just wanted to be with him. We knew he was trying to do the best for us, but you can see how that can be a trap."

The prince nodded. "Yes, maybe it can be. I believe I've fallen into that same trap with working too much. I'm going to make some changes so I can spend more time with Anna."

Kaylie's eyes lit up. "I think that's wonderful." When they shared a smile, she felt her whole body tingle, but warning bells were also going off in her head. *He's a prince. Walk away. Run away. Remember, concentrate on your career...*

She stared down at the floor and took a deep breath to steady herself. "I need to get going. It's late and I have a lot more work to do, but thank you for the hot chocolate and the cooking lesson about what not to do with a potholder."

The prince laughed a little. "And thank you for the help."

"Any time," Kaylie said, and then realized how foolish that sounded because she knew there wouldn't be other times like this for them. Once she returned to New York in a few days, all this would just be a distant memory, but one she knew she would remember and cherish forever.

"I'll see you in the morning," she said as she started to walk away. She'd only taken a few steps when the prince stopped her.

"Kaylie," he called out.

Her heart raced as she turned around. "Yes?"

Their eyes met and held. Kaylie saw the prince struggle like there was something he wanted to say.

"Sleep well," the prince finally said. "We have a big day tomorrow."

Kaylie nodded, trying not to be disappointed. "You, too. Good night." As she headed down the hall, she thought about how, in just a few hours, it would be Christmas Eve, one of her last nights at the castle. For the first time in a long time, she didn't wish Christmas would hurry up and be over; she wished she had more time for Christmas, and if she were being honest with herself, more time with the prince and his family.

Back in her room, it was well past two in the morning when she finished the Tolvania Christmas feature and sent it to Rachel. She'd also made some good headway on her fairy tale for the princess.

She was truly surprised at how much she'd enjoyed working on both stories. The Tolvania story had come together so easily. She'd found the hardest part was picking and choosing what to include because she had so much great material. The outline for the fairy tale had also been a lot easier than she'd thought.

But right now, what she knew she needed the most was a few good hours of sleep before all the Christmas events began, with the tea at ten in the morning. After putting her computer away and turning out the lights, she snuggled underneath her covers and smiled up at the tiny gold sparkling stars covering the canopy of her bed. They twinkled as they caught the moonlight. It was magical, just like her whole day had been.

She reached out and took her phone off the nightstand and scrolled through the video she'd taken at the Christmas tree lighting. She quickly found what she was looking for. The video that showed the prince and his family singing along with the carolers. She played it back several times. Seeing the family's love and joy filled her heart with happiness, and she knew this time in Tolvania would be a memory she would cherish forever.

Chapter 30

The next morning, Christmas Eve Day, Kaylie woke up and was filled with anticipation and excitement. This was the big day, a huge day when they'd be having the queen's Christmas tea, the Christmas Crown event, and that night, a spectacular Christmas ball. It all felt so surreal but exhilarating, and she couldn't wait to get started.

But first, she wanted to make sure Rachel got the feature she'd sent last night because she hadn't heard back from her yet. She quickly sent her a text. *Did you get everything okay?* She'd also sent Rachel a list of exclusive story ideas to give Gerry, hoping to impress him with a range of stories she'd gotten from her top law enforcement, government, and even celebrity contacts.

She waited for a response from Rachel but when one didn't come right away, she remembered it was the middle of the night there, so she started getting ready for breakfast.

An hour later, when she walked into the dining room, fifteen minutes early, the only person there was Chef Jake. She gave him a guilty look. "Morning, Chef Jake. Sorry again about last night's little…incident. I hope you weren't up all night cleaning up after our mess?"

"I was," Chef Jake said with a laugh. "And I was getting ready for this morning's Christmas tea. I can sleep after Christmas."

"Oh, no," Kaylie said, feeling worse.

"Hey, don't blame yourself," Chef Jake said. "We both know who the real culprit is. How did you sleep?"

"I was like you, mostly working, not sleeping, but I got a lot done, so I would say the night, minus trying to burn down your kitchen, was a huge success." Kaylie quickly stopped talking when the queen, followed by the prince, and princess entered the room.

The princess was beaming. "Good morning, Kaylie. Merry almost Christmas."

"Good morning, princess." Kaylie smiled back at her. "Merry almost Christmas to you, too. Are you excited for today?"

"Oh, yes," the princess said. "We all are. Are you?"

Kaylie nodded. "I am *very* excited. What can I do to help?"

"Do you have time to help?" the queen asked, giving Kaylie a knowing look. "I know you have that little project you're working on for Christmas tomorrow. How is that coming along?"

"It's coming along great," Kaylie answered the queen with a bright smile.

"Fantastic," the queen said, with a cheerful smile.

"I know there's a lot going on today and I'm happy to help with anything I can," Kaylie offered. "I can get a behind-the-scenes look at these traditions."

"Just not in the kitchen," Chef Jake muttered under his breath.

"What was that?" the queen asked.

The prince rushed to the rescue. "Nothing."

Chef Jake nodded. "Nothing at all."

The queen turned her attention back to Kaylie. "That's very kind of you to offer, but everything has come together beautifully. We should be all set. People start arriving for the Christmas tea in two hours, at ten. We have several different seatings until two, and then we open up the castle and allow people to come in to see the Christmas Crown. The Christmas Crown viewing ends at five and then our Christmas ball starts at eight. It's quite the schedule."

"Wow," Kaylie said, impressed. "It sure is."

"And I have three different outfits to wear," the princess said proudly.

"And so do I," the queen said and then looked at Kaylie. "And so do you."

Kaylie laughed. "I'm afraid I don't have three different things to wear. I only have one basic little black dress so I can just blend into the background."

"I don't see you blending in," the prince said. The way he said it, Kaylie wasn't sure if it was a compliment or not. She saw the princess and the queen exchange a knowing smile. "What?" she asked them. "You two look like you're up to something again."

The princess, delighted, clapped her hands. "We got you dresses!"

"What?" Kaylie laughed. "No, you didn't." She looked at the queen.

The queen's eyes twinkled. "Oh, yes we did. It's part of our tradition, so we had to, right, Anna?"

"Right," the princess agreed happily. "You can't dance at the ball without a ball gown."

"Oh, I wasn't planning to dance," Kaylie said.

"Everyone dances at my ball," the queen said, leaving no doubt she was serious.

"And I helped pick out your dresses," the princess said. "They're dreamy."

When Kaylie looked to the prince for some help, he just shrugged. "I'm staying out of this one. Fashion is their department, not mine."

"I don't know what to say," Kaylie replied.

"Just say thank you," the princess said, sounding just like her grandmother.

Kaylie laughed. "Okay, thank you. Thank you so much."

"You're welcome," the queen said graciously. "But first, let's all sit down and have a good breakfast. We need the energy to get through this day."

Kaylie couldn't believe how fast the next hour flew by. After they'd finished their breakfast, she'd helped the queen put the finishing touches on the decorations for the Christmas tea, adding beautiful centerpieces of white lilies and red roses to all the tables that were set up in the drawing room.

By the time they were done, she had just enough time to run upstairs to get ready. When she stepped inside her room, she gasped when she saw three beautiful party dresses hanging on a pretty gold clothing rack. The rack had a big red Christmas bow tied around it.

"This is amazing," she said in awe. She knew the queen had said they'd gotten her something to wear, but these were no *ordinary* dresses, these were some of the most beautiful gowns she'd ever seen.

She touched the first one, a stunning rich red velvet sheath cocktail dress that had tiny pearls along the neckline. When she looked closely, she would have sworn the pearls were real. The next dress was even fancier. It was all gold sequins, floor-length, with a slit up one thigh, and a halter style neck. It was extravagant and classy all at the same time. But it was the final dress, the spectacular ball gown, that truly took her breath away. It was white, with exquisite gold beading on the bodice shimmering in the light, and a layered tulle skirt that added dramatic volume.

With each dress, she also found amazing shoes and accessories, and there was an adorable note from the princess. She read it out loud...

"Thank you for spending your Christmas with us."

It was signed by the princess, the queen, and the prince, and they had each signed their first names, Anna, Isabella, and Alex, and there was a painted paw print with Blixen's name under it.

She was so touched. She held the card to her heart. While she loved the dresses, what she appreciated the most was how everyone was including her and making her feel like part of the family, making sure this Christmas was also magical for her.

The moment was interrupted when a call from Rachel lit up her phone. She grabbed it quickly.

"Rachel, Merry almost Christmas! You're up early."

"Wait, did my Grinchy friend just wish me a Merry Christmas?" Rachel asked, stunned. "I must still be sleeping. I must be dreaming..."

Kaylie laughed. "You're not dreaming. Sorry for sending everything so late, or early your time, but I just wanted to make sure you got the feature draft I sent you. If you did, did you get a chance to read it? Is it too fluffy, too sweet, too much Christmas?"

"Wait, so many questions." Rachel laughed. "I need my coffee." She took a deep breath and a sip of her coffee. "First, I got the draft and it's great! I can't wait to see what you're going to write about the Christmas Crown, we'll just add that and we'll be ready to go."

"You really think it's okay?" Kaylie asked, nervous. "This is my first feature story in like...forever and I'm not sure..."

"Stop it," Rachel interrupted her. "It's perfect. It's Christmassy. It's supposed to be a feel-good, fun story, that's the whole point and you nailed it and the pictures were fantastic. You really should take more of your own photos, but I'm still waiting for the video. You said you had some, right?"

Kaylie stared into the camera. "I have a lot of videos and I sent them after the photos. You didn't get them?"

Rachel shook her head. "No, send them again, right away, so I can get them to Gerry. He was asking for them. I also passed on your exclusive story ideas for the investigative reporter job, including the pharmacy drug scandal. He has some follow-up questions, and wants to talk, so that's a good thing."

"This is great news. I'm so relieved," Kaylie said.

"And I'm relieved that one of my best friends is finally not acting so Grinchy anymore," Rachel said with a laugh.

"That's right," Kaylie said proudly. "Check this out. You can now call me Christmas Kaylie." Kaylie held up her new red velvet sheath cocktail dress. "This is what I'm wearing to the Christmas tea." She flipped the camera around so she could show Rachel her other dazzling dresses. "I'm wearing this gold dress to the Christmas Crown event and of course, this incredible ball gown to the ball."

Rachel's eyes grew huge. "No way! Those are all yours? Where did you get them? Let me guess. The queen?"

Kaylie grinned and nodded, excited. "And the princess. She helped pick them out."

"Then can I hire her for my stylist? Those are amazing," Rachel said.

"I know, I really am starting to feel like Cinderella…" Kaylie stopped talking when the alarm went off on her phone. "Oh, no, I have to go. I totally lost track of time."

"Okay, send the videos right now and call me later. Have fun!"

"Wish me luck!" Kaylie said.

"You don't need it," Rachel said. "It looks like you finally found your Christmas spirit."

As soon as Kaylie hung up, she grabbed her first beautiful dress to change into and rushed to send the videos to Rachel. "Please get them this time," she pleaded, waiting for a text back from Rachel.

Got the videos! Have fun! Rachel texted back.

"Yes!" she said, taking a deep breath. "Done and done, and now it's teatime!"

Kaylie wasn't sure what to expect for her first Christmas tea. She guessed it would be a pretty formal affair since it was a tea at a castle, on Christmas Eve Day, and the queen and princess had picked out a stunning cocktail dress for her to wear.

As she looked around the drawing room, there were certainly extravagant Christmas decorations and wonderful gourmet treats from Chef Jake, but she'd been surprised and delighted to find that the vibe of the tea, despite everyone being dressed up, was relaxed and laid back.

Kaylie liked seeing how all the guests, the teachers, military members, and first responders, were thoroughly enjoying themselves and looked like they felt very comfortable around the queen and princess. No one seemed nervous or intimidated at all.

When it came to dressing up, the queen and princess didn't disappoint, and were both wearing exquisite matching jeweled tiaras to mark the occasion. The tiaras were simple but striking, adorned with dozens of tiny pearls and diamonds. Kaylie had been fascinated when the queen had explained that, in many royal families, there were rules about where, when, who, and even what time of day you were allowed to wear tiaras and crowns. She'd also explained that every family had different rules and, in her family, they all believed in wearing the tiaras and crowns for special events, no matter the time of day, because it made people happy to see them. It was also a way to share part of the family's history with everyone.

When the prince made his entrance, smiling and greeting all his guests, Kaylie felt herself falling even harder for him. It wasn't just because he was gorgeous in his immaculately-cut designer suit, but because of the way he was so kind to everyone and went out of his way to talk to every single guest. She also noticed how he'd taught the young princess to do her part by making sure everyone felt at home and welcomed.

Kaylie became even more impressed when the prince delivered a sincere and heartfelt speech thanking everyone for their daily sacrifice. As she looked around the room, she saw how much his words meant to every single person. She felt honored to be part of this Christmas tradition that so clearly made a difference by simply letting people know how much they were appreciated.

After his speech, the prince made his way over to her, holding two glasses of champagne. He handed her one.

"So, what do you think of the Christmas tea?"

"I think it's been wonderful," Kaylie said. "Truly, this is amazing. What a special Christmas tradition to honor and give thanks for the people in your community who give back every day in their jobs. I thought your speech was great."

"I'm sure you could have written a better one," the prince said.

Kaylie shook her head. "No, I couldn't have, because what you said was from the heart. It was real, and everyone felt that and you made them feel special."

"Thank you," the prince said, looking like her words meant a lot to him. "I always feel like I don't say enough to convey how appreciative we are for what everyone does."

"I think they understood that very well," Kaylie said. "You could tell you were sincere and genuine, and that's what matters most to people."

The prince looked into her eyes. "Is that what matters most to you?"

Kaylie's heartbeat quickened. "Yes, being honest and genuine—that's what's important to me."

"Well, I'm glad you could be here to be part of this," the prince said. "I don't know if this Christmas tradition fits into a fairy tale, but I know it's important to my family, so my mother wanted you to see it."

"I'm so glad she did," Kaylie said. "And I think it should definitely be in the fairy tale because it's about giving thanks and giving back, and that's so important at Christmas."

The prince nodded. "I couldn't agree more. Thank you."

"Thank you and your family for including me, and for my dresses."

"You look beautiful," the prince said before he took a sip of champagne.

"The dress is pretty incredible…"

"I wasn't talking about the dress," the prince said, looking into her eyes.

Kaylie blushed as she felt her pulse quicken. "I don't know how your mother did it, everything she's gotten me, or how she does all this, all these amazing Christmas events. She definitely knows how to make things happen. She's a force to be reckoned with, in a good way."

The prince laughed. "That's a very good description. So how would you describe me?"

The words that instantly came to Kaylie's mind were, *smart, kind, caring, reliable, loyal, and gorgeous*, but she was saved from having to say anything when a group of teachers came up to talk to the prince. "I'll talk to you later," she said as she slipped away.

By the time the tea was over, she felt like she'd talked to almost everyone in the room. They had all been very curious about the royal family's American guest and she'd made sure not to mention she was a reporter.

After the queen said goodbye to their last guests, and it was just the four of them in the drawing room, Chef Jake and Elsa appeared with champagne, and sparkling water for the princess.

"Congratulations," Chef Jake said, giving them all a glass. "From what I saw, the Christmas tea once again looked like a huge success."

"Thanks to your delicious menu, Jake," the queen said. "And for all your impeccable planning, Elsa. Thank you both so much. You always make this family so proud."

The prince held up his glass. "I'll cheers to that, and to you, Mother, for all your hard work for making this happen." He turned to Anna. "And to my beautiful daughter who was a wonderful host talking with everyone. I was very proud of you today."

The princess's face lit up with joy. "Thank you, Father. You did a very good job, too, with your speech."

The queen nodded her approval. "And to Kaylie for helping us with all the last-minute details."

Kaylie was surprised by the compliment. "I didn't really do anything…"

The queen gave her a look. "You've done more than you know by just being here and helping us celebrate a very special Christmas when I have both my son and granddaughter home with me again."

"I'll drink to that," the prince said and they all toasted and drank.

As Kaylie sipped her champagne, she caught the prince smiling at her and she couldn't remember a moment where she'd felt happier. She lifted her glass again. "And to all of you and how much you care about the people of Tolvania and each other. You are an inspiration."

"To the Christmas tea," the prince said, leaning down to clink his glass with the princess.

"To the Christmas tea," the princess echoed her father before drinking her sparkling water. "Now, do we get to go change into our Christmas Crown dresses?" the princess asked, excited. "I love my next dress."

The queen nodded. "Yes, but we don't have a lot of time."

The prince took the princess's hand. "Come with me, my beautiful girl, I'll take you back to Ms. Meyers who has your next dress all ready." The prince turned and smiled at his mother and Kaylie. "I'll see you both soon."

Chapter 31

Back upstairs in her room, Kaylie stared at herself in the mirror and barely recognized the woman staring back at her. She was wearing the stunning, shimmering gold dress and her cheeks were flushed and her eyes were sparkling. She felt beautiful, and it wasn't just the dress. She genuinely felt like, for the first time in a long time, she had found her Christmas spirit again and she was filled with a sense of joy and gratitude.

She took a deep breath and refused to let herself think about how her stay at the castle was quickly coming to an end. "Tonight, I'm going to live in the moment and enjoy every second."

She left her room smiling and that smile only grew when she found the prince waiting for her at the bottom of the stairs. He had also changed and she thought he was now even more handsome, if that was possible, wearing a black tux.

As her heart raced, her legs suddenly felt like jelly as he gazed up at her. Her hand shook as she reached out to hold onto the banister as she carefully navigated the stairs wearing her new high heels that had come with the dress.

It was the way the prince was looking at her that made her stomach do somersaults. He held out his hand to help her down the last stair.

When Kaylie put her hand in his, the spark she felt went from her head to her toes. She quickly told herself to get a grip. "Well, this is quite the service," Kaylie said with a nervous laugh, trying to get her mind off how gorgeous he looked.

"My mother wanted me to escort you into the Grand Hall," the prince said with a sexy smile that made Kaylie forget everything else. "And may I say, you look stunning."

Kaylie blushed. "Thank you. So do you. I mean, you look very handsome."

Blixen ran up to them and barked, interrupting the moment. Kaylie laughed when she saw he was also dressed for the occasion, wearing a red satin Christmas bowtie with gold sequins.

"And don't you look handsome," Kaylie said, leaning down to pet Blixen.

"It looks like I have some competition," the prince said.

Kaylie laughed. "You sure do, because this guy is wearing gold sequins. He's bringing the sparkle."

The prince laughed. "He sure is." When he held out his arm for Kaylie, she didn't hesitate before taking it.

"Shall we?" the prince asked.

Kaylie looked into his eyes and for a moment got lost. "Yes," she finally said breathlessly. "I'm ready."

After walking a few steps, Kaylie turned to the prince. "Your mother didn't have the chance to tell me much about the Christmas Crown, just that your ancestor Henry made it to propose to his girlfriend Mary. Your daughter, the princess, says it's magical." Kaylie laughed.

The prince nodded. "The people in the village have always believed it's magical, and that's why they come to make their wish."

"Their wish?" Kaylie asked, confused. "What wish?"

"A Christmas wish for love," the prince said, as if it was the most normal thing in the world. "Things were complicated for Henry because he was royal and Mary was a commoner, and Henry's parents didn't approve of the marriage."

"Oh boy," Kaylie said. "That's not good. I feel like this story is as old as time."

"Unfortunately, yes," the prince said. "Mary loved Christmas, so Henry had the Christmas Crown made using priceless rubies that his uncle gave him as a gift. He wanted to help support Henry's dream of marrying for love. When another uncle heard what Henry was doing, he gave Henry some diamonds for the crown. It turns out both uncles had great loves in their lives they hadn't been able to marry because of family pressure to marry someone suitable. They had always regretted this and didn't want to see the same thing happen to Henry. They wanted him to be free to marry whomever he wanted."

"So, the family came together to help Henry," Kaylie said, loving this story. "Everyone but his parents. They couldn't have been happy about this."

"Not at first," the prince said. "But, with the encouragement of the rest of the family and as the story goes, with the magic of Christmas, they came around and gave Henry their blessing. Henry asked Mary to marry him on Christmas Eve."

"I love this story. I'm totally using the Christmas Crown in the fairy tale," Kaylie said, excited.

The prince nodded his approval. "I think my daughter would love that. Everyone in Tolvania believes the Christmas Crown is a symbol of love and hope. It's also a reminder how anything is possible at Christmas if you believe. So now every year people come here to see the Christmas Crown, on the same day that Henry's parents gave him their blessing, and they make their own wish for love."

"And you believe in all of this? All of this…magic?" Kaylie asked.

The prince looked into her eyes. "I believe in love."

Kaylie's steps faltered. "Sorry, it's these high heels." She wasn't about to tell him his words had gone straight to her heart.

"Just hold on to me and I'll make sure you get there in one piece," the prince said making Kaylie's heart beat even faster.

She gave him a grateful smile. "Thank you."

When they arrived at the Grand Hall, Kaylie's eyes were immediately drawn to the end of the hall where there was a four-foot-tall glass case that was surrounded by a red velvet security rope and lit up with lights.

Mesmerized, Kaylie couldn't take her eyes off the case as she walked toward it. As she got closer and the Christmas Crown came into view, her breath caught in her throat. "Wow," she whispered, in awe, barely believing what she was seeing.

Inside the glass case was a spectacular, sparkling crown that had large teardrop rubies surrounded by hundreds of glistening diamonds.

"It's incredible," Kaylie said, still staring at the crown, knowing "incredible" didn't even begin to describe it.

"It is very special to us and everyone in Tolvania," the prince said with pride. "You will have to make a wish."

"I have to wish for something?" Kaylie asked, looking up at him.

"A Christmas wish for love," the prince answered. "That's the tradition."

Kaylie was thankful she was saved from responding when the princess ran up to them. The queen also joined them.

"Do you like our dresses?" the princess asked, modeling her dress next to her grandmother. The princess and queen had similar versions of the same dress. Both were a luxurious red satin, the same color as the ruby red gemstones in the crown. Where the queen's dress was sleek and chic, the princess had a petticoat under hers that fluffed it up and made it look more age-appropriate. There was also a pretty black velvet belt and a bow that was tied in the back.

They were wearing matching tiaras again. This time, their tiaras had rubies and diamonds that danced in the light, paying perfect homage to the Christmas Crown.

"You both look fabulous," Kaylie said, smiling at the princess and queen.

"Thank you," the queen and princess said at the exact same time.

"So, what do you think of our Christmas Crown?" the queen asked Kaylie.

"It's spectacular, amazing. I really can't find the right words to describe it. It's just…"

"Magical?" the princess offered.

Kaylie smiled at the princess. "Yes, that does describe it very well. Magical is the perfect word."

The queen walked over to a small table that was next to the crown, where a festive wooden antique chest was displayed. It was a deep, rich maroon color and had dozens of tiny gold stars painted on it. She picked up a little gold basket that was filled with tiny white scrolls, tied with gold ribbon.

"When each person enters the castle through a special door that's attached directly to the Grand Hall, they're given one of these. A little scroll that has a red pencil inside, so they can write down their Christmas wish and leave that wish here in our Christmas Wish chest." She pointed at a small opening at the top of the chest. "They can keep the pencil as a souvenir if they like. It has the family crest on it."

"Does the crest and the two swans have a special meaning?" Kaylie asked.

The queen nodded. "Our crest, with the two swans forming a heart, is our family's symbol representing love, the love we have for each other, and for our community, a love we hope will always be honored for generations to come."

The prince put his arm around his mother. "It will be because you do so much to make sure our traditions will live on forever. Like bringing Kaylie here."

Kaylie was touched by the prince's words.

The prince knelt down so he was eye to eye with the princess. "Are we ready to open the door and invite people in?"

The princess looked down at Blixen, who was faithfully sitting by her side. "We are, Father, we're ready, aren't we, Blixen?"

They all laughed when Blixen barked his approval.

"Then let's open the doors," the queen said as she picked up the gold basket of scrolls and handed it to the princess, and then started walking toward the door. The princess and Blixen happily followed her.

But when Kaylie glanced back at the Christmas Crown, she felt like it was drawing her in and she stepped closer to get one more look.

The prince joined her. "You look like you're a million miles away," he said. "New York City, maybe?"

Kaylie shook her head, walking around the glass case, admiring the crown from different angles. "No, actually, I was thinking about your family and Tolvania and how special it is here. Like this tradition with the Christmas Crown—how you open the castle up to everyone to come and see this historic piece of your history and heritage. But not only do you make it available for people to see, you also encourage them all to make a wish, sharing your family tradition with everyone."

"The Christmas Crown is priceless," the prince agreed. "But we've always believed, like our ancestors, that it was meant to be shared with as many people as possible. Yes, we are the royal family and therefore we own the crown, but the people of Tolvania are the jewels in the crown. They are what makes us shine."

Kaylie was moved by his words. "Are you sure you aren't the writer? That's really beautiful. I think I'm going to use it in the fairy tale."

"By all means, use whatever you like," the prince said. "I'm going to go join my family."

"I'll be there in just a moment," Kaylie said.

They shared a smile.

As the family took their position by the door to greet everyone, Kaylie snapped a few quick pictures of the Christmas Crown, capturing how it sparkled in the light, and quickly sent them to Rachel.

Rachel immediately texted her back. *Love this! It's perfect!*

Kaylie took a selfie with the crown in the background and sent it, too, along with a text that said, *Living the Royal Life!*

She was about to take another picture when she saw the door open, and people start to enter. She quickly backed away from the crown as the crowd eagerly walked toward the glass case.

She was impressed by how orderly and respectful everyone was, and how they all lined up to put their wish in the Christmas Crown wish box. It was clear that everyone took this tradition very seriously and seemed genuinely excited and hopeful about making their own wish for Christmas love.

The event ran almost one hour over the scheduled time, but the queen insisted on keeping the doors open until everyone who had come had a chance to see the crown. It was just one more thing Kaylie decided that she liked about the queen: her sense of compassion and empathy for other people.

When everyone was finally gone and it was just the family left, Kaylie watched, fascinated, as the queen, prince, and princess all stood around the crown and wrote out Christmas wishes of their own. After the princess put her wish into the Christmas Wish chest, she walked over to Kaylie and held the gold basket up to her.

"You still need to make your wish," the princess said as she picked up a little scroll and gave it to Kaylie.

"That's okay. I don't have a wish," Kaylie said as she dropped her scroll back into the princess's basket. When she saw the princess looked disappointed, she rushed to continue. "But maybe later." She was relieved when she saw the princess smile in return.

"So, what did you think of our Christmas Crown event?" the queen asked Kaylie.

Kaylie shook her head in amazement. "It was really something seeing all the people who came here and how much they love this crown. I talked to so many people who told me they come every year as their Christmas Eve tradition. Everyone had stories to tell about how the Christmas Crown has brought them, or someone in their family, luck in finding true love."

The queen's smile was nostalgic. "It is, by far, our most beloved Christmas tradition."

"And now I can see why," Kaylie said. "Thank you for including me. This was really special."

"We are glad you enjoyed it," the queen said. "Although, I'm afraid we are now running late. I'm having Chef Jake prepare something so we can have a quick meal in our rooms while we get ready for the ball. I hope that's all right?" the queen asked, looking at Kaylie.

"That sounds great to me," Kaylie said as they all started walking toward the door.

The prince took the princess's hand. "Okay, Anna, let's get you upstairs or I'll be in trouble with Ms. Meyers because you won't have enough time to have dinner and change." He turned back to Kaylie. "We will see you soon."

Kaylie kneeled down so she was eye to eye with the princess. "I can't wait to see your dress for the ball."

The princess's eyes lit up. "It's my favorite one so far."

"Then I bet it's beautiful, just like you," Kaylie said, touching the tip of the princess's nose.

The princess giggled and then spontaneously gave Kaylie a heartfelt hug. "I'm glad you stayed."

Kaylie felt her heart melt as she hugged the princess back. She looked up at the prince and smiled. "So am I."

Chapter 32

Back in her room, Kaylie felt like it was a Christmas Groundhog Day, in the best way possible, as she changed into her third dress, the stunning ball gown. It was the most exquisite piece of clothing she'd ever had the privilege to wear. The white strapless ball gown, with its shimmering gold embroidered beading and fitted bodice and waistline that lead to a full dreamy skirt, fit like it was made for her. As she did a slow turn in front of the mirror, she knew she'd completely gone down the Christmas Rabbit Hole and she was loving every minute of it.

She was surprised when she heard a knock on her bedroom door, and was even more surprised to find the queen on the other side of it. Kaylie stood back, in awe of the queen's own magnificent gown. It was a classic A-line emerald green sequin ball gown that somehow managed to look both chic and festive at the same time. The next thing that caught Kaylie's attention was that, for the first time, the queen was wearing a crown, not just a tiara, and the extraordinary diamond and emerald crown sparkled regally.

Kaylie felt like she needed to curtsy or bow or do something royal, but instead, just opened her door wide. "Please, come in. You look amazing. I don't even have the words, and that's saying something for me."

The queen laughed. "That is, and thank you. You look stunning as well. I knew that dress would suit you perfectly."

Kaylie, giddy, did a little twirl. "I feel like a princess..." She froze, embarrassed. "Sorry, wrong word. I keep forgetting where I am and who I'm with."

The queen took her hand and gave it a reassuring squeeze. "It's fine. You would make a wonderful princess."

Kaylie felt her face flush with even more embarrassment. "I don't think so. I'm just a girl from New York City."

The queen looked into her eyes. "It's not where you're from that matters, it's what's in here." She tapped Kaylie's heart. "I wanted to talk to you before the ball and thank you again for being here and all that you are doing to help make my grand-daughter's Christmas so special."

"The fairy tale is coming along great," Kaylie said. "I'll have it to you in the morning to look over in case you want to make any changes before giving it to the princess at the Christmas dinner..."

"I'm not just talking about the fairy tale," the queen said. "I'm talking about the time you've spent with her and my son. You've helped my son remember how special Christmas can be. I haven't seen him this happy in a long time."

"I don't think I had anything to do with that," Kaylie said quickly.

The queen looked into her eyes. "You've had everything to do with it."

Kaylie's heart beat faster. She fought to find the right words to say because the last thing she wanted was for the queen to figure out the truth, that she was falling for the prince. As much as she'd tried not to, and fought her feelings, in the end, as much as she hated to admit it, her heart had won out. Now she knew the only thing she could do was to try and make sure no one found out so she didn't embarrass herself or anyone else.

"My son has feelings for you, and I think you feel the same about him," the queen said. It was a statement, not a question.

"I think you're mistaken on both counts," Kaylie said adamantly, starting to panic. "We are two different people from two different worlds, and I'm about to go back to mine in New York. There is nothing between us at all. I have my career and life back in New York and that's all. I'm focusing on right now and the prince...well, he's a prince, enough said." Kaylie inhaled to catch her breath since she'd been talking a mile a minute. She squirmed under the queen's eagle eye.

"My mistake," the queen said. "I'm sorry."

Now Kaylie felt even worse. She hated lying to the queen and to herself. "There's nothing to be sorry about," she rushed to continue. "I'm very thankful for the time I've had here. You, your son, and granddaughter have helped me remember how much I love Christmas and spending time with my family. And now because of that, we're going to all start celebrating Christmas again. That's the best gift anyone could ever give me. So, truly, thank you, for everything."

"You're welcome," the queen said. Her expression was impossible to read. "We should be going. The guests will start arriving in the next half-hour." The queen held out her hand. "Are you ready for one more of our Christmas traditions?"

Kaylie happily took her hand. "I'm ready."

A few minutes later when they entered the ballroom, Kaylie's eyes immediately were drawn to the incredible upside-down Christmas tree that she'd gotten with the prince and princess. It looked magical dangling from the center of the ceiling, surrounded by a canopy of white twinkle lights. On the tree, the red glass heart ornaments caught the light and shimmered. Adding to the festive ambiance was an orchestra playing a classical arrangement of the Christmas song, "It's the Most Wonderful Time of the Year."

Kaylie was happily humming the song when she saw the prince and princess enter from the other side of the ballroom. She couldn't take her eyes off the prince, who looked gorgeous in his royal uniform with all his gold medals. When she saw the queen watching her, she quickly turned her focus to the princess, who was wearing an adorable emerald green ball gown that was similar to her grandmother's, and a miniature version of the same crown as well.

Kaylie smiled when she saw the princess, head held high, regally walk over and join her grandmother, and then smile at Kaylie.

"Father, doesn't Kaylie look pretty? I helped pick out the dress."

"She looks perfect," the prince said, looking into Kaylie's eyes.

Kaylie felt her whole body tingle from his compliment. Embarrassed, knowing she was blushing, she quickly looked at the princess. "I would say you're the belle of the ball, princess. You look so grown up and your crown, wow, it's amazing."

The princess grinned from ear to ear. "Thank you. Have you ever worn a crown?"

Kaylie laughed. "No, never."

The princess, excited, took off her crown, ignoring the bobby pins that were sent flying everywhere, and handed the crown to Kaylie. "You can try mine on if you want."

Kaylie was touched as she carefully took the crown and admired it. "Wow, it's heavy."

"It's a solid gold frame with four hundred and twenty diamonds, three hundred and ten pearls, and one hundred emeralds," the queen offered.

Kaylie's eyes grew huge realizing she was probably holding something that was worth more than her parent's house. She quickly handed it back to the princess. "I think you'd better take this. I don't want to hurt it."

The princess grinned back at her. "You can try it on later, if you'd like, and I have other crowns you can pick from, and lots of tiaras that aren't as heavy, and…"

The queen interrupted, taking the crown from the princess. "And now we need to get this crown back on you—our guests are about to arrive."

The prince was already retrieving the bobby pins. He handed them to the queen.

The queen took the princess's hand. "We'll be right back."

Kaylie smiled, watching them go. "Your daughter has such a kind heart," she told the prince. "She gave me her crown to try on and I also saw her at the Christmas tea letting people try on her tiara."

"She is very generous," the prince agreed. "Just like her mother. She has a way to connect with people that I envy. I wish Sophia were here to see how Anna is growing up."

"I believe Sophia is watching over Anna and you," Kaylie said. "She lives in your heart, so she is with you always and I'm sure she'd be very proud of you both."

The prince looked moved. "Thank you for saying that. Every day I try and think about what Sophia would do. Still, I never feel like I'm doing enough."

"I think you're doing a wonderful job," Kaylie said. "The fact that you think you're not doing enough and always want to do more proves that. Anna is lucky to have you."

"We're lucky to have each other," the prince said, taking a deep breath. "I thought this Christmas was going to be rough, being back here for the first time since we lost Sophia. But you're right. Being surrounded by so many memories has brought a sense of comfort. It has reminded me that we must go on and it's okay to be happy. It's what Sophia wanted."

When the orchestra started playing a new song, it was "The Christmas Waltz." Kaylie smiled and sighed wistfully.

"They're playing your song," the prince said.

"How do you…" Kaylie started.

"You told me the other day," the prince said. "You said it was your father's favorite."

Kaylie nodded. "It is. We used to dance to it when I was little."

The prince held out his hand. "Then let's dance."

"Oh, no," Kaylie said, shaking her head. "It's been years…"

"All the more reason," the prince said, taking her hand. "Besides, it's one of our Christmas traditions, dancing with a prince."

Kaylie's eyes widened as she let the prince lead her out to the dance floor. "Really?"

The prince laughed as they started to dance, and he pulled her closer. "No, but it should be."

Kaylie laughed and felt her body relax as she let the rhythm of the music take over and trusted the prince to lead her as they twirled around the dance floor. They were laughing and enjoying themselves when the prince started singing softly in a rich baritone voice.

> *It's that time of year*
> *When the world falls in love*
> *Every song you hear seems to say*
> *Merry Christmas*
> *May your New Year dreams come true...*

When Kaylie looked into the prince's eyes, she didn't know about the world falling in love, like in the lyrics of the song, but she knew she was falling in love. The way the prince was looking at her gave her hope that maybe the queen was right, maybe he was starting to feel the same way.

When the orchestra finished the song, the prince pulled her even closer. She held her breath knowing he was about to kiss her. She knew the kiss would change everything, but for the first time, she didn't care. She didn't think about all the ways their relationship couldn't work. All she thought about was how she wanted that kiss more than anything she'd ever wanted before. Just as his lips were about to touch hers, they heard Anna and the queen come back into the ballroom.

They both pulled apart quickly, but when Kaylie saw the queen's knowing smile, she realized not quick enough.

All of a sudden, the lights in the ballroom dimmed.

The princess, smiling, ran over and took her father's hand.

"It's time," the queen said.

When Kaylie looked at the prince and they shared a smile, her heart skipped a beat.

An hour later, the party was in full swing. The ballroom was filled with dazzling guests who were dancing, drinking, talking, and laughing.

Sipping champagne, Kaylie was enjoying watching the prince dance with his daughter until, at the end of the dance, she saw the beautiful woman from the village jewelry store, Madeline, walk up to them and give them both a warm hug and kiss on the cheek.

Kaylie's smile faded when she saw something sparkle on Madeline's wrist and recognized the diamond tennis bracelet the prince had bought at the jewelry store as a Christmas present.

"What…no," Kaylie said, her heart breaking.

Chef Jake and Elsa, who were putting out new appetizers, overheard her. "What's wrong?" Elsa asked.

As a wave of jealousy hit her, Kaylie could only motion toward the prince.

"Ah, Madeline. She and the prince go way back," Chef Jake said.

"How far back?" Kaylie asked, watching the prince put his arm around Madeline. "They look very…close."

"They were high school sweethearts before the prince went off to college and met Sophia," Elsa answered.

Kaylie felt sick to her stomach. From what she could see, Madeline was doing her very best to rekindle the relationship, and the prince didn't seem to be minding one bit. He was laughing and looked like he was having a great time. Kaylie couldn't take her eyes off Madeline's sparkling diamond bracelet. As it caught the light and sparkled, she felt like it was mocking her.

Kaylie was so angry with herself. She couldn't believe she had been so blind to think the prince might have real feelings for her. He'd just bought another woman, this Madeline, a diamond bracelet for Christmas. Obviously, there was something between them. Now, she sadly realized, the prince was probably just being nice to her to keep an eye on her. The whole 'keep your friends close and your enemies closer' thing because from the start he'd told her he didn't trust reporters. When she saw the queen walk over and also hug Madeline, it was another knife in her heart. She felt sick. She needed to get some air.

She wasn't sure how she ended up back in the Grand Hall. She'd left the ballroom, upset, and had just started walking. When she arrived, she saw Thomas standing by the Christmas Crown, getting ready to move it. He looked surprised to see her as she walked toward him. "If you're looking for the ballroom, it's two corridors down," he offered.

"I know. I was there," Kaylie said with a sigh. "I needed a break. What are you doing?"

"Moving the Christmas Crown back to the vault," Thomas said. "It's the safest time to do it, when everyone's at the ball."

Kaylie watched as Thomas carefully lifted off the top of the glass case that was protecting the crown. She found herself holding her breath as he leaned in and carefully picked up the Christmas Crown. As he was in the process of carefully transferring it to a black velvet-lined box, the crown slipped out of his fingers and started to fall.

"No!" Thomas and Kaylie cried out at the same time.

Kaylie lunged forward and caught the crown just before it hit the ground, but when she grabbed it, one of the giant tear-shaped rubies popped out and fell to the floor.

"Oh, my God," Kaylie exclaimed.

Thomas grabbed the ruby. "I got it."

That's when Kaylie noticed how light the Christmas Crown was. It didn't make any sense. It was gold, just like the princess's crown, and it was twice as big, but it didn't weigh anywhere near what the princess's small crown had weighed. When she saw there was glue where the ruby had fallen out, her eyes widened.

"Can I see that?" she asked Thomas, pointing at the ruby he was holding. Before he could answer, she took the ruby out of his hand. She felt its weight. She held it up to the light. Her jaw dropped to the floor. She looked at Thomas, shocked. "This isn't a ruby. This is just…glass."

"What are you doing?!" the prince demanded, arriving in the hall. He marched toward her, like a soldier going to war.

She waved the crown at him. "This Christmas Crown isn't real. It's a fake!"

Chapter 33

Prince Alexander, upset, grabbed the crown and ruby out of Kaylie's hand.

"You don't know what you're talking about," the prince insisted.

Kaylie, dumbfounded, stared back at the prince. "I don't know what I'm talking about? Me? Seriously? You remember what I do for a living, right? I'm an investigative reporter. I make a living going after people who are frauds and try and rip other people off with counterfeit goods, like the Santas in New York I told you about. I know a fake when I see one, and that crown is a fake. You don't use glue on gemstones like rubies and diamonds. They're too smooth and polished for glue to work, because glue needs some little rough spots to hold on to, and anyone who felt how much this weighed would know it isn't real."

"And that's why no one is supposed to touch it, outside of Thomas and myself and my mother," the prince fired back at her. He handed Thomas the crown. "Thomas, please put this away quickly. I don't want anyone else walking in here and seeing it like this."

Kaylie's eyes grew huge. "So, you admit it?! It *is* a fake?!"

"Please, lower your voice," the prince demanded. "Do you want everyone to hear you?"

"Do you mean everyone that you've been lying to about this crown for who knows how long?" Kaylie asked, getting more upset by the second. "I can't believe this. You and your family tell me this whole story about how much this Christmas Crown means to the people of Tolvania, and how for centuries it has been part of your Christmas traditions, and how the priceless jewels, the special rubies and diamonds, that were used to make the crown, were to celebrate the belief and power of true love. You even have people believing this crown is magic, and making their own wishes for Christmas love when none of this is true…" Kaylie shook her head in disbelief as she watched Thomas put the crown in the black velvet box and hurry away. She had even started believing in the Christmas Crown, and how love could conquer all.

"I can explain," the prince said.

Kaylie crossed her arms. "I'm listening. Please tell me the real crown is safely stored somewhere because it's too valuable to display, so you use a fake one for this event to symbolize the real crown, and that everyone knows this?"

The prince took a deep breath. "No."

Kaylie's eyebrows arched. "No, as in the people don't know you're using a fake while the other one is stored away?"

"We're not hiding the real crown," the prince finally said. "We use this replica because we don't have the real crown."

"Then where is it?" Kaylie demanded. "Where is the real Christmas Crown, or is the entire story made up?"

"No, the story is true," the prince said. He looked over his shoulder again to make sure they were alone and walked closer to her. He lowered his voice until she could barely hear him.

"The real Christmas Crown was stolen about a hundred and twenty years ago."

"What?!" Kaylie exclaimed. "It was stolen?!"

"Shhh, please." The prince took her arm. "Not so loud. I can't have anyone overhearing and knowing this. Come with me." Still holding Kaylie's arm, the prince started walking.

Twenty minutes later, alone in the drawing room, Kaylie didn't know what she was more shocked to learn: that the Christmas Crown had been stolen one Christmas Eve during the Christmas Ball and had never been recovered, or that the royal family had hidden this secret from everyone in Tolvania for more than a hundred years.

"How did you ever keep something like this a secret?" Kaylie asked, still trying to wrap her head around the story. "Surely, when police started looking for it, the word got out?"

"And that's why we never had anyone look for it," the prince replied.

"What?!" Kaylie asked. "You never looked for it? This priceless family heirloom?"

The prince inhaled a deep breath before continuing. "Our royal family, going back generations, has always only allowed its head of security to move the crown. When it was stolen, there was only one security person who knew about it outside of the family. While it was unimaginably devastating, the family knew what a scandal it would be and how much it would upset the people of Tolvania if they found out the Christmas Crown was gone. The other grave concern was the safety of the royal family. If the word got out that the family's security had been breached, it would put everyone at risk. So, the family decided it would be safest and best for everyone to never tell anyone what happened."

"And the security guard never told anyone?" Kaylie asked, sounding skeptical.

"That security guard was Thomas's great-great-grandfather, and his family has continued to be head of our security all the way up to today, so our secret has stayed safe, until now."

Kaylie gave the prince a stunned look and laughed. "And now you expect me to keep your secret, too? This is insane, and it's not right," Kaylie said with conviction. "You are lying to everyone in Tolvania, to everyone anywhere who knows about the Christmas Crown. I understand a hundred years ago not telling anyone for security concerns, but after the family was safe, why weren't people told the truth, explaining what you just explained to me?"

The prince shook his head. "That can never be done. People would lose faith in us. If they thought we didn't tell them the truth about the Christmas Crown, they'd think we were hiding other things from them."

"Are you hiding more things?" Kaylie asked.

"You don't understand…" the prince started.

Kaylie shook her head. "No, you're right, I don't. I've made my living fighting for the truth, and this lie you're telling seems pretty self-serving to me. I think people deserve to know the truth. They shouldn't be coming here every Christmas thinking they're seeing something special. They're making silly Christmas love wishes when it's all a big fat lie. It would be like the Mona Lisa not being real, and all the people who have traveled from all over the world to come and see it don't know. It's just not right. People need to be told the truth…"

The prince's eyes darkened. "What are you saying? That *you're* going to tell them? I can't let that happen."

Kaylie bristled. This wasn't the first time someone had threatened her when she was about to expose them, and it instantly triggered her reporter instincts to try and protect herself. She glared at the prince. "What are you going to do? Lock me in your dungeon? You said you really had one, or was that just a lie, too?" She was about to say more when the prince's cell phone started sounding off with a string of texts.

Annoyed, the prince glanced at his phone and Kaylie saw his expression change from shock to fury, and then she heard Christmas carolers coming from his phone that sounded familiar. She stepped closer to see what was upsetting the prince so much and she froze when she saw he was watching the video she'd taken at the tree lighting ceremony of the Christmas carolers and the crowd singing along. Only the video clip he was watching was the one that she'd taken that included the prince, the queen, and the princess, with their backs to the camera, singing along with the carolers, arm in arm.

"No!" she gasped, her heart stopping. She couldn't breathe. "No! No! No! This can't be happening. I never meant for anyone to see that video…"

The prince, shocked, turned his anger on her. "You did this?! This is your video? My daughter is in this video, and my mother. What have you done? This has gone viral. It's everywhere!"

Kaylie, horrified, rushed to try and explain. "No one was supposed to see that video except me. I swear. I didn't mean to send it. It must have gotten sent with the others by accident…"

"There are others?!" the prince fumed.

"Just some of the village, for my story. That's all," Kaylie answered.

"Your story?!" the prince asked, looking like his head was going to explode. "I knew it! I knew you were here to get some undercover story…"

"No, wait," Kaylie jumped in, trying to explain. "It's not a story about you or the family, it's just about Tolvania and the Christmas traditions. That's it. It's just a feature on the village. I would never write a story about your family after what you told me…"

"Just like you'd never take a video of us and post it around the world," the prince said with a scornful laugh that cut to Kaylie's core. "How do you expect me to believe anything you say? I can't believe I trusted you when I knew better, and now, I've put my family at risk…"

Kaylie fought to find the right words to say to try and make it better. "That video only shows the back of you. No one will know…"

The prince held up his phone that had dozens of texts. "Everyone knows, including all the other media outlets that are running the story."

Thomas entered, looking as upset as the prince. "You saw the video, Prince Alexander?"

The prince's jaw clenched. "Yes, Thomas, I did. Please escort Miss Karlyle to her room and have her pack her things immediately. Stay with her. Don't leave her alone for a moment and get her out of here as fast as you can."

Kaylie, upset and filled with guilt, touched the prince's arm. She had to try and make him understand. "I am so sorry. This was an accident. I swear. I can fix this. I can call right now and have them take the video down immediately…"

When the prince jerked away from her touch, she flinched.

"The only thing I want you to do is leave, immediately," the prince said. "Before I have you arrested and don't think I won't do it."

When the prince locked eyes with her, she saw he was deadly serious. She felt a chill down her spine. "I'm so sorry…" she whispered.

The prince didn't wait for her to finish before he strode over to Thomas. "Don't let her out of your sight." A second later, the prince was gone.

Kaylie's eyes filled up with tears. "I swear, Thomas, this was an accident…"

"We'd better hurry, before the prince changes his mind," was all Thomas said.

Chapter 34

Back in her room, knowing Thomas was waiting for her in the hallway, Kaylie rushed to change out of her ball gown and put on the clothes she'd originally arrived in. She packed in record time, wanting to get out of the castle just as much as the prince wanted her gone.

After the initial shock and numbness had worn off, she knew the prince wasn't bluffing about calling the police. Her heart was broken. First, it turned out the prince had a girlfriend, and now she'd found out that he and the entire royal family were living a lie.

She'd called Rachel and told her to tell Gerry the video needed to be taken down immediately. She also told her to hold off on running the feature she'd turned in earlier because she'd just learned something new that could potentially make her story huge and be something exclusive.

When Rachel had pushed to find out more, Kaylie hadn't wanted to say anything yet, because she was still deciding what to do. She didn't know if she should tell the truth about the Christmas Crown being stolen, or let the feature run, as she'd already turned it in.

Her entire career was based around reporting the truth not ignoring important facts. She also knew if she told the real

Christmas Crown story it was the kind of juicy exclusive that Gerry would love, giving her a real shot at her dream job.

Rachel had told her she had until midnight to decide because the story, whichever one she decided to do, needed to go live on Christmas morning.

She felt terrible that she hadn't had a chance to finish the Christmas fairy tale for the princess but in reality, knew the last thing the prince would want now is anything from her.

Thomas knocked on her door. "Are you ready?"

"Coming," she called back to him as she quickly hung her ballgown up next to the other dresses she was leaving behind, along with everything else the queen had given her. She was heading for the door when she stopped at her dresser and picked up the painting of the Christmas tree she had painted with the princess. It was one memory she wasn't willing to leave behind.

The ball was still going on as she left the castle with Thomas having no idea where he was taking her. She was relieved and embarrassed when he'd pulled up to his own quaint home in Tolvania and said he and his wife were going to take her in for the night.

When she'd tried to insist that she didn't want to impose, especially on Christmas Eve, he'd insisted it was fine and had also added it was their only choice since the few small bed and breakfasts and tiny inns in Tolvania were already booked through Christmas.

After introducing her to his lovely wife, Susan, who welcomed her warmly despite the circumstances, Thomas had excused himself to return to the castle. He was still on duty.

"So, what happens next?" Kaylie asked him. She was almost afraid to hear the answer.

"The prince has arranged for you to fly out of Tolvania first thing in the morning."

Kaylie nodded. She didn't know why it hurt so much. She shouldn't be surprised. She knew she should be relieved that she was finally going back to New York City.

Thomas checked a text that came in on his phone. He took a deep breath before turning to Kaylie. "Miss Karlyle, I'll need to take your phone."

Kaylie's eyes grew huge and she took a step back. "What? No…"

Thomas held up his phone. "I'm afraid I don't have a choice. It comes from my boss."

Kaylie ricocheted from shock to anger. "The prince told you to take my phone? He can't have my phone. Everything is in my phone."

"I think that's the point," Thomas said. "And while you're here in Tolvania, I'm afraid what he says goes. Your phone, please."

"I have a password," Kaylie said. "He's not going to be able to get into it and see anything…"

"I don't believe he cares about seeing anything," Thomas said.

"He just doesn't want me to have it," Kaylie said, exasperated. "What does he think I'm going to do?" Kaylie held up her hand. "Don't even answer that." She reluctantly gave Thomas her phone. "This isn't a fairy tale. This is a nightmare."

An hour later, sitting on the bed in Thomas's guest room, Kaylie was still upset. She had her computer on her lap when she called Rachel and was relieved when she picked up right away.

"Well?" Rachel asked when she came up on the screen. "Are we just using the story about Tolvania's Christmas traditions that you sent me this morning, or do you have something else?"

Kaylie sat up straighter. "I just wrote you a new story. I'm sending it now and I want you to use this one instead."

"So, you have an update on the Christmas Crown?" Rachel said, excited. "I can't wait to hear it."

"I do have an update." She took a deep breath and then looked determined as she pushed the send button on her email. "I want to make sure you get this. Tell me when it comes in."

Rachel stared at her screen for several moments, then a smile broke out. "Just got it." Her eyes widened when she read the title. "A Royal Family's Christmas Crown Secret."

Kaylie nodded. "That's it."

"Oh, this sounds juicy," Rachel said.

Kaylie leaned in closer to the computer. "You have no idea."

It was early Christmas morning and the sun was just coming up as Thomas drove Kaylie into the Tolvania airport and up to the private plane she'd originally flown in on.

She knew she should be relieved to be going home, but her heart hurt from everything that had happened the night before. Normally, when dealing with difficult emotions, she could just go numb and power through her feelings, but this morning none of her usual go-to defense mechanisms were working. She felt exhausted, emotionally and physically. She took a deep breath before reaching for her door handle with a shaky hand.

Thomas turned in his seat to look at her. "If you could please wait. We're not quite ready."

A small, hopeless sigh escaped Kaylie's lips as she sat back in her seat and continued to fight off the tears that had been threatening to fall ever since they'd pulled up to the airport. At this point, she just wanted to go before she broke down in front of Thomas. She wasn't sure how much longer she'd be able to act like she was okay when she most certainly was not.

When she saw Thomas watching her in his rear-view mirror, she offered him a wobbly smile. "Thank you again, Thomas, for letting me stay last night. That was very kind of you and your wife."

"You are welcome," Thomas said. "I'm sorry about the circumstances."

Kaylie nodded. "Me, too. I'm sorry about a lot of things." When she saw the pilot step out of the plane and motion for them to come, her stomach hurt.

When Thomas got out of the car and started walking toward her door, she quickly wiped a tear away and put on a brave face. She wasn't sure who she was trying to fool, herself or Thomas.

"Thank you again," she said before rushing to the plane, trying to escape the icy wind that had her shivering right down to her toes. As she started climbing the stairs to get into the plane, she heard a car drive up and turned around. Her heart raced with hope when she saw it was the same car the prince had been in the first time she'd met him at the airport when she'd accidentally jumped into the car, landing on his lap. She held her breath as she watched Thomas open the car door, but was instantly disappointed and then startled when it wasn't the prince that stepped out, but the queen.

Kaylie gulped. "Oh, boy…" she said under her breath. She slowly descended the plane's stairs and tried to summon her courage as she walked toward the somber queen.

"Good morning," the queen said, breaking the awkward silence.

"Morning," Kaylie said in a voice that cracked with emotion.

The queen reached in her coat pocket and brought out Kaylie's cell phone and handed it to her. "I thought you would want this before you go."

Kaylie, surprised, took the phone. "Thank you very much." Kaylie looked into the queen's eyes. "I just want to say how sorry I am, for everything. I know what the prince believes but I swear to you I never took that video of your family with any plans of it ever being seen by anyone but myself. All I was doing was writing a positive feature story about Christmas in Tolvania that I thought could be good for the village and help bring in more tourism and show how very special it is to everyone. I was never writing a hit piece on your family…"

"I know," the queen said. "I believe you."

Kaylie's eyes grew. "You do?"

"Yes," the queen said. "From what I've seen, you have very strong convictions and you feel it's your duty to report the truth, just like we, as a royal family, feel it's our duty to protect the people of Tolvania and our family. In a sense we are the same, driven by duty and honor, so when you tell me you were never trying to hurt my family, I believe you."

Kaylie dropped her head. "But I did hurt you. That video that was accidentally sent…"

"Was an accident," the queen said. "And I saw your online Christmas Tolvania feature. Your story about the Christmas Crown secret."

When Kaylie lifted her eyes to the queen, she was relieved and thankful when she didn't see judgment, just admiration.

"I thought your story was beautifully written," the queen said. "I will say the headline had me worried for a moment, A Royal Family's Christmas Crown Secret, but you kept our secret and for that, I thank you. I thought it was wonderful how you explained the crown's secret is all about how it symbolizes the magic of Christmas and always believing in true love. The way you shared the stories of people who had found love after seeing the Christmas Crown, I thought it was uplifting and powerful, and above all else I think it will bring people hope. For people who may not have found their great love yet, your story will hopefully encourage them to keep an open heart and believe that love will find them when they're ready."

Kaylie didn't realize she was crying until the queen took off her glove and gently wiped a tear off Kaylie's cheek.

"So, are *you* ready?" the queen asked.

"For?" Kaylie asked, confused.

"To come back home with me because you still owe me a fairy tale for my granddaughter. It's Christmas and that was our agreement, was it not?"

"Yes," Kaylie said nervously. "But I didn't get a chance to finish it…"

The queen looked confident as she linked arms with Kaylie. "You're a storyteller. I'm sure you'll come up with something fast."

Kaylie shook her head, worried. "But the prince, he doesn't want me there. He said…"

The queen interrupted by opening the car door for her. "The prince says a lot of things. You let me worry about him. Please get in. Chef Jake is making our Christmas gingerbread pancakes and we don't want to miss that tradition, do we?"

When Kaylie didn't know what to say, the queen reached out and took her hand and gave it a reassuring squeeze. "And I want to thank you again personally for not reporting the story about our Christmas Crown being stolen. It would have broken so many people's hearts right now. I know as a family it's time we address this, but now you've given us the time to do it properly…"

But Kaylie didn't hear the rest of what the queen was saying because she was too busy staring at the queen's glittering diamond tennis bracelet.

"Your bracelet…" Kaylie said, not realizing she'd said it out loud.

The queen held it up so it caught the light. "It's my Christmas present from my son. He had a jeweler in the village make it special, to be just like the one I've always admired that our family friend, Madeline, had, that her parents gave her."

"I saw him with Madeline in the store. I thought he was buying it for her," Kaylie said.

The queen laughed. "Oh, no, my son isn't interested in Madeline. They've always been great friends. He thinks of her like a sister."

Kaylie shook her head, processing the news. "I really thought they were into each other…"

The queen studied her intently. "And did that bother you?"

"Yes," Kaylie answered honestly.

The queen smiled a knowing smile. "Good. Now, let's go celebrate Christmas."

A few minutes later, as they walked toward the door of the castle, Kaylie could honestly say she had never been more nervous in her life. She understood that the queen had forgiven her for the video and wanted the Christmas fairy tale for the princess, but she didn't think the queen understood exactly how furious the prince had been at her.

Before she could worry anymore, the door was flung open and the princess greeted her with a huge beaming smile. "Merry Christmas, Kaylie!" the princess said and surprised Kaylie when she opened her arms for a big hug.

Kaylie felt a rush of love as she quickly knelt down to hug the princess, and when she felt the princess's little arms hug her tight, her eyes misted up with tears again.

"That was so nice of you to stay with Thomas and his wife and keep them company on Christmas Eve," the princess said.

When Kaylie stood up and gave the queen a confused look, the queen shrugged and whispered so the princess couldn't hear, "You're the storyteller, not me. I did the best I could."

Kaylie couldn't help but laugh and that's when she noticed Blixen was wearing a bright red Christmas sweater that was covered with white snowflakes. He was holding his leash in his mouth. "Well, it looks like someone is getting ready for a walk," Kaylie said, smiling at Blixen.

When Blixen, excited, dropped his leash and barked, they all laughed. Everyone but the prince, who had just come to the door looking stunned, and not in a good way.

"What's going on here?" the prince demanded, locking eyes with Kaylie.

Kaylie shivered when she saw his demeanor toward her hadn't changed one bit. Her eyes flew to the queen for help.

"Anna, would you like to take Kaylie on your quick walk with Blixen before our Christmas pancakes?" the queen asked.

The princess's face lit up with joy. "Yes, Grandmother. I can take Kaylie for a walk, too."

"I don't need to wear a leash, do I?" Kaylie asked with a chuckle. She purposefully avoided looking at the prince.

The princess giggled. "Of course not. Only Blixen needs the leash. Come on. Let's go!" The princess took Blixen's leash and Kaylie's hand and led them both out the door.

As they left, Kaylie looked nervous but the queen just smiled a self-assured smile. "Have fun."

Chapter 35

The prince could barely wait for the princess and Kaylie to walk away before he started in. "Mother, what in the world are you doing, bringing Kaylie back here?!" he demanded. "After what she did to us…"

Seeing Kaylie again had been a shock to his core and his heart. He'd been up all night thinking about her and trying to convince himself he'd done the right thing by sending her away. He'd thought it was the only thing he could do to protect his family. When he'd seen her feature story come up online, and it was a wonderful tribute to Tolvania's Christmas traditions, he'd been temporarily relieved, but was still waiting for the other ball to drop, or for her to report the truth about the stolen Christmas Crown.

The queen crossed her arms. "And what exactly did Kaylie do to us that is so terrible? She made a mistake about the video. She didn't mean to send it. She apologized. She kept our secret. She came here to help write a fairy tale for Anna, to give Anna a special Christmas. We should be thanking her for writing that fantastic story honoring our Tolvania Christmas traditions. Do you know the story has gone viral?"

"Oh, I know," the prince said, upset, raking his fingers through his hair.

"But do you know that I've been flooded with emails all morning from people around the world, everyone from dignitaries and politicians, to other royal families, celebrities, and just regular people who were so inspired and touched by the story that they felt compelled to reach out? I've also been hearing from the press," the queen said.

The prince's eyes flashed with anger. "And that's exactly what we don't want!"

When the queen started walking down the hall, the prince followed her. "Where are you going?"

"To the drawing room, so we can talk," the queen said. "I have a lot to say."

The prince instantly knew by his mother's tone that he'd be wasting his time if he tried to fight her, so he followed her in silence. By the time they got to the drawing room, he had a long list of things he wanted to say as well, starting with how Kaylie needed to go, immediately.

But when they walked into the drawing room, the queen walked over to the Christmas tree and started looking at the cut-out snowflakes. "Anna did these snowflakes with Kaylie. It's one of Kaylie's family's Christmas traditions to write a word on each snowflake that represents something important about Christmas. Here are some that Anna wrote." The queen started reading the snowflakes. "Anna wrote family, angels, pets…" She chuckled, then continued. "And she wrote traditions." The queen looked at a few more snowflakes. "And here are some that Kaylie wrote, she also wrote family, joy, hope, and…love."

"I'm not sure I'm getting your point," the prince said. "What does this have to do with Kaylie being here?"

The queen walked over to her desk and picked up a piece of paper and scissors and expertly cut out her own snowflake and wrote her own word on it. "Forgiveness," the queen said. "That's my word that I think is important at Christmas."

The prince shook his head, dumbfounded. "You want me to forgive Kaylie?"

"Yes," the queen said. "But it's also time you, me, all of us, forgive what's happened in the past with the paparazzi."

"You want me to forgive the press, after what they've said, what they've done to us?" the prince asked, shocked.

The queen took his hand. "Please, hear me out. We have been so isolated for so long by running from the press and not traveling, for fear of the negative media coverage we would get. We've even banned the press here in Tolvania to try and control it, but that also means we've cut ourselves off from the rest of the world, and that's not good for us or for Anna as she grows up."

"We've done this to protect Anna," the prince shot back quickly. "I've done this to protect you and Tolvania."

"And I appreciate all you've done and sacrificed," the queen said. "But we can't live in this bubble forever. It's not realistic or healthy for any of us. That video that Kaylie accidentally sent didn't hurt us. It helped show us as a family who loves each other and loves to celebrate Christmas together. It's time we stopped hiding from the world and reenter it on our own terms, and that includes talking to select members of the press that we trust, when it's in our best interest to do so, for our family and for the people of Tolvania."

"But how will we ever know who we can really trust?" the prince asked. "I don't want to make a mistake and put this family at risk."

"And you think Kaylie was a mistake?" the queen asked. "As someone in the press, or as someone you've started to care about?"

The prince's eyes flew to his mother's. "I don't know what you're talking about. I don't have feelings for Kaylie." As he walked over to the window and looked out at the lake, he knew he wasn't fooling his mother or himself. The fact that he was starting to care for Kaylie was why he had gotten so upset thinking she'd betrayed him and the family. He sighed. "I don't know how this happened. She's going back to New York. She's a reporter. She's everything I've tried to avoid…"

"Including love," the queen said, stopping to get another snowflake from the tree before joining him. "Sophia wanted you and Anna to be happy, and to find love again. There's always a risk when you fall in love. There will never be any guarantees, but wouldn't you rather try with Kaylie, be honest with yourself, and tell her how you feel, and whatever happens, happens, instead of always wondering what if?" She handed the prince the snowflake.

He read it. "Believe." He looked at his mother. "That's what you're asking me to do?"

"To believe and have faith that anything is possible at Christmas? Yes, that is what I'm asking. You can call it my Christmas gift." The queen gave him a hopeful look.

"I already got you the bracelet," the prince said, but then kissed his mother's cheek. "Thank you for always caring so much. I love you, you know."

"I know." The queen smiled back at him and gave him a heartfelt hug. "I love you more. Merry Christmas."

After she had taken a quick walk with the princess and Blixen, Kaylie found herself back in the princess's art room after the princess said she had something to show her. As soon as they'd walked into the room, Kaylie had instantly noticed that there were even more paintings showing different Christmas scenes around Tolvania that had been put up for display. She had been captivated by the wonderful paintings of the village, the church, the Christmas trees by the lake, the Christmas carolers, the upside-down Christmas tree, and lots of paintings of Blixen in his Christmas bowties and sweaters.

"This is amazing," Kaylie said, taking it all in, impressed. That's when she noticed even more paintings on another wall that brilliantly showed the Christmas tea, the Christmas Crown event, and even the Christmas ball.

The princess followed her gaze. "My mother painted those. They're my favorite."

Kaylie walked closer to admire them. "They're so beautiful."

The princess smiled and nodded. "My grandmother always says my mother really captured the heart of Christmas. I'm trying to do that, too, in my paintings."

"And you're doing an amazing job," Kaylie said, pointing at another painting of Blixen where he was sitting by the fireplace. "I see so much love here."

"And here's a new one I just finished," the princess said, picking up a painting that was on the table. She gave it to Kaylie. "I made it for you. Merry Christmas."

"For me?" Kaylie asked, touched, and then her breath was taken away when she saw the painting was of three people making snow angels by a big Christmas tree.

"That's us," the princess said proudly. "That's my father, you, and me, and the angel on the top of the tree is for my mother, because she's always with us, too."

Kaylie didn't realize she had tears in her eyes until one rolled down her cheek.

"Are you sad?" the princess asked, concerned.

Kaylie gave her a big hug. "No, I'm just so happy. This is beautiful. I love it so much. Thank you."

The princess looked delighted. "You're welcome, and look, I added Blixen even though he wasn't there, so he wouldn't feel left out."

When the prince walked in, Kaylie instantly tensed, fearing the worst.

He smiled at the princess. "Chef Jake says the gingerbread pancakes are ready."

The princess, excited, grabbed Kaylie's hand. "We have to go! The pancakes are ready!"

The queen appeared and held out her hand to the princess. "Anna, why don't you come with me? Kaylie and your father have to talk about a surprise for you."

The princess's eyes lit up as she looked from Kaylie to her father. "A surprise? For me? This is the best Christmas ever!"

The queen laughed as she led the princess out of the room, leaving Kaylie and the prince alone.

Kaylie, nervous, held up her pictures and showed the prince. "You have a very talented and thoughtful daughter. She just gave me this for Christmas."

The prince appeared surprised. "She usually only paints pictures for the family."

Kaylie's heart was racing. The suspense of what the prince was going to say or do was killing her. "Your mother made me come back here," Kaylie blurted out. "I didn't want to come, but you know how impossible she is to say no to."

The prince nodded. "That's true."

They stared at each other in silence for a moment before both saying the same thing at the same time. "I'm sorry."

"Please," the prince said. "After you."

Kaylie shook her head. "Oh, no, if you were about to apologize, then by all means *you* go first."

Kaylie watched the prince walk over to the wall of paintings that had been done by the princess's mother. "Anna takes after her mother. Not just in her talent for painting, but in how she loves with all her heart, and how she enjoys socializing and being around other people. The last few years, I've kept her very sheltered. We went away for Christmas, just the two of us. I thought it was for her own good, to protect her, but now I'm realizing I was wrong, she needs to be around other people, and to travel, and to experience life to the fullest."

"I don't think you were wrong," Kaylie said. "You did what you thought was best at the time because you care and love her so much."

"That's very kind of you to say," the prince said. "But I've learned sometimes love can blind us, making it impossible for us to see things that are right in front of us. The things that really matter the most."

When the prince took a step closer to her, her heart started to race. "I'm sorry for jumping to conclusions and for not believing you about sending the video on accident," the prince said with a sigh. "I've had a very combative history with the press, but that still didn't give me the right to attack you like I did. It wasn't fair and I'm truly sorry."

Kaylie could see in his eyes that he was sincere, and she was so relieved. She gave him a grateful smile. "Thank you. That means more than you know, and I owe you an apology for telling you how you should deal with the Christmas Crown story. I had no right passing judgment about something I know so little about, something your family has been dealing with for years. I was self-righteous and I went right into investigative reporter mode and that was wrong."

"But you weren't wrong about how it's time we share with the people of Tolvania the truth about what happened to the Christmas Crown," the prince said. "For generations, we've felt like it was our story and our secret, but like your feature story showed so eloquently, the Christmas Crown and its legacy belongs to everyone, so everyone has a right to know the truth."

"I agree," Kaylie said.

"I'm glad," the prince said. "Because I'd like to ask if we can…start over?"

"I would like that," Kaylie said. "So, a new truce?"

The prince thought about it for a second. "No, a truce means an agreement between enemies to stop fighting for a period of time. You're not an enemy and going forward, I want to concentrate on things that are going to last."

Kaylie's pulse quickened as hope filled her heart. "Me, too," she said with a radiant smile as she held out her hand. "To new beginnings."

The prince took her hand and, never taking his eyes off his face, kissed it. "To new beginnings."

When he finally let go of her hand, Kaylie still felt warm and tingly from his touch. "Since we're talking about new beginnings, I have a question," Kaylie said. "After you tell people about the Christmas Crown and when you're ready, will you let me help you find out what happened to it? Figuring out mysteries like this is what I'm good at. I really think you need to find the crown and bring it back to your family and the people of Tolvania, and I'd really like to help you do that, if you'll let me?"

The prince looked into her eyes. "Yes, I think that would be wonderful but right now there's one thing we need to take care of right away," the prince said. "We have Christmas pancakes waiting for us."

"It's a family tradition," they both said at the same time and laughed.

Chapter 36

At the dining room table, Kaylie took her last bite of gingerbread pancake and sat back in her chair, stuffed.

The princess gave her a look of respect. "You had three gingerbread pancakes *and* you had frosting. I've never had that many."

"And they were delicious," Kaylie said with a laugh as she held her stomach. She was interrupted when her phone lit up with a video call. When she saw it was her parents, her eyes flew to the queen.

"I'm sorry," Kaylie said. "I know this is so rude but this is my parents calling, and it's in the middle of the night for them, so something could be wrong…"

"Please, answer it," the queen said.

Kaylie picked up the call. "Is everything okay?" she asked in a panic.

"Merry Christmas!" Kaylie's mom and dad called out joyfully, and then Kaylie was shocked to see her sister Amelia pop into frame.

"Merry Christmas!" Amelia said, laughing.

"What's happening?" Kaylie asked, confused. "Where are you guys?"

"In Germany!" Kaylie's mom said. "We decided to surprise Amelia."

Kaylie shook her head, confused. "I thought you were going back to Vermont?"

Kaylie's dad laughed. "We were, but we got to the airport and thought, Vermont, Germany, what's the difference, let's go to where we can see our daughter for Christmas, and then when you're done working you can come join us. You can join us, right?"

"Yes." Kaylie laughed. "I can come as soon as I'm done here tomorrow." Kaylie looked up and was embarrassed when she realized everyone at the table watching and listening. "I'm actually working right now," Kaylie said. "I gotta go…"

"In the castle?" her sister jumped in. "With the handsome prince?"

Kaylie, mortified, tried to turn down the volume. "You're on speakerphone, and the royal family is right here with me." She hoped that would give Amelia a clue, but it only made things worse when her mom chimed in, too.

"Is the queen there?" Kaylie's mom asked, excited. "I would die to meet the queen!"

"What about the princess?" Kaylie's dad asked.

The excited princess leaned closer to Kaylie so she could see the screen. "I'm right here. I'm the princess," she said, thrilled to be included in the conversation.

"Anna, please, give Kaylie some privacy," the queen said.

Kaylie laughed. She'd given up at this point. "It's fine. Okay, everyone, I have to go. I'll call you later."

"And Kaylie ate *three* whole gingerbread pancakes with frosting, all by herself!" the princess chimed in, gleefully.

Kaylie's family laughed. "And she's not even a breakfast person. So that's saying something," Kaylie's dad said.

Kaylie held up her phone. "Okay, that's it. Bye, everyone. I'll call you later. Merry Christmas."

"Merry Christmas," Kaylie's family all shouted back. "Merry Christmas royal family," Kaylie's mom said.

"Merry Christmas," the princess called back to them and waved until Kaylie hung up.

"I am so sorry," Kaylie said to the queen and prince. "I thought I turned my phone off and…"

"It's fine," the prince said. "It's Christmas."

"Thank you for understanding," Kaylie said.

"I like your family," the princess said. "They're nice."

Kaylie laughed. "And I'm sure they loved you, too." She turned to the queen. "If it's alright, I thought I'd go to my room and work on that Christmas project we talked about."

"Is it the surprise for me?" the princess asked, bubbling over with excitement.

Kaylie stood up from the table and gave the princess a teasing look. "I'll never tell."

"Do you need any help?" the prince asked.

"Thank you, but I think I'm good," Kaylie said. "I'll let you know if anything comes up." She turned to the queen. "What time would you like to see our little project to check it out and make sure it's okay?"

"I don't need to check it," the queen said. "I trust you. I will look forward to being surprised like everyone else. Take all the time you need and let's all meet back in the drawing room at four before our dinner. Does that work for you, Kaylie?"

"That works great," Kaylie said, taking all the time she could get. She was excited but also scared. She didn't want to disappoint the family.

Back in her room, Kaylie couldn't believe how fast the afternoon flew by.

At first, she'd had a hard time concentrating on writing the fairy tale because her mind kept going back to the last conversation she'd had with her real-life prince.

She wasn't sure exactly what that meant to "start over" with the prince, but the look in his eyes made her wish for things she didn't even know she wanted. For once she'd decided to stop being afraid and take it one day at a time and see what happened.

Even though her head kept telling her any kind of real relationship was impossible because he was a prince and she was a girl from New York City, she chose instead to listen to her heart that was telling her to go for it and to hold on tight to any happiness she could find. She'd even decided to be brave and, after dinner, tell the prince how she felt about him. She knew if she was going to go for it, she needed to go all in for love and not hold anything back.

"Love," she said the word softly, shaking her head in amazement. But it was the truth. She knew that's what she was starting to feel for the prince, and also for the princess, the queen, and even Blixen. She knew it was crazy, but the entire royal family had found a place in her heart.

A video call from Rachel brought her back to reality. She answered with a big smile. "Merry Christmas, Rachel."

"Merry Christmas," Rachel said, excited. "And I have the best Christmas present for you. Gerry loved your Christmas feature! And he looked at your tape and he wants to talk to you as soon as you get back here tomorrow about sending you to Mexico to do that exclusive story you pitched him about the fake pharmaceutical company selling knock-off drugs."

When Kaylie didn't respond right away, Rachel looked worried.

"Did you hear me?" Rachel asked. "Do we have a bad connection?"

Kaylie shook her head. "No, I heard you." She'd heard everything Rachel had said, but all she could think about was how she'd told her parents she would meet them in Germany at her sister's place. The idea of going to Mexico and chasing after criminals had also lost its appeal. She knew it was her dream to work as a national investigative news reporter, but during her time in Tolvania, she had truly enjoyed focusing on more uplifting and positive stories that fueled her imagination and made her feel better about the world, not worse. Maybe she was just feeling burned out and needed a break. All of a sudden, her future, and what she thought she really wanted, didn't seem so clear.

"Kaylie, is everything okay? Why aren't you jumping up and down, telling me I'm the best friend ever for getting you this job?"

"You *are* the best friend ever," Kaylie said with a grateful smile. "So, I hope you'll understand when I say I need a minute to think about all this."

"What's there to think about?" Rachel asked, baffled.

"Everything," Kaylie said. "And right now, I only have a few hours to write this fairy tale. Can I call you back later?"

"What do you want me to tell Gerry?" Rachel asked.

"Just buy me some time and don't tell him anything yet," Kaylie said. "It's Christmas, he'll understand."

Rachel laughed, surprised. "Uh, we always work Christmas in the news business. You know that. Who are you and what have you done with Kaylie Karlyle?"

Kaylie laughed. "I gotta go. Merry Christmas. I'll talk to you later."

After the call, Kaylie got up and started pacing around the room, trying to get herself back in the mood to write a magical fairy tale. She walked over to the stereo panel and turned it on, and the orchestra version of the Christmas song "Angels We Have Heard on High" filled the room. She hummed along and then saw the little crystal angel that was holding a red heart on her nightstand. She smiled thoughtfully as she walked over and picked it up. "Maybe you can help me, because I'm thinking a Christmas fairy tale needs an angel, right?"

The hours flew by, and before Kaylie knew it, it was almost four o'clock and time to meet the family in the drawing room. Luckily, the angel and Christmas music had inspired her and the more she wrote, the more she fell in love with the fairy tale she was creating for the princess. Somewhere along the line, it had stopped feeling like a job and more like a gift.

She'd found the hardest part was trying to pick from all the special Christmas traditions she'd learned about. She had so much amazing material, she could do an entire Christmas fairy tale series.

As she did one last quick copy edit, she took a bite of the gingerbread cookie Elsa had brought her when she'd also dropped off some lunch. And that wasn't the only thing Elsa had surprised her with. After helping to print up the fairy tale for her, Elsa had also presented her with a sparkling gold garment bag that had a giant red satin bow on it and a note from the queen that said…

Fit for a Fairy Tale. Merry Christmas, XOXO, Isabella.

Once again, Kaylie was touched by the queen's thoughtfulness and generosity. Inside the bag, she'd been delighted to find a stunning red satin cocktail dress with sparkling rhinestone heels.

Now, standing in front of the mirror, wearing her new spectacular Christmas dress, she really did feel like she was living inside a Christmas fairy tale. As she looked down at the fairy tale she'd rolled into a scroll and tied with some of her red ribbon from her present, she was both nervous and excited to share the story she'd written.

She checked the time on her phone and got a sudden rush of nerves when she saw she only had five minutes until she was due in the drawing room. She took a deep breath and gave herself a little pep talk. "You got this. You did the best you could. You wrote from your heart."

When she heard a bark at her door, she quickly opened it to find Blixen waiting. He was wearing a red satin bowtie that matched her dress. She looked around but he was all alone.

"Are you my escort?" Kaylie asked him with a laugh.

For an answer, Blixen barked and wagged his tail.

"I'll follow you," she said as she picked up the fairy tale and her phone and shut her bedroom door behind her.

When they got into the hall, Kaylie smiled brightly when she heard the Christmas song, "I'll Be Home for Christmas" start playing…

I'll be home for Christmas
You can plan on me…
Please have snow and mistletoe
And presents by the tree…

Kaylie was still happily humming the song as she followed Blixen into the drawing room. "I'll be home for Christmas, if only in my dreams…"

But she suddenly stopped singing and blinked in disbelief when she saw her parents and sister in the drawing room with the queen, prince, and princess.

"Merry Christmas!" everyone shouted and then her parents and sister came running up to her and embraced her in a huge hug. "Surprise!"

"What is happening?" Kaylie asked, stunned, as she hugged her dad like she never wanted to let go. "Is this real? Are you really here?"

Kaylie was laughing and crying, and she wasn't the only one. When she looked over at the queen, she saw the queen was also misty-eyed.

"How did you do this?" she asked the queen.

But the queen shook her head. "I didn't. My son did."

Kaylie gave the prince an amazed look. "What…"

He nodded and smiled. "You've given so much to my family, I didn't think you should have to wait another Christmas to be with yours," the prince said. "Merry Christmas, Kaylie."

Kaylie ran over to the prince and without thinking threw her arms around him and kissed him with all the love in her heart. When he passionately kissed her back, Kaylie felt the kind of love she had never dreamed possible and knew she was ready to believe and embrace in her own happily ever after.

When they pulled apart the prince looked into her eyes and smiled. "I like the way this new beginning is starting."

Kaylie laughed and quickly kissed him again. "So, do I."

"Yes!" the queen said, delighted. "And so do I."

Kaylie's family looked surprised but equally excited for her.

The princess, overjoyed, ran over to her father and Kaylie who both knelt down to give her a heartfelt hug.

"My Christmas Crown wish came true!" the princess said merrily.

"What was your wish?" Kaylie asked the princess.

The princess grinned back at her. "I asked the Christmas Crown for love for my family."

"I asked for the same thing," the prince said as he shared a smile with Kaylie.

"Wait, where is this Christmas Crown?" Kaylie's sister asked. "I'm a single girl, too. I need to make a wish. Prince, do you have a brother?"

Everyone laughed.

"I still don't understand how you're all here," Kaylie said in awe.

"Christmas magic," the princess said.

"And we called your old boss, Bob, this morning," the prince said.

"Bob had your parents down as your emergency contact," the queen continued. "He was more than happy to help us. Since your parents were already visiting your sister in Germany, and they were only a few hours away, the rest, as you say, is history…"

"I helped, too," the princess said, running up to Kaylie. "I showed them around and took them for a walk."

"She was the perfect hostess," Kaylie's mom said, smiling at the princess.

Kaylie shook her head in disbelief. "So while I was upstairs working…"

"We were down here planning your surprise," the princess said, smiling ear to ear. Kaylie's dad walked over and handed Kaylie a gift.

"What's this?" Kaylie asked. "We usually don't exchange Christmas gifts."

"And we usually don't get together at Christmas," her dad agreed. "But since we're starting all kinds of new traditions this year, I wanted you to have this."

Kaylie felt all eyes on her as she opened the present and was stunned to find it was her *Someday Trips Journal* that she used to write in with her grandmother about all the places they'd visit someday.

She held it to her heart as her eyes filled with tears. "I thought this was lost years ago…"

"We found it, and we've been saving it for you," Kaylie's mom said.

"Look on page two, middle of the page," her dad said.

Kaylie flipped to page two. It was her grandmother's original list of places she had written down as a young girl that she always wanted to visit. The writing was faded, but when Kaylie looked at the middle of the page, there was one word underlined twice.

Tolvania.

She looked up at her dad, speechless. "Grandma wanted to come here? To Tolvania?"

Her dad smiled and nodded. "Yes. I know you always regretted that you never got to take a 'Someday Trip' with your grandmother, but you're here now, a place she always dreamed of visiting. You were meant to come here, Kaylie, and I know she is with you here, and always."

When a tear rolled down Kaylie's cheek, she hugged her dad, mom, and sister. "I love you guys so much. Thank you for being here. Thank you for being my family, and thank you for bringing me this."

"Grandmother, can we do a book like that?" the princess asked, excited.

"I think that's a wonderful idea," the queen said, smiling at Kaylie. "It will be a wonderful new Christmas family tradition."

Kaylie flipped through the pages of the journal. "I'm going to do these trips. This is what I want to do. I want to write stories like the one I wrote about Tolvania."

"What about the investigative reporter job you wanted?" her sister asked.

"It's time for a change," Kaylie said, smiling at the prince. "I want to do stories that uplift and inspire people. I think that's so important right now, more than ever. This *Someday Trips Journal* is going to help show me the way and I can write from anywhere."

"Anywhere?" the prince asked, his voice full of hope.

"You can write from Tolvania," the princess said eagerly.

"It certainly seems like a great place to start," Kaylie said.

"I agree," the prince said and when his face lit up Kaylie knew she was on the right path.

"It's the perfect place," the queen chimed in. "And now, princess, are you ready for *your* surprise?"

The princess nodded, excited. "I'm ready!"

That's when Kaylie realized that sometime during all the commotion, she'd accidentally dropped the fairy tale scroll she'd been holding.

"Oh, no. Where did it go…" she said as her eyes darted around the room, and finally came to rest on Blixen, who was sitting by the fire with the scroll in his mouth.

When she leaned down to get it, he happily dropped it and wagged his tail. "Good boy, Blixen," she said as she patted him on his head.

"Are you ready?" the queen asked, looking as excited as the princess.

"I am," Kaylie said with confidence.

"Then everyone, please, let's all take a seat around the fire," the queen said.

As Kaylie stood up by the fireplace next to the queen her dad winked and she winked back. When the princess saw it, she winked at her father and the prince winked back. Kaylie laughed, loving them even more.

When the queen started talking, all eyes were on her. "Anna, I wanted to give you a present that you could cherish and share with your family for generations as part of your legacy and a way to always honor the true meaning and magic of Christmas. So, I invited Kaylie to come here, all the way from New York City, to see and experience all our family's Christmas traditions and use them to help create a very special Christmas story just for you."

"A fairy tale," Kaylie added, and saw the princess's face light up with joy.

"I love fairy tales!" the princess exclaimed. "And I've never heard a Christmas fairy tale before."

"Well, this one is just for you," Kaylie said. "But before I start, I was hoping you could help me with something, if your grandmother and father approve?"

"Okay!" the princess said, growing more excited.

The prince and queen gave Kaylie a curious look. "What do you have in mind?" the queen asked.

"I've written the fairy tale, but one of the most magical parts will be the illustrations, bringing my words to life," Kaylie said. "The princess showed me the paintings she did with her mother, of Tolvania at Christmas, and I think we should use them for the fairy tale."

"I think this is a wonderful idea," the prince said, giving Kaylie a grateful look.

"I couldn't agree more," the queen said. "Thank you, Kaylie. This will be a truly special memory for generations to come."

"And Kaylie can paint, too. I can teach her how," the princess said.

The scared look on Kaylie's face had everyone laughing.

"I think I'll leave the painting to my little expert here, seriously, thank you for allowing me to write this story, and sharing all your Christmas traditions with me. It's been a true gift because it's helped remind me of what truly matters most at Christmas." Kaylie glanced over at her family and felt so much love. As she slowly started to unroll the scroll, she smiled when she saw the princess's eyes grow huge with anticipation.

"Princess, may I now present to you your very own Christmas fairy tale…"

Before she started, Kaylie shared a smile with the prince and glanced around the room that was filled with everyone she loved the most, her family, and her new royal family. She felt so thankful and blessed, and she knew with all her heart that her own fairy tale was just beginning.

She took a deep breath and looked down at the words she'd written and smiled as she started reading.

"Once upon a time…"

Acknowledgments

I've always lived by the thought, "we're all in this together," but since the global pandemic started these words have become even more poignant and powerful. I am truly thankful for all the essential workers and unsung heroes who continue to tirelessly dedicate their lives to helping others, and for every single person who is reaching out to help someone in need.

When I was writing this novel, I suddenly found myself in a hospital, alone, waiting hours for surgery. I was so touched and comforted by all the nurses who made the time to stop by my room and make sure I was okay. When they learned I wrote Christmas movies and novels they shared how grateful they were for uplifting, heartfelt, feel-good Christmas stories to help stay hopeful even during the most challenging times.

This was a very special reminder of why I do what I do. I believe that we all have the power within us to create our own happily ever afters. This inspired me to write my first Christmas royal romance, in 2017, the Netflix Original, *A Christmas Prince,* and now a new holiday story, *A Royal Christmas Fairy Tale.*

Before I write any story, I have to "see" it and I'm very thankful for designer Mary Ann Smith who helped bring my vision of Tolvania to life by creating this magical book cover and to Ramesh Kumar Pitchai for the beautiful interior design. Also, a heartfelt thank you to Justine Bylo, Leigh Pierce, and the entire Ingram family for continuing to create and distribute quality books all over the world. I couldn't ask for better publishing partners. I'm grateful every day for the support and guidance of my brilliant literary agent Christina Hogrebe and her team as Jane Rotrosen Agency, including Sabrina Prestia and Hannah Rody-Wright in subsidiary rights, and for my fabulous film and TV manager, Sydney Blanke with the Fourth Wall Management group, and my powerhouse entertainment attorney Neville Johnson.

I am very blessed to have the ongoing unconditional love and support of my family. To my moms, Lao Schaler, and Kathy Bezold, who read and help edit every single draft. I could never do this without you. Thank you to my dad, Harry Schaler, for your creative ideas and plot twists, and Margaret Schaler for our daily inspirational talks that have meant everything to me.

To Jon Clark, David and Margaret Crane, Nathan, John, Maddy, Marcus, Taylor, Debbie, and Wynn, I am grateful to have you as family. To my friends that are like my family, Brenda, Bryan, Anna, Carolyn, Jeryl, Clint, Geoff, Lorianne, Greta, Samuel, Louise, Lamar, Amy, Tim, Marybeth, Heather, Lee, Delia, Tom, Denise, Rob, Hope, Sue, and Carol, thank you for always being there.

To my stars in the sky that I know are watching over me, John Bezold, and my grandparents, Pat and Walter Crane, and Irene and Harry Schaler, I miss you every day, but you're always with me in my heart.

And to you, my dear readers, thank you for allowing me to share my stories with you.

I hope you always know how thankful I am for all your support and kindness. We truly are all in this together. Have a safe, healthy, and happy holidays.

Meet Karen Schaler

KAREN SCHALER is a three-time Emmy Award-winning passion-ate storyteller, screenwriter, author, journalist, and national TV host. Karen has written original Christmas movies for Netflix, Hallmark, and Lifetime, including the Netflix sensation *A Christmas Prince*, Hallmark's *Christmas Camp*, Lifetime's *Every Day is Christmas* starring Toni Braxton, and *Rediscovering Christmas*. Karen is currently working on several more Christmas movies based on her novels that have so far included *Christmas Ever After, Finding Christmas, Christmas Camp, and Christmas Camp Wedding*. Karen has also created a real-life Christmas Camp experience for grown-ups, held around the world, where she carefully curates and hosts magical holiday activities from her movies and books. Traveling to more than sixty-eight countries, Karen is the creator and host of Travel Therapy TV that airs nationally on top TV and streaming outlets where she features the most inspiring and empowering trips to take based on what you're going through in life. Karen believes in always paying it forward and giving back, and all of her stories are uplifting, filled with heart and hope.

Visit www.karenschaler.com to sign up for Karen's newsletter for special book giveaways and deals, Zoom chats, sneak peeks, and so much more!

More Books by Karen Schaler

Christmas Ever After, 2020

Finding Christmas, 2019

Christmas Camp, 2018

Christmas Camp Wedding, 2019,
(novella)

BONUS CONTENT
FOR
A Royal Christmas Fairy Tale

*A Royal Christmas
Fairy Tale*

 **RECIPES**

If you've read my Christmas novels or watched my movies, it's no secret that I love writing about holiday treats and special dishes, because I believe they're part of our traditions and bring back wonderful memories. In my first novel *Christmas Camp,* where I also wrote the Hallmark movie, I included some of my family's favorite original recipes and have continued to do this with every Christmas story I write. For *A Royal Christmas Fairy Tale,* I'm sharing with you the gingerbread pancakes I always make my dad at Christmas, and my own unique easy version of the gingerbread biscuits I heard that Queen Elizabeth II likes to have at Christmas, and the delicious and delectable dark chocolate-covered cranberries, a new family favorite.

I hope you enjoy these as much as I enjoyed creating them for you, and would love to hear what you think.

Merry Christmas!

Royal Christmas Gingerbread Pancakes

Makes 8 pancakes you'll want as your new holiday tradition!

Ingredients:
- 1 ½ cups of all-purpose flour
- 1 teaspoon ground powdered ginger
- 1 teaspoon ground cinnamon
- ⅛ teaspoon of nutmeg
- 1 teaspoon baking powder
- ¼ teaspoon baking soda
- ¼ teaspoon sea salt
- ¼ teaspoon orange zest (optional, but brings the ginger flavor out)
- ¼ teaspoon pure vanilla extract
- ¼ cup of 100% pure maple syrup
- 1 egg
- 1 ½ cups of water
- 16 oz. container of cream cheese frosting (optional for topping)

Instructions:
- Combine flour, ginger, cinnamon, nutmeg, baking powder, baking soda, and sea salt with a whisk in a medium bowl.
- In a separate large bowl, add the syrup, vanilla, and the egg and beat until smooth. Then add the water and mix thoroughly.
- Add all the flour mixture at once to the syrup mixture and combine slowly so you don't over mix. Batter will be lumpy and that's fine.
- Let batter sit for 10 minutes so gluten in the flour can relax for the secret to light and fluffy pancakes.
- Lightly oil a griddle or pan with olive oil and place on medium-high heat. Drop the batter for whatever size pancakes you want and let them bubble before flipping.
- OPTIONAL: For a delicious cream cheese frosting, melt a ½ cup of frosting in the microwave for 10-15 seconds and drizzle on top of your gingerbread pancakes and enjoy!
- OTHER TOPPINGS: I also love sprinkling cinnamon on top, and of course, you can always use the traditional warm melted butter and syrup.

Enjoy!

Royal Christmas Gingerbread Biscuits

Makes 20 chewy, soft, delicious cookies

Ingredients Cookies:
- 2 cups of flour
- ¾ cup of unsalted butter
- ½ cup dark brown sugar
- 1 teaspoon baking soda
- 2 teaspoons ground ginger
- ¼ teaspoon fresh grated ginger
- ¼ teaspoon salt
- ¼ teaspoon fresh grated orange zest
- 1 egg
- ¼ cup pure maple syrup

Ingredients Cookie Topping:
- ¼ cup white sugar
- ¼ cup cinnamon

Instructions:
- Over low heat in a saucepan, melt butter, sugar, grated ginger, and syrup and set aside to cool.
- When cool, add egg and whisk together all the liquid ingredients in a large bowl.
- Combine all dry ingredients in a medium bowl.
- Stir dry ingredients into the large bowl of liquid ingredients.
- Roll into a ball, wrap in plastic wrap and chill for 40 minutes in the refrigerator (the more the dough is chilled the less the cookies will spread).
- Line cookie sheet with parchment paper.
- Combine sugar and cinnamon for the topping.
- Roll dough into Ping-Pong-sized balls and roll in topping.
- Preheat oven to 350 degrees F and bake for 10-12 minutes. They will be soft inside. Do not overcook for the best chewy, soft texture.

Berry Christmas Dark Chocolate-Covered Cranberries

Makes 1¼ cups of this favorite tangy, tasty Tolvania Christmas treat

Ingredients:
- 10 oz. of dark chocolate chips for melting. I like using the Ghirardelli brand.
- 10 oz. whole cranberries
- ¼ teaspoon cinnamon
- ⅛ teaspoon vanilla

Instructions:
- Melt chocolate chips over very low heat stirring constantly, or in a microwave starting at 30 seconds and then doing 10-second intervals. Do not overcook the chocolate. Once melted add cinnamon and vanilla.
- Using toothpicks, dip cranberries into the chocolate and place cranberries on a cookie sheet lined with parchment paper.
- Put in the refrigerator until firm.
- Enjoy and be sure to leave some out for Santa, we hear he loves Tolvania treats!

NOTE: This is a fun project to do with your kids. The more little hands you have to help dip the cranberries before the chocolate hardens, the better.

*A Royal Christmas
Fairy Tale*

 **ACTIVITIES**

I really love carrying on my tradition of always including some fun, easy, and affordable Christmas activities you can do at home for the holidays. The snowflake idea came when I asked friends to make me a snowflake instead of giving me a birthday card or gifts one year so I could decorate with them and be surrounded by loving, uplifting thoughts. At brunch, everyone presented their snowflakes and shared some holiday stories. I also have a snowflake theme in my Lifetime movie *Rediscovering Christmas*. The *Someday Trips Journal* is something I wish I'd done with my grandma who loved to travel. We'd always talk about trips we wanted to take. I hope it inspires you to start your own journal and to find ways to make your *Someday Trips* and travel dreams come true...

Royal Christmas Snowflakes

Equipment:
- White paper in a square, sizes 8x8, 10x10, 12x12
- Scissors
- Red felt tip pen

Directions:
- If you're starting with regular 8.5 x 11 paper, just fold it into a triangle and cut off the excess to make your square.
- Take your square piece of paper and fold it into a triangle.
- Fold into another triangle.
- With this triangle, fold in thirds. First, fold the right edge toward the middle. Flip the snowflake over and do the same on the other side, folding the edge just to the middle, leaving you with two loose tips at the top.
- Cut off the loose tips at the top, leaving you with just a triangle you fold into one last triangle.
- Start making your cuts! You can also sketch them out first, if you like.
- The beauty of making snowflakes is no two are the same, so be sure to try new things!
- TIP: If you're someone (like me) who needs to learn visually, there are lots of great videos online showing you how.
- Once your snowflake is finished, write one word on it with your red pen about what Christmas means to you (and I like to date it). Continue until you have a whole collection of snowflakes that have a special meaning for you.
- Hang with ribbon or string on your Christmas tree to always remember what truly matters most at Christmas.
- TIP: If you're having a party, you can make the snowflakes as fabulous party gifts and encourage everyone to write down what matters most to them to take home for their own Christmas trees.

Someday Trips Journal

Equipment:
- Journal or notebook
- Pen

Directions:
- You can create your *Someday Trips Journal* any way you like that inspires you. I like starting on the first page by making three columns. The first column is the date I'm doing the entry. The second column is the trip I want to take, and the third column is the date I took the trip (being optimistic).
- You can also write one page for each trip you want to take and put down the reasons you want to visit and the specific things you want to do.
- The key is to actually write down where you'd like to go, in any way you like. This is the first step to making your dream *Someday Trips* come true.

Merry Christmas, XOXO